D1297552

Ashes by Now

Ashes by Now

by

Barry McKeown

Barry McKeown

RIVERCROSS PUBLISHING, INC.
NEW YORK • ORLANDO

Copyright © 1996 by Barry McKeown

All Rights Reserved

Printed in the United States of America. No part of this book may be used or reproduced in any manner whatsoever without written permission, except in the case of brief quotations embodied in critical articles and reviews. For information address RIVERCROSS PUBLISHING, INC., 127 East 59th Street, New York, NY 10022

ISBN: 0-944957-59-5

Library of Congress Catalog Card Number: 96-10418

First Printing

Library of Congress Cataloging-in-Publication Data

McKeown, Barry.
    Ashes by now / by Barry McKeown.
      p. cm.
    ISBN 0-944957-59-5
    1. Southern States—History—1775-1865—Fiction. 2. Man-woman relationships—Southern States—Fiction. 3. Women slaves—Southern States—Fiction. 4. Mulattoes—Southern States—Fiction.
    I. Title.
PS3563.C37553A93 1996
813'.54—dc20   96-10418
                                                         CIP

In memory of
JAMES R. McKEOWN

Dedicated to
THE BAZARTE FAMILY
(and all the love we share)

Acknowledgements

My wife Judy, who meticulously dressed the wedding party, typed, edited and perservered through more hours then I care to remind her.

My daughter Anna, those teenage years that you and your friends spent in our house flew by far too quickly.

In countless ways so many little things are reenacted in this story. I could never have written it was that wonderful if we hadn't experienced it.

To my Mother, who stood behind us unconditionally (always). This wouldn't have happened without you.

Greg, we greatly appreciate all the time you spent working with us on this project.

Barbara, what an incredibly talented girl you are. I could never tell you how much I appreciate what you did for my story.

Lacy, for your editing assistance and the sweet gift you sent me. We are all so happy to know you.

Henry and Susan, whose interest and support (wine and music) made it all a most enjoyable experience.

Aja, whose unending enthusiasm and from-the-heart conversations are my special source of joy.

Misty, how else could I have known there could be a girl like her.

Table of Contents

Introduction

You are about to enter the lives of people you will never want to forget.

One in particular will enter your heart; you will not want to let her go.

Born in one world, raised in another, she brings the two together with a love so strong that no amount of time or prejudice or even death itself could destroy.

This story is about love; may we come to know it as they did.

PART 1

Mariah

Early October 1841. They arrived a day later than planned, but nobody seems to mind. The magnificence of autumn is all around them. It was a warm clear Saturday afternoon when their cariole pulled up in front off The Histand, perhaps the finest hotel in all the city.

How good it felt to arrive at their destination, after what seemed a never-ending journey, a journey that had brought them from the sweet easy pace of Georgia to the bustling metropolis of New Orleans.

They had all been there before, for Mr. Tanner this had become a ritual, to meet with the bankers and lawyers and merchants of the world. He hated the trip and the time away from home, but he did love the time spent at the negotiating table.

Mrs. Tanner, on the other hand, hadn't come along for several years, not since the birth of her last child, and while she suspected she was pregnant again, it was early on, and there were friends she had missed for too long.

The moment they pulled up the house manager, Melton Farra rushed towards them. With outstretched hand and a smile that went from ear to ear he cried out, "Hubert Tanner, how fine it is to see you again! I trust your trip went well sir?" Not waiting for an answer he turned his attention to Mrs. Tanner and with a wink of his eye said, "I'm glad to see you've come along this year, Mrs. Tanner. You know Hubert can get a mighty unruly when he's here alone." As the laughter and hand shaking were going around, porters flocked from everywhere, helping the children out of the buggy and grabbing up luggage as quick as could be. As the party made their way up the stairs toward the porch, Mr. Farra turned to one of the porters and pointing toward the buggy said, "Go with the boy round back to the barn and wipe the horses down and feed 'em good."

The "boy" was hardly a boy in years, a man of at least sixty, if not more. His name is Henry. He has made the trip to New Orleans more times than he can count starting with Hubert's father Josiah. Henry has been owned by the Tanners all his life, being but a child when Josiah began building the family empire. He lives a life now that any slave in the south would envy, but what he has didn't come about without cost. With sweat and blood, pick and shovel, he worked shoulder to shoulder with the Tanners in the early years putting up the buildings and clearing the fields. But, of course, none of that matters to anyone else. Henry will sleep in the barn where any other Negro would sleep after driving their masters to town.

This time they will be in New Orleans about a week, enough time to take care of business, visit old friends and, of course, do some shopping.

Sunday was spent partly in church, partly visiting and dining with friends. Come Monday morning, six handsomely dressed men were seated at a table in the conference room on the second floor of the hotel. One was Hubert Tanner, primed and ready to make things happen. Mr. Tanner loved talking business. It just seemed to come naturally—the negotiating, the attention to details, the deal making. Few other things got his blood up the way business sessions did. At the table also, was Mr. Tanner's lawyer, Scott Franklin, a young man, but one Mr. Tanner had a great deal of confidence in. With them were two bankers, their lawyer, and a northern gentleman who liked to refer to himself as an industrialist, Albert Cooper.

The trip to Orleans this year was threefold. First on the agenda was the meeting already in progress. At stake was a great deal of money, both Mr. Tanner's and his soon-to-be partners', our two banker friends. Also at stake might be a reputation. This meeting involved a substantial investment by a southerner into the industrial-minded north, something that surely would have been considered foolish by his peers. Be that as it may, all went smoothly. Papers were signed, hands were shaken, and Mr. Tanner was on his way.

The rest of the day, as well as the next two were spent doing what any lady and two young girls be they northern or southern, would do, visiting the shops that lined the streets of New Orleans.

On Thursday afternoon part two of this business trip got underway. Mr. Tanner, along with Mr. Franklin, were negotiating a large sale of cotton to several importers from England. The demand has never been greater, and the Tanners black-seeded cotton was the finest produced anywhere. With each successive year the demand from England grew greater. Mr. Tanner's ability to neither flinch nor change his expression during these negotiating sessions left all with the utmost feeling of confidence that all contracts would be carried through as smoothly as the demeanor of the man who sat before them.

All left the meeting feeling satisfied (and somewhat richer) from the day's event. Mr. Tanner and Mr. Franklin now went to the lawyer's office to finalize and double check their work. As they sat in the small room at a desk looking over their papers and sipping Kentucky bourbon they talked about what the next few years could bring. With the sale of cotton being more lucrative now than anyone would have dreamed even five years ago, and the possibilities of the northern enterprise, the two stood to make a great deal of money.

Thursday evening was a time to relax and enjoy. Dinner was at the Franklins' and Gloria Franklin put on a feast that won't soon be forgotten. Scott and Gloria were both in their mid-twenties. Scott had worked hard the past few years, and with Gloria's support had done well. Hubert met Scott at a dinner three years back. Impressed with his enthusiasm and sense of humor, Hubert decided to put the young man to task, a decision neither of them has regretted.

As the evening drew to a close, Mrs. Tanner and Gloria were happy to learn they would meet again in late January or February in Georgia. Hubert and Scott would have some business to tend to and the Franklins would spent a fortnight on the plantation, where Mrs. Tanner promised lots of good old southern hospitality and relaxation.

Early Friday morning the Tanners were up, packed and ready to go. They would stop over at Leesway; a large plantation in Alabama owned by Mrs. Tanner's sister and her husband. But before leaving New Orleans there was one more business transaction to be tended to. This one Hubert Tanner would do with Henry at his side instead of his lawyer. Matter of fact, he wouldn't even discuss it with him, because this was the one area they didn't agree on.

19

They had both stated their views on the matter a number of times and now found no need to bring it up again.

A plantation the size of the Tanner's required a great many hands, and that translated into many slaves. The clearing of additional land required young strong slaves. So their destination this morning was the auction house. It's said a ride down the Mississippi River is an event never forgotten. This is true for slave as well as free man. The free man rides in luxury on the top decks, the slave in chains down below. At the end of his ride is the auction house, where he is sold body and soul to the highest bidder.

A large group of Negro men, women, and children had been brought down over the past several weeks. At the auction house slaves are well fed and rested. The auctioneer knows the better his merchandise looks the more money it will bring in.

Mr. Tanner directed Henry to park the buggy a short distance from the auction area, this out of regard for his wife's feelings. Mrs. Tanner considered slavery a necessity to running large plantations. But in her way of thinking, slaves should be allowed to marry within their ranks and produce offspring, thereby making the horror of the auction house unnecessary. The screams and cries as mothers and fathers and their children were torn apart and sold to different owners were common occurrences. How anyone could watch this with indifference was beyond her.

As Mr. Tanner and Henry stepped from the buggy, so also did Susan the eldest of the two Tanner girls. Mrs. Tanner immediately protested, not wanting the child in the company of her father when he was conducting this type of business. Mr. Tanner, however, insisted it was healthy to satisfy the curiosity of a young mind, and off they went, Mr. Tanner with Susan's hand in his one hand and an umbrella in the other. The morning had brought a change in the weather. A light mist and cool breeze greeted those at the auction house. How quickly the ground can turn soft.

It was nearly 10:00 a.m. and a good sized crowd had formed in front. The "items for sale" were brought out and led to a platform for all potential buyers to examine. Some had the practice of looking inside the mouths and feeling for defects in body parts, on the women as well as the men. All seemed to agree that this was an unusually good lot for sale here today. Not only in quality but in quantity as well. Judging from the appearance of many of the men here, Mr. Tanner knew the bidding could be fierce. The cost of slaves had risen sharply the past few years, and supply was hardly keeping up with demand. He set in his mind if he could get a dozen or more strong hands this morning it would suffice for now.

In a few minutes the bidding would begin. The last few potential buyers were looking the lot over closely. One man stood out amongst the rest, a rather tall man, with long hair and beard, not dressed very nicely and particularly rough in his examining of those in line for sale. As he made his way down the line he grabbed with huge hands the faces of those in front of him pulling open their mouths and checking the teeth. Then he squeezed shoulders and arms and legs with a lot of pushing and shoving about, causing many to lose footing and fall. All the while he had a cold look in his eye and a constant murmuring of complaint. All were struck with fear at the thought of being bought by this man. Many were the tales of horror told among slaves about men such as this. No one in the crowd knew him, but a few knew of him. One was overheard saying he was about the meanest tempered man they'd ever come by and that he must have more money than brains. He worked his slaves to death years before their time.

As the man made his way to the end of the line he looked at those in back. These were the ones to be sold next. Among them were the women and children. As he was about to turn away to take his place with those ready to begin, he caught sight of a face partially hidden in the crowd. When she saw him looking at her she tried to sink down below the shoulders of the people in front of her, but it was too late. To get a better look he walked to the back and pushed his way through. On reaching her he half smiled as he said, "Come here, wench. Let's get a good look at ya." Since she was too frightened to move he reached out and grabbed hold of the dress she had been given that morning by the auctioneer and pulled her to him. He opened her mouth, then placed his hands on her shoulders and moved them over her breasts, then down to her legs causing her to jump backwards and fall, much to the displeasure of the man. Grabbing now on the chain that was connected to her ankle braces he dragged her forward toward him and pulled her to her feet with one swift tug on her arm. At which point she fainted.

The auctioneer and two assistants quickly made their way over to straighten things out. Hot with anger that this man had not only been holding up the proceedings, but now appeared to be damaging the merchandise, the auctioneer directed his assistants to carry the girl to the rear and get her back on her feet. He directed the man

21

to go to the area reserved for potential buyers, informing him he could "do as he pleased" with any he chose after he had first laid down his money. The auctioneer was particularly disturbed because this action had taken place in view of all those present. He knew this girl would have brought him a good sum of money; but now she might be considered unhealthy or damaged goods.

The girl was a mulatto of about fifteen years and, as is often the case with most mulattos, she was pretty, with fair skin and long flowing black hair. She was somewhat tall with the physical attributes of a more mature woman. Mulatto women often brought a high price being preferred by some for housekeeping and tending the master's children. Some of the more low-minded had other reasons.

The auctioneer had done his best that morning to make her look as pretty as possible hoping for a good sum when the bidding began. But if one were to closely examine the girl's eyes and the expression on her face, or notice her lack of energy, it would be quickly discerned that this girl was ill. The abusive fellow didn't see it because his mind was preoccupied with other thoughts. The auctioneer didn't see it, but then he never did. It was strictly business with him.

As the bidding began, the attendants readied the girl for her time. They had gotten her to her feet, but she was not very stable. As an incentive, they offered the threat of a good beating, if she fell. Having been subjected to years of abuse she understood the alternative all too well.

Mr. Tanner considered Henry an asset at these dealings. Henry was a pretty good judge of character and would often advise which to buy and which to pass on. Henry's judgment of character extended beyond that of fellow slaves. He had been noticing for some time the child, Susan, Mr. Tanner's daughter, who was accompanying them today. Susan was not affected by the mistreatment of people the way her mother and sister were. As they witnessed the harsh treatment of the mulatto girl Susan seemed, at least in Henry's mind, to be unmoved by the event.

After about forty minutes Mr. Tanner had purchased eleven of what he and Henry considered good field hands. As they waited for another lot to be brought up, some women and children were being auctioned. Mr. Tanner had no need this year for women and children, which were plentiful to the plantation. As he stood talking with some other men Henry watched with Susan as women and children were sold to the highest bidder, the air was periodically filling with heart-wrenching cries as mothers and young ones were sold to separate owners. No matter how many times Henry saw this happen, it never failed to bring a tear to his eye. Susan, though, seemed not bothered at all.

The mulatto girl was now brought center stage. Not able to hold herself well she tried to make eye contact with a man and his wife who had just purchased two women, but as the bidding began they make no motion. The pleading look in her eyes could not hide the fact that she was not very well. Very quickly the bidding was left to the tall bearded fellow and one other. Henry, in an uncharacteristic move, interrupted Mr. Tanner and suggested he buy this girl saying that with a little rest she'd make a good field hand. The words were hardly out of his mouth when Susan replied that a sick Negro could be found on any plantation, and that her father need not buy one and so far from home at that. Mr. Tanner, ignoring the girl's comments, said only that he needed strong young Negro men for the clearing of new fields.

The word "sold" then rang out. Henry looked up to see what he had feared. The bearded man had bought the girl. Attendants placed her off to the side and removed the braces and chain as was their custom. The man paid and took possession of the deed. On returning to the girl he attempted to bring her to his wagon where four men and a woman purchased earlier sat rechained. He motioned for her to walk, but she didn't, or couldn't being too ill or too frightened. This immediately brought out the despotism in her new owner. Placing his huge hand behind her neck he gave her a mighty shove while loudly demanding the wench "start walking." As though her legs were tied in knots she fell again, this time not on the platform but in the mud. Infuriated, he placed his muddy boot on her side and gave one swift kick, causing her to roll onto her back, Yelling now at the top of his voice all attention was focused on this scene. Lifting her to her feet by her hair he raised up his hand to strike her.

A strange mix of emotions now permeated the air. Totally appalled were the women in attendance. A disgusted look came over the face of Hubert Tanner, as well as most men watching. And Henry, poor Henry, to be a man, strong, fit, ready to do good by everyone, standing by watching as a man abuses a child, knowing there's not a thing that can be done on his part. It touched deep into his heart.

The man released his powerful hand and hit the side of the girls head dropping her once again to the wet ground near his feet, screaming for her to get up and walk. Using all the strength she could muster, she got to her knees, at which point, she vomited,hitting the legs and feet of the despot who now wished he had never laid eyes on her. Several men in attendance had seen enough. Confronting the man one exclaimed, "The proceedings have been held up long enough. Conclude your business quickly, sir, we all have better things to do today." Another motioned for two attendants to come and give a hand. They carried the girl to the wagon and dropped her inside where she lay in cold wet clothes partially sullied by her own vomit. As the man pulled away, the proceedings began again. Mr. Tanner thought only about the business at hand. Henry, however, could think only about what would become of the poor souls who were chained in the back of that wagon.

A half hour more and Mr. Tanner had finished his business. It was time to head home. As their small caravan pulled away Susan told her mother and sister what she had seen, but she did not mention the mulatto girl. Mrs. Tanner listened intently, troubled by the child's enthusiasm.

They had been longer then they planned and they had a distance to go before they would reach their lodging place of the night. The wet ground would also slow them down.

Three days journeying found them well into Mississippi. The warm days of autumn had returned and traveling was going smoothly. Mr. Tanner drove the wagon in front with his young son sitting next to him. His wife and youngest daughter lay in the back reading and talking, enjoying a beautiful day. The wagon in the rear was larger, driven by Henry with Susan at his side. The two sang every song they knew and laughed and carried on as if they didn't have a care in the world. This wagon held the young Negro men and four teenage boys, along with some new pieces of furniture and other supplies.

It was Mr. Tanner's custom to allow the newly-purchased slaves to travel unchained once they had been in his company a few days. His words to them were few and simple. Anyone not behaving would be shot, though he had no intention of shooting anyone. It was Henry's job to see to it they believed he would. This made for trouble-free traveling.

Late afternoon and not far from the Alabama border Mr. Tanner decided to stop for the day. A slow-moving stream would supply some needed recreation for the children and refreshment for the slaves, as well as an hour with a good fishing hole. Walking with his young son along the creek bed he spotted a wagon a short distance ahead. Thinking it might be another family with the same intentions as his, he went up to introduce himself. On arrival he was given quite a surprise. Cooking over a small fire a short distance from the wagon was the fellow who had caused such a stir at the auction house in Orleans. Never a man of intentional ill manners, he introduced himself and his son, inquiring of his needs, to which the man responded, "I got all I need thank ya, I'll be home by midday tomorr."

"Alabama?" Mr. Tanner asked.

"The plantation Eznor, cotton producers we are, I've been to several auctions buying niggers. Business been good!" As he continued to talk the name Eznor kept ringing in Mr. Tanner's head. He was sure that was the name his brother-in-law had mentioned. Two brothers had inherited the family estate and made a reputation for their cut-throat business practices. Meanwhile Roscoe had walked over to the wagon where a group of slaves huddled together in chains. After a brief conversation, Mr. Tanner excused himself to return to his campsite. Rising to get his son he knew the man had not recognized him from Orleans. Curious about the mulatto girl he said, "Looks like you got yourself a healthy lot of Negros."

"I spects the ones on the ground are fine enough" (referring to fourteen men of various ages, five women and some children), but there's a wench in the back of the wagon that's good for nothin'. Laid out cold cash for the nigger and I spect I'll be leaving it for the birds any hour now."

Walking up to the boy he took his hand then walked to the back of the wagon. The stench was strong. Bearing it he pulled back the curtain and peered in. Lying on her stomach her long hair covering her face, she looked all but dead already. The dress he had last seen her in, was now covered with dried mud and bloodstains and wet with tears. Her hair was heavily knotted and filled with dirt and leaves. Mr. Tanner wondered, was he perhaps letting her die because she was not able to fulfill the purpose for which he so obviously had bought her? Turning to depart one of the Negro women said softly, "Massa, da po child ain't had nutin to eats or drink. I's tried to help her but he won't let me."

On returning to his campsite Mrs. Tanner inquired about his visit. Before stating it was the obnoxious fellow at the New Orleans auction he asked if the plantation Eznor was near her sister. She replied, "Yes, I'm certain I have heard them speak of it before? Is that the owner?"

"I believe it's one of them for certain," said Mr. Tanner. Then he related the rest of the story. Henry sitting nearby was listening anxiously. He still was thinking about the poor girl and what would become of her. Mr. Tanner had not mentioned her, not wanting to upset his wife. Henry, not realizing Mr. Tanner's intention asked, "The girl Master. Is the girl all right?"

"What girl, Henry?" asked Mrs. Tanner.

"The light skinned girl the man bought. She was a might sickly, and he beat her so in Orleans!" Henry said excitedly.

"Does he have this girl, Hubert?"

"I'm afraid he won't for much longer. There's nothing can be done for her," Mr. Tanner said rather sadly. Of course, he wasn't speaking from a medical standpoint. His reference was to the fact that she was the man's property and he could do what he pleased. Henry's body relaxed and he said, "Lord have mercy on her soul."

Things like this happened all the time and many people just accepted it as part of life. But not all. Mrs. Tanner had not been raised that way, nor did she want her children to be. She accepted slavery, but not the harsh methods with which some treated their slaves, particularly the young ones.

She tried to get the young girl out of her mind but couldn't. Finally, going to her husband she told him she had to look in on the child. Knowing her well, he knew she wouldn't rest till she did.

Taking Henry and Susan they walked to the campsite. Sitting up against a large oak tree smoking a pipe the man appeared to have little interest in Mrs. Tanner's concern. However, he did have a considerable investment in the girl, so he half reluctantly agreed to her request. The three approached the wagon and pulled back the canvas flap to get inside, but the stench was so great that Susan quickly turned and walked several feet away. Mrs. Tanner went in as Henry stood in the entrance looking on.

Mrs. Tanner herself was not ready for what she found. Gently pulling her by her shoulder, she rolled her onto her back. The girl moaned some as she fell back and looked up to see who was there. For the first time in who knows how long she saw eyes filled with compassion and kindness, all she could do was stare at them. Mrs. Tanner took control. "Henry, set loose the woman outside there. Have her fetch water in a pail. Then come around and open the

26

front flap. This child needs fresh air." Pushing back her hair off of her face she kept saying in a soothing voice. "It'll be all right, child. It'll be all right. You just try to be calm. I'm going to clean you up."

The air inside the wagon was so heavy you could almost feel it move when the flap in front was opened. Along with the fresh air came light, and Mrs. Tanner could see fully what lay before her, and a heart-wrenching sight it was. To the woman with the water she said, "Help me remove her clothing so we can wash her and tend to her wounds." But, the girl had lain too long in the wagon. Lying in her own urine, mud and blood dried to her skin and hair, it would be impossible to do anything with her there. With Henry's assistance they carried her out and laid her on a blanket and began washing her. After nearly an hour she was clean. She looked to be somewhat relaxed now; however, she spoke not a word.

Several times Mrs. Tanner asked her what her name was, but got no response. Meme, the Negro woman assisting her, said the girl had not spoken at all, even when he had beaten her.

The man was nowhere around, having walked off into the woods. Mrs. Tanner sent Henry back with Susan to their own wagon to get food for the girl as well as Meme, who had eaten only once a day since leaving New Orleans.

Mr. Tanner returned with Henry and the supplies. Looking down at the young girl he could only shake his head and feel sorry that the girl wound up at the wrong place at the wrong time. But, what also troubled him was the expression he saw on his wife's face. They had seen situations similar to this before, but she had never reacted quite this way. As he was thinking it she began to speak, "Hubert, you must persuade this man to give us this child. If we leave her here I know she'll die. I'm sure we can make her well, and we can find plenty at home for her to do."

"I don't know, Emily," said Mr. Tanner. "It's not our place to be interfering with this man's property. And, why should he want to give her up to me anyway?"

"We will pay for her of course, I wouldn't expect not to. You must do this Hubert! I cannot! I cannot leave her here! Please, offer him one of the slaves you purchased in exchange for her. Surely you can convince him to take a strong young man for this dying girl!"

"Perhaps I can Emily, but I'm not sure why I would want to."

"Please Hubert do this thing for me." And with a smile of delightful satisfaction, Mr. Tanner conceded.

27

As he went off to find the girl's owner, Meme began to plead with tears coming down her face, "Oh, Missis, please buy me too, I's promise to work real hard for ya, I's can pick cotton seed, I's can do wash, tend to youngins, I's never be no trouble to ya. Dis man mean, and I knows he'll whip a lot. And, oh, Missis you're so kind and I's promise to work real hard. Don't leave me with dis here man."

"Meme if I could I'd take all of you out of here, but I can't, and I'm sorry, I'm truly sorry."

Henry had taken some food also for the men chained near the wagon. Talking with them he found that none of them knew where the girl had come from. All he learned was that when they woke in the morning she was there at the auction house.

Mr. Tanner returned, looking at his wife who was sitting on the blanket where the girl was lying and said, He'll give me the girl for three, Emily, three of my best hands! And he'll hear of nothing else. I'm sorry Emily, I know you wanted to help." Reaching out his hand he said, "We better go back now." Taking her husband's hand she rose to her feet and started to walk. She couldn't look back. If she had, she would have seen the first real response from this sick girl. Sitting upright with the most forlorn look on her face, she watched Mrs. Tanner slowly walk away.

It was well into the night before Mrs. Tanner fell asleep. In a few short hours it was daylight again. She was up sitting by the fire with a cup of coffee in her hand. She knew it was a formidable task, separating this girl from that man. In a few hours he or they would be moving on. Putting her cup down she went to Henry, gently woke him and told him to bring one of the slaves, a strong one, and meet her in a minute near the front of her wagon. She then went inside the wagon and to her leather hand bag, and took out a small box. Inside this box was a pair of earrings. Small nuggets, but pure gold, the most expensive jewelry Mr. Tanner ever purchased. One she put back in the box the other she pulled off the hook and placed into her pocket. Then she went out to meet Henry. As the three of them hurried across the trail Mr. Tanner watched, totally perplexed by his wife's actions. He waited a few moments, then followed only to be near enough if trouble arose. His wife's tenacity intrigued him and he wondered how on earth she would try to persuade such a despot to release the girl, and for only one slave, when he, unbeknownst to his wife, had also offered two hundred and fifty dollars along with a strong young slave.

Mrs. Tanner approached the man, who she found sleeping rolled up in a blanket near a fire that had long gone out; As she called to him he half rolled over. An empty flask fell to the ground. He opened his eyes but didn't speak. Mrs. Tanner knew then he had been inebriated the night before and sought to take advantage of the situation. Speaking loudly she said, "Are you feeling all right sir?" Not waiting for a response she said; "I fear you and the rest here might also be coming down with cholera."

"Cholera;" he repeated. "What are you talking about, lady?"

"I believe;" said Mrs. Tanner, "the girl has cholera. She has the symptoms doesn't she?" "I don't know, she's just sick;" he replied.

"And you?" asked Mrs. Tanner, "your eyes are puffy. Do you have a fever?"

"No, I have no fever. What do you know about cholera?"

"I know if the girl has it you'll be burying her before this day is over, and if she doesn't have it she looks like she might die today anyway. I'm going to give you this boy here and this gold nugget and take the girl with me and try to save her." Thrusting her hand quickly toward his face he reached out and took the nugget. He thought just to look at it, but he no sooner had it in his hand then Mrs. Tanner, Henry, and the young man with them were heading for his wagon.

The girl lay sleeping on the blanket with Meme nearby just as they left them the night before. Awakening her, they got her to her feet, wrapped a blanket around her and began to walk her away from the wagon. Several feet away they sat her down on a log and Mrs. Tanner went back to the man to exchange deeds for proof of ownership.

It was happening so fast the man looked as though he still wasn't sure what was going on, but if there was any doubt in him it ended quickly. As the girl sat with Henry she turned her head, doubled over and vomited. Deeds were exchanged.

After walking a short distance Henry carried her. He placed her in the back wagon covered her up, and left her to rest.

Mr. Tanner approached his wife and said with a smile, "Emily, my dear, the emancipators of the north could use someone of your capabilities."

"Time we be moving on Hubert," she said slyly.

The wagons moved on. Mr. Tanner, his wife, and young son drove in the first one. It looked like another beautiful day dawning.

He hadn't asked her yet, but he was wondering why his wife had reacted the way she did about the mulatto girl.

Henry was riding with two of the new boys at his side and wondering the same thing. He was happy the girl had been rescued, but he too had never seen Mrs. Tanner react that way.

Is it so odd a woman of Mrs. Tanner's disposition should want to save the life of a young and sick girl, one perhaps only a year or two older than her own daughters? There was also a fact that Mrs. Tanner had yet to relate to anyone. When she undressed the girl to bath her, she immediately realized the girl was three or four months pregnant just as she was. From that moment on there really was never a question. Mrs. Tanner was taking this young girl to Mariah!

Mariah

One of the premier plantations in all of Georgia. A house so big and beautiful you might think the Governor himself lived there, boasting spacious grounds with gardens and orchards and pastures abundant with livestock, and cotton fields as far as the eye could see. Cotton fields, worked six long days a week, producing the finest black-seeded cotton the earth can grow. Cotton pickers, upwards of three hundred slaves, lived on the plantation. As grandmother Tanner often said, "It's gotten to where you can't get a drink of water without passing two Negroes and three more are watching you from somewhere else."

The plantation was named after Naomi Tanner's mother Mariah. She died there shortly after Josiah and Naomi purchased the land in the late seventeen hundreds. A young and strong man, Josiah was in those days. And a hard worker, too, turning woods and wet lands into productive fields and trees into lumber to build cabins and storage sheds. They never dreamed what it would all amount to. But there they were highly respected by all who knew them as both gentlemen and sharp businessmen. Local politicians for some time have been trying to persuade Hubert Tanner to run for the governor's office, but so far to no avail.

Inside the house is the elegance one would expect, but with an atmosphere of homeyness and comfort, like a fine southern plantation should be.

Josiah and Naomi occupied one wing of the house. Hubert and Emily with the children took up the bigger part. Henry had a small apartment on the ground floor and Aunt Molly had a small apartment off of the kitchen. Aunt Molly too, has been with the Tanners since the early years. She is nearly seventy five now with a heart as big as the entire plantation. Widowed more than thirty years she spends her days cooking and cleaning and teaching the younger ones from her vast supply of wisdom. There are two things Aunt Molly insists on looking after herself. The kitchen, and everything else. Several other housekeepers live within the main house, and all contribute to making the Tanner household a warm and happy place.

A short distance from the house are the gardens. You would think with all the slave labor on hand you'd never see a white face in the gardens, but the Tanners have a love of the land. And from planting to harvest you will almost always find at least one of them picking and pulling and adjusting during the day and strolling in the evening.

The job of overseeing the orchards and gardens rested on the shoulders of Lester. Over the years he had proved himself to be a top notch gardener. He lives in a one room shack next to several barns at the far end of one of the gardens. His wife Willy Mae spends most of her day doing wash from the main house, as well as for her own four young ones.

Some months ago when the Tanners got back from New Orleans, she was given someone to help her with her chores. But the helper first needed to regain her health, and this has yet to happen, despite the attention from both Mrs. Tanner and Aunt Molly.

It's March now, 1842, spring is in the air. A few more weeks to make it official, but it's definitely in the air. Spring on the plantation is a busy time, everywhere you look there's planting, and pruning, and fixing things up. But, if you're young it's time to play. Roscoe's nearly four now and he's got nothing but play on his mind. There's no shortage of playmates; Negro children of all ages are plentiful on large plantations like Mariah.

Sunday evening just after dinner, Mrs. Tanner rises from the porch and walks to Lester and Willy Mae's house. She is in search of her friend whom they have called Lydia since bringing her home. At the sight of Mrs. Tanner, Lydia smiles. It's taken several months but a trusting relationship is developing. As they walk through the garden paths deciding where to plant tomatoes and potatoes and squash, they talk about motherhood and happy times. Lydia still

32

says very little. All that's really known about her is sad, a life of constant abuse. This may not be her first child.

Two women, as big as any should be when eight months pregnant, walk side by side through the garden. If you were a stranger you would not be able to tell that one was really a slave, a Negro, owned by the other. Though Mrs. Tanner never thought in those terms, they did live in Georgia, and a Negro is a Negro regardless of how much white blood he or she carries.

One difference was very noticeable. One woman walks deliberately strong; the other walks slowly, often on unsteady legs. Though looked after constantly, Lydia is not well and spends a great deal of time lying in bed. The baby inside her moved and kicked the same as Mrs. Tanner's and all hoped things would turn out well.

They sat on a bench in front of what in just a month or so would be a beautiful flower garden. As was always the case Mrs. Tanner did most of the talking, Lydia the listening, and more and more often smiling. Mrs. Tanner was saying, "The baby will be a month old or better before the annual May party. I should be able to do all I want by then, and you too Lydia, will have your strength back. There is so much to do. Aunt Molly, she tries so hard to do like she used to, but she can't. I see it in her more and more. She's slowing down poor thing, but you can help, Lydia. It would please me so and make things easier for Aunt Molly, and Aunt Molly can teach you so many things. She loves you, you know, she just talks about you and your baby all the time."

"She do?" questioned Lydia with a tone of confusion.

"Why of course she does Lydia. Can't you tell that?" asked Mrs. Tanner.

"I don't know, Missis. Why do she love me?"

"Sometimes, Lydia, there aren't words to describe feelings. Love is a natural thing that God made for people to have and share. Aunt Molly loves you. You're special to her heart and I love you, Lydia. When you were born and your momma held you to her breast she loved you very much. Why she is living somewhere, Lydia, and can't a day go by that she doesn't think about you, and her love for you."

For the first time, tears ran from her eyes and while Mrs. Tanner felt sad she also felt glad, glad to see emotion, glad to see she touched her heart. Lydia leaned over and placed her head on Mrs. Tanner's shoulder and sobbed uncontrollably. Finally getting a small measure of control she said, "I's want to love my baby real bad. I's scared Missis cause I's don't know how and I's scared my baby will be sold away from me."

"Lydia, Lydia, you poor child, I give you my word, my promise, your baby will never be taken away from you. You're gonna stay right here on Mariah, and one day someone's gonna marry you like Lester and Willy Mae, and you'll have more babies. So you stop your worrying right now. Things are gonna be just fine."

Mrs. Tanner helped Lydia to her feet and they started back to the house. They were joined by Naomi, the youngest of the two Tanner girls, and several playmates. "Aren't you feeling well today, Lydia?" asked Naomi.

"She's just tired;" replied Mrs. Tanner, "making a baby is a lot of work."

"Did I make you tired like that mother?" asked Naomi. To which Mrs. Tanner gave a motherly smile. "I hope both of you have baby girls," said Naomi. "Mother is going to name hers Isabelle, what will you name your baby Lydia?"

"I spects I want to name it Aunt Molly," replied Lydia with a certain firmness in her voice.

Naomi's first response was that child-like laughter that comes so spontaneously. Then she said"Oh, Lydia, aunt is not a name. Her name is just Molly. We call her aunt because we love her. And, what if it is a boy? Aunt Molly would be a funny name for a boy." This made all the children laugh and carry on. Lydia first looked confused then smiled and laughed with the rest.

As they lay in bed that night, Mrs. Tanner related the evening's events to Mr. Tanner. How delighted she was at Lydia's show of emotion. To her husband she said; "Don't you think it must be a strange feeling being a mulatto? Do you think sometimes they feel the way white people do, and other times like Negroes do?"

"I guess a lot depends on where one lives. If you're a very light skinned mulatto and live in Europe there are places that treat them as if they were white. Up north they are not quite as tolerant as that, but they don't have the restrictions that full-blooded Negroes have. And here in the south? Well, they know they're Negro and I suspect that's better for them. No confusion about what they are or where they belong. Emily, I know we have had the same thought about Lydia's baby. I'd bet a year's wages that a white man fathered the child. Those mulatto girls are usually too good looking for their own good. And when your Lydia was a might healthier, she was surely better looking than most."

34

"I know, Hubert, I know, that poor child."

The next couple of weeks brought plenty of rain, especially for March in the south. It also meant more than the usual amount of time Grandmom Tanner spent in the kitchen, a thing Aunt Molly enjoyed as much as a thorn in her side, still she was so busy running to Lester and Willy Mae's all hours of the day and night, she didn't complain. Lydia wasn't doing well at all. Although Mrs. Tanner couldn't neglect her own health, she would sit with her as often as possible. A persistent fever took all the strength from the girl. It became increasingly impossible for her to keep any food down. Aunt Molly and Willy Mae were doing all they could, but there was no hiding the worried look on their faces.

The twenty-fifth day of March. The sun has been shining all day. Mrs. Tanner didn't go out today, plenty of rest, that's what everyone keeps telling her. Her midwife has been staying with them since the weekend past, and no one expects she'll have to stay much longer, least of all Mrs. Tanner. Having done this three times already, she's had enough experience to know her time had come. The reports coming back with Aunt Molly weren't good, and this troubled her so, but she knew she had to stay close to the house today. She spent her day as normally as she could. The morning and most of the afternoon were spent with the children doing their lessons. By evening she was worn out and retired early.

Whenever left alone like this, Mr. Tanner, that highly respected, successful, wealthy business man who many thought should be the next governor, became, Hubert the Giant. Tables and chairs were pushed back to expose a large oriental rug which became Badman's Island. Young Roscoe's job was kill the giant and free the people. Not one to abandon her little brother at such a time of crisis, Naomi closed her book and attacked. Susan, who would insist to any and all that she was too old for such playing, wasn't!

Grandmother Naomi sat knitting in her chair by the window watching and smiling at the sounds of the children's screams and laughter. In the study there was a small glow coming from the fireplace. Josiah and Henry played chess. Josiah's patience in teaching Henry the game years ago have brought may hours of satisfaction. Josiah has boasted to his friends that Henry could beat any of them fifty percent of the time. They, of course, for the most part don't believe he can play, let alone win.

About 5:30 the next morning and nearly light Mr. Tanner was awakened by his wife. He opened his eyes and found her sitting on the edge of the bed. "You might want to get Marie, Hubert. I'm about to make you a daddy again," said Mrs. Tanner with a smile. "Send your mother and the girls in too, and I think you better hurry." As Mr. Tanner was doing just that, Mrs. Tanner called out to him to send up Aunt Molly.

Not quite 6:30 and down the stairs came two young girls at full speed calling out for their daddy and running from room to room. They've got a message. The kitchen was the place to look. Mr. Tanner, his father, Henry, Lester and a half dozen children sat around looking at one another while every five minutes someone different came to the back door to inquire. Finally, the kitchen door swung open and in rushed the girls each trying to get the words out first. "It's a girl, papa! It's a girl! She's beautiful! She has lots of hair! Go and see her papa! Mother is waiting for you!"

When he entered the room his eyes became misty. Sitting up in bed, his wife was nursing his newborn baby girl. What a sight to behold. "Come and say hello to Isabelle, Hubert;" said Mrs.Tanner. "Such an easy delivery this one was."

"It certainly was;" said Marie, "I can only wish they were all like that."

"Oh Missis never had too bad a time wit any of um;" exclaimed Aunt Molly. "And she sure do make um pretty. You come on down to da kitchen Master Tanner when yous' a ready. Ya old Aunt Molly is gonna make ya yo favorite breakfast." Mrs. Tanner smiled, she knew her husband couldn't resist that invitation for long.

After a few moments of talking Mr. Tanner's mother hurried him out of the room. There were still many things yet to be done, and his wife needed her rest.

When he arrived in the kitchen, Willy Mae was there. "Aunt Molly says de baby is a pretty one. I spects it be a while for anyone can see the Missis."

Mr. Tanner looked her in the eye with as straight and serious a look as he could make, held it for a second then said, "Well, ya going up or not?"

She almost was out of the room before she got all the words out. "Yessum Master. I sure is." Following close on her heels were two young children. Aunt Molly snatched them up before they could get out of the room. "You little critters a goin no where. You see the baby soon enough." Children, no matter who they are, or where they live, know how to take advantage of a good situation.

About midway through breakfast, Mr. Tanner came to realize every seat at the large kitchen table was filled. Aside from the four men, the seats were filled with happy, giggling children drowning Aunt Molly's flapjacks in expensive maple syrup. He placed his hand on top of a woolly head sitting next to him and said, "boy, I think you like Aunt Molly's flapjacks. Aunt Molly give these youngins some orange juice, we're having a party, aren't we son?" The kitchen filled with laughter. Joy is such a contagious thing.

Willy Mae sat on the edge of the bed as Mrs. Tanner handed her the baby. The two women are close in age, both now have four children, both have lost two. Years of living as closely as they do, and working the gardens as often as they do, has produced a friendship they both value. Willy Mae has a strong sense of motherhood, perhaps because she, too, like many, was sold away from her mother when very young, spending her teenage years in hard labor in cotton fields. The conversation quickly turned to Lydia. In response to Mrs. Tanner's inquiry Willy Mae said, "The po child don't eat hardly nutin. One time she hot with fever, then she got chills. Can't keep awake no how. I's been prayin everyday fo da baby be born. Then maybe she be well."

"I hope so Willy. I'm scared for the baby though. I pray too that everything's going to be all right."

The third morning after the birth of Isabelle Mrs. Tanner was feeling fine. She put the baby in her crib and left Mother Tanner to watch her. With her girls, and little Roscoe, they walked over to Lester and Willy Mae's. Lydia was sitting up in bed eating when Mrs. Tanner came in. Her eyes immediately became teary. You could almost feel her joy as she sat straight up smiling freely, without the hesitation that was characteristic of her just a few months ago. Delighted to see her sitting up and eating, Mrs. Tanner went to her bed and sat next to her. Lydia listened excitedly about the baby Isabelle.

Mrs. Tanner hoped she was hiding the despair she was feeling as she looked at the large dark lines under Lydia's eyes and her drawn face. Her lungs sounded congested as she coughed repeatedly. Why does this child have to be so ill? Mrs. Tanner asked herself. If she had been born in another place and time a girl as beautiful in appearance and possessing so sweet a disposition would have married a fine gentleman, raised a family and lived a happy life. But that will never be. A white father, a Negro mother, made pregnant against her will produces only forlorn children of which Lydia is one.

Both women needed their rest, so the visit was short. The next day Dr. Myers came to check in on Mrs. Tanner and on the baby. Both received a clean bill of health and the good doctor was in a hurry to move on. Mrs. Tanner, in expectation of his visit, had asked her husband to have Doc Myers look at Lydia. Because it was such a highly unusual request, she dared not asked herself. Mr. Tanner thought it a good idea and approached it from the standpoint of his concern for his wife and children being around this sick girl, and their not knowing what she may be infected with. Dr. Myers was an easy going man and would apply his skills anywhere if it would help someone. Also, his friendship with the Tanners went back a good many years.

The two men left the house and walked together to Lydia's house. Dr. Myers went in alone and sent the children out, but had Willy Mae stay to reassure Lydia that everything was all right. A few minutes later the doctor came back out. Rather then have his cariole brought to the house, the men walked off toward the stable. "I couldn't examine her too well Hugh. My touching her seemed to frighten her a great deal. I was afraid I was doing more harm than good. I believe though, she has pneumonia. The lungs are awfully congested. I couldn't check too well, but I found some broken ribs that hadn't healed right. I'd say she's been badly abused. How'd you come across her?"

"Emily came across her," said Mr. Tanner. And, she's taken her under her wing. It's been several months and the girl can't seem to get better. What about the baby?"

"I can't say, Hugh, pneumonia isn't what made her this sick. It could well be what's keeping her from getting well though. It's a hard enough thing to shake on its own, but what with being pregnant, and whatever else ails her, I don't know. I'd say she's due to deliver any day. I'll gladly come by if you need me. Have Emily see that Willy gives her the medicine on time."

"Tell Victoria, Emily will be calling on her soon. Seems like they start planning the spring ball earlier every year." The two men parted company. Dr. Myers drove off to his next call, and Mr. Tanner headed toward the back buildings looking for his field manager.

The next few days brought no change for Lydia. Mrs. Tanner and her newborn though were doing quite well. With each passing day the baby grew stronger. She wanted so badly to take the child to Lydia to boost up her spirit, but knew she couldn't do that.

One week to the day since the baby was born, about mid afternoon, one of Lester's young boys came charging into the house, calling out loudly for Mrs. Tanner; "Momma says y'all better come right now! Miss Lydia sick summum alful!"

"You go fetch Aunt Molly and tell her to come quickly!" said Mrs. Tanner as she quickly rose to her feet. Calling into the next room to the elder Mrs. Tanner she said, "Please watch Roscoe and the baby, and ask Hubert to come over when he gets in." The two younger girls headed out with their mother and the three hurried across the yard.

Mr. Tanner and his father came in the front door missing his wife by not even a minute. His mother relayed the message, then repeated what she had said before (though never to his wife). 'I don't know why she insisted on bringing a sick one home anyway, and all the time it's taking up could be better spent with her own youngins. The Negroes take care of each other just fine without us meddling in." He wasn't going to get into a conversation about it, but he too had often wondered about the whole situation.

When he arrived at the house where his wife was, he was greeted by several children who were quick to fill him in on what was taking place inside. Sending one in to get his wife, she came out to see him. "Oh, Hugh, his wife said sadly, "the baby is ready to be born and she's unconscious. Been like that all day. She shakes terribly, then lies perfectly still."

"Emily," Mr. Tanner said compassionately, "I'll send Henry to fetch Doc Myers, but it may be that no one can do anything for her. You have all tried your best. Robert didn't seem to think she could get well."

"She's just a child, a poor child alone and scared," said Mrs. Tanner. "God only knows what she's been through. In a few years our own daughters will be the same age. It's just all so sad."

The day slowly moved into evening. The noticeable change was that Lydia's breathing grew more and more labored. Mrs. Tanner's thoughts had shifted now from trying to save Lydia, to saving the baby. As darkness set in, she knew Lydia would not survive the night.

Henry arrived at Doc Myers' some hours ago, but the doctor was out calling on others and all Henry could do was wait. It was well past midnight and he was sleeping in the buggy when the doctor woke him. "Henry, are Mrs. Tanner and the baby all right?" asked Dr. Myers.

Getting himself upright he said, "yes 'em, they's fine. It's the Negro girl, Lydia. She real sick. Master Tanner sent me out dis here afternoon to fetch ya. He spects she gonna die today."

"I'm gonna get a few things and be right back. I'll ride with you."

By the time they arrived it was nearly five o'clock in the morning. Lester had taken the children with him to sleep in the hayloft of the barn. Willy Mae and Mrs. Tanner had been taking turns wiping a cool rag over Lydia's head and neck. Doctor Myers began to examine her. Her lungs were heavily congested and she was barely breathing. He knew right away the girl was dying. He slid his hands over her stomach. She wasn't as big as she could have been, but he felt that the baby was fully formed and ready to be born.

He rose up, went over and sat next to Mrs. Tanner. She could see he was exhausted and the look on his face said it before the words came out. "She's not going to make it through the night Emily," he said in a sorry tone. "She won't go into labor on her own, but maybe we can save the baby. We could lose her, and maybe the baby too. But, she's going to die without delivering the child anyway. We can only try."

"Please, Robert," said Mrs. Tanner. "Do what you can." As he picked up his bag and went back to the bed he asked that someone ready hot water. "Emily, I'll try to induce labor. Let's pull the bed away from the wall. I'll need you on that side to hold her leg toward you. Willy Mae, you stay by her head in case she starts moving around."

Reaching now inside her, the doctor attempted to cause her water to break, and to try and determine if the baby would indeed be able to deliver naturally. This caused her to stiffen her body which brought pain and considerable groanings. Dr. Myers looked at Mrs. Tanner with concern but said, "She's very dilated. If she weren't sick, this baby would have been born already. We'll just have to wait a while and see what happens." Again her body stiffened, relaxed, then stiffened again. As the doctor started to speak she let out a low soft moan and exhaled completely. Her body lay still for a second. Then drawing in a breath that half filled her lungs, she released it again and lay perfectly still. The girl died.

As Mrs. Tanner was rising to a standing position and the words were coming out of her mouth, "Oh God no." Dr. Myers whipped around lashing out to grab his bag. He failed to get a good hold of it and upset the small table it sat on. When his bag hit the floor it opened, partially emptying its contents. Scrambling in an instant he recovered his instruments. One was a scalpel. Placing his hand on the girls stomach he took the scalpel and began to cut. Willy Mae, already with tears racing down her face, immediately turned and went to the other side of the room. Within just seconds of that final breath the doctor had laid open her stomach and was reaching inside in a desperate attempt to save the baby. Mrs. Tanner as though frozen, did not move a muscle. Her face was pure white. The odor was almost unbearable, she seemed to be in shock, just staring at what was taking place, unable to say a word.

There was blood everywhere. Mrs. Tanner's eyes widened as she leaned back against the wall. It was such an awful mess, but between the doctors blood-covered hands, was a baby. He quickly snipped the umbilical cord, then gave the baby a light smack on its rear end. Getting no response he did it again. This time the baby's legs kicked. It made a gargling sound and then it cried. Dr. Myers took it to the table and laid it on a towel. Calling to Willy Mae to bring warm water and towels, he cleaned the baby's nose with cotton swabs, then began washing it off.

He looked over to Mrs. Tanner. She had slid down to a sitting position on the floor. He quickly took the blanket at the top of the bed and covered Lydia's body, then reached out and took hold of Mrs. Tanner's hand and helped her to her feet. "Emily;" he said, "we've got to get this baby cleaned up so I can examine it." Although it was really Mrs. Tanner he was concerned with.

The baby appeared to be fine. The distraction worked, Mrs. Tanner went to the baby and began wiping it clean with the warm rags Willy Mae had prepared. Dr. Myers next instructed Willy Mae to fetch her husband and have him remove the body from the house. "It's a girl," Mrs. Tanner said out loud, but to herself, "a girl. Lydia wanted a girl. Is she all right Robert?"

Doctor Myers half smiled and said, "She's crying like a healthy newborn wouldn't you say Emily?"

After the baby was cleaned Dr. Myers checked her over. Satisfied all was well he returned her to Mrs. Tanner. The door opened and Willy Mae entered with her husband and another man to remove Lydia's body from the house. There would be no delay in burying her. The wagon was out front, they would take her to the slaves' cemetery immediately. Dr. Myers now instructed Willy Mae to go fetch a slave who was nursing a child and bring her up to feed the baby. He went outside, sat down on a bench, leaned back and closed his eyes. He was totally exhausted.

Mrs. Tanner had the baby wrapped in a small white blanket and holding her tightly she paced back and forth across the floor waiting for Willy Mae's return. It was a considerable distance to the slave quarters, and while the baby had managed to survive within its sick mother it couldn't wait for nourishment now. Really there was no need to wait. Mrs. Tanner already overdue to feed her own little girl had a ready supply of milk. Enough for this baby and her own. Sitting down in a chair she turned the infant to the side position, withdrew her arm from her blouse and placed the baby at her breast. In an instant the baby took hold. What can be compared to the moment when a mother and child make this life sustaining connection for the first time. When their eyes meet in an unbreakable stare, and without uttering a word they convey to each other love, commitment and trust in a way that words could never do.

As the eyes of this baby focused on the eyes of Mrs. Tanner, she was overcome with emotion. All the events of this night came rushing in on her and her eyes filled with tears that rolled down her cheeks and dropped softly on the child's blanket. When a tear landed on the baby's face Mrs. Tanner wiped it away with her thumb and in doing so realized the magnificent beauty of the baby for the first time. With her thoughts turning back to Lydia, she rested her head back against the chair and closed her eyes.

Several minutes passed and the door opened slowly. Aunt Molly had already heard the news. It was nearly 6a.m. and the night's activities were being related throughout the plantation. She came in to comfort Mrs. Tanner, though she herself needed some comforting since she had grown quite attached to Lydia during the months they were together. Sitting in a chair nearby, she spoke softly. "Lydia's wit de Lord now misses, and He'll take care of her. Da po child suffer much, now she gonna rejoice much." At that moment Aunt Molly realized what had taken place. The baby had stopped nursing and fallen asleep just beneath Mrs. Tanner's breast. Never one to hold back a word she said, "And de Lord bless your soul. I's an old woman, misses, and I's see lots the time when a Negro woman nurse a white baby for its sick mother, but I ain't never seen a white woman nurse a Negro baby. The Lord himself will rejoice when you goes to be wit him."

Mrs. Tanner opened her eyes and said, "Is that Master Tanner I hear outside Aunt Molly?"

"Yes em, he talkin to Doc Myers."

"Hold the baby for a spell while I go and see him." As she walked out into the daylight her husband put his arms around her and she held on to him with what little strength she had left. "Take me home, Hugh;" she said. "I've got to tend to Isabelle and get some rest." Turning to Aunt Molly who was standing in the doorway, she said, "Stay with the baby, Aunt Molly. She needs you."

"Don't you fret none bout dis here baby. I's not taken my eye off her today," Aunt Molly said in a reassuring voice.

"I'll send someone to take you home Robert," said Mr. Tanner. "I'll be in to see you in a couple of days." Aunt Molly went in and made a bed of blankets and straw where one of the children slept and placed the baby down gently where it lay asleep.

Rarely do white folks involve themselves in the lives of their Negroes. To many their slaves were only property unable to feel love and desire like white people. But not all. Some were like Mrs. Hubert Tanner whose hearts possess something different, and a few got to benefit from it. But, by and large the vast majority lived and died never having met one of these. Lydia did, if only for a brief moment. But so powerful can love and compassion be that in that brief moment, years of abuse were overcome and a heart was rescued.

The night is over now, some things have come to an end. Some things will never be the same again. Some who have known each other for many years will look at one another differently now.

For a few saw something that some never see in a lifetime. They saw the innermost feelings of another, the secret person of the heart.

The morning has arrived, bringing with it as always, new beginnings. Sleep now little baby, for not always when you close your eyes will you feel such peace.

End of Part I

PART II

Bonds of Love

The years have been good on the plantation Mariah. Harvest after harvest of that prized black-seeded cotton has brought a considerable fortune to the Tanner family. The family has grown some and taken the years well. Hubert Tanner has continued to steadfastly refuse requests to enter the political world. Business takes up a great deal of his time, and it all rests solely on his shoulders now. Josiah, his father, passed on a few years back, and Roscoe isn't ready yet to share the responsibility. Emily Tanner's years have also been good. She's seen fine results for the time spent raising and training her children. And she's a grandmother now. Two boys by her eldest daughter Susan. Wesley is six, and David not quite four. Their father, Edward Ramsay who captured Susan's heart some years ago, graduated near the top of his class with a degree in law and political science. He comes from a wealthy family in Georgia. Some say they were meant for each other, though there is always a tinge of sarcasm in that statement.

Naomi has grown into a fine young lady, with a heart full of wisdom like her mother and a head full of knowledge like her father. She is a very good seamstress and an even better accountant. Sometimes she works with her mother creating dresses and gowns, a hobby they've practiced for years. Other times she helps her father so he is not buried under his mounds of paper work. But always she waits for the return of her fiancee, Zachary Johnson. He's the son of Nathan Johnson, who owns several cargo ships which the Tanner's have used regularly to transport their cotton to England. On a ship now, he'll return in May, and a June wedding is planned.

Roscoe Tanner is seventeen now, six feet tall with broad shoulders and handsome features. He possesses the fine characteristics of his father. There are plans to send him abroad in a year to finish his education in England.

Then there's the baby, little Isabelle. She is a true picture of what a southern belle looks like, with as pretty a face as one could have, long flowing blonde hair and a personality and disposition as pleasant and comical as one would want a young teenager to be. She's up to something this morning and her father knows it. He also knows he would be thinking the same thoughts if he were fourteen and had a day such as this looming before him.

Early May brings days like this—the sweet smell in the air, the warmth of the spring breezes around your head. Isabelle's making breakfast for her parents this morning. Flapjacks, bacon and grits, the way Aunt Molly used to. All the while she is suggesting how she could better do her studies later in the day after getting this horse riding urge out of her system. Placing breakfast before her father she says, "Listen." Then she cups her ear with her hand. "Do you hear it? The meadows are beckoning me. 'Isabelle-Isabelle ... have your brother saddle your horse ... come gallop through our wild flowers and stir up the birds and bees ... come Isabelle, ride' ... Do you hear it father?"

"That's just the grits sizzlin in the bacon fat, Isabelle," her father replies with a smile. "But it does seem to be saying something." Cupping his ear with his hand he says slowly,

"Isabelle ... put me on your brother's plate, because you know he eats more than the biggest work horse on the plantation." Kissing her father on the top of his head, she says, "You're very funny this morning, father. I'm sure I'll still be laughing as I ride the length and breath of the meadows."

"Yes Isabelle, it's a beautiful morning for doing just that," said her mother.

"Well, then," declared her brother, "if I'm gonna be saddling her horse I might just as well throw a saddle on my own. Let him get a look at the meadows too."

"Your horse boy, could go through the meadows sleeping, he's been getting so many looks at it lately," added his father.

Off they went to the stables to ready their horses for riding. The use of the word saddle was for the benefit of their worrying parents. The fact is they rarely used their saddles. Leaving their shoes behind with the saddles, they ride bareback and barefoot with only the reins on the horses.

The Tanners have been breeding horses for years. Isabelle's is a two-year-old large brown and white one. Her brother's grayish with a patch of black near its hind quarters. The third one is thought to be Roscoe's, but he has given it to a friend. This horse is a black, two-year-old filly. Holding the reins of the third horse he leads it along as he and his sister depart from the stable. Round the back of the orchards they go in a pattern repeated many times. To the back of Lester and Willy Mae's house.

The house is bigger now, having been enlarged by two rooms to accommodate the growing family. Lester's off working in the gardens, which have also increased in size. It takes more and more each year to feed the Tanner household, as well as his own the year round. His wife is at the main house where she spends a good part of each day. Since the death of dear old Aunt Molly, Willy Mae has done most of the kitchen work, while her daughters have tended to the wash.

Back behind the house three girls are hard at work. Lilly Mae is washing clothes in a large wooden tub. Her older sister is hanging some on the line. The third girl is carrying a basket load to Elsa to hang, but at the sound of the horses' feet she looks up to see what she's been waiting for. Hurrying to Elsa, she drops the basket at her feet and takes off running toward the oncoming horses and her friends who ride with them. Elsa hollers to her, "Y'all just asking fo trouble girl. Y'all know what yous been told." Elsa wasn't really mad though. She knew it wasn't worth giving much thought to. This scene has been going on in one form or another for as long as she can remember.

As the girl reached her friends, young Roscoe jumped down from his horse. Standing next to the black one he cupped his hands. She ran up and in one motion placed a slightly dirty barefoot in his hand. He heaved, she sprang, and without ever stopping she landed on the horse's back. Gathering the reins and placing them in her hand, she turned the animal around, gently kicked its side and with a loud laugh took off in a gallop towards the forest and the meadows. As Isabelle turned her horse and kicked she said laughing, "Beat you to the meadows, Ros," and took off. He heard what she said, but his thoughts were elsewhere. This was going to be a beautiful day.

By the time he caught up with the two girls, they were well into the woods. The girls were sitting on a rock near a stream where they often stopped to water the horses. The air was filled with the sound of birds singing out their mating calls. Everything was green and alive. He sat on an old tree log near the rock and threw little stones in the water at their feet. "Bout time you got here Ros, we though y'all got lost," said his sister, sarcastically, then both giggled and kicked up water at him.

"I was just taking my good ole time, little sister, enjoying the morning air."

"Taking your time indeed, if you go any slower the horse will be sleep walking," said a still giggling Isabelle.

Getting up from the rock and stepping from stone to stone, the other girl entreated them saying; "Let's ride and get to the meadows while it's still early." Placing her hand on Roscoe's head she jumped down from the log and headed for her horse.

The rest of the morning and early part of the afternoon was spent at what they call the meadow, an area of wet lands and ponds interconnected by land bridges. A small boat Josiah built for Susan and Naomi when they were younger sat tied to an old dock.

About mid afternoon, and Isabelle had to return. They rode together as far as the orchards, where Roscoe said, "Leave the bridle on the fence, Iz. I'll put it away with mine. We're gonna ride through the pastures for a while. I'll see you at dinner."

There couldn't have been a nicer afternoon for riding, Isabelle rode slowly through the grove. She would have rather gone riding the fields, but knew it would have displeased her mother if she didn't return for her lessons. Watching as they rode off she waved again. Then a smile came over her face. She was happy for them. Happy they could keep on enjoying this day this way. Happy, too, for another reason. She was beginning to realize something, something her young innocent mind saw only good in. Seeing this picturesque scene from her eyes: a young boy, a young girl, riding their horses bareback through the lush green pastures. The girl's long black hair reaching down to the horses back. The boy sitting big and strong leading the way.

Yes, Isabelle was growing up, coming into a new age. They all were, but they weren't the only ones to know it.

When Isabelle returned to the house her mother asked her of her brothers whereabouts. Her reply was no surprise to her mother who said nothing. But Isabelle's grandmother, who was sitting across the room quickly responded saying to Mrs. Tanner, "Emily, your son is just asking for trouble. It's getting to where the boy ignores his lessons and chores and everything else. He needs to be put right." Mrs. Tanner didn't respond. They had had this conversation before. She just told Isabelle to bring her books to the study.

Mrs. Tanner didn't respond out of respect for her mother-in-law. She knew the remarks were not made to be cynical, but were out of concern for her family. She too could see what the elder Mrs. Tanner could see, but it was her hope that when Roscoe went off to England to finish his education all things would work out for the best.

As Isabelle and her mother sat down at a table in the study, the two young riders sat on the ground under a large cypress tree. A gentle breeze moved the moss that hung down from the branches. Butterflies and bees flew from flower to flower. The fresh smell of spring was all about them. Sitting there the girl pulled her long hair from behind her, draped it over one shoulder, and rested her head against the tree. She said to him, "Ros, isn't it lovely? I know there's not a more lovely place in all the world then right here, right now." Leaning on one elbow and facing her he said, "There's no doubt in my mind. I've never seen anything as lovely." Feeling him looking at her she realized what he meant. Responding as any teenage girl would, she pulled up a clump of grass and threw it at him. This was all he needed to start a wrestling match. Out here, far from everyone else, they were free to be themselves. Their roles in life had been taught to them from their earliest years, and they never had reason to question them, but things were changing quickly now.

Rising to his feet and stretching out his hand, he took hold of hers and brought her to her feet. She shook back her hair. They stood frozen for a moment. Then he lightly tugged her hand. "You want to walk for awhile?" As they walked toward their horses they continued to hold onto each other's hand. Gathering up the reins they started walking through the high grass.

"Isabelle says your family is going to meet the new family that bought the Dollin plantation on Sunday;" she said. "We heard two of their children are around our age. What's the matter, Ros? You don't look very interested."

I haven't given it any thought. I'd rather not even go, but I have to."

"I don't know why you're like that, I think it would be so much fun. She says they moved down from Kentucky. What did you hear?"

"Nothing more than what you just told me. I'm sure it'll be all right, but I could think of other things I'd rather do."

"Oh could you now;" she said with a smile. "Let's see, is it building a bigger boat for the meadows like you've been saying for, let's see now, three years? Or, how 'bout that hope chest for Naomi you've been working on since last year. Um, or is it . . . ?"

"Enough of your wise cracking remarks, girl. Besides, I'm gonna work on Naomi's chest this evening. I have to get it done soon."

Mounting their horses they headed back to the stable. After putting the horses in the barnyard, they parted company. Walking just a short distance, she turned and called out to him, "Ros . . . ?" As he stopped and turned around, she said, "I liked it when you held my hand today."

Not waiting for a reply, she turned and started walking again toward home. He watched till she rounded the corner of a building and was out of sight. She liked it he thought. Well that's good, cause I sure liked it too.

It was about all he could think of during dinner. He hoped she would come to the wood shop that evening while he worked on the hope chest.

Come Sunday afternoon, the Tanner family set out to visit the Cambridges, the family that bought the old Dollin plantation. The Dollins had been good friends for many years. When the elder Dollin passed away, the children having all grown, and now living off on their own, decided to sell. The Cambridges bought the plantation with the hope of restoring it to its once productive state.

It took just a little under half an hour to arrive. They were greeted by the entire family when they pulled up at the house, Wendall Cambridge and his wife Laura, two older sons, both married, and two younger children, Wendall Jr. seventeen, and Addie thirteen. They were a fine looking family and gave the Tanners a nice reception.

Mr. Tanner commented immediately on how much they had accomplished already. Though it was not one of the larger plantations, it was a beautiful one, consisting of several hundred acres, and a large stately house. Lunch was served in typical Georgia fashion after which the adults reclined on the veranda. Mr. Cambridge was interested in hearing about Mariah. He thought some of what he had heard might be exaggerated. To Mr. Tanner, he said, "How many acres do you possess over there, Hubert?"

"Oh, little more then a few thousand, but it's not all good for planting," replied Mr. Tanner.

"How much of our crop here would you say should be in cotton?" asked Mr. Cambridge.

"We hold to about eighty percent cotton. The price today has never been better," said Mr. Tanner.

"When we bought here, we were told you had discussed leasing the fields for planting. I hope we didn't cause you a problem?"

"No, not at all;" said Mr. Tanner. "I would have done it because they were sitting dormant for two years past and old Jonathan wasn't up to it anymore. Besides that he didn't have the slaves that it would have required and sending any of mine right now would have been a hardship."

"It must take a lot of slaves to work on a plantation the size of yours."

"We've about three hundred or so, but it would take a lot more if it weren't for the cotton gin."

The young ones sat respectfully listening. Then young Wendall asked his father if he could show the others about. Within a moment they disappear. As they are walking, they pass by a small group of slaves, three men and two women, sitting outside one of the huts used to house them. When they looked their way, Isabelle smiled and waved. Roscoe nodded and the slaves responded in kind.

Wendall and Addie looked away. "If they weren't such lazy critters we'd have been further along here by now," said Wendall to Roscoe. Roscoe didn't respond, he had heard that slaves were lazy all his life, but the ones he knew the best, Henry and Lester, and others seemed like hard workers. He just paid it no mind.

Then Addie said, "Poppa's gonna sell off the nigger children next week, and buy some young bucks. He wants to get this place in top shape as quickly as possible. Poppa says its easy down here to buy and sell niggers. He says the abolitionists aren't a problem like in Kentucky."

"Stupid abolitionists," says Wendall. "How on earth would all the work get done if it weren't for slaves? They can't do nothing else anyway."

Neither Roscoe nor Isabelle wanted to keep this conversation going. They had grown up knowing the warmth and affection of Henry, and Lester, and Willy Mae. Roscoe was old enough to have known Aunt Molly. All these people are a part of their lives and they were not taught to think ill of them. The others were field hands. They neither thought good nor bad of them. Isabelle suggested they meet next Saturday to ride together. Roscoe pointed toward an opening in the woods, and gave directions on which way to go. They decided to meet about half way.

When they returned to the house they learned they would be having dinner together again next Sunday when the Cambridges were coming to Mariah for the day. When Isabelle mentioned riding together on Saturday, Mrs. Tanner suggested they bring a change of clothing and spend the night. With all in agreement the Tanners headed for home.

On arriving there they were greeted by anxious faces, all wanting to know about their day with the Cambridges. What were they like? What changes have they made? What did they serve for dinner? And so on. Roscoe and Isabelle slipped away. He said, "After you change, meet me in the kitchen. We'll take a walk."

It wasn't necessary to say where. If she wasn't there to meet them they would go to get her. So off they went to Lester and Willy Mae's. But she wasn't there either. Willy Mae said, "Ain't seen her since da meetin dis mornin, I reckon she be at Goldies. She took wit her clothes she been workin on."

"I'm too tired to go that far, Ros, said Isabelle. "I'm going back to the house and read for awhile."

The house that Goldie lived in was among the row of shacks that housed the slaves, about three-quarters of a mile from the main house. Roscoe had walked it many times before, and he'd do it again this evening. "Come on Digger," he said to the dog. "I know you'll walk it with me." As he walked he thought about what his sister had said about Addie. How she did nothing but talk about him when the girls were alone, and the way she kept looking at him. He knew he liked it, but it didn't mean anything to him. There have been other girls who had taken a liking to him. Doc Myers' daughter, Rebecca, who he considered a very nice girl, had a crush on him several years back. But more and more with each passing day, he felt his heart swelling within him. Only one person ever dominated his thoughts and feelings, and all he wanted to do right now was be with her.

On arriving at Goldie's hut he stood in the open doorway. Sitting on a bale of straw at an old table, teaching several young ones to read, sat the one he had waited all day to see. With her back to him he looked at her long shiny black hair, and listened to her voice as she sounded out words and letters for the children to repeat. When Goldie looked up and saw him there she said, "Evenin Massar Tanner," at which all at the table looked around to see him.

"Evening Goldie," he said. Then looking at the girl and smiling, he said to Goldie, "You know Goldie, the sheriff will come and take her away if he hears she's teachin Negroes to read."

"I's be tellin her dat Massar Tanner, but she don't listen no ways. An what fer dem kids gonna read anyway, I's ask her? But, she say so dey read to me. Lor Massar Tanner, I's don't see it no-ways," Goldie said in an excited voice.

This caused the girl to laugh. "You'll see, mammy. They'll be reading books to you soon, and the Bible at Sunday meetings." To the children she said, "That's all for now, you practice what you learned tonight. You're all doing real good." Turning about she said, "I guess I better stick close to you, Ros, so that the sheriff doesn't get me. Is that why you came looking for me? You gonna hide me away so they don't take me to jail?"

"Maybe I've come to take you to jail," he said to the still laughing girl. "No use trying to talk me out of it. Better just come along peacefully." Bouncing up off the bale of straw she said, "I'll do anything you say, just don't let that ferocious dog get me." Digger had spent the whole time going from one child to another, his tail wagging so hard his entire rear end went back and forth. They departed laughing and saying to the dog, "Come on Digger before you hurt someone with that tail."

Once outside, she said to him; "Let's go to the meeting house, I want you to hear something." The meeting house was a room connected to a large barn the slaves used as a church. When not in the height of planting or harvesting they were allowed Sundays off from work. These days were spent mostly in this room. Once inside, she went to the old black piano. Having been taught along with Isabelle by Mrs. Tanner, she could play well, oftentimes coming here alone and playing for hours. "I made up a song I want to sing to you."

"Okay." Roscoe sat down on a bench near the piano. Softly she started to play. This old piano sounded nothing like the white marble grand piano in the Tanner house, but to two kids who had waited all day to be together it was the sweetest music there ever was. And, whatever the piano lacked, she more than compensated for with her voice.

Nothing about this girl said she was only fourteen, with the physical appearance of a mature woman and the singing voice of an angel. She started her song.

> *"I dreamed of a house on a hillside;*
> *in the open door stood mother dear.*
>
> *The sun was shining brightly in the blue sky.*
> *She reached out her hand and took me near,*
> *I heard her say my name; she said it sweetly.*
> *I threw my arms around her held her tight;*
> *She told me that she love me with her whole heart;*
> *And never would we ever have to part."*

As she continued singing, he stared at her, falling deep into thought. There had never been any question in his mind that she was the prettiest girl he'd ever seen, but now, he was seeing something else. She is so beautiful he kept telling himself, how could he ever want any other girl? But how could he ever really have this one? Thoughts he had never allowed to enter his mind before, he couldn't keep out now. Realities came rushing in on him like flood waters. His heart started racing, his hands were sweating, he shifted in his seat trying to get control of himself. Finally he stood up, wiped his forehead and walked around behind her and placed his hands on her shoulders. She played the final few notes very softly and then stopped. Her head was slightly bowed, he reached around putting his fingers under her chin, and raised her head. She was crying and it almost overwhelmed him. Brushing the tears away with the side of his thumb, he bent over and kissed her gently on her head. "That was a beautiful song," he said softly.

"Thank you;" she said as she squeezed his hand.

"I should get you home, it's getting late," he said. "I want you to play that song for Mother."

"I will;" she said as they departed.

That night Roscoe couldn't sleep. He tossed and turned for hours, unable to get the thoughts he had had earlier that evening out of his mind. If he could only change things he kept telling himself. Or if people didn't know he thought, it's none of their business anyway. But nothing can be done or changed. It's not fair! It's just not fair! Before falling asleep, he decided he would talk with his mother about this tomorrow. If anyone would understand she would.

At the breakfast table the next morning, Roscoe found his parents having a conversation about his grandmother. They had been talking a lot lately about bringing someone into the house to live in the apartment Aunt Molly used to have, to help with the household chores, and keep an eye on his grandmother's needs. Of course, they couldn't tell her that. She was an old woman now, but her mind was sharp as ever. Roscoe didn't want to trouble his mother with his problems right now, so he ate and went about his chores. Maybe later he thought.

Day after day went by, and he never did say anything. Before he knew it, it was Friday. Isabelle wanted to go to town to bring Rebecca Myers home for the weekend. Henry and Roscoe readied the cariole, picked up Isabelle and were well on their way before noon.

When they pulled up in front of the Myers' house, Rebecca and her mother were sitting on the porch waiting. As the girls went in to gather up Rebecca's things, Mrs. Myers invited Roscoe and Henry to relax a while. Going back into the house to get them a pitcher of cold water she called for her husband. "Hello, Ros, Henry," the good doctor said as he walked up onto the porch. "I didn't expect you here so early. Victoria getting you something to drink?"

"Yes, she is;" replied Roscoe. "How have you been Dr. Myers?"

"Been just fine Ros. Delivered the Dayton girl's baby the other day. They were asking about y'all."

"Who'd she marry Doc?" asked Roscoe.

"A young man from Kentucky, seems like a fine sort;" said the Doctor.

"You don't say, the folks that bought the Dollin plantation, the Cambridges, are from Kentucky. Rebecca's gonna meet em this weekend," said Roscoe.

"That's what I hear. I've been meaning to call em myself. Guess we ought to do that this weekend," the Doctor responded. "And Henry you're looking right well," the doctor continued. "Been getting any fishing in this spring?"

57

"I's get in a time or two when I can;" said Henry. The doctor and Roscoe looked at each other and laughed. Henry was known for his fishing. Years ago when Roscoe's grandfather was alive, he would tell his wife that Henry had snuck off again, and he was gonna hear about it right now. Off he'd go to the fishing pond where Henry would conveniently have an extra fishing pole. "Now never mind, never mind;" Henry said, laughing. "Someone gots a catch em or dare gets a be too many in da pond."

"Yes, Henry;" said Roscoe. "You're doing that pond a big favor." And the men sat and joked a spell enjoying a warm and pleasant afternoon.

That evening back at Mariah, the entire house had gathered after dinner in the family room, sitting around the piano singing, and laughing, and reading poems the girls had written. After dark the young ones, along with Willy Mae's youngins, and several other of the Negro children played games with the little ones till nearly ten o'clock. They retired, satisfied by the days pleasures, and anxiously looking forward to tomorrow. Roscoe went to his room and fell fast asleep. The three girls went out on the upper veranda with blankets to sleep there. At almost midnight, Mr. Tanner appeared at the doorway, "Are you girls going to talk all night?" Still barely able to control their laughing, Isabelle said, "Sorry, Father, we didn't realize we were being so loud. Goodnight Father," she said, knowing he wasn't really upset.

"Goodnight Father," said a voice from a bundle of blankets.

"Goodnight, Father," said yet another giggling voice. Mr. Tanner returned to bed and soon all were fast asleep.

In the morning Isabelle and Rebecca headed to the dining room for breakfast. The other girl, too excited to eat she said, went off to the stable to brush down her horse. About midway through their meal something unexpected happened. Mr. Tanner entered the room leading Wendall and Addie behind him, "Look who I found at our front door," said Mr. Tanner.

Isabelle exclaimed, "How on earth did y'all get here?"

"We started out a little earlier then we said we would," answered Wendall.

"Ros' directions were easy, and we were here in no time," added Addie.

Mr. Tanner called for Willie Mae and said, "You kids must be hungry, Willie Mae will take care of y'all. Addie asked only for juice and a biscuit, and Wendall said he was fine and wanted to know where Ros was. "I'm not sure," said Isabelle. "He may have gone to the stable." After getting directions, he departed to find him. Roscoe, however, had gone on an errand for his father, and was nowhere near the stables. Wendall was strolling along, taking in the beauty of the plantation, a beauty unlike any he had seen before. He envisioned himself owning such a place one day.

Rounding the chicken coup he was now facing the stable. What he saw almost brought him to a standstill. Who in the world is that? he thought. Walking much more slowly now, he was fixed on the sight in front of him, almost next to her before she turned and saw him. She took a deep breath. "You startled me, I didn't hear you coming," she said touching her heart with her hand.

"I'm sorry," he said, "I didn't mean to scare you." Staring into her almond shaped green eyes he was without words (something quite unnatural for Wendall).

"Are you looking for someone?" she asked.

"Yes," he said.

She waited a moment for him to say more but he didn't. "Who are you looking for? Maybe I can help you," she said as she began brushing the horse's mane.

"Oh, I'm trying to find, ah . . . ah . . . I can't think of his name, but I know he lives here," Wendall said laughing.

"Ros?" she asked.

"Yes, that's who I'm looking for, I was told I'd find him here." Is he about?"

"I saw him a little while ago at the house, but I do expect him here anyway. We're all going riding this morning," she said.

"Oh, you're going riding too? I'm glad to hear that. Forgive me, I haven't introduced myself, I'm Wendall Cambridge. We are the new owners of the Dollin plantation, and you are?"

"My name is Misty. I'm pleased to meet you Wendall. I thought we were gonna meet you and your sister along the trail later."

"We got an early start and seemed to arrive in no time. Are you a Tanner?" he said as he patted the horse.

"Well, yes. I've lived here all my life," she said with a slight laugh.

"My," he said. "When they made mention of you last week I got the impression they were talking about someone much younger. You must be at least seventeen, maybe eighteen?" Busy brushing the horse, she didn't respond. "I'm sorry you didn't come with the family last week. Were you ill?" he asked.

"No;" she said, "I don't go everywhere they do." Though he thought that was odd he didn't question her.

"Perhaps if you'd like I could come over some morning, and bring you to our plantation, and show you about. If your father would approve of course," suggested Wendall.

"Thank you, Wendall, that's very nice of you," she said.

"That's a beautiful horse you have," Wendall said looking the horse over with one eye and her with the other.

"Ros gave her to me the day she was born. I love her;" she said giving the horse a kiss on the cheek.

"I've got an idea," he said. "How about I go fetch my horse. I'll tell the girls we'll meet them on the trail. I'd love to ride with you a little."

"I guess we could ride through the orchard. They'll catch up pretty quickly," she answered.

Once back at the house he poked his head into the dining room and said, "I didn't find Ros, but I found your sister."

"My sister?" Isabelle said looking at Rebecca. "What's she doing there. I thought she and mother went for material goods."

"No, she's brushing down her horse," Wendall said. "We're gonna ride ahead. We'll meet up later on the trail." As quickly as he came he was gone. At the same time, Isabelle and Rebecca realized he was talking about Misty, and both started to laugh. Rebecca said, "That explains why his eyeballs are coming out of his head," and the girls laughed even louder.

"Well, is Misty your sister or something?" asked Addie. "Everyone talks about her like she is."

"I couldn't love her anymore if she were my flesh and blood," answered Isabelle.

"Well, is she related to you Rebecca?" asked Addie, uncertainly.

"Well, in a special kind of way," replied Rebecca. "My father brought her into this world. If he hadn't been there she would have died with her mother. There's a bond of love between Misty and my dad, between all my family really. Since we were little girls she would come with Isabelle to my house and I would come here, we've just always been together."

"Who was her mother? A cousin or something?" asked Addie.

"No;" said Rebecca looking at Isabelle and laughing. "One of us . . . Iz . . . better tell her the whole story before her curiosity kills her."

"Yes, please do," replied Addie.

"Misty," began Isabelle, "was born one week after I was. Her mother . . . her mother . . . was a mulatto who was very ill."

"You're saying," interrupted Addie, "Misty is a mulatto?"

"Well . . . her mother was a mulatto. Her father had to be white. Just one look at her and you'll understand why we say that. You know Addie, many Negro women are . . . well . . . let's say a lot of slave owners, the men, well they ah . . ."

"Go on with the story, Isabelle;" said Addie, "I know what some of them do."

"Mother bought Misty's mother from an abusive man, who surely would have killed her. She brought her home and they tried to get her well, but couldn't. Rebecca's father saved Misty at birth, but could do nothing for her mother. Mother said she was a very beautiful girl. When you meet Misty, you'll know it was true. She has to be quadroon, you wouldn't know there's Negro blood by looking at her," said Isabelle.

"Yeah, but quadroons are still niggers. It is peculiar I do say," said a surprised Addie.

"Peculiar? Maybe," said Rebecca. "My older sister Susan, now there's peculiar," responded Isabelle. She and Rebecca laughed, but Addie seemed taken back by the whole thing, and didn't say anymore.

Soon Roscoe returned, and they headed for the stables, and their horses. In no time, they were off. Misty and Wendall were beyond the orchard now. Upon reaching the stream where they normally stopped, Misty said they could wait there for the others. "Misty, that's a pretty name," he says, "I don't recall ever hearing it before."

"That's nice of you to say that Wendall." she said to him as she walked into the water. "My Aunt Molly gave me the name. I don't know where she got it from. She died when I was quite young." Wendall sat down on the ground as Misty walked about in the stream. She was wearing a white cotton dress that came just below her knees. Isabelle and Rebecca were wearing the same thing. They had made them for riding. Loose fitting and cool, the white seemed to glow next to her skin, a very light golden brown. Her long black hair, braided, reached to the bottom of her back. Every time she looked at him, he was staring at her. She thought, maybe he thinks I'm silly walking around in the stream, so she came out and started looking anxiously for the others. "My sister Addie," he said, "has Ros said anything to you about her?"

"He said he thought she was a nice girl, and I'd like her," she answered. "I'm sure you'll like her, but does he? She has just talked about him all week, a big crush I'd say." She didn't respond, she was starting to feel uneasy. Where could they be, she thought. They should have been here by now. Wendall kept talking about one thing after another as she paced about until finally he said, "Misty, would you like us to go look for them?"

"Yes, I would," she answered.

Getting up and walking toward the horses he said to her, "Let's ride then." He cupped his hands to help her onto her horse. She stepped into his hand and flung herself up on the horse. Not letting go of her foot, he slid one hand up to her ankle and left it there. Looking up at her he said, "I didn't think I was gonna like living down here in Georgia Misty, but things are looking up." Looking down at his smiling face she now knew why she was feeling so uncomfortable. It was Wendall. She looked him in the eye, smiled and with her other foot kicked the horse and said, "That's nice Wendall," and took off to a gallop.

Once out of the woods, and into the clearing, she could see the others coming. Seeing Roscoe she felt a great sigh of relief. Soon they were all riding together, and the morning seemed perfect. They rode for several hours before going to the meadows. There they spread blankets and brought out the food, and enjoyed a fine picnic lunch. After lunch Isabelle went to her riding bag and brought back a deck of playing cards. "What should we play?" she asked.

"I don't feel like playing cards," said Wendall. "I'd rather take a ride in that old boat there . . . Misty . . . you feel like going for a boat ride?"

"Not right now Wendall, maybe Ros does," she said looking at Roscoe.

"Nah, us two in that boat together will surely sink it," Wendall said as he stood up and reached for her hand. With a gentle tug he brought her to her feet. "You sit up front and direct the way."

At this his sister Addie looked at him, and said in a somewhat stern voice, "Wendall . . . just stay here and play cards . . . that old boat doesn't look safe anyway."

"Nonsense, little sister," he said, "the boat's just fine. And we feel like riding, don't we Misty?" Not waiting for her answer, and still holding onto her hand, he led her to the boat. As they went off, the others played cards. Roscoe had a hard time concentrating. He didn't like Misty in the boat alone with Wendall, and by the look on her face, he knew she had wanted him to do something. Now all he could do was stare out into the meadow waiting for their return.

By day's end, they were all back at the house and sitting at the supper table. As they were enjoying the meal and their conversation, Mrs. Tanner noticed the way Addie kept looking at Misty. There was something unfriendly about her conversation too, though the others didn't seem to notice it.

After dinner they all went into the family room. Isabelle, Rebecca, and Misty stood around Mrs. Tanner who played the piano as the four of them sang along. Mr. Tanner listened for awhile then slipped out in search of Henry and a game of chess.

Roscoe asked Misty to play her new song for them, but she declined saying she would another time. Wendall now stood up and said he would sing a song if someone would play it on the piano. "Can you play from sheet music Misty?" he asked.

"Just a little," she responded.

"Now Misty," said Mrs. Tanner, "you play just fine, and you're getting better all the time." Standing up and moving to one side she said, "Come on, Misty, you've played this one a hundred times." Opening the book to a certain page and placing it on the piano stand she said as she gently clapped her hands, "Ladies and gentlemen, I give you Mr. Wendall Cambridge." Misty played as Wendall sang, and he sang very well. About midway through he walked the few steps to the piano bench and sat down singing the remainder of the song as though there were no one else in the room other than Misty. At the conclusion all heartily applauded, and Wendall quickly began turning the pages looking for another song.

Addie stood up and said to her brother. "Wendall you'll keep us here all night once you get started. Let's take a walk or something before it gets too dark."

Immediately, Misty sprang up from the bench and said, "That's a wonderful idea, Addie. Let's go by way of the work shop, Ros is making Naomi a beautiful chest."

Mrs. Tanner added quickly with a motherly look, "Yes, he is. He may even finish it some day. Isn't that so son?"

Looking at his mother and laughing he said, "You're funny, Mother. Yes you are."

Turning to Mrs. Tanner, Misty said, "Come with us Mother. It's a lovely night for a walk."

"No;" she said, "Naomi and Lilly have been sewing for hours, I'm going to check in on them." Once again she noticed the queer way in which Addie was looking at Misty, but now she knew why. Misty calling her mother had set that look off. She could only hope that as Addie got to know everyone better she would see things differently.

Out the door and across the porch they went. From the far end of the long porch Mr. Tanner waved. he had found Henry, and they were in the middle of a chess game. Seeing this Wendall said to Roscoe, "Your father has quite the sense of humor."

"What makes you say that Wendall?" asked Roscoe.

"Playing chess with that ole nigger. He must have to tell him every move to make." Then laughing out loud he said, "Ah, but then you can't lose that way can ya Ros?"

"Henry has been playing chess for years, Wendall. My grandfather taught him."

"Ros," said Wendall, "you think I can be fooled easily? Come on now, ain't no nigger smart enough to play chess."

"Well," said Roscoe, "see it your way Wendall, but if you ever should play old Henry, don't be bettin nothing you're fond of on the outcome."

"Indeed," said Wendall.

The wood shop was just a short distance from the house. Lester was there working on gardening tools when they arrived. "Say hello to Wendall and Addie, Lester. They're the new owners of the Dollin plantation," said Isabelle.

"Evenin youngins'. That's a mighty fine plantation it is. I's been over dar before. Levi still there is he?" asked Lester.

Addie looked at Wendall and said, "That's that ole nigger papa said he was gonna get rid of."

Wendall said to Lester, "Not for long boy. We need young strong bucks over there; there's a lot of work to be done."

Looking back at what he was working on Lester responded, "Yes, sir, I reckon dar is."

Misty called attention to Roscoe's wood chest, pointing out some of the finer details. "I once made a chest for my older sister, Ros," said Wendall. "I put a compartment in it that lifts out to hold some smaller things. You ever think of putting something like that in there?"

"No, I can't say I did," answered Roscoe.

"He's gonna put these nice handles on the side. Aren't you, Ros?" Misty said holding up two brass handles.

"Misty, I'll get my wood shop set up, and maybe I'll make you a chest," Wendall remarked.

"Thank you anyway Wendall, but Ros is going to make one for me when he's done with Naomi's."

"The way I hear it," Wendall said laughing, "that could be awhile. A handy girl like you ought to have two anyway. I'll have my tools hanging in no time." Walking over to Lester, Wendall stepped in front of the vise he was using to hold the tool he was sharpening. "Ya have it sideways, boy," Wendall said as he loosened the vise and turned the tool. "Here, this is the way it's done." Pushing the file along the tool he said, "There now, ain't that the better way to do it, boy?"

"Well, look it there," said Lester. "Now whys didn't I think of that? Yes sir, that's a better way." As they all headed out the door Lester kept saying as he slid the file over the tool, "Yes, em, that's a fine way, just a fine way of doing," until they were out of sight, and then he quickly loosened the vise and put the tool back the way he had it before. "Yes, em, that's a better way, if y'all wants a be here all night."

When they got back to the house, it was getting dark, the girls wanted Roscoe to bring his guitar out on the veranda so they could sing songs. Isabelle said she was chilly and was going for a shawl; Rebecca and Misty were going to do the same. "Can I get you something to wear Addie?" asked Isabelle.

"I have a shawl in my bag, I might have brought it to your room," answered Addie. On the way to the stairs they found her bag in the hallway.

Misty reached in and pulled the shawl out saying, "I'll just give it to her now." When she reached the doorway, she stopped as Addie said, "Wendall, you big dummy! I've been trying to get your attention all day. What on earth is wrong with you, behaving like one of them disgusting-minded field overseers!"

"Little sister, you're making no sense. What are you talking about?"

"I'm talking about the way you've been acting around that nigger girl."

"Nigger girl? Addie y'all ain't making no sense at all. I think y'all got too much air in your head, and it's making y'all dizzy;" Wendall said as he laughed at his sister.

"The only one dizzy here is you dummy, and you got that way over that nigger girl Misty!" Misty leaned her shoulder against the doorway. A lump formed in her throat so hard she couldn't swallow, and her heart sank with a feeling she had never known before.

"Addie, you're out of your mind. Why would you say such a thing?" said her now angry brother. "I can't believe you sometimes."

"Look at her," said Addie. "That black hair, green eyes, does she look like any of the Tanners to you?"

"She told me she's a Tanner," Wendall said, though sounding less convinced.

"Of course she's a Tanner. Slaves always take the master's last name when they got none of their own, and she never had one of her own," said Addie.

Still not fully convinced that his sister knew what she was talking about, Wendall asked, "How do you know so much anyway?"

"Isabelle told me all about it this morning, said she loves her like a sister. I find it quite disgusting myself."

"Just shush up a minute Addie. Let me think," said a very confused young man.

Misty, having been in the company of white people as often as Negroes, had heard expressions like those all her life, but they had never been directed at her, nor had she ever thought of herself that way before. Tears slowly fell from her eyes. She dropped the shawl and ran in the other direction. Wendall and Addie heard her and he quickly jumped up to see Misty rounding a corner toward the kitchen. Turning to his sister, he said, "That's just great Addie. Misty was right in the doorway. Who knows how much she heard."

"Just like a nigger to be eavesdropping," Addie said as she turned away from Wendall to hide the worried look on her face. Wendall didn't say anything. He just sat back in his chair and looked straight ahead.

When the others returned they found Addie's shawl on the floor. Isabelle picked it up and took it outside. "Where's Misty?" she asked.

"We haven't seen her," Addie responded as she took the shawl and wrapped it around her shoulders. Roscoe came out next but she wasn't with him either.

"Have you seen Misty?" his sister asked.

"I thought she went with y'all upstairs," he said.

66

"Maybe she went to the kitchen for something," Rebecca offered. Roscoe tuned his guitar and played a song, after which, Isabelle and Rebecca sang a few, but they were concerned because Misty had not returned. Isabelle asked her brother to go look for her. On entering the house his sister Susan asked him what was wrong with Misty.

"Why, where is she?" Roscoe asked.

"She came through the kitchen white as a ghost, crying too. I asked her what was wrong, but she went right out the door," answered Susan.

Roscoe went out the side door and walked over to Lester's, figuring Misty must have gone there. When Willie Mae opened the door he could hear crying. "Lor Massar Tanner, what's wrong with Misty?" asked Willie Mae.

"I don't know," answered Roscoe. "That's what I came to find out. Tell her I'm out here. I want to see her." Willie Mae returned to tell him Misty didn't want to see anybody. "She's all rolled up like a baby and a cryin like I's never seen her do before." While they were still talking, one of the young children came to the door and said Misty had run out the back door. Roscoe went around the back of the building but she was gone. He called out for her, but she was nowhere around.

His first thought was to go looking for her, but he knew if she didn't want to be found, he'd never find her. He decided to go back to the house and find out what had upset her. Thinking that Susan might have said something he went looking for her. It was getting late now and the girls were in Isabelle's room. Roscoe went in only to say Misty was going to stay the night at Lester and Willie Mae's, and that she was upset about something, but they'd have to wait until tomorrow to find out what it was.

The next morning all were up early and ready to go to the Sunday meeting. All except Roscoe. He told his mother about the night before, and said he was going to see Misty. He walked to Lester's house but no one was there. They must be on their way to the meeting house, I'll get our horses, he thought. A morning ride will make her feel better. But when he got to the meeting house, Misty wasn't there either. Going inside, he approached Leo and Goldie, who told him she had come to their place late last night and was sleeping when they left this morning.

When he arrived at Goldie's, he knocked lightly on the door, then opened it. In the corner of the small hut was a bed made of straw and blankets where she was sleeping. He sat down in an old chair next to her and called her name. She was so deep in sleep it didn't waken her. He got off the chair and sat on the floor next to her, gently rubbing her back, he called her name again. Although she was still not moving, he knew she had opened her eyes. "What's wrong, Misty?" he asked. "Why did you leave last night, and then you wouldn't come out, and then you ran off again? I don't think I slept ten minutes all night. Did I do something to upset you?"

Closing her eyes again she rolled over onto her back. "No, Ros, you didn't do anything. I'm sorry I didn't come out to you last night," she said in a low soft voice.

"Then what is it Misty? I've never seen you like this," he said as he picked up her hand and held it in his. A tear formed in the corner of her eye, then rolled down the side of her face and disappeared into her hair. Another tear fell, then in one motion she covered her face with her hands, and rolled onto her side and began to cry. "Why are they like that, Ros? I just wanted to be their friend."

"Edward and Susan," Roscoe said. "I should have known. I'm gonna punch him right in his eye. They've really been getting on my nerves lately!"

"No Ros, it's not them;" she said brushing the tears from her face. "Wendall and Addie, Ros, I heard them talking about me on the porch. Saying I didn't belong there and criticizing Isabelle. Oh Ros, sweet Isabelle, I love her so much."

"But why did they feel that way?" asked Roscoe.

"You know why," she said in a very low voice. "I don't know about Wendall, but Addie sure feels that way. I felt like someone stabbed me in my heart."

"Stupid people. I'll never spend another day with them again," Roscoe said angrily.

"No Ros," she said looking him in the eyes, "it's not their fault, not really. They were raised that way."

"Bred that way is more like it," answered Roscoe. "It wasn't just that they said it anyway Ros," she said, now putting her hand on his, "it was what it meant. It was like the blinders I put on, that we all put on, were ripped from me, and forced me to face the reality of things that must come, and they are coming quickly now." As her eyes began to fill with tears, Ros shifted around, sat next to her head and leaned against the wall. Lifting her head onto his lap he slowly brushed her hair with his hand, and stared deeply in thought.

"Maybe it was good. Maybe it's time I start preparing myself for the future and the things that must take place," Misty said.

"Good?" responded Roscoe. "I won't hear of it. Our lives have been nothing but happy and if others try to change that, I'll run em off quick."

"You can't run the world off, Ros, and you can't run away from the world either." Rolling onto her back and looking up at him she said, "Our lives have been happy, more wonderful than anyone could ever imagine, and I'll have those memories always."

"Stop talking like that Misty, their parents will take them home today, and things will be as they always were," said Roscoe in a reassuring tone.

"Oh Ros, you always make everything all right, but the day will come when Isabelle marries, and Rebecca too, and I know they'll marry good people, but their husbands won't want someone like me around." Turning back to her side, she lay silent, and then he realized what she was thinking. After a long silence he said, "You think that is going to happen with me too don't you?" She didn't answer, she just nodded her head slowly.

They fell silent. They had both shared the same dream for as long as either could remember and though they never said it, they had always seen themselves together. But they weren't children anymore, and on this day they could no longer ignore the reality of their situation.

"So what are we saying here Misty?" Roscoe asked as he helped her to a sitting position.

"I guess we're saying that no matter how good a dream is, you have to wake up," she answered in a solemn voice.

"No! I won't accept that!" Roscoe said. "And I won't give up or give in!"

"What are you saying Ros? I don't understand?"

"I'm saying, that nothing, or nobody, is going to separate us." Sliding forward and sitting face to face he looked deep into her eyes. "Misty, with my whole strength, body, and soul . . . I love you. If I have to live in a wooden hut with a dirt floor like this one, I will, if that's what I have to do to live my life with you." She leaned forward and for the first time, they kissed. He put his arms around her. She lay her head on his shoulder and said, "I have always loved you, and I always will. No matter what happens I always will!"

69

* * * * *

A whole year has passed since that night. Things never were the same again after that. Their time spent together now, meant more to all of them. Especially to Misty. She knew this kind of time would end one day and so she was storing up memories to last a lifetime. At Misty's request, little was ever said about that weekend to Mrs. Tanner. Although she said nothing, Mrs. Tanner was well aware of all that had taken place. The relationship between Roscoe and Misty also did not escape her notice. When she had set out her plan for Misty's future, this situation had not entered her mind. She hoped each day the remaining time would be favorable for her.

But right now everyone's attention was being diverted. There will be a wedding this weekend and a reception the likes of which this plantation has never seen. The wedding was to have taken place a year earlier, but the ship Naomi's fiancee was with had been damaged in port across the ocean in England. The wedding was moved to the fall. Then Naomi became ill, giving everyone quite a scare, especially Zachary Johnson, her fiancee. She recovered fully by winter, but Zachary was to set sail again in February, so a June date was set. And now it has finally arrived.

As preparations are being made, and people are rushing to complete one job after another, Naomi sits perfectly still in a high back wooden chair in the study. Sitting several feet away is Mylo Topaz. Mr. Topaz has made a reputation for himself amongst the wealthy as a painter of portraits. He has already painted Mrs. Tanner and Susan, and is to return in mid summer to do a family portrait of Edward and Susan with their children as well as one of Mr. Tanner.

The wedding will be Sunday afternoon at three o'clock. It is Friday evening now, the last time the entire family will sit together for a meal for some time to come. Tomorrow the family from Leesway will arrive, and a small party is planned for the evening.

After dinner all retired to the family room. Hubert and Emily, Grandmother Tanner, Edward , Susan, and their children, and Naomi, Roscoe, Isabelle, and Misty. This is the way it had always been. The Tanners were a close family, and as they sat this night and reminisced about years gone by, tears were shared along with laughter. The past couldn't be talked about without the mention of Aunt Molly. "Oh if I could have one wish," said Naomi, "I'd wish

70

for Aunt Molly to be here for my wedding. If I close my eyes I can see her smiling, and feel her arms hugging me."

Mr. Tanner piped in and said, "And I can hear her saying, "Massar Tanner, you be right proud of dat girl, da good Lord don't make a whole lot like dat."

Mrs. Tanner added, "Yes, Naomi, she would have spent the last month telling you all the things a good wife should do, and I'm sure she would have been right about all of them."

"Oh, I wish so much I could have known her," said Misty.

"I wish I had known her longer," added Roscoe.

"If you had," said Susan, "she would have taught you how to make tomato sauce." While everyone was laughing, Mr. Tanner asked Edward if he had ever heard the story of Aunt Molly's salty sauce?

"No, I never heard that one," he replied.

"Well, we were entertaining friends one evening," Mr. Tanner said, "and we were going to serve a meal that night with some fresh picked tomatoes. Aunt Molly spent the better part of the afternoon making sauce, and it smelled great throughout the entire house. Roscoe was about two and a half, and Aunt Molly loved the children around her. Well she took the sauce off the fire. It was just right, only needed to sit a spell. Roscoe had been watching her put in this and that and stirring, and he climbed up on a chair and dumping about a pint of salt into it, he stirred it up good he did. When Aunt Molly got to it and tasted it, she knew right away something was wrong. She probably looked at that chair, and the empty jar of salt, then at the boy. He came a running out of that kitchen as fast as those little legs could run, and Aunt Molly was behind him with a big ole wooden spoon."

"Did she catch ya Ros?" asked Edward.

"No," said Mr. Tanner. "He was at the top of the stairs before she reached the bottom. She gave up on him that time."

"Ros was the only one she would ever give a licken to," said Susan.

"That's because we never deserved it, Susan," Naomi said laughing.

"I'm pretty sure that's not why," said Mr. Tanner. "Aunt Molly couldn't read the Bible, but she sure could quote it when it benefited her. She'd say, 'The good book say don't spare the rod on a boy,' and, she took it for what it said."

"So I got it, and they didn't," said Roscoe. "You'd no sooner get a wopin then she'd have you on her lap feeding you pie and cream," said Mrs. Tanner.

"Oh, I wish I could have known her," said Misty.

"I can picture her now Misty," Mrs. Tanner said in a soft voice, "sitting on her rocking chair on the veranda holding you in one arm, and Isabelle in the other. Rocking and singing, and talking to you both about anything and everything. She'd bring one of you up and kiss your head, then the other, then in a few moments back to the first for another kiss. You were special to her heart Misty. The morning you were born, I left you with her while they looked for a nursing mother. She never left your side. Willie Mae told me she only let Goldie hold you long enough to nurse you, then she held you till you were asleep again."

"I remember walking to that little hut you lived in, I don't know how many times," said Susan.

"That first year when you stayed with Goldie," said Mrs. Tanner, "Aunt Molly must have walked there almost everyday."

"She didn't only go with the children, Misty," said Mr. Tanner.

"Yes, I guess we did walk there a lot, Hubert," added Mrs. Tanner affectionately.

"I remember how she was always washing me up. Every time she saw my face, or hands, or knees dirty, she would run right in the kitchen, and get a wet rag. Scrub my face so hard, I'd think my nose was coming off, and all the while saying, 'Tain't right ya carryin on like ya was a boy, it tain't proper,'" laughed Susan.

"Well of all the girls, Susan," said Mrs. Tanner, "you were the one to be dirty. Get your clothes so dirty, they'd never come clean."

"One night, I was sick with the flu," said Naomi, "Momma and Poppa had looked in on me and went to bed. Pretty soon Aunt Molly came with warm milk. She sat in the chair next to my bed, and talked to me till I fell asleep. When I woke up in the morning, she was still there, sleeping in the chair. I started to cry because, well I guess because, I don't know why, seeing her sitting there, knowing she wouldn't leave me when I was sick. She was always going to be there if I needed her. We couldn't have had a better Auntie, could we?"

"No indeed Naomi," said Mr. Tanner, "we were blessed with her."

"I bet I know what your favorite memory is, Poppa," said Isabelle. "Flapjacks."

"I couldn't say no to that, Isabelle, but along with those flap-jacks and grits were many years of early morning conversations. She was a wise old woman, and never one to hold back her opinion."

"I say amen to that," added Grandmother Tanner laughing, "and she had an opinion about everything."

"You knew her the longest, Grandmother," said Naomi, "tell us what comes to your mind about her."

"First thing to my mind, is how stubborn she was. We'd come back from the depot with new things for the kitchen, and show her how they worked, and we'd never see em again. Stick em away somewhere she would, and never use em."

"We sure did find all sorts of things when we remodeled that kitchen," said Mr. Tanner laughing. "But, come now mother, you know she was good for us. I sometimes think you missed her most when she was gone."

"I'll say it was not the same without her," she said.

"Only time mother went in the Negro church in her entire life," said Mr. Tanner.

"I didn't know that, Grandmother, you went to see Aunt Molly's funeral?" asked Isabelle.

"My head hurt me for two days after that. All that fussin and singing, and carrying on," said the elder Mrs. Tanner. "But, I will say this," she continued, "the day Josiah died, I was sitting on the veranda that night after everyone was gone. Molly came out and sat next to me, and she started talking, oh . . . do you remember this, and do you remember that, and this and that, and it made me feel good. She even had me laughing a little, and as I was lying in bed later that night, I realized that she was talking so much, because of her own grief, and I don't think we ever, well, we never saw things eye to eye, but we didn't argue as much after that night."

About this time, Mr. Tanner tuned his violin. Mrs. Tanner took her place at the piano and the family enjoyed a beautiful evening together.

The wedding

Late Saturday morning, her chores are done and she is walking down the road picking wildflowers. It's been a long while since Misty has seen Mrs. Tanner's sister Leah. They should be arriving any time now, and Misty has set out with Digger to meet them at the covered bridge.

When the cariole comes into view she stands up on the stone wall at the edge of the bridge and waves excitedly. The cariole comes to a stop, and Misty jumps from the wall as the others disembark from the coach. Leah embraces Misty with the biggest hug, "Oh Aunt Leah, I've missed you so much," exclaimed Misty.

"I've missed you too my dear," responded Leah, "and look how much you've grown, you're a young lady now."

"And, about as pretty a one I've ever seen. How about a hug for your ole Uncle Samuel."

"I'm so happy to see y'all, I know I'm gonna cry," Misty said as she hugged and greeted everyone. "And I know who you are," she said to the little girl she had never seen before, "You're Sage."

"Say hello to Misty, Sage," said the child's Father, Paul. "She's two years old now Misty, and quite a handful on a trip like this."

"Well, let's not stand here all day, all this riding has made me a mite hungry" said Mr. Eichner. Misty climbed into the cariole with the Eichners and they headed for Mariah.

Midafternoon while all were sitting in the family room, a young Negro child who had been stationed on the front steps of the house came running in excitedly announcing, "Deys here Massa," repeating it several times while all scrambled to their feet and headed for the door. The Franklins had arrived. It had been some time since all these families were together so the hugging and hand-shaking went on for a good time before they even made their way to the porch. When Gloria Franklin reached the top of the stairs she embraced Misty, then holding her at arms length she said, "When Emily last wrote she said you were becoming quite the young lady. I do declare, Misty, you have arrived!"

"Oh my, it's so good to see you again," said Misty holding back tears. "I sometimes read your letters over and over. It seemed like this day would never arrive."

Mrs. Franklin and Misty had been together only a few times in their lives, but a friendship had developed through letters they would send with messengers who transported legal documents between Mr. Tanner and Mr. Franklin. The Franklins would be spending a fortnight on the plantation after the wedding, and there would be lots of time for everyone to be together and strengthen the bonds of love they had spent years developing.

After dinner everyone went outside and sat on the veranda. A bit warm it was, but not muggy. Willie Mae and her daughters Elsa and Lilly were serving lemonade. The men were talking about business and the women about the wedding. Down the road a bit the young ones spotted Henry coming. He had taken Isabelle to town to bring Rebecca home for the weekend. Henry carried her luggage upstairs, and then went to the kitchen for a drink of water. Mr. Franklin came in looking for him. The last few trips the Tanners made to Orleans, Henry hadn't accompanied them. Entering the kitchen Mr. Franklin said, "Henry my good fellow, a pleasure to see you again," and stretched out his hand.

"Massa Franklin, ain't seen y'all in a coon's age, you's lookin fit as ever."

"Well you're looking fine yourself, Henry." Mr. Franklin responded. "We're gonna be staying a fortnight. That's a lot a time Henry, don't know what I'm gonna do with it all."

The smile on Mr. Franklin's face was easy enough for Henry to read, and in that old familiar laugh that sounds something like, He . . . He . . . He . . . Henry said, "I spects I's could find some time fo some fishin, if in y'all got a mind fo it."

Laughing and heading for the door, Mr. Franklin said, "We'll talk about this matter again Henry, real soon."

As evening wore on all made their way to the huge room in the west wing of the house. This was where the wedding would be tomorrow. Mrs. Tanner is busy pointing out where the orchestra will be, where Naomi will enter, where she'll stand for the ceremony, and a thousand and one other details. It's a perfect room for a wedding with many large windows with drapes from ceiling to floor, an abundance of marble and brass, and the most beautiful chandelier one has ever seen hanging from the high ceiling in the center of the room.

Once a year a spring party is held here. Susan's wedding was here, as well as the Myer's eldest daughter's. One point of preparation Mr. Tanner has taken delight in is acting in an official capacity. Obed and Daniel, twin Negro boys about six years old, caught Mr. Tanner's attention at the screen door of the kitchen where they appear at least three mornings a week. Their parents are cotton pickers, and live in the second community of huts. Many children come looking for food at the door, but these two stand out. Identical in appearance, he can't tell one from the other. They've learned they can make him laugh, and so they capitalize on it to the point that he now looks into the crowd for their faces. Fitted with little matching tuxedoes, they'll stand one on each side of the entranceway, and announce in unison as the family enters to take their seats, culminating in the announcement for all to rise for the bride's entrance. They have yet to get it exactly right, but they have kept the family amused all week. Mr. Tanner sent for them, wanting to show his family and friends the good results of his hard work.

After a few minutes the twins come in grinning from ear to ear. They go straight to Mr. Tanner. "I've told everyone how hard y'all been working, and they'd like to see y'all in action, now which one of you is Obed?" At this both boys step forward to the delight of all in the room. One lets his hands hang loosely at his sides, the other covers his mouth with his hands. Both laugh along with the crowd. Mr. Tanner now said, "I been told Obed was sneaking jelly rolls and ought to get a lickin. Now which one of y'all is Obed?"

Pointing at each other they said, "He is," and laughed all the harder. They've played this game with Mr. Tanner every day, and seem to enjoy it more each time they do it.

As he has them take their positions in the large doorway, Mrs. Tanner says to Gloria, "They've been over and over this and have yet to get all the way through it. I've tried to tell Hu they're too young for it, but he swears he can get them to do it."

"They are so cute, it's not going to matter what they say," Gloria responded. "Everyone is going to be looking at their faces."

"I know," responded Mrs. Tanner, "Hu's had them staying at the house most of the week. They're always up to something that keeps him amused. We had them in one of our spare rooms with single beds, and every morning we'd find them with all the blankets off the beds sleeping on the floor next to each other. Now they're sleeping on the floor in Henry's room, and he's not too happy about it."

While the adults were talking the young ones made their way to the piano that had been brought in from the family room for the wedding. Isabelle and Misty sat on the bench. Rebecca stood behind them. As they sang together Mrs. Eichner said to her sister, "My word Emily, listen to that child's voice." It wasn't just Mrs. Eichner who noticed it. Everyone's attention had been caught. When Misty sang her solo parts, it was no longer with the voice of a child, but because the girls hadn't noticed the others watching, they were cutting up and laughing as much as they were singing.

"You'll hear that voice tomorrow, in a way that won't soon be forgotten," said Mrs. Tanner.

"How's that Emily?" asked her sister.

"The girls have always written stories and poems and songs. They would play a game where one would write the first verse, then another would write the second, and so on. Well several weeks ago, Naomi and I heard Misty playing the piano alone, and singing a song. Naomi recognized it as a poem the girls started and never finished. Misty finished it, and put it to music. It's quite a beautiful love song. Naomi asked her to play it right before they exchange vows."

"Oh, what a wonderful touch that will add to the ceremony Emily," responded Leah, gently taking hold of her sister's hand.

"Our only concern," said Mrs. Tanner smiling, "is whether she can get through it without being overcome by emotion."

Looking over toward the children, Leah said, "Remember when we were girls and we had that old piano that was so out of tune? We would spend hours at that thing, with Poppa and Mother looking on, and sister Ruth singing so sweetly. I think of her often."

"Those were wonderful times Leah," her sister responded. "I wish we didn't live so far apart. Sometimes I sit and play those old songs of ours, and picture you and Ruth singing and laughing. I do miss her so."

"Come Emily, let's play. Let's play the song that Mama and Poppa liked so much."

"The one about three boys a callin for your little girls?" asked Emily laughing as they made their way to the piano. "Poppa was so amused by that, remember?"

"Like it was yesterday!"

* * * * *

The meeting house was filled to capacity Sunday morning. Many of the friends there had prepared a light lunch for the Tanners and their guests, after which, they hurried home to make final preparations. By two o'clock the guests were starting to arrive. Henry was positioned at the front door to greet the guests and direct them to the gardens outside the west wing where refreshments were being served. Many of those coming had known Henry for many years, and his presence and greetings were a planned part of the day's events.

The patio gardens began to fill with quite a variety of people—politicians and businessmen, as well as many of those who lived nearby. The past week had been a busy one around the house. Many slaves had been brought up to work on the grounds and Mariah had never looked so beautiful. The day was warm, but not too hot. This was especially good since everyone was dressed in their very best.

The bell sounds. Henry appears in the doorway and requests that everyone take a seat. The wedding will soon begin. With so many people entering the room, the temperature quickly rises. Overhead are six fans that start turning, three on one side of the room, and three on the other side. Each set of three is connected to a thin rope and several pulleys. The rope runs along the ceiling, and through two square holes in the back wall of the room at the ceiling. Behind the wall in a small hot room sit two young Negro men on contraptions like bicycles. A large pulley at the ceiling directs the rope down to a wheel, the servants start pedaling, and the fans begin cooling the guests.

All is set. The long awaited moment has arrived.

In the front row on the right is the Johnson family, on the left the Tanners. Young Zachary takes his place before Reverend Brown, who now announces that it is time to begin. The orchestra takes its cue and begins playing softly and quietly.

The time has come to see if Mr. Tanner's young friends, Obed and Daniel, will get their parts right. The large double doors are opened. The young boys take their places in the doorway facing each other. The orchestra leader motions and the wedding song begins. First to step up to the doorway are Isabelle and Roscoe Tanner. Roscoe wears a tuxedo and leads his sister by the arm. There is no doubt in anyone's mind that he is a most handsome young man, the look on every girl in the room is a testimony to that fact. Isabelle, her long blond hair arranged in lovely curls, looks beautiful in a full length gown, which glides gracefully along the shining wood floor. Already fighting back tears, and holding tightly to her brother's arm, she is the picture of a true southern belle.

Roscoe can't hold back his amusement as he looks at Obed and Daniel and waits to see if they will get it right. A rather large wager rests on their performance. Since the boys have never gotten it right once from beginning to end, father and son have bet on the outcome. When the boys hesitate to make their announcement, Roscoe looks back at his father and smiles coyly. But before that smile leaves his face, their words ring out in perfect unison. Facing each other and lifting their heads slightly they say, "Ladies and gentlemen, Massa Roscoe and Lady Isabelle." As Roscoe walks by he playfully smacks the child on the side of his head and says to himself, they'll never do it.

Next up to the doorway, are Edward and Susan Ramsey. The boys announce "Massa Edward Ramsey and Lady Susan." Attention is focused on the entranceway. Stepping up to the doorway are Naomi's nieces, Melissa and Sage. Again the announcement is made in perfect unison, "Lady Sage and Lady Molissa." The two little girls in pretty dresses, carrying flowers, smiling from ear to ear as they walk down the aisle are a perfect touch. The next announcement rings out, "Massa Nathan Johnson and Lady Rosemary Cochran." Mr. Johnson, a widower, is proudly walking down the aisle today with his sister Rosemary. The assistance provided by his sister in raising young Zachary is something he knows he could never repay her for. This is as much her day as anyone's.

The two grandchildren David and Wesley, go to the rear of the aisle and take their positions, one on each side of the aisle. The anticipation can be felt in the whole room. The moment everyone is waiting for is nearing. But there is one last announcement before the final call. Taking their cue from Mr. Tanner, who is standing out of sight of the doorway, the boys announce, "Hear ye, hear ye! The honorable Massa Hubert Tanner and Lady Emily."

As they step up to the doorway the crowd applauds. Emily Tanner is simply beautiful. Her long blond hair is netted evening style, a jeweled tiara adorns her head. Her gown of satin and lace flows elegantly over the large crinoline. With a smile that can be felt as well as seen, she holds the arm of her husband and walks with the poise and confidence that so many admire. Mr. Tanner, so handsome in his tuxedo leads his wife to the rear of the aisle where her grandchildren, one on each side, accompany her to her seat. Mr. Tanner remains at the top of the aisle. This is it! All eyes are focused on the entranceway. The orchestra has played softly throughout all the introductions, but now changes slightly, and begins to build in tempo. As the music rises, so also does the anticipation of those whose eyes are locked on the doorway. The music rises to a crescendo and stops. All in attendance loudly applaud and then are silent.

Mr. Tanner, unable to control the smile on his face, motions to his doorkeepers. They in turn look at each other and, nodding their heads with each word, they say slowly and clearly "Please rise ladies and gentlemen." And then as they look at each other waiting for the other to start the next word the smile leaves their faces as neither knows what to say. Roscoe looks to his father hoping to catch his attention with an "I told you so look" on his face. The two boys, now looking worried, look to Mr. Tanner who, still smiling gives them a reassuring nod and mouths the word welcome. Instantly a broad smile returns to their faces, and nodding their heads they say, "Welcome to the plantation Mo-riah and the wedding of Miss Naomi Tanner." As Naomi steps up to the doorway the guests applaud.

Expense was not a factor, neither was time, nor preparation. The young woman, wearing a wedding gown the likes of which few if any have ever seen, had almost a glow about her. Naomi was always a beautiful person, both in appearance and in her heart, and that combination seemed to radiate from her on this day.

At this moment, she looked toward the front of the room at Zachary, who was hard pressed to fight back the tears of joy that threatened to overwhelm him. As she looked at her family and all their friends, and then at her father, a strange feeling came over her. At the rear of the aisle stood her daddy, and she knew he was looking at his little girl. At the front was her soon-to-be-husband, who saw her as the beautiful young woman she is. She reflected for just a moment before she started walking, about how wonderful life can be.

She walked to the rear of the aisle where her father waited with an extended arm. She stopped alongside him and took his arm, then paused. Lilly Mae following behind, gathered up the long train of her gown and placed it in position for her to walk down the aisle, as her father looked down at her and she looked back at him through her veil. In a few moments she would leave from under the protected wing that had given her shelter and security all her life. She said to him softly, "Poppa, I love you." And giving her that so familiar reassuring look, they started down the aisle. The orchestra again began to play softly. Mr. Tanner had taken great delight in choreographing the events that have thus far taken place, all went perfectly well. A few more steps and he would be handing over his daughter to a fine young man, and his part in this day's events would be coming to an end.

When they reached the front Mr. Tanner placed his daughter at the side of her fiancee, stretched out his hand to Zachary, grasped it firmly, gave him a nod of his head, then turned and walked to his seat. Reverend Brown had married Mr. and Mrs. Tanner, he had married Susan, and now stood ready to do the same for Naomi. He opened his book and the ceremony began.

All listened intently as he read the scriptures about family life. About the husband's role and then the wife's, explaining what these things meant, and how they could apply them to their lives. He talked with them for about twenty minutes, and then looked to the audience and said, "Dear friends, having considered these things today, and knowing in my heart they understand them, and want to fulfill their roles as husband and wife in accord with God's marital arrangement, I say before you all today, I see no reason why this couple should not be bound by holy matrimony today. How does ye respond?" With that a thunderous applause filled the room. Turning to Zachary and Naomi he said; "So be it." Then looking to Mr. Tanner he said, "Who gives this young woman to this man?"

Rising to his feet Mr. Tanner responded, "I do."

Looking again to those seated behind he now said, "The exchanging of marital vows, is indeed, the most important agreement one will ever enter into. That time has arrived for Zachary Johnson and Naomi Tanner. At the request of Miss Naomi, before the vows are said, a song will be sung."

A large high backed wooden chair with arms is brought forward from behind Reverend Brown, then one from each side is brought up for the bride and groom. Several attendants detach the train from Naomi's gown and lay it neatly on the floor. Zachary and Naomi sit facing each other. Reverend Brown takes his seat. The piano had been placed near the front of the room next to one of the large windows. Misty now rises from her seat and begins walking toward the piano. All attention focuses on her. She too has spent a great deal of time preparing her dress for this day. She is wearing a soft blue satin with dyed lace around the edges and embroidered lace coming down from each shoulder forming a medallion on her chest. Her long black hair was pulled back and up highlighting her green almond shaped eyes. Ringlets hung from the back of her head, interwoven with ribbon which accented the lace on the edges of her gown. Some who have known her since she was a child are looking on in awe. This is no child walking across the floor. What they are seeing is a beautiful young woman, moving with a graceful stride bound in determination and purpose. Taking her seat at the piano, she first looks at Mrs. Tanner who gives her the look of a mother who says without words, 'I'm so proud of you my child.' She then looks at Naomi whose seat faces the piano. They smile warmly at each other.

The time has finally arrived. As her fingers touched the ivory keys mouths were leaning toward ears as those who knew said to those who didn't, "It's the Negro girl Emily raised." Others weren't as kind, but when she started to sing, quiet fell over the room.

> *"In the peaceful calm of morning*
> *song birds rise early, and give warning,*
> *unbridled and unceasing*
> *their hearts they are releasing*
> *loves too strong a thing to hold inside.*
> *so - I -*
> *think that, we should be*
> *as uninhibited as thee, melodious sounds*
> *of the dawning day.*
>
> *And when it's touched you, and it's moved you*
> *mind and heart go places ever new.*
>
> *When vernal and vivacious, oh,*

we, long for, it to take us
and be held in the chambers
of its will.
Oh songbird, come to my window,
let your song, oh let it fill the air,
and may it be heard, forever more,
I'm in love - I'm in love,
what a glorious day is dawning.
When the heart has been excited
by another's love invited
then surely like the birds
that heart will sing.

And this is my song to you
come quickly while there's morning dew
while songs of love are in the air
I'll sing to you my heart I'll bare.
The birds will make the melody,
the words for my love will be,
forever, forever, I'll love you forever.
for always - and - a day."

When she had played the last note and the piano fell silent, she looked again toward Naomi. With tears in her eyes, Naomi sprang from her chair applauding. Misty hadn't noticed the effect she had had. She was too overwhelmed with emotion herself to see what had occurred. But something extraordinary had happened. She had captivated the audience. So involved they were with her song, and more so her voice, they had forgotten for a moment what they were even there for. The entire room rose to its feet. The applause was long and loud. Almost frightened by it all, she looked to Mrs. Tanner who motioned for her to curtsy, which she did, but the applause didn't stop. Mr. Tanner sensed she was frozen in place, he walked over and put his arms around her, as he hugged her he said; "That was magnificent young lady, simply magnificent;" then led her back to her seat. Not until she sat down did the applause stop. Roscoe turned in his chair and reached back, taking her hand he squeezed it firmly.

Reverend Brown now stood up and said to Zachary and Naomi, "Rise children, and make your vows." The room again gave way to silence as the young couple exchanged vows and Zachary placed the ring on her finger. Reverend Brown then said those words, "By the authority vested in me, and in the presence of Almighty God, I pronounce you man and wife. What God has yoked together, let no man put apart. Son, you may kiss your bride."

And kiss her he did, lifting her veil from before her face he looked deeply into her bright blue eyes and said just before he kissed her, "There is no happier man alive on this whole entire earth."

At the conclusion of their kiss, Reverend Brown presented to them on a silver platter a marriage certificate. First Zachary dipped the pen in the ink well and signed, then Naomi, after which, Reverend Brown signed. Henry, who was seated against the wall now came forward. With his mostly gray hair and tuxedo he was looking very distinguished. Reverend Brown handed him the certificate and holding it as if he were reading he announced, "Hear ye, hear ye, on this day the twenty-eighth of June, eighteen hundred and fifty seven, Zachary Johnson and Miss Naomi Tanner were married on the plantation Mariah." Rolling up the certificate and handing it back to Reverend Brown, he looked at the audience and said, "Ladies and gentlemen, Mr. and Mrs. Zachary Johnson." A thunderous applause filled the room as the couple made their way down the aisle and exited through the double doors.

The next ten minutes were spent with hugs and hand shakes until Mr. Tanner announced that refreshments would be served just outside in the courtyard. Dinner would be served in an hour. The doors were opened allowing the guests to move freely, some stayed inside, while others made their way outside to enjoy the late afternoon breeze.

The patio is large with many benches and plants and tables. A few steps down and you enter the courtyard, a beautifully landscaped area surrounded by large stone walls. Walkways lead around flower gardens and ornamental shade trees. There are several goldfish ponds and in the center a large gazebo.

Isabelle, Rebecca, and Misty go upstairs to freshen a bit. Once inside Isabelle's bedroom she turns to Misty and says, "You really did it down there."

"Did what?" she responds.

"Did what!" says Rebecca as if she can't believe Misty's response. "That performance Misty. You were really something."

Sitting down on the edge of the bed Misty says, "Oh, I did want everything to be perfect for Naomi today."

"It couldn't have been more perfect," said Isabelle, "and I swear you never sang more beautifully."

"I was so nervous when I first sat down. I didn't think my hands were going to play," commented Misty. "Then I looked at Naomi. She was so beautiful sitting there. I had to think about not crying, so I just started to play."

"Here, Misty, let me see what these look like with your hair up," Isabelle said as she came toward her with a pair of earrings made of shining gem stones.

"If we let just a little hair down by her ears, the earring will sparkle through;" said Rebecca.

"There," said Isabelle, "they are too long for me, but they look good on you."

"Did you see the boy with the red hair sitting about halfway back?" Rebecca asked Isabelle.

"I did, I don't know who he is, I'll ask Poppa who his family is." Looking at Rebecca with a coy smile she says, "And how about my big brother? Ros sure is handsome today." With a wink to Rebecca she adds, "And was there a little hand holding going on in front of everybody today?"

"I know your teasing ways, Iz, and I refuse to succumb," Misty said as she bounced up from the bed. The three continued to poke fun at each other as they departed to join the rest.

Once outside they were quickly surrounded by the other young ones. Many compliments were paid to Misty for her fine performance this afternoon. Some wanted to know if she would be singing more this evening. Every time she said no, Isabelle or Rebecca would say maybe. Once Isabelle said, "If we could find the right person to ask her, maybe she would."

Rebecca responded, "Um, now who could that be?" No one knew who they were talking about, but Misty herself who said, "I'm getting out of here, I know that look in your eyes. You two are going to get crazy today."

She left them and walked down the steps into the courtyard. Sitting on a bench under a mimosa tree were Roscoe and Wendall Cambridge. Misty hadn't seen Wendall or his sister Addie for quite some time. Whenever they came over, she would find things to do to keep her away. As she approached they both stood up to greet her.

"Hi Misty," said Roscoe.

"Hi, Ros, Wendall," she said.

"Your musical score was wonderful. Everybody was talking about it."

"Thank you Ros."

"You held me in awe Misty," said Wendall, "I don't think I ever heard a voice as lovely as yours."

"That's nice of you to say, Wendall, but I think people were already on a high note. The wedding was staged so beautifully. I'll get to meet your parents again today. I'm looking forward to that, and Addie looks lovely today." Several others now join them. The talk quickly changes to schooling, travel, and the like. Misty excuses herself and goes off to find Mrs. Tanner.

Back in the house, Obed and Daniel are having the time of their lives walking about, conversing with the guests, picking at the many trays of food being passed about, and smiling non stop as many tell them how well they did today at the door. As the word spread that jugglers were performing on the patio, the two boys filled their hands with all they could carry and followed the rest of the children out.

Misty was trying to make her way through the room again in search for Mrs. Tanner. One person after another stopped her. Some to compliment her on her performance, others out of curiosity. Some were extremely kind, others not so kind. Those without hesitation would say, "You don't look at all like a Negro," One lamented, "I wish our mulattos were as well bred as you my dear." To those she would comment, what a lovely day for a wedding, and then excuse herself. Mrs. Tanner had told her beforehand to expect some of this. Some people she said are well meaning but ignorant, others she laughed are ignorant but have to be invited anyway.

Just as she made her way to the door leading to the hallway, Mr. Tanner appeared and took hold of her arm. "Come with me child. Someone would like to meet you." He led her to Tom Sweeney the orchestra conductor.

"I wanted to compliment you, young lady, on your performance this afternoon. I was truly taken back with your style of singing, and your voice as well. Did you have more than one teacher?"

"Mostly Mother Tanner, but there are some slaves who play quite well and do have a style I guess you'd call their own," said Misty feeling somewhat embarrassed by the attention.

Handing her a small stack of papers he asked, "Do you know these songs?" Paging through she saw a number of them Mrs. Tanner also had and said, "Yes, some of these we sing."

"Would you do us the honor of selecting three or four and performing them with the orchestra this evening?"

"Oh no sir, I couldn't," she said shaking her head. "I've never done anything like that before. I'd be scared to death."

"Nonsense Misty," said Mr. Tanner, "you'll do perfectly well. Pick out a few you feel good about, and just let it go natural, the way you always do."

"I don't know if I can," she responded hoping they would let it go. Perhaps they would have if someone hadn't come at that moment and asked if she would sing again this evening.

"Now there Misty," said Mr. Tanner laughing, "you don't want to disappoint the friends." The gentleman then turned to his wife who was several feet away talking with others and said, "She is going to sing again tonight dear, this time with the orchestra."

"Which will be your pleasure dear?" asked Mr. Sweeney gently touching her shoulder in a reassuring manner. After looking the music over she selected three songs saying she knew these the best, then quickly excused herself. Hurrying back outside, she gave up the thought of finding Mrs. Tanner and was now looking for Isabelle and Rebecca. Finding them sitting on a bench on the patio she sat down alongside of Isabelle and slumped back against the wall, lifted up her leg and said, "someone please break this leg."

"Would that be above the knee or below?" asked Isabelle.

"Oh that wouldn't do anyway, they will only make me sit in a chair."

"What are you talking about Misty?" asked Rebecca.

"I'm in big trouble, BIG TROUBLE," she said, "Poppa Tanner just volunteered me to sing with the orchestra."

"Sing with the orchestra! That's wonderful!" said Isabelle.

"Oh good, I'm glad you feel that way, Iz, we'll do a duet," Misty responded.

"No, Misty, what I think is wonderful is that he asked you and not me," Isabelle said laughing.

"We'll sit up close to the front if that'll make you feel any better," said Rebecca.

While they were talking two elderly women approached them. One asked, "You're Hubert's youngest?"

"Yes, I'm Isabelle. This is Misty, and this is Rebecca Myers."

The other woman said, "You must be the doctor's daughter. Pleasant young man your father is."

'Thank you," responded Rebecca. Turning their attention to Misty one said, "And you're Emily's quadroon?" Misty, fighting back a smile, she nodded her head. Isabelle looked at Misty and rolled her eyes.

The other woman said to Misty, "You people sure have the gift of song. We had a mulatto once, didn't look white like you do, but she could sing. We'd bring her in sometimes, have her sing for us."

Rebecca said to her with a twinge of undetected sarcasm, "I'll bet she liked that just fine."

"Of course she did." Looking at Misty she said, "Emily did a remarkable job. Why you'd never know."

While they were talking, Addie Cambridge and another young girl approached.

"Hi Addie," said Rebecca.

"Hi Rebecca, Isabelle. What a lovely day for a wedding. Do you know Ellen?"

Before anyone could answer, one of the older women asked, "Where are you girls from?"

"I'm Addie Cambridge. We own the plantation that connects to the east side of Mariah."

"And you, young lady," she asked the other girl.

"A cousin of the groom," she said offering no more.

"Well, said the other woman, "dinner will be served soon."

"Yes," responded the first lady, "we should be getting back inside."

As they walked away Misty said to Addie, "Hello Addie, you look very nice. It's nice to see you again."

She responded with one word, "yes," then turned her attention to the other girls.

Misty excused herself. She couldn't stop thinking about what she would have to do later that night.

In an uncharacteristic move she approached Roscoe as he was talking with other young men and asked to see him alone. They exited through a gate at the rear of the courtyard. As they walked through the open yard Roscoe began reassuring her the evening would go okay. Stepping behind a large oak tree they were concealed from the house. She stood with her back to the tree, he stood directly in front of her. Placing his hands on each side of her face he said, "Did I tell you today how much I love you?"

"Yes Ros," she said with a smile.

"I did? When?" he asked as he moved in close and kissed her.

"When you reached around and held my hand after I got back to my seat, I think you told everyone who saw it."

"That's just fine with me," he said. "Why there isn't a boy up there who wouldn't like to be standing where I am right now. Most of all Wendall Cambridge."

"Why are you always poking fun at Wendall, Ros? You don't like him very much," she said.

"He's okay I guess. Besides, I can't blame him for the way he looks at you," said Roscoe.

"He does not," Misty said laughing.

"Does too;" responded Roscoe, "I was watching him do it today." The sound of the dinner bell rang out, and they headed for the house. As they walked holding hands they were unaware someone was watching from a window on the second floor. Gloria Franklin saw them come out from behind the tree and watched them strolling so leisurely across the yard then disappear through the gate.

After everyone sat down, Zachary and Naomi entered the room. Greeted by loud applause they smiled and waved and made their way to the main table. They and all the guests then enjoyed roast pork, roast chicken, red potatoes and yams, collard greens, string beans, and cream of broccoli soup. When the meal was finished, cakes and pies and cookies with cider were served. Some ate so much they just sat back in their chairs no longer able to move.

When all was cleared away the men moved the tables from the center of the floor and chairs were set in rows facing the orchestra. A musical program had been prepared by the family and friends. Mr. Tanner would serve as coordinator of this program, as well as beginning it with a song. With everyone now comfortable in their seats he began. "Friends, Emily and I greatly appreciate your presence here today. It has been a wonderful day so far has it not? And it is not over by any means. There will be much entertainment this evening. Mr. Sweeney and his orchestra will return shortly, but first we would like to present our own little arrangement that we have worked up." Mrs. Tanner began to play as Mr. Tanner said, "This song is for my little girl." He paused for a moment then said, "It's hard on us fathers, isn't it men, seeing our little ones grow up and marry? Well at any rate, this song is for you Naomi." Mr. Tanner began his song, his strong masculine voice filled the room. His song a show tune many were familiar with, was quite pleasing. At the conclusion of his song he said laughing, "Now that I got that over with I can relax and enjoy the rest of the evening. Next up Emily, Susan and Isabelle will entertain you with several songs, one of which Isabelle will sing solo." The next hour was spent with various family members and friends performing for Zachary, Naomi and all the guests. The concluding number had Isabelle playing the piano and singing with Rebecca and Misty a comedy song they had made up themselves, drawing on different moments in Naomi's life when she did the kind of silly things we all do, but hope everyone has forgotten.

"Friends," Mr. Tanner announced, "I know you're going to enjoy the next portion of the evening. So many have commented about the musical number Misty performed here this afternoon, she has graciously agreed, with a little arm twisting I might add, to perform a few numbers with Mr. Sweeney's orchestra. So without further ado, I'd like to turn the remainder of the evening over to Mr. Sweeney." As the members of the orchestra took their places, Mr. Sweeney took Misty by the hand and led her to the spot she would sing from and said to her in a low soothing voice, "Just relax and concentrate on the music. Let it come freely."

"I'll try," she said as she looked at Mrs. Tanner for reassurance.

"Don't start till I cue you;" said Mr. Sweeney. "We'll let the orchestra take it around once. Just feel the music and watch for my cue." Turning to the audience he said, "I was quite taken this afternoon by this girl's lovely voice. I'm happy to say she has selected three songs she will do with us this evening. The first is a number I'm sure you are all familiar with, 'Where the Road Ends.'" Looking at Misty he asked, "Do you know it well enough or would you like the sheet?"

"I do know it quite well sir," she answered, "but I am so nervous I might forget."

"Here child;" Mr. Sweeney said. "You hold onto the sheet, but I don't think you're going to need it." As the music began she closed her eyes and listened intently to the orchestra. When it came time to cue her Mr. Sweeney saw there would be no need to. She began to sing precisely on time. Most were familiar with this song, but none had ever heard it like this. With an orchestra behind her, her voice was angelic. She moved through her next two numbers with

90

ease and grace. At the conclusion the room filled with loud applause, many rising to their feet. Then something unexpected happened. As Misty was about to step down from the small platform that held the orchestra, Wendall Cambridge stepped up, took hold of her hand and turned her toward Mr. Sweeney. The three stood in a circle while the two men talked. Misty looked troubled as if she desperately wanted no part of this, but that was not what was being considered. After a moment Mr. Sweeney reached for his stack of sheet music and pulled one out handing it to an obviously delighted Wendall. He looked it over and had some conversation with Misty, at which point Mr. Sweeney announced, "We have one more number we would like to present to you. Mr. Wendall Cambridge and Miss Misty Tanner will perform a duet. A very lovely song has been selected, it's called 'Here at Last'."

Misty quickly resigned herself to this arrangement. Never had she experienced anything like the thrill of singing with the orchestra. As the music began Misty started the song. "When the daffodil is in bloom" Wendall followed with; "You know that spring will be here soon;" Misty turned to Mrs. Tanner and unable to hold back her feelings she wiped a tear from the corner of her eye. Many times they had sung this song together when she was a child. She sang, "When the butterflies arrive." Wendall responded, "and the woodchuck comes outside."

Misty	*Fireflies in the night*
Wendall	*Full moon shining ever so bright*
Misty	*Dogwood trees in floral array*
Wendall	*Birds are coming back this way*

Wendall had the kind of deep voice that fit so well this type of slow song where hitting both high and low ranges were so important. The chorus they sang together. He moved closer and took hold of her hand.

chorus	*It's a lovely time of year,*
	that wonderful season is here;
	it's here, it's here at last;
Misty	*We waited the winter long*
Wendall	*To hear the bluebirds song,*
Together	*It's here at last.*

91

Misty was swaying to the sound of the orchestra, all the fear she thought she'd have was nowhere in her mind now. She raised her other hand pointing her fingers toward the ceiling and sang her next line;

Misty   *Will you hitch the surrey*
Wendall   *I will in a hurry*
Misty   *Will you drive us through the pines;*
Wendall   *Yes I would, I'd like that fine.*
Misty   *Listen to the hoofs on the wooden bridge*
Wendall   *Look at the sun setting over the ridge;*
Misty   *The grass is green and growing tall*
           soon will be the springtime ball;
           and we will dance
Wendall   *And we will dance;*
Together *It's a lovely time of year*
           that wonderful season is here;
           it's here, it's here at last
           we waited for the winter long
           to hear the blue birds song
           it's here, it's here at last.

Misty   *Daffodils and butterflies*
Wendall   *Woodchuck coming back outside*

Rising up on her toes and lifting her hands shoulder high Misty sang;

Misty   *Dogwood trees and birds and bees, lovely time*
Wendall   *It's a wonderful time;*
Misty   *Lovely time*
Wendall   *It's a magnificent time*
Together *Welcome back, spring time, spring time.*

It was an incredible performance. The crowd rose to its feet. Wendall took hold of her hand and bowed to the audience, turned, raised Misty's hand and she bowed also. Then they bowed once in unison before leaving the platform.

The chairs were pushed back against the wall. The orchestra played and everyone danced. One after another approached Misty to congratulate her on her performance this evening. While the

92

group of young ones stood off to the side conversing Wendall entered in saying, "That sure was a lot of fun Misty. I hope we get to do it again sometime."

"It was fun Wendall," she replied, "but next time give me some warning. It's not good to scare people like that." As they stood laughing the orchestra started another number. A slow one. Wendall clicked his heels together, bowing slightly and said, "Honor me please with this dance." Catching her totally off guard her mouth moved but nothing came out. In an instant Roscoe stepped forward and moved Misty toward the dance area. As he did this he said to Wendall, "She can't. She's dancing with me."

"Ros, what are you doing? This is not a good idea," Misty said in a near frightened voice.

"He'll be dragging you out under the moonlight next, the big toad," said a somewhat angry young man.

"I don't think people are going to appreciate this Ros," said Misty. As they started to dance Roscoe smiled and said, "That's just too bad. I'm going to appreciate it very much."

"I'm glad one of us is, I already feel like the whole room is staring at us," said Misty.

"I'm sure they are my dear;" he said with much satisfaction. Off to the side Gloria Franklin and Mrs. Tanner were watching too.

"How can you blame them?" Mrs. Tanner asked her. "What could be done to keep it from happening?"

"It's really sad;" Gloria said looking at them dancing. "They're so in love. And it's going to lead to such sorrow. I saw them earlier outside the courtyard and I think Emily you had better consider moving your plan up a couple of years."

Watching her son's face she said with a slight sigh, "Perhaps tomorrow."

"That may prove to be more serious than not," replied Mrs. Franklin. "We're thinking the same thoughts Gloria. We'll talk tomorrow. I love them both so much. We'll do what's best for them."

As the evening wore on, everyone danced to their heart's delight. Roscoe danced with his mother and sisters and again with Misty. Mr. Tanner danced with his children and his wife till his legs could hardly hold him any longer. Wendall got his dance with Misty and Addie pursued Roscoe till he finally asked her. Getting close to nine, Mr. Sweeney announced the final number. The bride and groom would dance the first stanza alone then all were welcome to join in. Many of the younger ones had by this time wandered off. Some were congregated in the courtyard, others were walking about the gardens under the moonlight.

When Misty was alone for a moment near the front of the house Wendall seized the opportunity. "Misty, would you walk around to our coach with me? I have something for you."

"Something for me Wendall?" she asked.

"It's a little something I made;" he said. When they reached the buggy he pulled a curry comb from a small wooden box. and said, "Remember the first time we met? You were brushing your horse with a broken curry comb."

"I remember that morning. That old comb has been around the barn as long as I can remember. This is beautiful Wendall. It must have been hard to make." "The ridges are always a problem, but I did enjoy making it for you, I'm always making something. I'd much rather work in the shop than in the fields. I like to tinker with machinery, things like turbines and steam power really fascinate me."

"I've seen Poppa Tanner reading things about steam powered trains and things like that. I think it fascinates him too," she said.

"There is something else that fascinates me," he said to her looking more serious.

"What?" she asked.

"You Misty," he answered.

"Wendall why on earth would I?" she asked, yet not understanding what he meant.

"You're different," he said.

"Yes, I am Wendall, but not everyone finds it fascinating," she said laughing.

"No," he said, "I don't mean different as to who your parents were or that kind of thing, you're different from others because of what you are on the inside. Your equanimity is something others your age don't possess, and that's what I find so fascinating about you. All day the others were saying she is so beautiful, curvaceous, and yes I think you are. I think your beauty is enthralling, but your personality is more beautiful to me."

"Wendall, I don't know what to say. It's very nice of you to say those things but . . ."

"You don't have to say anything, Misty," he interrupted. "I know Ros has strong feelings for you. And you for him. He probably tells you these things all the time."

"Well, no, not exactly," she said.

"Well, I think he should be," he said indignantly. "I would hate to think that his feelings for you would not be befitting of the person you are."

"Oh Wendall don't think that way of Ros. He would never think that way of me," she said.

"Yes, I guess I know you're right. Just the thought of it though could anger me. Misty, I'm not going to remain long in the south. The world is changing fast these days. The south doesn't want to keep up. It's the things I read about in the north that excite me."

"Poppa Tanner owns things in the north," she replied.

"I'm going to own things in the north too. There's a bundle of money to be had, and land even more beautiful than in the south."

"It sounds wonderful I guess," she said to him.

"It *is* wonderful Misty, and when I go I'd like to take you with me," he said.

"Oh Wendall, I think you're a very nice young man, and I know you'll do well for yourself up north, but I couldn't go with you, I don't ever want to leave Mariah. This is my home, and these are the people I love. Wendall you certainly are full of surprises," she said with a kindly smile.

"Misty I understand, really I do, but you know if you stay here you'll never be able to marry a white person. For Ros to marry you he would have to leave the south, and Mariah. I don't know if he could do that, and what if he married someone else, you couldn't live with that could you?"

"I know what you're saying Wendall, I don't have all the answers, I pray about it everyday. Anyway, you're the one who said the world is changing fast, and Poppa says that the abolitionists will one day win out and slavery will take on a different form. Only God knows the future." With that they walked back to the house and joined the others.

By now many of the guests had gone. Others were making their way to the various carriage houses and guest rooms for the night. Several of the young folks were sitting on the veranda when Wendall and Misty returned. Roscoe was there looking a bit uneasy as the two came up the front stairs. "Where have you been?" he asked. Misty sat down and handed him the curry comb saying, "We walked to the carriages. Wendall made me a gift. Isn't it beautiful?"

"My goodness," said Addie who was sitting a few feet away, "you really finished it. He must have made a hundred of them till he got it right. Probably used the whole tree up to make that curry comb."

"It will get put to good use," Misty responded, "I'll introduce my horse to it in the morning."

"I did have a lot of trouble getting the ridges right on the teeth. Don't know how many I broke till I got it right," Wendall said.

Addie started laughing as she said, "Wendall used to make broken things on purpose, like nigger Jone's chair, right Wendall?"

"Never mind Addie," Wendall said, obviously not wanting to talk about it.

"Come on Wendall," Addie said, "The three legged chair was funny and you know it. Wendall would take an old wooden chair and cut one leg off near the top, then set it up so it looked okay. He'd call this old nigger over and tell him to try the chair he was fixing. We would tell him we needed someone bigger than us, and he'd sit in it everytime. Down he would go backwards. Funniest thing you ever saw. Dumb old nigger never caught onto it."

Wendall could see that most there found no amusement in this and he said, "Childishness, Addie, that's all it was."

"Nigger Jones was about the dumbest character there ever was," Addie responded, "and I dare say the rest ain't much better."

"To say all people are like one, Addie would have to be just a matter of opinion," Misty said, looking her straight in the eye.

"Excuse me miss," Addie said indignantly, "You would contradict me?" Then with a coy smile Addie said, "Oh yes, I see, self defense is a natural reaction."

"This is not an evening to discuss the politics of the south," Isabelle interjected.

"I understand Olivia brought up two baby coons today Iz, how young are they?" asked Roscoe.

"Can't be more than four, maybe six weeks. Cutest things ya ever saw," said Isabelle responding to her brother's lead to change the conversation.

"This girl Olivia," said Roscoe, "teenage girl maybe sixteen or so, parents are field hands, but she has such love of animals, we put her to work in the stables. Before we knew it, she had cages all about with orphaned critters in em. Bottle feeding em like you would a baby, early spring she had baby squirrels nursing on a barn cat."

"She once had a fox, beautiful thing it was," said Rebecca.

"Tell em bout the fox Ros," said Misty.

"It was beautiful all right," he said laughing, "had a pretty good appetite too."

"For chickens," said Isabelle. "A fox in the chicken house won't live long round our house," said Wendall.

"That's the way Poppa Tanner thought too, Wendall," said Misty.

"Did he get it?" asked Wendall.

"Well we kind of protected it," said Roscoe. "Olivia raised it from a pup, but we all got attached to it. When it came time to let it go, it didn't want to go, and when she stopped feeding it to try and get it to leave, it started eating chickens."

"Father was so mad after about the fifth chicken," Isabelle added, "he came down to the barn looking for the fox. When he didn't find it he turned to Olivia and pointing his finger at her he started yelling about the chicken-eating fox. Well, Olivia covered her face with her hands and dropped to the ground crying hysterically. Father was so dismayed he just turned and walked away."

"What happened to the fox?" asked Ellen.

"I was made to take it for a long ride and let it go. It never did come back," said Roscoe.

"It was nearly old enough to find a mate anyway," said Misty.

With that everyone started saying goodnight. Misty told the girls she would be right up, then sat a few moments talking to Roscoe. Their conversation was kept light as they talked about the day's activities. Finally Roscoe said he could stay up no longer, said goodnight and headed in. Misty took a few moments to enjoy the quietness of the night, and then headed in herself. From the bottom of the stairs she saw Mr. Tanner sitting alone in the room. Walking in quietly she asked, "Did you fall asleep in the chair Poppa?"

"No my dear," he answered, "I think I'm too wound up to sleep."

"I was going to bed but, I don't think I'll fall asleep too soon either," Misty said as she sat down on the floor in front of his chair.

"It seems like only yesterday Misty," he said placing his hand lightly on her shoulder, "Emily called me into this room so excited. Aunt Molly had Naomi's hand and she was taking her first steps. I thought of that today as I walked her down the aisle."

"Oh, I was so happy for her, walking down the aisle holding on to your arm. She kept saying this evening that you made this day so wonderful. And you did. And not just for Naomi, Isabelle had to be thinking that one day you will do it for her too," Misty said in a soft voice.

"Not too soon I hope," he replied. "Susan will be going north while Edward runs the business there. Naomi will be sailing the seas, and Roscoe will be at the university in England. I didn't build such a big house to get lost in. It's been my dream to see him take over the plantation and have my family here, and grandchildren all about the place, and happily grow old with the wife of my youth. How does that sound Misty?"

"Perfect," she responded, "I want to grow old here too, I want to see Naomi's children, and Isabelle's too."

"What about your own children my dear?" he asked.

"I don't think about that," she said.

"Don't think about it huh. Why not?" he asked.

"Maybe I can't be pregnant, maybe I would get sick and die like my mother Lydia;" she said looking down toward the floor. "No, no Misty, I know that you know better than that. That poor girl was sick a long time and didn't have a chance. No, that's not why you don't think about it." Misty looked up into his eyes and felt her whole body relax. His look of love and reassurance was exactly what she needed.

"Emily always said that girls mature faster than boys, and I see it clearly with you and the boy."

"I don't understand what you mean;" she said to him.

"I mean, dear, you take a much more realistic view of things than he does. Don't you think Emily and I know how you two feel?" he said.

"Poppa, I never meant to be displeasing to you," she said as she looked away.

"Child you have never been displeasing. I don't think it's within you to be. How about you and I go to the kitchen and pour a cup of tea and talk for a while."

Once their tea was poured they sat down at the table. Facing each other, he asked "Is there anything you might want to talk about?"

"I guess being really confronted with this I'm seeing more clearly now, more honestly maybe. I love Ros, I always have. But I wouldn't have ever said anything about it. I knew long ago it wasn't right, but when he told me how much he loved me I couldn't, I didn't want to hold back my feelings. But I didn't know then how serious it could be, and everytime I try to put it in perspective and be honest with myself, he says they'll be a way for us to be together." She paused and looking at him with a slight smile

98

said, "That's what you meant isn't it, when you said I matured faster than Ros? Because I know don't I, it can't be, but he doesn't. You're worried he would leave Mariah. I can tell."

"Oh yes Misty I am. I can see more than ever before that I have reason to be."

"That's funny, Poppa, because I can see more than ever before you don't have to worry about that. I owe you two my life, and I love you more than my life. I would never, ever betray you, nor give you pain for my own comfort's sake."

"You know," he said, "I wonder just how much you are like your mother. I never really took an interest in knowing her, and I doubt she ever spoke more than a word or two in my presence. But I wonder if Emily saw in her what I'm seeing in you tonight, this whole day for that matter. I can't blame my son for loving you." He stopped talking and a silence fell over them for a moment. Then he asked, "Did I ever tell you about well digging?" She laughed and said, "Did I ever tell you we poke fun at you and your parables?"

This brought out the laughter of a father who knows his children well.

"But please, Poppa," she said, still laughing, "teach me to dig wells."

"That's not exactly what the story is about, but here it is anyway. When a man starts to dig a well he's on level ground with shovel in hand. As he digs the hole he has to stand in it. Pretty soon the hole is so deep he can't throw the dirt up over the top. What does he do?"

"He gets buckets and ropes, I've seen it done."

"Exactly," he said, "do you get the point?"

"No."

"Well, what worked perfectly well in the beginning doesn't work at all anymore. So to complete the project the old method has to be put aside and a new one, completely different, has to be used."

She reached over and touched his hand and said, "That's very interesting, Poppa. Thank you for sharing that with me," and then they laughed. "No Poppa, I'm sorry," she said trying to stop laughing. "Tell me what you mean by it. I do want to know."

"Sometime dear, before the Franklins leave, Emily was going to talk with you about going home with them," Before he could get another word out she drew back, a frightened look came over her.

"Please! Please!" She said anxiously. "I'll do anything you say, but don't send me away. I wouldn't want to live if I couldn't be here."

"Send you away? No child we couldn't ever do that," he said reassuringly. "Think of the well, one method works well for a while, then another is employed to finish. Emily raised you to be a white person, and indeed you are. Nobody could ever look at you and think otherwise, except the law. The law says you're Negro, and the law won't see it any other way. Emily doesn't want, nor do I want to see you unhappy or hurt because of this. I'd give up this right arm, Misty, if you and the boy could marry and take possession of this plantation."

"But, you always say the abolitionists are going to change things," she said hoping for a positive answer.

"Yes, I believe they will, but who knows how or when, and in the meantime you could be finishing your training with a new method. Living in Orleans as Misty Tanner, with no explanation to anyone, and I know Gloria could use the help with all the packing and moving and arranging they'll be doing once their new house is complete. Stay for the winter, come home in the spring. Now that's not so bad is it?"

"No, I guess it isn't, but I've never been away before. It's kind of scary," she said.

"It'll be fine dear, even exciting," he said.

"Does Ros know about this?" she asked.

"No, nobody does. I'll tell you truthfully, this was something planned for a later time, but we really think it best that it be done now," he replied.

"You mean to separate Ros and me" she said sadly.

"Not just that honey, but for you. Nobody ever expected you to grow up so fast, or mature so quickly. We want what's best for you, and for Ros too." He paused for a moment. "I know what you're thinking, and you're right, and I too wish it could be different. I'll take my well story one step further. It doesn't matter how much the man wants his well in that spot, if he digs deep enough and still finds no water he has to fill in the hole and dig elsewhere. That's the way life is, we sometimes have to accept things we cannot change. Think about it for a while Misty, and we'll talk again. But say nothing to Ros or Isabelle just yet."

"Poppa I'll do anything you want me to, you know that don't you," she said with eyes full of tears. He stood up and walked around the table and raised her up.

Putting his arms around her he said, "I know you will dear. Trust me in this. I think it is for the best."

She put her head against his chest. "Poppa could I please not go until autumn, till after Ros leaves for England?"

With all his heart he knew he should say no, that she should leave next week with the Franklins, but he couldn't. How could he hold this innocent child, whose pleading words came with tears, whose heart he sensed was breaking. He held his hand on her head and lightly pressed it to his chest near his heart and said okay, then bowed his head down and tenderly kissed the top of her head.

The very next day Mrs. Tanner took Misty for a long walk. She would not delay talking to her after her husband told her of their conversation. Having had time to think about it, Misty felt somewhat better. It would be only for six months or so, and Ros would be overseas anyway. That evening the family sat down with the Franklins and discussed the plans in detail. Isabelle expressed both excitement and sadness. It would be the first time they were ever apart. Gloria Franklin did her best to make Misty feel that she was needed and wanted in their new home. Roscoe sat quietly doing much more listening than talking. As the evening wore on, Misty became more relaxed about the idea and started thinking in terms of helping Mrs. Franklin and being needed there, and that it could be an exciting experience.

Another week and the Franklins were gone, plans were to bring Misty in late October, or early November. For now though things went back to normal. July came and went, August was all but over and the hot muggy days were best spent in the swimming hole. Roscoe, Isabelle and Misty spent all the time they could together, and more and more Roscoe and Misty sneaked off to be alone.

Misty had been so sure of things the night she sat and talked with Mr. Tanner, but it took only one time alone with Roscoe to change her thinking back around again. She wanted so much to believe what he said, that one day he would find or make a way for them to be together. Soon they would be parted for the first time, and for a long time. So why not she thought, just let time pass and see what another year would bring.

Roscoe would be the first Tanner to go to a university, and receive a college degree. It is necessary now, considering the vast empire the family is building and the responsibility that will rest on his shoulders. Time is quickly running out, it's September 1st: twenty one days till he departs. School won't begin till January, but he'll be leaving with Zachary and Naomi and a cargo of their own cotton. This will also give him time to adjust to England and become acquainted with those who import Tanner cotton.

Mylo Topaz has returned to paint Mr. Tanner's portrait. When he has completed this he is commissioned to do both Mrs. Tanner's portrait and Isabelle separately. Roscoe has come up with an idea to make Mr. Topaz a little extra money. When not working on Mr. Tanner, he has him doing sketches of Misty, some charcoal, some water colors, others pencil. All the while he stirs their hearts with stories of men marrying mulatto women in France and England, even in parts of this country, and raising children and not being bothered by the ignorance of others.

As the days move on, a friendship develops between Mr. Topaz, Roscoe and Misty. He has finished his portrait of Mr. Tanner and his wife, and is now working on Isabelle. Unbeknownst to the others he has also been working on a portrait of Misty in the evenings. Isabelle does know, however, she has been fixing her hair and helping with her gown, the one she wore at Naomi's wedding. Isabelle's been conveniently unable to sit for long stretches of time, and Mr. Topaz has had to stay longer, giving him the needed time to finish Misty's portrait. Roscoe plans to wrap the painting and seal it in a wooden box and store it in the attic for a future time.

The days are winding down quickly. Saturday the twentieth of September, two days till his departure. This evening there will be company. The Myers family and the Cambridges are coming for dinner and to say farewell to Roscoe. In the morning he, Isabelle and Misty rode their horses in to get Rebecca. They've taken the long way home riding through places they haven't been for years, perhaps in an attempt to make the day last longer.

They rode into an old apple orchard they used to ride to years ago at this time of the season to pick apples for themselves and their horses, but when they got there, there weren't any apples and not many trees. It was left untouched for some time, and overrun by thickets and trees. The few apple trees left were without fruit and dying. The four of them sat quietly on their horses all thinking similar thoughts, and all feeling saddened by the meaning they were putting to it. Finally, Rebecca spoke up, "Let's make a plan. Let's come back in the spring after next with a dozen seedlings. We'll clear out a piece and plant the orchard again."

"Yes," said Roscoe. "And in ten years we'll be back with our children picking apples. Come on let's ride, the day is still early."

Off they went, not looking back, but thinking back. As they stop in one familiar place after another they talk about the past and the things they had shared together. Although determined not to show it, Misty's heart was growing sadder with each hour. What changes would the next year bring? Would they ever be together like this again? It somehow felt like the beginning of the end. She wondered if maybe the others didn't feel the same, but she laughed and told stories with the rest. This was a day she wanted to remember as a happy one.

That night back at the house a big dinner was served. The guests brought gifts and were full of praise for Roscoe, going off to England at such a young age. You'll come back a different man they told him. Roscoe smiled and listened and agreed with them all, but his heart was hardly in it. Now that the time had come he really didn't care whether he went or not. The adventure excited him, but being away from Misty for so long—they had been together practically every day of their lives—was not a thought he could get use to. Not wanting to disappoint his parents however, he pretended all was well and did his best to enjoy the party.

Later in the evening Roscoe, Isabelle and Rebecca went to the stable to hitch a surrey for a moonlight ride. Wendall offered to help Misty prepare cider and snacks to bring along. Alone in the kitchen he asked, "Do you think it would be all right if sometimes I rode with you girls? I really haven't found too many people down here I enjoy being with, and Addie's friends, well let's say twenty minutes in their company is long enough."

"That would be fine Wendall," she answered, "I'm sorry Addie wasn't feeling well today."

"She's feeling all right, she just didn't want to come, so she said she was sick. I don't know why you're so kind to her when she's so odious to you. She doesn't deserve it you know."

"Mother Tanner always said, those that show love the least need love the most, and not to say that you are like Addie, but you don't seem to view things like you used to."

"Thanks Misty," he said. "I'm glad you think that, after coming to know you, well never mind, but thanks."

The next morning, all were up early for breakfast. Roscoe didn't want to go to the meeting, but his mother convinced him he had to. Everyone would want to say good-bye and they would be disappointed if he didn't come. After the meeting was over and everyone left, the Myers family walked to their coach with them, while the older ones talked. Roscoe and Rebecca walked off a short distance saying their good-byes. They embraced. Roscoe held her tight for a moment then moved her back to arms length and said, "I want you to be at the house the day I get back. Promise you'll do that."

"I promise Ros. I'll be there the day before just to be certain," she said as she hugged him one last time. On their way home as they neared the covered bridge they could see Misty and several children sitting on the wall waiting for them. Bringing the coach to a stop, they climbed on. Up over the embankment came Digger dripping wet from walking in the stream.

"Move on horse," Mr. Tanner called out. "That dog tries to get in smack'em."

What was Reverend Brown's sermon about this morning Ros?" asked Misty.

"He wouldn't know, Misty," said Mr. Tanner laughing. "His body was taking up space, but his mind was somewhere else."

"He talked about God," Roscoe responded. "He talked about abolitionists to father again," Roscoe added.

"Yes, he did son," said Mr. Tanner. "How'd he put it? Keep their northern noses in their own affairs, and stop meddling where they're not wanted. Set in his ways ole Reverend Brown is, but a lot of truth in what he says."

At the house Roscoe and Isabelle quickly changed, grabbed a bite to eat and headed with Misty to the stables. In just a few minutes they were galloping through the orchards and heading for open fields. They had planned to go to the meadows one last time, but the weather was not going to cooperate. It had been overcast all day, and when the rain came, it came hard and steady. Forced to turn back, they rode to an abandoned hut once used by a group of slaves. They huddled in a corner and wrapped themselves in the blanket they used for playing cards on.

"Fine way to spend our last day together," Isabelle said as she pulled the blanket tighter and cuddled closer to her brother.

"Could be worse," Roscoe responded.

"How so big brother?" Isabelle asked.

"Roof could be leaking on this side too," Roscoe said laughing. Before Isabelle could respond a drop of rain hit the top of her head. As she wiped it off, they laughed uncontrollably. "Misty," Roscoe said, "I want you to have James ride my horse at least a couple of times a week. I don't want him to get lazy." James is a slave in his early twenties. A very big fellow, handy with tools, he does repairs on equipment and buildings and the like.

"I'll do that Ros, I thought I would ride him myself sometimes."

"I hope it is the quickest year of my life," said Roscoe.

"I can understand you wanting to get back home," said Isabelle, "but what a marvelous opportunity it is to see other parts of the world, and to learn so many things. I'm excited for you."

"As much as I don't want you to go, it is important that you do," Misty said trying to reassure herself. "Poppa said to me one night when we were talking about you going to school, that he would like to buy out his partners in the north and have everything run from within the family."

"Edward will be leaving soon to learn the business up there," Isabelle added.

"Edward learn the business?" Roscoe said. "I've not seen my father make too many mistakes, but sending Edward north may be one."

"He seems to drink a lot," said Misty.

"Drunk is more like it," said Roscoe.

"Maybe Poppa feels he will stop it if he's given more responsibilities," said Isabelle.

"Drinking is not his only problem Iz," Roscoe said in a disgusted tone.

"What do you mean Ros?" she asked.

"Never mind Iz. He'll hang himself one day." Misty clutched Roscoe's arm tightly and pressed up against him.

The conversation went back and forth between the future and the past and a couple of hours went quickly by. The rain slowed down to a drizzle and they headed home for dinner.

During the course of dinner, Edward, who might have already been sipping at his pocket flask, suggested that if the family wanted to separate Misty from the south for the winter, why not New York instead of Orleans? "She can accompany Susan and me." he said. "What with Susan being pregnant again, and totin these youngins, she could be a might big help."

"Edward, I think we should discuss something like that in private first," Susan said sternly.

"Edward," Isabelle said, "in New York you have to do things for yourself. There's no slavery where you're going. You have to teach him to change diapers Susan."

"No . . . no," said Edward, "that's the beauty of it. No one will know she's a nigger. They won't know why we brought her."

"We'll end this conversation here," said Mrs. Tanner. "Misty will be in Gloria's house by December. There's no point in discussing any other arrangement." Pushing her chair back from the table, Susan stood up and said, "Excuse me y'all." Then turning a cold eye to her husband she said, "Edward would you be so kind to see me upstairs when you've finished?"

"Yes dear," he said. "I'll be there directly."

After dinner was over Roscoe and Misty quietly slipped out the kitchen door. "Where are we going?" she asked.

"I don't know. Let's just walk a while," he said.

"I can't believe this night has arrived," Misty said as he took her hand. "We are both going to be so far from home, and for such a long time. I wish we never had to grow up, that we could just keep doing what we've always done. That way we could just stay together." Roscoe pulled her close to him. She reached around his waist and leaned her head against him as they walked.

"My father had one of those father-son talks with me yesterday. He'd never come right out and say we couldn't be together, but he tried to reason with me so I'd see it that way. Same as he did with you, right?"

"He only wants what's best for you Ros. You know that."

"Oh yes Misty, I do know that, and I don't mean anything other than that. My father is a very smart man. He knows in his heart that I won't stay here or in the south or even in this country, if it means not marrying you."

"Oh Ros," she said with a sound of despair. "I guess that old expression Henry uses about being between a rock and a hard place is where I am now. I told Poppa I would never cause them heartache and I won't. Not for anything. Oh if only things change."

"What would cause more heartache? Them knowing I stay on to live my life the way they wanted, or my being happy? Think about it Misty. Don't you see what he would have done to have my mother. In his heart he knows what he really wants me to do. He just hasn't come to grips with it all yet. But he will. I know him."

"Oh I don't know, I just don't know," she said. "I want to just stay here and wait for you to come home. I'm afraid if I leave things will never be the same again."

"Come on now girl," he said trying to reassure her, "the time will go by in a flash, and Zach will bring our letters back and forth."

"That's another thing Ros. How will I ever write to you from Orleans?"

"We'll work something out," he answered.

They walked to the old building the slaves used as a meeting house. They've spent much time here over the years, sitting at the piano, playing and talking endlessly. They lit a couple of oil lamps to give just enough light for the area they were in. "Play my song Misty. It would be nice if we finished it tonight," he said as they sat down together on the piano bench. They played and sang and joked around like they always did, not really wanting to think about tomorrow. After a while he turned and sat on the bench sideways with one leg on each side and facing her, he pulled her close, and gently rocked her. Suddenly he sat straight up bouncing her head off his shoulder.

"Ros what's wrong!" she asked.

"Wrong!" he said excitedly. "It's not what's wrong, it's what's right. I've just been hit with a bolt of lightning."

"It must have hit the back of your head, cause I didn't see it;" she said laughing.

"Misty," he said, "marry me tonight."

"Ros stop it. Don't play like that," she said.

"I'm not fooling. We can get married right now," he said looking at her with a serious expression.

Knowing he was joking she put her hand on his face and said, "My poor sweet Ros, you couldn't take leaving and now you've gone crazy. I'll come to the stable and visit and feed you everyday and see that Olivia gives you clean bedding every morning."

"You think I'm kidding. Well I'm not," he said. The look on his face was more serious and it frightened her some. "Misty, we'll get Toby to marry us. He's a minister." She started to cry and tried to get up, but he grabbed hold of her hand.

"Stop it Ros, just stop it right now. Why are you upsetting me like this? Don't do this to me on this night. Why am I . . . who I am. Why didn't I just die in my mother's belly."

"No! You stop it and you stop it right now!" he said quickly. "Don't you ever say that again. I want to marry you tonight. I love you Misty. If having Mariah meant losing you I'd hate Mariah and I'd be miserable. I love you more than I love my life. Marry me tonight. We won't tell anyone for now."

"Ros you're crazy, we can't do that," she said not looking at him.

"I say we can, what's to stop us?" he responded.

"Let's start with the facts. A Negro can't perform a marriage for a white man," she said.

"We don't need people's approval, it's God's approval that matters," he said.

"Then we would have to go to Reverend Brown and you know we are not doing that," she said.

"Not so Misty. Is Toby minister in this here church? Does God hear the prayers that come from here? Isn't that all that really matters." he said.

"You're really crazy," she said as she turned and looked at him face to face.

"Crazy am I?" he said as he kissed her. "Toby will do as I tell him and I'll tell him to keep it to himself. No one need know anything for now, and what ever has to be done later we'll do."

"Ros I want to really I do, but I'm scared. What if we get in trouble?" she asked.

"No one will know until we want them to, or until we can make it official in their eyes. Trust me Misty, it'll be all right."

They went first to the woodshop where he placed a small block of cherry wood in the vice and drilled a small hole through it. Then he went to work with a hand saw, knife and file. Misty sat on the work bench watching him work and feeling more excitement now than fear. If no one knows it will be all right she reassured herself, and this will surely help her through the time they are apart from each other, and from Mariah. Sanding the finished product, he takes her hand and slips the cherry ring on her finger. It's a little loose, but she says it is fine and they go to get Toby to bring him to the meeting house. Once there, Toby, too, puts up some opposition, but he'll do as he is told and the wedding takes place. Sworn to secrecy, Toby leaves quickly and they are left alone.

She throws her arms around him and he holds her tight. "Oh Ros, I can't believe we did this. I feel like my head is spinning around," she said.

"My wife! You are my wife," he says shaking his head, "no man ever had a more beautiful girl for a wife. We'll always be together Misty. I won't allow anything to come between us." Then laughing he said, "as Grandmother Naomi would say, 'Not hell or high water'."

When they went outside Misty stopped and looked up at the full moon. "Ros, isn't it an amazing thing, how it's only round like that certain times of the year. I think it is very romantic, so serene. Whenever I see a round moon it will remind me of this special night." As they walked slowly holding each other's hand she started singing. "When I see the bright moon, big and strong and round, I will be listening carefully for the melodious sound, of my lover serenading me." Letting go of his hand and putting her arm around his waist she said, "Doesn't it make you want to sing?"

"You want to be serenaded to? Well let's see," he said pulling her close. "If it was my calling, that I should be a king, have my very own empire, and all the wealth it would bring, [but not have you], I would walk away this evening, never would I return. I would go the course of poverty, let the whole world know, [it's you alone I live for]; more beautiful than corals, more precious than fine gold. I'll have you for my lifetime, and when I have grown old, I'll be with you."

"That was nice Ros, I'm going to write that tomorrow," she said.

"I'll have to build you another chest just for all the things you write," he said.

"You may very well have to," she said. "By the time a year goes by I'll have a library written."

As they walked Roscoe was directing the way. He led them to the barn. "See if you can find a lamp, I'll get some blankets," he said. She picked up the lamp and the old King James Bible that lay on a shelf. Roscoe found three clean blankets and they climbed up into the hayloft. He broke open two bales of hay and spread them into a small thick pile and lay one blanket over it, made a pillow of another and wrapped the third around them. "I can't believe we did it Ros," she said.

"Stop saying that. You are my wife now, we did do it."

"We've done some crazy things before, but you topped em all tonight," she said resting her head against his shoulder.

"I topped em?" he asked laughing, "don't you mean we?"

"I'm practicing Ros. If anyone finds out after you're gone, I'm blaming it all on you." They laughed awhile, then held each other and kissed, tenderly and passionately. Feelings of endearment and passion were stronger than they ever knew them to be. Nothing could be more natural on a wedding night.

"Ros . . . Ros," she said as she rolled on her back.

"I know Misty," he said.

"Oh Ros, I want to be your wife in a complete way tonight. More so Ros, than words could ever say."

"I'm going to go to them Misty and tell them what we've done, and that I'm taking you to England with me when I leave tomorrow."

"Oh no Ros," she said in her soft voice, "that would be wrong. It would be wrong to do that to them, as wrong as me becoming pregnant tonight. We said we would wait, and doing so will work out best, I know it will. Let's just enjoy the rest of our time together."

She picked up the Bible and opened it to the book of Ruth and said, "We used to read this book a lot. It is such a beautiful account of love." She started reading. As they became engrossed in the lives of Ruth and Naomi, they relaxed and their minds were once again at ease.

Soon the rooster's crow called their attention to dawn. Climbing down from the hayloft they walked to the pond and got in the rowboat kept tied at the dock. Misty rowed lightly, Roscoe sat in the back facing her. Both were hungry now, but they knew if they went up to the house their time together would be over. They rowed around the small island over and over again, then docked the boat and walked some more.

It was just another day for the rest of the plantation. People could be seen moving about and the day's activities had begun. To Roscoe and Misty this meant that his departure time, nine o'clock, was coming all too quickly. Off in the distance they saw Mr. Tanner coming their way. "Do you think he is mad Ros?" she asked.

"He has no reason to be mad. Smile girl," he said with a laugh. "You look guilty, like a criminal."

"You two must have gotten up early this morning," Mr. Tanner called to them. "You could say that father," Roscoe replied.

Mr. Tanner then laughed and said, "I did say that. Why do you look like a fox that's been caught in the hen house?"

"Looks guilty like a criminal I'd say," Misty said laughing at him.

"It's half past seven son. Y'all come up to the house. Your mother is in the kitchen with Lilly Mae. They're gonna fix y'all something special."

"We'll be right along father," Roscoe replied. They sat on an old tree stump and holding her hand Roscoe said, "I wish we had this day to be together."

"Then we would want the next day too," she said.

"It seems like this time arrived so quickly, I hope to find it in the past just as quickly," he said.

"We will Ros, it'll go by fast. I know it will."

"A year is a long time Misty. I'm going to take some of Mylo's sketches with me. I'll let the other fellows see how beautiful you are. Then I'll say, this is my wife."

"I don't have any drawings of you Ros, but I can ride your horse. It does look a lot like you."

As he put his arm around her shoulder and pulled her close he said, "You did say before the horse was better looking anyway."

"No Ros," she said smacking his leg, "I said the horse was easier to get along with, and you deserved it that day and you know it."

One bad day in years and you won't let me forget it," he said as they both laughed.

"We'll have two full months together when you get back," she said.

"Yeah, then off for another year," he replied.

"But when those two years are over you'll be nearly twenty-one and have a university degree. Things may change a whole lot by then."

"We'll never be apart again after that. I promise you today, we'll live as man and wife." Saying that to her he turned to face her, they embraced and kissed, continuing to do so for some time. So involved were they that they failed to notice the little children who were gathering a short distance away. Soon the laughter of the children was loud enough for them to hear, and turning their attention in that direction they saw a small audience of five or six children giggling. Roscoe motioned for them to come near. After he chatted and joked with them for a moment, Misty sent them off telling the eldest to find Sarah and bring her to the kitchen door.

Once back at the house, a breakfast fit for a king was served. The entire family, minus Edward was there. Everything he liked was prepared and the family enjoyed their last meal together. Shortly after nine, James came to the door and announced the cariole was packed and ready for travel. They eventually made their way to the front porch, where last hugs and kisses were exchanged. Roscoe asked Susan if they ought not to get Edward up to say goodbye? She said no, because he was not feeling well this morning. Roscoe looked at Isabelle as he hugged Susan and winked, but said no more about it. When he walked down the steps his mother looked on with tears in her eyes, his father with a broad smile, excited for his son, and proud of him. No greater joy can a father have than to see his son become a man.

James was seated at the reins, Henry has grown too old to drive long distances, and James has proven himself a competent young man. Isaac, a teenage slave has been sent along to provide a companion for the long ride home. Roscoe climbs into the cariole followed by Isabelle, Misty and the young child Sarah. They will ride as far as the covered bridge. James gives the command for the horses to start walking. Roscoe stands up and waves one final time as the cariole takes him away.

At the covered bridge the four disembark, a final kiss and hug for his little sister, a kiss for the child Sarah, and a long hard embrace and kiss for Misty. With Roscoe looking back they wave good-bye as he rides down the road and out of their view. As the girls turn to walk home Misty asks, "How will I ever get through this day?"

"Let's do something . . . anything," responds Isabelle. "Let's just be busy today."

They walked slowly, picking a flower here and there, taking turns carrying Sarah and trying to keep their minds occupied with other thoughts. As they walked along the stream, Misty picked up a small smooth stone and showing it to Sarah she said, "Look Sarah, I've found the alchemists stone. I'm going to transform you into a butterfly. A monarch butterfly. So you can fly alongside of Ros' carriage and watch over him for me. Are you ready?" Sarah had no idea what she was talking about, but it amused her, and Sarah's laughter made them laugh.

If ever there was anything that could make the young women forget their troubles it was the laughter of a young child, and this child Sarah was just what was needed today. At three, her laughter is spontaneous and her mind inquisitive. Too young to know how the girls are feeling, she was without trying, a delightful distraction.

Sarah was born to a young slave girl a few years back, a very pretty mulatto with thick reddish hair. Many know who fathered the child, but no one dares talk about it openly. Several months after her birth the mother was called in from the fields, loaded onto a wagon and taken away. The field overseer was instructed to sell the child with its mother, but through his negligence the baby was left behind. She is being raised now as an orphan among the slaves. Isabelle and Misty love being with the children, and Misty has a special fondness for this one. She leaves her as often as possible with Goldie, the woman she herself calls Mammy.

Days seem to pass by slowly, but the weeks are rolling on. It's coming into the rainy season. As autumn nears, night arrives early and a chill is in the air. Many of these evenings are spent in the family room with a crackling fire, a little music, a game of cards, conversation, and now crocheting is their latest hobby.

If the Tanner house seems different with two gone, what will it be like after Edward and Susan are gone, followed shortly afterward by Misty's departure for the Franklins. The thought makes Isabelle sad. Though her father tries to reassure her that in a few short years their household will once again be a hub of activity, she would rather it never change at all. She knows it will never be the same again. As for poor Misty, she can't fool Isabelle, acting like she's looking forward to going to Orleans. Isabelle knows better, for Misty more than herself, things will never be the same again. And what if it doesn't go well for her in Orleans? Things just seem to be moving too fast.

Early one morning Mrs. Tanner, Isabelle and Misty go out to the orchards to harvest. Lester and others are there picking and sorting. Mrs. Tanner and the girls want to make pies and fruit salad today. Lester helps them to sort through the baskets and pick some from the trees. While doing this he asks Misty if she has seen Olivia?

"Isabelle and I were talking about that last night. We haven't seen her in days, but her work's been done. Have you seen her?"

"Yes em, been doin her work. I's tend to it early," he answered.

"What's wrong with Olivia, Lester?" Misty asked with concern.

"She's been hurt Missy, restin now;" he said.

"Well, is she all right?" Misty asked trying to get more out of him.

"I reckon she be fine in a day or so," he said.

"Lester what happened to her?" she asked. He looked first at Mrs. Tanner making sure she was out of hearing range, but then he looked away saying only that he didn't know. That was enough of an answer for Misty. She didn't press him further.

After collecting all they needed Mrs. Tanner instructed two men to take the baskets to the house. They strolled through the garden picking a few things along the way. After which, Misty and Isabelle departed saying they would be along shortly. Filling Isabelle in on Lester's conversation, they headed down back in search of Olivia. One look at her confirmed what Misty had been thinking. Lying on a straw bed, Olivia's face was swollen and bruised. She wouldn't respond to their questions, and they could see she was frightened so they left her alone. After leaving the hut she was in they approached a woman nearby and asked when this happened? "Two night back," she answered. "Someone beat her, forced her to lie down. Po child, it happen again." That statement confirmed what Misty suspected a few months back. "Poor Olivia," she said to Isabelle. "How can people act so ugly?"

113

There was nothing anyone could do. Sometimes this happened amongst the slaves themselves. Other times the field overseers, who were white men, took advantage of their power and abused the young slaves. And then there was one other possibility that they both thought, but neither mentioned.

Mid October now, and what Henry calls an Indian Summer. Bright skies and warm weather. It is Sunday, and Henry will have company to fish with today. Isabelle is going home from the meeting with Rebecca, and Misty wants to go fishing with her little companion Sarah. They bring several bamboo poles with them and take the boat to the center of the pond. This was just the kind of day Misty needed. Sitting back and relaxing, listening to Henry's stories and laughter, and hearing Sarah recite the songs as Henry sang them to her, just like they did when she was a little girl.

"Rebecca has a beau Henry, did you know that?" she asked.

"No, I's can't say I did," he replied.

"She has been wanting Iz and me to meet him. I think she wants Iz to meet his friends too. You know what I mean Henry?"

"I reckon I do. I's know about how youngins think," he said with a smile. "How's come you don't go?"

'I wanted to stay home today." Henry didn't say anything. He just looked off into the water and nodded his head. "She did ask me Henry," she said.

"I's know she asked y'all. Myers' good people, always do what's right," he responded.

"I was worried the others wouldn't want me around and that would make Iz and Rebecca feel bad. I didn't want that to happen. Besides I really did want to stay home." Then sitting up straight and smiling she added, "And when was the last time we were together fishing? Don't you know I miss that too?"

"You always be my little girl," he said. "Ole Henry loves you mo than he loves anybody. You's always remember dat."

They drifted on the pond for hours, catching fish, singing songs and telling stories. At afternoon's end Misty took Henry and Sarah to Lester and Willy Mae's and cooked them a fine meal. As evening set in she was more at peace now than she had been in some time, and decided to stay the night there with Sarah.

At the main house Mr. Tanner and his wife enjoy a quiet meal together. They then stroll out through the courtyard to sit in the gazebo. When summer like days appear in October there is no finer way to enjoy them then this. Autumn colors are starting to appear. This has always been their favorite time of year. Taking his wife's hand Mr. Tanner holds it between his and says, "Look at us Emily, sitting out here in peace and quiet." He then adds with a smile, "And we didn't have to sneak off to do it. Why I don't remember the last time we ate supper alone and walked about with no one around."

"Did we ever?" she asks smiling back. "Ah, it is a lovely night Hugh, and it is nice to have a little quiet time."

"I know. I feel that way too, dear," he said. "But I'm surprised to hear you say it. We must be getting older Emily," he said.

"I'll accept getting older if along with it I get wiser," she says.

"You don't have to be worried about being short on wisdom. My goodness, Em, look at all you've accomplished," he said resting his back against the wall. "Our children are as fine as the best I've ever seen. And that there big old house. Why it is so full of love and happiness. And now grandchildren, with the potential for many more. How many times you had the answers I was struggling to find." He put his arm around behind her. "Emily you're the smartest woman ever was, cept Aunt Molly of course."

"I wonder if things would have been different if she were around when they were children. She was always so straightforward about speaking her mind," Mrs. Tanner said.

"Roscoe and Misty? I don't know, Em, she loved that baby, and she would have had a strong influence on her, but who can say. With Roscoe off in England, and Misty gone to Orleans, young minds and hearts change. And the talks I've had with her, well it's like I said before, she's a very smart girl and she knows her limitations. She'll do the right thing."

"Oh Hugh, I don't know quite how to tell you this, but the time you spend reasoning with her, well she does see it all clearly and knows exactly what she should do, then two minutes after she walks away her heart mixes all up, and she's finished off by a reassuring session with your son," Mrs. Tanner said matter-of-factly.

"Two minutes Em, I get farther with her than I do with you."

"What do you mean by that?" she asks. "It only takes you a minute sometimes to rearrange my reasoning," Mr. Tanner said amusing himself.

"Right now Hugh, my bigger concern is Susan and Edward. I smelled liquor on his breath this morning, "What is wrong with him that he drinks so much?" There are many things about Edward's behavior that troubled them. His drinking was on the rise, and any conversation Mr. Tanner had with him about it always

115

had the same results. Edward would say yes, he would drink less, and then he would drink more. They were bothered too, that in the evenings after dinner he would go for a walk alone rather than join the family and his own children for a while. Mrs. Tanner was troubled too by a recent confrontation she had with him. At Willy Mae's request, Mrs. Tanner insisted that Edward not have Lilly Mae in the room with him when he bathed, suggesting that even in Susan's pregnant condition, she could scrub his back. Edward protested to no avail, that he had always had a Negro to wash him. Mrs. Tanner did not relate any of this to Mr. Tanner for fear of his reaction. Willy Mae had reason to believe he was giving liquor to Lilly, but of yet has said nothing to anyone except her daughter.

Mr. Tanner questioned more and more in his mind sending Edward north to oversee his investments there. With so much time and work and money involved already, could he trust him to handle the responsibility of both the business and his daughter. He was rethinking it all the time. Also he knew things about Edward that he had not shared with his wife, things that had the potential to cause his daughter unhappiness.

Several nights back he had Henry follow Edward on his evening walk. The report came back that he had entered the cabin of Tom Louder, the plantation's agricultural manager, or 'Boss Master,' as he has slaves refer to him. Mr. Tanner does not hold this man in high esteem; however, he knows his job and left to do it, he makes a higher yield each year. Henry's report also included others in Louder's house, Lilly Mae and two other young girls were seen entering. To Mr. Tanner whatever Louder did was his own business, but he wouldn't tolerate his daughter's husband doing the same. A private, and somewhat heated discussion took place the next day.

The more Mr. Tanner listened to his wife talk, and the more he thought about what he knew, the more trouble it gave him. Perhaps it might be good to follow through on an idea that kept coming to his mind—closing up the house and going north with the whole family. Have Scott Franklin meet them in New York City, and take a week or two going over his investments there and seeing to it that Edward gets down to business. Then go onto New Orleans to leave Misty with the Franklins for the winter.

It had been many years since the two of them were to New York. Isabelle had never seen it and a vacation might be good for all. It was an idea that was sounding better all the time. This was

116

as good a time as any he thought, and he began discussing it with his wife who, to his surprise not only agreed wholeheartedly, but proposed an even better idea. Sending Edward ahead alone, giving him a month or so to get established, and seeing what he is going to do before leaving him there in a more permanent position. They would follow later with Susan and the children. Mr. Tanner thought it perfect. He wanted to get Edward away from the plantation in hopes it would be good for him, he had serious concerns about Edward's ability to handle responsibility. He didn't know what Edward's problems were, but he knew they were getting worse.

Returning to the house they reclined in the sitting room, and for the next hour worked on their plans. It was decided that Edward would leave in the early part of November, and they in the middle of December. If the weather wasn't too awfully bad, they would be in New York the early part of January.

Isabelle, just back from the Myers', came into the room filled with news from the outside. Her parents listened intently, after which they shared some of their news with her. Isabelle exited the room more excited then when she came in. Off she went to share this good news with Misty. Misty wasn't hard to find. Once away from the house Isabelle could see the glow of a bonfire off toward the gardens. Most Sunday evenings a small group of slaves, men, women, and children gathered by a fire near the flower gardens with musical instruments and sang the evening away. These were considered the house slaves. They lived in huts closer to the main house. They worked the fields only during harvest. Their jobs consisted of tending the livestock, maintaining the fences and out buildings, farm equipment, making furniture and clothing, doing maintenance on the main house, and many other chores. They worked directly under the Tanners. Most of their instructions came from Mrs. Tanner. These slaves worked on the reward system; the better they performed the more privileges and material things they were given. The others took their instructions from Louder; he worked under the punishment system.

As Isabelle approached she grabbed up a small girl and held her as she sat down on the bench with Misty and Henry. Jason an older man who spent most of his time building and repairing wagons asked what she wanted him to play. "Something happy and fast," was her response. "Wait till I tell you the news Misty, you're gonna love it," she said, then turned to hear Jason play. With just his harmonica and voice he belted out a tune that had everyone tapping their feet and smiling. When the song was over Misty quickly said, "What is this news that has you so gay? Don't tell me Rebecca is getting married?"

"No, no nothing like that," Isabelle responded, "I'll tell you about them later. Come on let's walk. We're got to keep this to ourselves for now."

The girls had for years read about New York City. Many times they sat and listened to people who came to visit Mr. Tanner on business talk about this unbelievable place. They didn't know what to talk about first. They would be able to see shows and plays they had dreamed about, hear songs sung from the stage that they had been singing since childhood, buy fabric from around the world, see buildings that reached up into the sky, and of course, take their very first train ride. "Best of all," Isabelle said laughing, "we get rid of Edward." When the girls got back to the house it was quiet. Mr. and Mrs. Tanner had retired for the day, so the girls sat in the kitchen, had cookies and cider and talked about Rebecca and her friends.

The next morning the family gathered for breakfast. The idea was presented to Edward and Susan, and received a mixed response. Susan thought it a wonderful idea and was genuinely excited. Edward however, scrambled for one excuse after another as to why he couldn't be ready that quickly. Each excuse was quickly put down by Susan, until she angrily cemented the fact that he was going. At which point Edward lost his appetite and left the table.

All the planning and preparing was good for Misty. It occupied some of her thinking and made the days go by a little easier.

The second Saturday in November was a clear cool morning. Isabelle is waiting in the kitchen for Misty to come down. They're going riding with Rebecca and a few of her friends today. Wendall and Addie have been invited and a full day's activity has been planned.

Mrs. Tanner and Willy Mae are working on a treat for the young ones, as well as readying provisions for Edward's departure tomorrow. "I hope Addie's behavior is better than it has been," Mrs. Tanner said to her daughter. "I think Misty is concerned about meeting the others this morning."

"Frankly Mother I'm concerned too," Isabelle replied. "Rebecca's boyfriend was nice, but the others I found a bit arrogant, and with Addie you never know what to expect."

"Well Isabelle my dear, if I wasn't worried enough already," said Mrs. Tanner.

"I'm sorry Mother. I'm sure it will be fine."

"I never thought I'd be anxious to leave home like this, but our departure date can't come quick enough. I know Misty's awful worried about being away from home, but I feel in my heart it is the right thing to do," Mrs. Tanner said as she stopped working. "How would anybody have known it would have turned out this way. Has she said anything more to you?"

"Well, I think she is hoping that by extending the trip now to Massachusetts, she can just come back home instead of going to Orleans. You know how much she wants to be here when Ros comes home," Isabelle said hoping for a positive response.

"Don't encourage her that it might be so," her mother said softly. "Our plans may be changing further, we'll talk privately this evening." Isabelle was notified that some of her guests had arrived and left the kitchen.

Willy Mae turned her attention to Mrs. Tanner and said, "You fret about dat girl like she was your flesh and blood. You taught her well Miss Emily, she gonna be fine."

"Oh I hope so Willy. I feel frightened. I feel guilty too. I can picture in my mind like it was yesterday, sitting in the garden with Lydia, promising her the child would never leave Mariah, and now she is," Mrs. Tanner said as she sat down, "I know she is scared and confused."

"Now stop, you're gettin yourself all worked up and a fussin. Taint no better people than the Franklins and she be back home in no time, and Masser Roscoe, be back and everything be like it was!" Willy Mae said in her excited voice. "Youngins," she went on to say, "Dey make ya so happy den make ya so sad. Lor Miss Emily I don't know, I swears I don't. My Lilly Mae she be pregnant and won't tell who da father be. Lester whipped her behind with a switch and she still won't be tellin anyways."

"Oh Willy, I'm sorry to hear that," Mrs. Tanner said "I'll call her in and talk with her. I'll see to it that she gets married."

"Good morning," Misty said as she entered the room, "are the others here?" Before she could get an answer Isabelle called to her, and off she went. Wendall and her sister had arrived and were meeting the others on the front porch. When Misty stepped out Rebecca hugged her and said excitedly, "I'd like you all to meet

119

Misty." The one courting Rebecca stepped forward and offered his hand, "Hello," he said, "My name is Tom Stevens."

"I'm happy to meet you Tom," she replied.

"This is Jeffrey Purcell and Adam Wyatt," Tom said of the two young men with him as they nodded hello. "And this is Amy Moninghoff." As the response from the others was noticeably cool, Wendall stepped in to quickly add, "Delighted to see you again Misty. It's been too long since we've ridden together." Isabelle took the girls inside to gather up the things they would need for the day, and to do the things that girls always do before they do something else, what ever that is, the fellows mused. Waiting on the porch Adam said, "Every man on his twenty first birthday should be given a Negro girl that looks like that."

"Just for domestic chores, right fellows?" Jeffrey replied, poking his elbow into Adam's side.

"You'd hardly consider her a Negro I'd dare say;" Wendall said trying to come to Misty's defense.

"I can tell you're not a born and bred southerner;" replied Jeffrey. "One ounce of Negro blood is all it takes to make a person Negro, but there ain't no denying," he said laughing, "she's better lookin than any girl I've ever seen, be they as white as snow."

They were soon off riding. Rebecca's friends wanted to see the plantation. None of them had ever seen an estate this large. Half the day was spent riding through the cotton and corn fields, and along the forest. For lunch they stopped in a hayfield and gathered under a large willow tree. Roscoe and Misty had sat many times under this tree on the soft green grass and looked out over their land and enjoyed the tranquility that this place offered, but not so today. At various times throughout the morning crude remarks and jokes were made. Because they were spoken so that Isabelle and Rebecca wouldn't hear it was obvious that Misty was the subject of them. Addie and Amy it seems, are two peas from the same pod. After the lunch was spread out on the blanket, Amy said to Misty, "I suppose you don't serve either." Not used to being treated or talked to in that manner it caught her off guard, but before she could reply Wendall did, saying that serving was his job today. Misty however, kept her composure and interjected, "No Wendall please, let me have that pleasure. Now everyone just sit back and relax," Misty said in a voice that made Isabelle and Rebecca smile. The girls had never liked Addie, and Isabelle wasn't too fond of Amy at this point. Misty's tone of voice meant she was about to be coy.

"Today," Misty said, "you have a choice. You can be served southern style, which is really European in the more sophisticated regions of the south, or you could be *anomalous*. I am as you are well aware, equally qualified to serve African style, or better yet, why not be of the Epicurean mind? Let it not matter, and I'll mix the two together. Amy, I'm sure you are a *multifarious* person, I'll serve you first."

"No thank you," Amy replied, "I think I'll just help myself."

"Addie," Misty asked, "what is your pleasure?"

"You wouldn't want to know dear," she replied.

"I think the problem here," Wendall interjected, "is the girls really wouldn't know the difference in styles. Now tell me, who really are the ones raising the good white folks of the south? Is it not the Negro? Truth is, whatever style Misty fixed would have been one and the same, isn't that so Isabelle?"

"Yes it is Wendall," she replied and then added, "If it weren't for the Negroes much of the south would starve."

"That could be Isabelle," Adam said, "I have a sister who can't hard boil an egg and makes a mess out of buttered bread."

Tom leaned over and pushed his back lightly saying, "Are you confessing that if it weren't for your Auntie you wouldn't be the man you are today? What a noble statement."

"No offense to those present," Jeffrey said, "but my taste buds prefer we keep white women out of the kitchen."

"No offense taken here," said Addie, "I'm in full agreement with that. Seems like a natural thing that niggers be in the kitchen."

"I love to cook," said Isabelle.

"So do I," said Misty.

"I rest my case," said Addie making herself and Amy laugh.

After lunch most of them played cards. Wendall and Adam played mumblety-peg with a pocket knife. They were joined by Misty who accepted an offer to play and sat down with the two of them.

"What is this word game you two are always playing?" Adam asked.

Wendall and Misty looked at each other and laughed. "We're epistemologists," Wendall answered.

"Okay what is an epistemologist?" he asked.

"It's a form of philosophy that investigates the nature and methods, the validity of human knowledge."

"Ahah," Adam replied with a laugh. "That's just what I thought it was."

"Misty and I challenge each other with words. It's a kind of brain game," said Wendall.

"You can read?" Adam asked Misty uncertainly.

"Yes," she replied.

"This is a kind of different arrangement than I'm used to. They punish Negroes in my neck of the woods for trying to learn to read."

"Then they'd kill me, Adam," Misty said laughing, "cause I can write too."

"I've seen lots of mulattos, but none as light as you are;" Adam remarked.

"Nor as pretty Adam," Wendall said with conviction and a smile.

"That too Wendall," he said.

"I'm most likely quadroon, but no one knows for sure," Misty offered.

"Tell the truth Adam," Wendall said, "if you didn't know, you would think her just a swarthy girl?"

"Swarthy?" asked Adam.

"You know, a white girl with a dark complexion. I know many that are darker than Misty come mid July," said Wendall.

"Did you teach yourself to read and write?" Adam asked Misty.

"No, I'm taught along with Isabelle, and I read a lot; I like to read," she answered. Then looking at Wendall with a smile she said, "Everything but thermodynamics."

"Steam power Misty," said Wendall. "You remember you heard it from me first."

"I rode on a train once," said Adam, "that was quite an experience."

"Thermodynamics is going to move more than trains," said Wendall. "It's my intention to go north, study and learn all I can about it. It won't be long before I do."

The others were cleaning up their things and preparing to ride some more. Misty told Isabelle she would be heading back now. There were things she wanted to finish. Wendall offered to ride back with her. She told him it wasn't necessary but he was insistent. As they were about to leave Addie told him Amy was riding home with her, so he would have to ride home alone. Once away from the others he told Misty he really didn't want to be around them today, but if she had things to do he would just ride home once they got back to the house. She really didn't want to be with them either. She had done it for Rebecca and Isabelle, but she knew it would be the same as it always was with Addie, and she worried about the others. Not for herself, but for Isabelle and Rebecca. The ignorance of others she is learning to deal with. It still hurt to be rejected, but her concern was that the girls didn't have a bad day because of it. When she and Wendall got back to the barn, they put their horses in the barnyard and sat on the fence talking.

"I think you're gonna love it in New Orleans," he said. "I hear it is quite an unusual place. Quite diverse in cuisine and music."

"Two of your favorite things," she said.

"I'd like to visit there some day," he said, "and pass myself off as an intellectual."

Laughing with him she added, "You have the propensity for it, that's for certain."

"I could be gone before you get back, I've sent to a number of schools for information," he said.

"Have you heard from any?" she asked.

"A few, but not yet from the one I'm most interested in," he replied. That one is in Pittsburgh, Pennsylvania."

"We're going there before we get to New York. Poppa has something to do with iron there."

"That is one smart business man that Mr. Tanner. It would be funny if someday Ros and I did some business together. Only God knows the future, isn't that what you say my dear?"

Jumping down from the fence she invites him to go with her. As they walk they talk about things of a more personal nature. Wendall does most of the talking but Misty too feels a need to talk to someone she can trust, and who she knows won't tell her lies to avoid hurting her feelings. They walk to the building the slaves use for their meeting house. "Wendall," she says as they sit on a bench near the rear of the aisle, "if I tell you something will you promise to keep it to yourself? If I don't talk to someone about this I don't know what I'm gonna do. It all happened so fast, then he was gone."

"You know you can trust me," he said. "I'd do anything to help you out. I hope you know that."

"It's funny. When we first met I didn't think you were such a nice fellow, and now, you're the best friend I have outside of Mariah." And then with a change of expression she added, "Wendall, you know what I just realized? You're the first person I ever made a friendship with on my own. Does that ever make me feel good. Maybe I was feeling sorry for myself, but I did feel bad about the

123

new friends Rebecca has, and of course she would want Isabelle and me to join in, but I knew they weren't going to accept me. Certainly they're not going to have me to their house for tea." Placing her hand on his she said, "Thank you Wendall."

Laughing a little uncomfortably Wendall replied, "Those words make me feel like a hero and a louse at the same time."

"A louse?" she asked.'Why?"

"Misty I have a great deal of respect for Ros Tanner, so I'll behave like a man. I also have the highest regard for your virtue, so I'll behave like a gentleman. But young lady, if given just half the chance I'd unleash my heart and fall more in love with you than David did with Bathsheba." Then patting her hand he said, "Enough of that. You're the one with something on your mind. Tell me what is troubling you."

"Now that you went and said that I don't know if I can."

"Tell me Misty. If something is troubling you I would like to help." Wendall paused a moment and asked, "You're not thinking of running away to England are you?"

"Oh no," she replied. "Oh, you don't know how crazy this is. My first response to that question would be, I couldn't do anything that would hurt the people I love, and yet that is exactly what I did."

"I can't believe you could hurt anyone," he said reassuringly.

"Oh but what we did is going to hurt a lot of people," she answered back in a tone more serious than he had ever heard before. Standing up and pacing she continued, "The night before Ros left we brought the preacher here and had him marry us. It all happened so quickly, I haven't told anyone, and now it's eating me up inside. I'm finding it difficult to look Mother Tanner in the eyes, and how will Isabelle react when she finds out? What if she thinks I didn't tell her because I didn't trust her? And that's just the beginning of it. I mean how will it all work out anyway?"

"Oh boy!" was Wendall's first reaction.

"Oh boy is right," she responded, "we really did it, didn't we?"

"Well my first thought, is to lash out at Roscoe for putting you in this predicament, but that won't help you now, and I really can't say I wouldn't have done the same if given the chance. What is it that you want to do Misty? That is the important thing right now."

"I want to tell Mother, but I'm scared," she said, "scared she will be angry, she's going to be hurt." Then she started to cry.

"What if this makes her sorry she ever brought my mother Lydia home, sorry I was ever born?"

"No Misty," Wendall said putting his arm around her, "I know Mrs. Tanner is not capable of such a thing, and you really know that too."

"What would you do Wendall?" she asked.

"It's not a legal marriage. They're not going to consider you two bound by it. It may not be nearly what you're thinking it will be. Talk to her Misty, I think that is what you want to do anyway."

The others had gotten back a short while ago. They saw Wendall's horse in the barnyard and wondered where Adam's horse was. Adam had left the others about mid afternoon to find Wendall and Misty. They thought they would see him here when they got back. After looking about, around the barn, they went to the house, but no one there had seen them either. Rebecca and the others set out for home. The sun was setting and it would be dark before long. They assumed Adam had departed ahead of them. Wendall and Misty talked awhile more before Wendall said he should be heading home. He told her he would come over the next day to see how she was, and how things worked out. They walked to the barn together, Wendall saddled his horse and said good-bye. He rode out the back toward the orchard. With half a moon lighting his way he would get home much quicker on the back trail.

Misty walked to the house and sat down on the veranda, wanting to go over in her mind what she would say before going in. Time though was not in her favor this evening, and Mrs. Tanner came through the door. "Hello my dear;" she said as she sat next to her. "Isabelle was looking for you. She might be in her room now."

"I'll go up in a moment, but first I need to talk to you," Misty said turning toward her.

"Isabelle told me you didn't stay the day with them. She told me Addie was being rude as always, and it sounds like the other girl wasn't much better," Mrs. Tanner said taking her hand. "I'm sorry Misty."

"It isn't that mother, I hope my leaving didn't make Iz feel bad," Misty responded.

"No of course not, she doesn't care at all for that kind of behavior, but Rebecca is very excited about this boy, so she made the best of it."

"I would have stayed, I was prepared for Addie's indiscretions, but I've been troubled by something, something I did," she said turning her eyes away toward the floor.

"Well my dear," Mrs. Tanner said brushing her hand softly over the back of Misty's head, "sometimes we think we did some terrible thing, and it turns out to be not nearly as bad as we think. And sweetheart, you've always been such a good girl, I couldn't ask any more of you." Misty broke down and started to cry. Those words meant to be soothing, were painful.

"Oh what have I done?" she said. "If only you had left me with Mammy. I don't deserve anything, least of all your love."

"Child," Mrs. Tanner said pulling Misty's head to her chest. "Don't ever speak that way. There's nothing you could do that would make me stop loving you. Tell me what this thing is that is troubling you so." Misty was silent for a moment, Mrs. Tanner could feel her trembling, felt her squeezing her arm tighter.

"We eloped," she said very softly, "I'm sorry, I'm so sorry."

"Misty, I don't understand. Try to calm yourself and explain this to me." Mrs. Tanner said holding her reassuringly.

"We married the night before Ros left. The preacher married us in the meeting house. We weren't up early that morning like everyone thought, we were out all night. I love him so much, I know I shouldn't have done it, but I couldn't stop. I didn't want to stop, it seemed like Ros' leaving was always so far off, then just like that, it was the eve of his departure and I could hardly bear it. It was the most wonderful experience I've ever had. I wanted that night to last forever, but it didn't and so quickly he was gone. I could barely look at you since then. I've felt so terrible; not only have I deceived you and disappointed you, I know there are going to be problems with others because of this, I wish . . ."

Mrs. Tanner stopped her there saying, "Oh Misty, what have you two done? You must know the kind of problems that this can lead to."

"Even breaking the law didn't seem to matter," Misty replied softly.

"That is the least of the problems, child," Mrs. Tanner said, "no one would recognize this as a legal marriage, but in God's eyes where it matters most to me, it certainly is. He loves you, Misty, I couldn't blame him for that, but he didn't do what was best for you, and what about his father? That is Hugh's only son and his dream is to have his son one day take over Mariah as he did from his father. But he loves you far more than he does even this place and he will leave it and that will break his father's heart."

"I don't want to do that," Misty responded sincerely.

"I know you don't my dear. If only you two had . . . oh it makes no difference now. I need more time to think about this."

'I'll go Mother," Misty said softly, rising to her feet.

"Does anyone else know about it?" Mrs. Tanner asked.

"Only Wendall, I told him today," she responded as she started down the stairs.

"Isabelle?" Mrs. Tanner asked. Without turning around she shook her head no.

"Misty," Mrs. Tanner called. She stopped and looked around. "Did you" she paused a moment, "consummate this marriage?"

Misty too paused a moment, then slowly shook her head from side to side and walked off into the dark.

Mrs. Tanner sat back in the chair and closed her eyes. She wished she could have hid her discountenance with Misty, but that she could deal with later. Right now she had to decide what to do about her husband. She had never kept anything of a serious nature from him before, but with Edward leaving in the morning, and their own departure three weeks away was it necessary to bring it up now? And what was going to happen to these two young ones? New Orleans, England, a year apart. Nothing would change the way they felt for each other. The tears started to form in her eyes. She could only see heartache for people that she loved.

Misty walked aimlessly. She knew Mrs. Tanner was dismayed with her and she now feared Mr. Tanner finding out. Then she thought of what Ros would think of her not keeping their secret. She stopped and sat down. It was foolish she said to herself, no one would ever think it more than a misalliance, and now it's going to cause problems in the family. She wished she hadn't said anything until Ros had come home. She covered her face with her hands and cried.

After a while she walked to the meeting house. Sitting down at the piano in the dark she played slowly. Not playing a particular song, just making an attempt to ease her mind. The door opened quietly and someone slipped in. With her back toward the door she neither heard nor saw anyone. He moved lightly along the wall and silently came up behind her. Dangling from his back pocket was a long cloth which he removed and wrapped around both his hands, lifting it up and over her head in one swift motion. It came down in front of her face and he pulled it tight across her mouth pulling her with great force off the bench to the floor. In an instant his knee was pressing down onto her chest and the cloth around her head was tightening. With all the strength she could muster, she let her arm fly striking his side and knocking him off balance. She scrambled to her feet only to fall over a row of benches behind them. He threw the benches out of his way, reached in and grabbed her by the hair, swinging her body around. With his other hand he struck her several times on the head and back, then threw her down flat to the floor and fell on top of her. With one hand he pushed her head hard on the wooden floor, his other hand began ripping at her dress. With her arm flailing, she struck repeatedly on his head and shoulder then grabbed his hair and pulled hard enough to rip some from his head.

In the dark she could see only a shadowy figure, and hear only his heavy breathing, and the sounds of her clothes tearing. He pushed her arm back over her head and her hand hit a stool. Wrapping her fingers around it she lifted it with all the force she could and brought it forward. A corner of it struck his throat and knocked him backwards. Desperately, she groped through the rows of benches falling and stumbling as she raced for the door. Not realizing her dress was badly torn and dragging she stepped on it and tripped falling onto the floor. Her assailant was at her again, lifting her by her arm and tossing her back into the benches. She landed on her side and rolled onto her back. With a forceful shove she kicked a bench in front of him, toppling him over, causing him nearly to fall on her. She managed to get to her feet and make her way again to the door. This time she pulled it open and ran out of the building. Tugging at the cloth around her head she pulled it free. Gasping for air she stopped at a large maple tree about thirty feet from the building and turned to see if her attacker was pursuing. In an instant his body slammed against hers and he pulled her to the ground. The back of her head hit hard and bounced, his body came down heavily, crushing her. In a desperate attempt to free herself as he ripped her dress the rest of the way off her shoulders, she bit into his arm, pressing her teeth so hard they almost touched. He let out a loud noise and pushed her face back until she let go. Rolling over in pain onto his back he grabbed his wounded arm, then rolled again and sprang onto his feet. She too rolled over and got to her knees about to stand and run when a bright light flashed inside her head. She heard a loud cracking sound and she fell to the ground. He stood over her for a second, looking down at her lying motionless. He dropped the object in his hand, a short thick piece of tree branch, and seeing blood coming from a gash on the side of her head he turned and ran.

Mrs. Tanner had retired for the night. Her husband lay sleeping alongside of her, but she could find no rest. It wasn't so much what they had done, but what they would do when Roscoe returned. She decided she wouldn't tell anyone about her conversation with Misty until they returned home. She would write to Ros about it, though she wasn't sure yet what to say.

The nights get cold this time of year, and things quiet down early. What light the moon offered was gone now as clouds rolled in. Lightning was off in the distance and a storm was coming. With everyone safe within their shelters there was no hope of anyone finding Misty tonight. The rain lasted through much of the night. By daybreak it had slowed to a drizzle. A light fog and the damp cool ground kept the day's activities from starting at their usual pace.

At nearly six thirty, a few women on the way to the hen house for eggs spotted Misty's body. Bare to the waist, her torn dress barely covering her legs, her hair soaked and bloody, they thought her dead. One went off for help as the other two made a closer examination. She was hardly breathing as the women covered her with their shawls and called out repeatedly for help. Within minutes people were coming from everywhere. Men carried her into a nearby hut and the women began cleaning her and removing what was left of her wet clothes. Word was sent to the main house.

Soon Mr. Tanner, his wife, and Isabelle entered the hut. He quickly ordered everyone out but the old woman who was holding a warm rag to her wound, and Goldie who was too hysterical to respond. Isabelle went immediately to Misty's side taking hold of her hand. Mrs. Tanner was taken back by what she saw and stood frozen. Mr. Tanner went outside and told one person to fetch Henry and tell him to make a fire in the boy's room. Another was sent for a horse and a wagon. Willy Mae who had just arrived was sent back to get the bed ready. Find James, send him here, Mr. Tanner told the rest of the group. Within a short time the wagon arrived and Misty was placed in it and taken to the house. James was sent to fetch Dr. Myers. Nothing more could be done now but to keep her warm and wait for the doctor.

Mrs. Tanner sat next to her fighting back tears. All she could see in her mind was the sad look on Misty's face as she had walked off the night before. It was not uncommon for her to stay the night at Willy Mae's or Goldie's, but not last night, Mrs. Tanner thought. She should have insisted she stay home. Isabelle sat on the bed holding Misty's hand and rubbing it, talking to her all the while, wanting her to open her eyes. Mr. Tanner left the house and went back to the hut to find out all he could about what had happened. The women had nothing to offer, but a field hand took him into the meeting house. One look in there told him what he had suspected, someone had tried to rape her. He next went looking for his field manager Tom Louder.

Isabelle told her mother how they couldn't find Misty or Wendall when they returned yesterday. Adam had gone off on his own wanting to find them rather than stay with the group, but they didn't see him either, not even his horse. "I spoke with her last night on the veranda," Mrs. Tanner said in a solemn voice. "Wendall had gone just after dark, but there was no mention of Adam, Isabelle. We'll see if Dr. Myers knows when he returned."

"Oh Mother he has to come soon;" Isabelle said looking back at Misty.

By the time James was able to find the doctor, it was mid afternoon. It was nearly four o'clock before he arrived at the house. He first checked her eyes. The look of concern on his face was evident to Mrs. Tanner and her daughter. He checked her heart and lungs then removed the bandage from her head. She had sustained a serious cut across her temple. He removed a small piece of bark from within it, and closed the wound as best he could. He knew she had gone too long without proper care. When he finished dressing the wound he said to Mrs. Tanner, "All we can do now is keep her comfortable. Someone will have to be with her all the time."

"She's going to be all right isn't she?" Isabelle asked. "There are several lumps on the back of her head. She was hit more than once. There is just no telling how she is going to be until she comes around. James says she was on the ground all night. She could be suffering from exposure. It's just too soon to tell."

The doctor took Mrs. Tanner by the arm and led her out of the room, Isabelle followed. Elsa had been waiting outside the room most of the day. She was sent in to sit by Misty and watch her. Downstairs Mr. Tanner sat in the family room waiting for Doc Myers. "Brandy, Robert?" Mr. Tanner asked.

"Please, Hugh," he responded, "Does anyone know anything about what happened?"

"Everyone will say it was one of the Negroes, but it wasn't, our Negroes would never do such a thing. It was that heathen animal, Tom Louder, that's who it was," Isabelle said with disgust.

"No Isabelle," her father answered.

"You know who did it Hugh?" Mrs. Tanner asked.

"I know it wasn't Louder, that's the first place I went. He wasn't alone last night and his alibi is reliable."

"I hate to think Hugh, but Wendall Cambridge was the last person with her other than myself," Mrs. Tanner said.

"I've sent Henry to ask Cambridge and the boy to come over here. It seems Misty and the boy went into the building together. Now the timing is in question, but it sounds like this was several hours before Emily spoke to her on the veranda. I'm not suggesting anything, but we need details." Handing the doctor a snifter of brandy he asks, "Was the child raped?" Isabelle nearly choked on the question and Mrs. Tanner sat straight up fixing her eyes intently on Dr. Myers.

"No Hugh, I'd say not. There are scratches on her back and legs, but her buttocks aren't marked in any way. Two of her fingers are broken. I'd say she put up quite a fight."

"What do you know about Adam, Dr. Myers?" Isabelle asked. "He left us at midafternoon yesterday to come back here, he wanted to catch up with Wendall. We never saw him again."

"Not much. He's only lived in the area a short time. His father died a year back, and he and his mother are living with her sister and her husband. Seems like an easy going young man, very polite and well spoken," the doctor responded.

"We'll have to talk with him too," Mr. Tanner said.

"You don't think it was one of the Negroes do you Hubert?" Dr. Myers asked.

"No, I don't Robert. Whoever did this left her for dead. I've not seen that kind of violence among the Negroes, and they consider her one of them."

"Rebecca told me of another young girl recently beaten pretty badly. Whatever came of that?" the doctor asked.

"I didn't get too involved in it Robert, I asked a few questions but got no solid answers. The girl wouldn't say a word, then she ran off shortly afterwards. I sent searchers out but to no avail."

"Was it similar to what we have here?"

"Someone smacked her around good, but not with the kind of force inflicted on Misty. Was it the same person? I have to think yes."

"That would reasonably eliminate the Wyatt boy," suggested Dr. Myers, "but not necessarily the Cambridge boy."

"I can't believe he would do anything like that. I know he didn't. He has kind of a crush on Misty, and while I don't think he is that much fun to be with, Misty has befriended him," Isabelle said.

"Do you find something peculiar about him Isabelle?" Dr. Myers asked.

"Not peculiar, but maybe too smart or too intellectual. The little things, the funny things seem to go over his head," she answered.

"No Hugh," Mrs. Tanner said, "I don't think for a moment it was Wendall, Misty took him into her confidence yesterday. She didn't like him much when they first met, but they became friends. I'm inclined to think it was one of the slave hands."

"There's so many down there now." The doctor set his glass down and went back to check on Misty's condition.

With the conversation growing quiet, the sound of small running footsteps could be heard coming from the front entrance. The grandchildren came racing into the room followed by Susan demanding they settle down now that they were in the house. "Susan," Mrs. Tanner exclaimed, "I forgot all about Edward departing today."

"With all the commotion going on around here this morning, he said it would be better if we just left quietly. Come on you kids, you gotta get a bath tonight. Is she okay?" Susan asked as she was walking out of the room.

"Dr. Myers is with her now, we don't know how bad it is yet," her mother replied. Slumping back into her chair Mrs. Tanner looked toward the ceiling and said, "If anything happens to that child I'll never be able to forgive myself. When I should have been putting my arms around her I sent her away. She has to be all right, she has to be."

As the next few days passed, it wasn't certain if Misty would be all right. She was never left alone for a minute. Someone sat at her side day and night, with a host of others constantly coming in and out of the room. On Thursday morning after Dr. Myers examined her, he spoke with Mrs. Tanner about his concern. The longer she remained unconscious, the greater the chance of permanent damage to her brain. He wanted to have her sent to a clinic in South Carolina where they worked with cases like this. Mrs. Tanner was ready to do anything the doctor recommended. She would speak with her husband about it, and they would get together in the evening.

When Dr. Myers returned after dinner that night, his wife and daughter were with him. Rebecca went up to see Isabelle and check in on Misty as soon as she arrived. Her parents sat down with the Tanners. Elsa served tea while Misty's condition was discussed. Mr. Tanner said they would set out for Carolina first thing in the morning. Dr. Myers would send a message ahead of them so someone would be ready to receive her. In time the conversation went to the cause of this whole ordeal, but there was nothing new to add. Adam Wyatt's story of losing his way through the woods and eventually finding the main road and just going home was conceivable. Mr. Tanner felt strongly he was telling the truth. Wendall Cambridge's story left some in doubt. No one saw him leave the area, on arriving home he went to work in the wood shop until eleven. No one could verify anything for him, and while Mrs. Tanner hadn't told anyone about what Misty disclosed to her that evening, she certainly hadn't forgotten. Did Misty telling Wendall trigger a different reaction than what she had perceived? The thought kept reoccurring in Mrs. Tanner's mind.

Rebecca had gone to Isabelle's room first. She found her sewing and sat down to talk with her while she waited for her to finish. Neither girl suspected Wendall of doing this horrible thing to Misty. Rebecca thought it was most likely one of the Negroes, and Isabelle still wasn't convinced Tom Louder's alibi was a hundred percent reliable. They also considered that it might have been someone else, but spoke about it only amongst themselves.

Together they went to look in on Misty. On leaving Isabelle's room they encountered the young Negro twin, Daniel, tip-toeing down the hall. He and his brother, Obed, and several other children had sneaked up and been chased back down a number of times the past few days. Isabelle took him by the hand telling him he could come in but only for a moment. Misty has always paid so much attention to the young ones, the look of concern on their faces is not to be ignored.

On entering the room they were given quite a surprise. While Lilly Mae had fallen asleep in the chair, Misty had awakened. Lying very still on the bed, she was looking up at the ceiling. Isabelle sent Daniel running to fetch the others and Rebecca hurried to Misty's side. Lilly Mae woke up startled and a great commotion took place in the room. "Oh Misty," she said sitting down on the bed next to her, "you're awake at last. You had us all so worried, how do you feel?"

"I don't know," she responded, "I feel like I've been here a long time. Have I?"

Dr. Myers came hurrying into the room smiling from ear to ear. "That's my girl," he said as he sat down and took her hand. "Do you hurt anywhere sweetheart?"

"Everywhere I think," she responded softly. "Am I cut here?" she asked reaching up slowly and touching the bandage on her head.

"It's healing fine," he answered. Then lifting up her other hand she asked, "My hand?"

"A couple of broken fingers that will be like new in no time," he answered. Mrs. Tanner who was standing behind the doctor asked if she wanted anything?"

"Sarah," she answered.

"We'll send for her in the morning," Mrs. Tanner said with a look of great relief. Dr. Myers asked everyone but Mrs. Tanner to leave the room now so he could check Misty over. He also wanted her to be able to rest.

The joy within the house quickly spread outside as the good news traveled from person to person. The many children who had congregated outside of the house were gone, each one wanting to be first with the message.

As Dr. Myers examined her he asked, "Do you know what happened to you?"

"I was sitting at the piano and someone came after me."

"Do you know who it was Misty?" asked Mrs. Tanner.

"No" she said softly.

"Is there anything at all you can tell us?" asked Dr. Myers. "Take your time and think about it a while. Maybe something will come to you. We would like to get this guy."

"My head hurts too much to think right now," she said. "It will feel better in the morning. Then Emily can get you up to walk a little," the doctor said as they got ready to leave the room.

"Mother," she asked, "can I talk to you for a moment?"

"You go ahead Emily," the doctor said. "I'll see you downstairs."

Mrs. Tanner sat down on the bed and brushed Misty's hair back from her forehead. "What is it dear?" she asked.

"Did you tell anyone about what we talked about?"

"No I didn't. I thought it best to keep it between you and me for now. I wouldn't have said anything without talking to you again. It will be awhile before Ros is home, let's let it be a spell, okay?"

"Thank you Mother, I'm so sorry that I hurt you."

"When did you hurt me Misty? When you fell in love with him? When you came to me to tell me because you were more concerned about my feelings than your own? You've never hurt me my dear. You better get some rest. I'll be back after the Myers leave."

As she stood up to leave Misty asked her one more question. "Mother, was I raped?"

Looking down at her she said, "No." Then with a smile she added, "All those years of wrestling you girls did with Hubert must have taught you something."

Misty relaxed her head on her pillow and gave a sigh of relief. Elsa was sent in to watch her. They talked awhile, then Misty fell asleep and slept the remainder of the night undisturbed.

In the morning they got her up from the bed and into a tub of hot water and bubbles. Little Sarah was brought in and quickly splashed into the tub with her. Other than feeling tired and sore she looked like herself again. She dressed and slowly made her way down the stairs, only to be greeted by a stern order from Mrs. Tanner to get back on her bed. However, she sad-eyed her way out of that and was made comfortable on the davenport, where she was fed and soon joined by Rebecca and Isabelle. After an hour or so of playing cards she fell off to sleep. The girls took Sarah with them, and went outside.

After several more days of eating and sleeping well, Misty regained much of her strength, though she was still troubled by occasional dizzy spells and tired quickly. With just a week before their departure for New York a decision had to be made.

The following Sunday the Myers' came over for dinner. The doctor hadn't checked on Misty for several days and he was concerned with the frequent dizzy spells she was still having. He was of the opinion that she shouldn't travel, that she should be watched until this lightheadedness subsides. Mrs. Tanner knew how disappointed she would be but doesn't want to risk her health. After dinner Dr. Myers took Misty and Mrs. Tanner into the study. He checked her fingers which seemed to be healing well. The cut on her head too is pretty well healed. Concerning the wound he said,

"It looks like it is going to be just a small scar. I was worried it was going to be much more."

"Isabelle says it gives a sign of character," Misty said laughing.

"Tell Robert what you remembered," Mrs. Tanner said to Misty.

"This morning I remembered grabbing a hand full of hair and pulling it hard. It was full and soft and easy to grab on to."

"That would eliminate any thought that it was one of the slaves."

"Misty," Dr. Myers said sitting down next to her and putting his arm around her shoulders. "It may take some time yet for these dizzy spells to clear up. I don't think they're serious, they will go away, but I'm concerned about your traveling. It might have a bad effect."

"I know I don't have the strength for it now but I have a week or so to improve. If I'm not better by then I know I should stay home, but I'm going to try real hard to get better, because I want to see New York badly," she replied.

"Well, if it has to be my dear," the doctor said reassuringly, "you'll come and stay with us. Until we find out who is responsible for doing this, you can't be left alone."

But the days went by without improvement. With the dizziness now come headaches and sleepless nights. She knows she is in no condition to go on a long journey, and does her best to hide her disappointment, especially from Isabelle who seems to feel worse about it than Misty does.

It is the eve of their departure and the family gathers in the family room after dinner. Misty has been feeling better the past two days. She and Isabelle are sitting at the piano singing and laughing, enjoying their last meal together. "I think we should all congratulate Misty," Isabelle says. "She has done a remarkable job of looking happy for us."

"Not true," Misty responds with a smile. "I *am* truly happy for all of you. I've just fixed my mind on meeting up with everyone in Orleans, if Henry doesn't get lost that is."

"It's not his getting lost that worries me," said Mr. Tanner, "but he drives so awful slow anymore, it may be spring before he gets there."

"I can't wait that long," Misty said. "Isabelle promised to bring back material and sheet music."

"I'm sure Gloria will be bringing back the same," said Mrs. Tanner. "We'll have enough for two years to come."

"What will you bring back Poppa," asked Isabelle.

"Cigars, my dear," he replied. "Cigars from Cuba."

"Hubert," said Mrs. Tanner, "you don't smoke cigars."

"I'm not going to smoke them. I'm just going to set that box on my desk with the lid up. Then when I'm conducting business with someone I'll take one out and roll it around in my fingers as I talk. Being a little intimidating can be good business," he said.

"Intimidating?" said Mrs. Tanner. "You and Henry will be sitting on the pond's edge wondering why the fish aren't biting, as you two go puffing like a couple of those steam trains you're always reading about."

After a while the elder Tanners retire. Isabelle and Misty sit and talk awhile. This will be the first time in many years they've been apart. They are trying to make the evening last as long as they can. Misty has one consolation. She convinced the Tanners to let her stay home till the weekend before going to the Myers'. She has stayed in Roscoe's room since her attack. Henry has moved out of his room and into one upstairs while they are gone. Martha, an elderly Negro woman who has been looking after Grandmother Naomi and serving as nanny to Susan's children, will move into Henry's room. Grandmother Tanner will move downstairs into the room next to Martha.

Morning arrives and Misty once again finds herself waving good-bye to those she loves. With each change that occurs she knows things will never return to what they were. Knowing she has to keep busy today she heads for the barnyard to bridle her horse and rides down back to visit the children. After playing some games and reading to them awhile she feels tired. Putting the little girl Sarah on her horse she climbs up behind her and heads back to the barn. Sarah was going to be her house guest for the week.

For the next couple of days, Misty didn't feel as well as she had been. On Thursday, Dr. Myers checked in on her, but couldn't persuade her to come home with him. He made arrangements for Rebecca to come out on Friday and bring her back on Saturday. He visited with Grandmother Tanner and was quickly on his way.

That evening when Misty awoke from a nap she went downstairs looking for Sarah. She followed the sound of her voice and laughter into the family room. What she saw on entering the room surprised her. Squeezed into the chair with Grandmother Naomi sat Sarah, holding the yarn and talking away as Grandmother Tanner crocheted. "There you are little girl, I've been looking for you," Misty said, then turned her attention to Grandmother Tanner. "Is she being a bother to you?"

"No, she has been quite helpful. A pleasant child this one is," she responded, "I've noticed you have her quite often, is she an orphan?"

"Yes," Misty answered.

"I presume she is a mulatto." Grandmother Tanner said.

"Yes she is," said Misty. "Can I get you anything from the kitchen?"

"No thank you dear. Perhaps the child would like orange juice," was Grandmother Tanner's reply. Once outside of the room Misty began shaking her head in disbelief, "Is this the same woman that I had to tip toe around all my life? It must be this big house being so empty that's getting to her. Anything that'll make her nicer has to be okay with me."

That evening was the first time that Misty had ever spent alone with Grandmother Tanner. Sarah fell asleep and the two of them talked for better than two hours. In the end Misty helped her back to her room and into her night clothes. They both finished that day with a different view of each other.

Rebecca arrived Friday around noon. They left her horse in the barnyard and took Isabelle's and Roscoe's out for a ride. In the evening they spent some time writing poems and baked a pie. They were both excited about Misty's stay at Rebecca's and were up early the next morning packing. Before leaving they were going to have breakfast and bring Sarah to Goldie's, but Grandmother Tanner and Martha who were at the table when they arrived had a different idea. Grandmother Tanner told the girls to leave the child. She could stay in Martha's room and help out with some of her chores. This news delighted Misty, and reaffirmed her notion that Grandmother Tanner did not like that big house childless. Misty kissed Sarah good-bye and the girls left the room. Just outside the doorway they heard Sarah refer to Grandmother Tanner as Grandmammy. They instantly stopped and waited, only to hear Grandmother Tanner reply to the question. The girls quietly walked off in disbelief, neither girl had ever addressed her in anyway other than Mrs. Tanner.

End of Part II

138

PART III

A View From the Outside

Staying at the Myers' was always a joy for Misty. This was the only place she knew aside from the plantation. The Myers lived on the edge of a small town, and the whole way of life was different. Several shops were on a main avenue in the town, including a trading post that supplied most of the people's needs for staples, animal feed, and a host of other things, a shop for fabrics and accessories, a blacksmith, a sawmill and, at the far end, a church and schoolhouse.

Most houses were like that of the Myers', somewhat large, constructed of wood with shutters and a porch across the front and around the side. The Myers' house had four large bedrooms upstairs, a living room, dining room, study, a big kitchen with a storage room attached, and a room used as an office for visiting patients. A spacious barn housed a cow, two goats, numerous chickens, three horses, and a tool room. A small front yard with mature maple trees separated the house from the road. Everyone knew the doctor and his family. Whenever anyone sat on the front porch, those passing by would stop and chat a moment from their carioles. For the most part it was a peaceful town filled with a pleasant people.

That evening Mrs. Myers, with help from the girls, prepared a roasted chicken dinner with corn and squash, biscuits and gravy, and apple pie and cream. It was all too much for the good doctor who fell off to sleep in his easy chair near the fireplace. They got out a photo album to show Misty photos taken recently by the town photographer. There were various newspaper clippings about Dr. Myers delivering babies or making statements concerning the laws and policies governing the town. There was also a collection of poems that Rebecca, Isabelle and Misty had written together over the years.

It was nearly nine o'clock. The doctor had already gone to bed and the girls were putting things away, preparing to retire for the day. "Victoria," Misty asked, "may I go to the meeting tomorrow?" Catching Mrs. Myers off guard she quickly added, "I know I have to sit in the rear. I don't mind. I haven't been since I was quite small. Henry will be there, I can sit with him."

"Of course you can my dear," said Mrs. Myers.

"I think she should sit right alongside of us," Rebecca said. "I don't see anything wrong with it at all."

"No Rebecca," Misty said, "I would be a distraction for anyone there who knows who I am, and it could cause some to be upset with your parents."

"But most people don't know who you are; that's gonna be a bigger distraction," Rebecca said. "They'll be whispering from ear to ear, 'Why is that white girl sitting in the Negro section?' "

"Someone may come and get you, Misty, and try to bring you up front where you belong."

"Oh my. I can see this is going to be interesting," Misty said as they went to bed.

Sunday morning was bright and clear. The air was still and cool as it often was this time of year. Rebecca and Misty had gotten up early. They wanted to look nice for the meeting and so they fixed each other's hair up and prepared their clothes carefully. Rebecca, of course had added reasons to look her best: Tom Stevens and his family also attended.

When they arrived the doctor let the girls out at the walkway and drove the cariole to the parking area. Small groups of people were standing about in front of the church. Many came over to say hello to Mrs. Myers and her daughter and to find out who the young girl with them was. As several of the young ones gathered around Rebecca and Misty, the older ones drifted off. Misty's beauty could not go unnoticed. If she were just working in the garden or performing household chores, she would stand out to a stranger's eyes, but fitted in a Sunday meeting dress with her hair up under a bonnet and morning sun lighting up her swarthy complexion, she was incredibly beautiful. Her large almond shaped eyes and bright smile seemed to draw people to her, many of whom were young men.

The Moninghoffs arrived and Amy quickly passed by motioning with her head for Rebecca to join her. Misty caught sight of Adam Wyatt parking his cariole and hoped he would say hello. Of the ones who had come riding at Mariah that day, she thought he was the nicest, but the bell sounded and it was time to go in. Dr. Myers and his wife went over to Misty to bring her in. Once inside they looked uncomfortable. They did not want to have Misty sit in the Negro section, but she seemed unconcerned and told them to take their seats. Then she walked off to the reserved section in the rear.

The Negro section was located closest to the doors. This was not only the coldest part of the room, it was also the farthest from the floor ducts that brought the heat up from the wood burner below. The benches were plain, flat-topped and backless. There were no accommodations for Negroes to hang their coats or hats, they held them on their laps. Conversation with white people was frowned on inside the building. Because Negroes had their own church services and meeting places, only those that had to be there—were, nannies and chauffeurs—mostly attended.

Misty saw Henry's face and started toward him. She then spotted sitting between Henry and Martha, Sarah, all polished and clean in a dress the girls had made for her out of remnants of left-over material. In her own excitement she failed to notice the excitement she was causing. Almost every eye in the building was following her, particularly those of several young men, who now looked confused. She made her way to her seat and picked up Sarah and placed her on her lap. Then she looked to see where Rebecca was to show her that the child was there. On doing so she was confronted with a room full of staring people. But who could blame them? Only a few knew who she was. The rest were in somewhat of a shock. "Why is this white girl sitting with the Negroes?" some were whispering. "She must be a Quaker." Others said, "She's an abolitionist." Still others knew she had to be from the north. Then many started looking to the Myers who only looked straight ahead, Rebecca doing so with a smile she couldn't get rid of. Although this was a bit more than Misty had expected, it didn't bother her as much as what was taking place in the section she was sitting in. For while the white folks wouldn't stop looking at her, the Negroes acted like she wasn't there. They perceived her to be white, and knew it was best for them not to speak to her, at least not while inside the meeting house.

Reverend Brown called for everyone to stand and open their hymn books to sing. Those in the Negro section stood. None except Misty had a hymn book, but since they couldn't read they didn't need one. However, they had the words memorized and sang out with a joyful cry. The good Reverend Brown was known to give a stirring sermon. Depending on his mood, it could be a real fire and brimstone follow-the-Lord-or-else sermon, or a lively political discourse. This morning it was politics. Misty listened intently as he heaped charges against the North for their meddling and self-righteousness, repeating over again the need for all southerners to be united in their stand on slavery and sovereignty.

After a while Misty began to look around and think about the people sitting there. She contrasted this beautiful brick building with fancy pews and windows and fine woodworking, with that of the meeting house that had once been part of a barn at Mariah. She thought, the people here have everything, yet they seem nothing but worried about how to keep it and get more of the same. The Negroes have nothing and they can't thank and praise God enough. And how much they love hearing the Bible read. She started to think about all of the things Henry had told her about God and started to wonder.

After a little more than an hour the meeting was over. Once outside the people were different than they had been before they went in. The majority of them now kept their distance. Dr. Myers went for his cariole much quicker this morning, and Mrs. Myers looked like she couldn't get out of there soon enough. Misty knew they were concerned about her feelings, but felt there was no reason for them to rush off. She asked Mrs. Myers if it was all right to visit with Henry and Sarah for a few moments, and went over to talk with them.

Rebecca was standing with a group of young folks who were questioning her at length about Misty. The young men who had talked with her before the meeting were afraid to do so now, but they couldn't keep their eyes off of her, much to Amy Moninghoff's displeasure. One of the young men in the group was Adam Wyatt. He suggested that instead of talking about her so much they call her over and question her themselves. "I think things have been stirred up enough for a Sunday mornin," said Amy. "She knows where she belongs and she's there."

"Well, Amy my dear," Adam said "I refuse to let your lack of hospitality rub off on me. If I have to go over there to extend a greeting and make an inquiry of her, I will." Then turning to the others he said, "And if there are any a Christian gentleman amongst this here group, they should do the same." At that Rebecca, Amy and Tom Stevens found themselves standing alone.

Adam being of a free spirited nature, was making a show of it all and thoroughly enjoying himself. He introduced himself to Henry shaking his hand and the hand of several other Negro men. He picked Sarah up and sat her on the seat of the cariole placing her at eye level. He then inquired as to how she enjoyed Reverend Brown's sermon? Sarah, of course, will talk to anyone about anything at anytime, so she quickly responded with something of an entirely different nature than what he asked, this to everyone's amusement. He then turned his attention to Misty and in a serious tone of voice asked how her recovery was progressing. "Did you know," he asked, "that they questioned me as to my whereabouts on the evening of your misfortune?"

"Yes," she answered, "I was told of it. I'm sorry."

"No need to be," he responded. "I'd rather y'all know I didn't do it than think that I might have."

"I never thought you did," Misty said to him.

"Are you coming to the bonfire tonight?" he asked.

"No, I don't think so," she said.

"I'm sure Rebecca is. Why don't you come? We'll roast some peanuts and tell a few jokes. It'll be fun." Not waiting for her answer he excused himself to join his family as they were leaving. The others departed quickly.

Back in the house they were joined by Reverend Brown and his wife Eleanor for lunch. With Misty present and the Reverend still being wound up by his sermon, he said to her, "You're a very fortunate person to be owned by the Tanner's. They're some of the nicest people in the whole country. I know it's a fact they treat their domestics good." Mrs. Brown added, "It's a wonderful gift they've given you."

"She's become quite a young lady," Dr. Myers said smiling to Misty. "She'll be leaving for New Orleans soon. Going to live with some friends of Hubert and Emily."

"I'm certain your services will be as much appreciated there as they are here," the Reverend Brown said. Misty looked at Dr.

Myers and smiled. He responded, "No, she is not going as a servant. She's going as a friend of the family, a white friend of the family."

"Oh," Reverend Brown said shaking his head as he said it. "Oh, yes I see." Then he changed the conversation.

After lunch the girls went for a walk. Misty asked Rebecca about the bonfire. She said she wasn't planning on going, she thought they would just do something together. "Rebecca," Misty said stopping and turning toward her. "I want you to go tonight. I know you want to see Tom, and I'm sure he wants to see you. You can't be with me the whole time I'm staying at your house. I've brought things to do."

"I know you have; you study so much I fear your brains are gonna explode one day," Rebecca answered.

"I love to read, Rebecca," said Misty laughing. "Besides I have other things to do. I'm crocheting a shawl and I'm keeping a diary for Ros so when I write him I'll be able to keep him abreast of everything that's taken place."

"Will you write him about your accident?" Rebecca asked.

"No not that. He'll learn about that when he gets home. But anyway, about tonight. I was invited to come."

"You were?" Rebecca said looking puzzled. "How did you know about it anyway?"

Adam Wyatt told me. He invited me to come."
"What did you tell him?"

"I didn't have the chance to tell him anything, he ran off."

"Misty if you want to go I don't think it will be a problem with the others."

"I would like to Rebecca, but, I wouldn't want your friends to not like you because of me."

"I don't think that will happen. Come tonight, we'll have fun Misty." With a little more persuading Rebecca convinced her to go. Misty was hoping that they might treat her better now that they had had time to adjust to knowing what she was. But regardless of what happened she made up her mind to accept anything, so as not to spoil Rebecca's evening with Tom.

About a quarter of a mile outside of town, a little clearing on the bank of a stream is where they'll meet. The girls baked some little cakes to bring with them this evening. After dinner they waited on the porch for Tom to come by. When Misty caught sight of him she began to have second thoughts. Her last time out with

146

him and his friends had not been very enjoyable, and now she wondered what she had gotten herself into.

When Tom walked up onto the porch he could see that Misty was set to go with them. "Is your friend joining us?" he asked with an uncertain look on his face.

"I asked her to come," Rebecca replied.

"Okay," he said. "Let's go." During the time it took them to reach their destination Tom never included Misty in the conversation. Rebecca tried several times, but Tom steered away from it by giving one word answers.

As they got near, the glow of a fire could be seen. As they got closer voices and laughter could be heard. When they arrived at the site a half dozen people were there. Three boys and three girls, they had a small fire burning and were sitting close to it on logs. Misty knew Amy would be there, but seeing her face made her question again whether she should have stayed at home. Even worse when those with their backs to them turned around, one was Addie Cambridge. She and Amy had become good friends since the day they first went riding together.

"Rebecca," Addie said, "it must be getting serious between you two. Your parents are having you chaperoned."

"Please Addie," she replied, "don't give them any ideas."

"Hello Addie," Misty said.

"Hello Misty," she replied, "did you find out who hit y'all on the head yet?"

"No," she answered. The third girl called for Tom and Rebecca to come and sit with her. This was Jane Hobart. She and Misty had never met, but since she was so obviously ignoring her, Misty felt sure the others had told Jane all about her.

Most of the conversation was about people that Misty didn't know or about places they had been to. She sat and listened as the others talked, sometimes poking at the fire with a stick she held in her hand. Looking at the couples sitting together made her long for Roscoe more than at any time since he had left. How good it would be, she thought, to be sitting here in front of this fire with just him. No longer hearing the words of the others she was deep in thought about happier days. Faintly she heard her name called. Then a second time. This brought her back to the present. "Misty," a voice called out. "Are you still with us?" She looked up and smiled. "The fire could use some wood," Amy said to her.

"Okay," Misty said. Is that a good area to look in?" Pointing behind them she started walking towards the woods.

Jeffrey said to her, "You'll have to go in about twenty feet or more. We've already burned everything close by."

Once she was out of ear shot Amy said to Rebecca disgustedly, "Really Rebecca, did y'all have to bring her with you tonight?"

"No Amy, I didn't have to, I wanted to."

"Well we were planning on going to my house later. Now I sure ain't gonna show up there with her," Amy replied angrily.

"You don't have to fret none about it, we'll go home," Rebecca said.

"I thought you were gonna be with me tonight," Tom said to Rebecca.

"I've known of other Negroes that looked kind of white," Jane said. 'They always stayed with their own. Why doesn't she?"

"Just send her home Rebecca. I haven't seen y'all for a couple of days. I planned on this tonight," Tom said.

"I didn't think it would be any problem," Rebecca said, trying not to get angry. "She's not bothering anyone."

"It's just the thought of it Rebecca," Addie said. "We know you like her, and I've seen how the Tanners raised her. But you can't expect others to be the same way."

"No matter how you cut it Rebecca, she's a nigger, and she doesn't belong with us," Amy added in a stern tone of voice. They all stopped talking as Misty came in from the woods with two pieces of wood under one arm and dragging a long piece in her other hand. She asked for help to get it to the fire. When nobody moved Rebecca got angry and went to her aid. Tom then got up and took hold of the big piece and dragged to the fire. "I found a couple more nice pieces that I couldn't carry," Misty said. "I'll go and get em, they'll make a nice fire."

"That's okay, girl," Tom said. "Rebecca and I will go get them." Tom wanted Rebecca alone, he was upset that she would go home because of Misty rather than go to Moninghoff's with him.

With Rebecca gone, Addie and Amy started in on Misty as she sat down again by the fire. "Why don't you do Rebecca a kindness and go home," Amy said to her. "We're going over to my house later, but she's gonna go home because of you."

"She really shouldn't have invited you, Misty," said Addie.

"She really didn't Addie," Misty responded. "Adam asked me to come. I had planned on staying home."

"Oh Adam did, did he," said Amy "Well I don't see Adam here, do you?"

"When she comes back I'll tell her I'm going home," Misty said.

"She is not gonna let you go alone, and you know it," Addie said.

Misty looked at the boys who were staring silently into the fire. Then she looked at the girls and said, "If you can tolerate my presence a little longer, I'll leave when it's time to go to your house and I'll persuade Rebecca to stay."

"I'm glad to see you're gonna do the right thing," Amy said. "You know I'd like to take y'all to my house, but ya know it ain't proper. I mean, it's not my fault y'all have nigger blood in ya. I personally think you would be better off just staying with your own kind." Misty ignored her comment and the few more that came her way before Tom and Rebecca returned. She patiently waited through the next hour until they all agreed to leave for Amy's. Misty did just as she said she would and with some persuasion convinced Rebecca to go. Amy put on a fine show for Rebecca and encouraged Misty not to go home, but to join them.

The next day the girls talked about the night before and about Rebecca's friends. Misty didn't mention the conversation she had had with Addie and Amy, but Rebecca sensed there was more to it than she saw or heard. Misty wanted Rebecca to feel free to join her friends and not worry about what she would do, but through most of the week the two girls remained together. By Friday they had earned enough money sewing to go into town and have their photograph taken together. One to send to Roscoe and two to keep for themselves.

On Sunday they went to the meeting house together again, this time without too much commotion. Misty sat in the back, but alone. The elder Mrs. Tanner didn't come this morning, so she didn't get to see Henry or Sarah as she had hoped to. After the service the four went home and had lunch together. Rebecca departed for the afternoon to visit with friends. Dr. Myers had to make a call on an elderly couple and his wife went with him.

Misty had been working on a collection of poems and letters to send to Roscoe along with the photograph and was happy to have some quiet time. She took her note pad and went out to sit on the porch, but before she got started writing a wagon with a load of fire wood pulled around to the side of the house. She soon heard a knocking on the back door and walked around to see if she could help. A Negro man with a young boy stood waiting at the door. "Hello," Misty called out as she walked toward him.

"Afternoon Missy. I's be lookin fer dey Doctor," he replied.

"He's not in now, and I don't expect him back too soon."

"I's brought dis here wood fo him. He be spectin it tommor but I's get it done quick and thought I bring it on today," he said.

"Have you brought wood for Dr. Myers before?" she asked. "Yes, em," he said with a proud smile. "The Doctor he don't buy no wood from nobody ceptin me."

"Well then I guess you can do whatever it is you always do with it," Misty said smiling back. Immediately he and his boy started unloading some wood into the small bin by the back door. After filling that he moved the wagon to the wood shed and stacked the rest. Later that day when the Myers' returned Misty told them of their wood delivery. She commented about the fellow who brought it, how polite and friendly he was. "That's Luther Sander, a hard working man he is, and as honest as the day is long. He has another boy and a girl."

"Lovely wife too," said Dr. Myers. "He cuts wood for me and does a lot of the repairs around the house. Things I either don't have time for or don't do them as well as he does."

"Who does he belong to?" asked Misty. "He's a free man Misty. If I remember it right, his father was on a small plantation some miles from here. He was probably a hard worker like Luther, but whatever the case, he was granted his freedom when Luther was just a boy. Ya know now that I think about it, it was an unusual thing to set the boy free with him. It was a very fortunate thing for Luther. Well at any rate his father died a few years after that and Luther came to this area and took what little money he had and bought a piece of ground that nobody else would have touched and turned it into something nice. He sells some vegetables, and fruit pies, and fire wood. He hires himself out as a handyman."

"And his wife," added Mrs. Myers, "she does some cooking and cleaning and runs errands for folks. Anything that will make some change for them. She's a real decent woman."

"I don't think I've ever personally met any Negroes that were free," said Misty.

"Well then I'll tell you what we'll do. You'll come with me tomorrow when I go over to pay for the wood. You can meet Luther and his family, and I think I'll order up some of them chicken pies, Victoria," he said.

"See what kinds of squash they have too," said Mrs. Myers.

The next morning as they were preparing to leave, a wagon came racing up to the house. A child had taken ill. Dr. Myers

150

quickly went for his bag and sent Misty to bring his horse up to his buggy. He hitched it up and told Misty to get in and off they went. "I'll let you off at the crossroads just outside of town," the doctor told her. "It's an easy walk to Luther's from there. Give him his money and ask for two of the large chicken pies. Tell him I'll see him before the week's up. In just a few minutes she was standing at the crossroads watching Dr. Myers' cariole hurry off. Following his directions she headed down the small dirt road looking for the pathway that would take her to Luther's. Her walk was cut short when a wagon coming up the road toward her turned out to be Luther and his family. He pulled the wagon to a stop alongside Misty. "Hello Luther, I was on an errand to your house for Dr. Myers."

"Mornin Missy," he replied. "I reckon we saves y'all walkin."

"The doctor wanted you to have this," she said handing up the money to him. "He also would like two large chicken pies for later this week."

"Dat Dr. Myers sure do like dem pies," Luther's wife Mary said to him.

"My name is Misty," she said to Mary.

"I'm Mary and this is Barry and Robin and the baby is Tammy."

"She's lovely," Misty said, "I'm pleased to meet y'all." Luther looked at his wife as they both sat quiet for a moment. He wasn't sure what to do. The problem however, was solved when Misty asked to ride with them back to town.

Very quickly into the ride Misty would see why the Myers' spoke so highly of these people. Sitting up front with them she held the baby and talked with them about their purpose in town. Mary had wash to deliver to three different people. Luther had a door to hang and a bench to deliver. Then he was going to pick up supplies and head back home. Head back home Misty thought, what a nice feeling they put to those words. She knew she felt the same. She wanted to go home badly, and being with these people made her want it all the more. In no time they were pulling up in front of the doctor's house. As Misty said good-bye she told Mary she would come for the pies Friday.

Inside the house she found herself alone. Two notes on the kitchen table were addressed to her. One from Rebecca said she would be gone till dinner, the other from Mrs. Myers had a small list of items for her to get from town. She tucked the note and the

151

money with it into a pocket and went to town. Her first stop was for sewing supplies. This was at the far end of town. After a couple more quick stops she was at Moninghoff's General Store. Luther's wagon was outside and she stopped briefly to chat with Mary. Luther and the boys were inside getting supplies. This was their last stop before heading home.

Inside the building Misty saw Luther waiting near the pay counter, his boys were looking at buck knives laid out on a shelf. Misty took a hand basket and began selecting the items on the list. As she was walking about she noticed that everytime Luther would step up to pay, another person would walk in and he would be told to back up and wait. He would simply nod and say yes and wait for another opportunity. This went on the entire time that Misty was selecting her goods. When she finished she walked to the counter, Mr. Moninghoff not knowing who she was told Luther to step back, which he did, until Misty said she might need something else and turned to Luther telling him to go ahead. Mr. Moninghoff was done writing down the figures when the next customers came in. He told Luther the total and started packaging his things. Misty looked at the slate board and in her innocence thought he made an honest mistake and pointed it out to him. He looked a little flustered and began to say something when Luther said, "Thank y'all Miss Misty, I's don't know rithmatic much, but I's know money's hard to come by. Thank you," Luther said to her. The name Misty rang a bell in Mr. Moninghoff's head. He quickly got angry and said, "I know who you are, you're the nigger girl from Mariah that the Myers' puttin up. You niggers never did know how to count, there's nothing wrong with these figures. Boy you give me what you owe me." Several more people were in the store now. Two men standing nearby were laughing at the events taking place. One said to Mr. Moninghoff, "Don't you have enough money Bill? You gotta be cheatin the niggers now?" And they laughed some more. Misty picked up the slate board and turned it toward her saying, "Excuse me sir, but these numbers aren't totaled right." She realized now that this was his practice for any Negro customer. By now there were six people inside the store. The laughter of the two men brought the attention of the others up front. Everyone thought this was quite amusing. Misty calculated the numbers correctly and told Mr. Moninghoff in a polite way what the figure should be. He again protested, this time he ordered them out of his building. Misty turned to a woman who was near her and held the

152

slate up so she could see it. "This isn't added right, is it?" The woman looked at it and then at Mr. Moninghoff but didn't reply. Moninghoff reached out to take the slate but one of the two men who was finding so much enjoyment in all this reached out and plucked it from Misty's hand first. "Look here Bill," the man said laughing, "the little woman's right." Then turning his attention to Misty he said, "I oughta have you count up my account. It's been seemin awful high. Y'all ain't been squeezin me have ya Bill?"

By now everyone was standing up front and laughing. Mr. Moninghoff was furious, he came around the counter and took back his slate board and erased it. "Get out of here nigger," he said to Luther. "Take your business somewhere else. I don't want y'all in here no more." Luther hesitated for a moment not knowing if he should say something or not. "Go on boy," Moninghoff yelled. "Get out of here." Luther walked out without looking back. Misty put down the basket she had on the floor and went out after Luther. Catching up with him by his wagon she said, "He's an awful person, he probably does that to all the Negroes who are free."

"Yes em Missy, I's sure he does," Luther said as he climbed up onto his seat. "I's know y'all was right cause I's know he always cheat me, but ya see Missy, I's not allowed to dey other places, he be dey only one that sell to me. I's have ta let em cheat me or I's can't git no goods."

"But that's not right Luther," Misty said.

"Tain't right Missy, but what's em I gonna do about it," he said as he slapped the reins and started the horses moving.

As she turned to walk back to the Myers' she saw several of the people from the store standing in the doorway watching. She could only imagine what they were thinking, but it made her angry. She turned back and walked up the three steps onto the landing and excused herself as she passed through the doorway and into the store. She never spoke a word, she just gathered the things she came for. When her items were totaled on the slate board Mr. Moninghoff didn't speak to her, he turned the board around for her to see. She laid down the exact change, picked up her purchase, and waited until he counted and picked up her money, then she set down on his counter a five cent piece and walked out.

When she got back to the house Dr. Myers was in his office working. She went to the kitchen and put away the things she was sent out for then went into the front room and sat down. Having never been in a situation like that before she was still shaken up, and what about poor Luther she was thinking. Will he be able to get his supplies elsewhere? What if he can't, maybe she thought, she should go back and apologize. Luther will be at a loss without access to the store. But that man won't care she said to herself. He's not gonna listen to me, but maybe telling Dr. Myers can help. As she rose up to go to his office the front door opened, and Mrs. Myers and Rebecca entered. They had met in town and walked home together. Rebecca looked at Misty standing there and walked away. Misty watched as she went upstairs, then looked to Mrs. Myers. "Come in and sit down Misty," said Mrs. Myers. "Do you know why Rebecca is upset?"

"No," Misty replied.

"Tell me what happened today when you went to town," Mrs. Myers said to her.

"At Moninghoff's?" Misty asked.

"Yes dear, what went on in there?" Mrs. Myers asked reassuringly.

"He was terrible to Luther, stealing his money. How could he take advantage of a poor person like Luther when he himself has so much?"

"You'll have to tell me what happened so I can understand," said Mrs. Myers. The doctor now came out of his office and into the room. Seeing how serious they looked he sat down and asked what was wrong.

"Well," Misty began, "I was in Moninghoff's store earlier and he was cheating Luther out of his money. When I told him politely of his mistake, he became very angry, and loud. Other people gathered around. They saw it too, but they were just laughing. All I meant was for him to correct the mistake, I didn't mean to cause a problem."

"What did Bill do?" the doctor asked.

"He was very pertinacious about it and ordered Luther out of his store. He told him not to ever come back," she answered.

"What did he say to you?" Mrs. Myers asked.

"He was hollering and swearing and calling me names. I just walked out. But poor Luther, Dr. Myers, he can't get his needs any-where else." She paused for a moment. "Did I do the wrong thing?"

Dr. Myers rested his elbow on his knee and his chin in the palm of his hand. He thought for a moment and shook his head no as he said, "You did nothing wrong Misty, I'll go have a talk with Bill. He also owns the feed mill. He hires Luther from time to time when harvests of various things come in so he won't stay mad at Luther long. He won't stop cheating either, but there's nothing anyone can do about that."

"Well I'll have a talk with Rebecca," said Mrs. Myers.

"What's the matter with Rebecca, Victoria?" he asked.

"She was in town with the others, Amy included, when the news reached them."

"Amy is Bill's daughter;" said Dr. Myers. Lifting her eyes up and nodding her head Misty said, "I know. Did it make a problem for Rebecca?"

"I'm afraid it did," said Mrs. Myers. "I'm sure also, when the story was related to them it took on entirely different proportions, but whatever the case they spoke to Rebecca harshly because of it."

"Should I go up and explain to her what happened?" Misty asked.

"Let me talk to her first Misty, she was quite upset," Mrs. Myers said. Dr. Myers went out heading for town. Mrs. Myers went upstairs to talk to her daughter and Misty just sat back in her chair wishing all the more to be home.

For the next few days she stayed close to home. Mrs. Myers included her in some of her projects and the two of them enjoyed their time spent together. This was especially important since Rebecca was still finding any excuse to keep herself occupied and apart from Misty.

On Friday afternoon Amy and Jane came for Rebecca. Misty was out back and never saw them. She knew Rebecca was spending the night at Amy's and thought she would bake a cake for Dr. Myers. After gathering the eggs she returned to the kitchen and found the flour can empty. She hadn't been back to Moninghoff's since that day, but Dr. Myers assured her it would be all right, and so she gathered up some change and walked to town. Everything went okay inside the store, she purchased flour and was treated decently, but when she walked outside, she found herself amongst a small crowd that included Amy and Rebecca. Before she had time to react Amy said to her, "Y'all got your nerve going into my father's store again." Misty didn't answer her or even look at her. Instead, she looked at Rebecca who was half standing half sitting against a horse post. Rebecca looked away. This reaction pierced Misty's heart. She quickly turned and walked away as fast as she could. Someone in the group called out to her, saying something ignorant and laughing. Misty never looked back. If she had she would have seen the look on Rebecca's face, a look so forlorn that Amy saw it right away and said, "Let the wench go Rebecca, she's not of our kind." Our kind, Rebecca kept thinking, over and over again, throughout that night. It wouldn't leave her alone.

The next morning Rebecca got up early. She had only one thought, to apologize to Misty, to make amends and to get far away from Amy and the rest of her so-called friends. Arriving at the house at half past eight she went directly upstairs to Misty's room. The door was open but no one was there. The bed was made and the room fixed as if there wasn't a guest staying in it. Hurrying downstairs and to the kitchen she found her parents sitting at the table. As she entered the room her mother said to her with a surprised voice, "Rebecca, we didn't expect you home this early." Her father added, "We were hoping it was Misty walking about upstairs."

"She's not up there."

"We know, Honey," her mother said. "She's gone home."

"Gone home?" Rebecca said sitting at the table. "We found this note this morning," her father said handing her a piece of folded paper. "I'm getting ready to hook up the buggy and find her, she can't be even halfway yet."

"You're bringing her back, right?" Rebecca questioned him. "I'll see what she wants to do. The letter sounds pretty definite," he answered. "I really don't like the thought of her out there without the others," Rebecca unfolded the paper and began reading it aloud:

Dear Dr. and Mrs. Myers,
I hope you won't be angry with me. You've been so kind to me, it would hurt me deeply to cause you any sorrow. I've packed up my things and I'm going home. Please don't worry about my walking there. I didn't want to trouble you, and I would like to walk anyway. You won't have to worry about my safety. I'll stay inside after dark and Henry will be there. Thank you for taking such good care of me and bringing me back to good health.

I love you *all* so much
Misty

Rebecca knew the line drawn under the word *all* meant her. It was all she could do to hold back her emotions. Her parents understood the look on her face. They had seen the strain in the girls' relationship and knew they both felt bad about it. Her father reached over and touched her hand saying, "How about I hitch the buggy and you go and find her?"

"Maybe stay the night at Mariah, Rebecca," her mother suggested.

"It'll just take me a minute to change," she said jumping up and hurrying from the room.

It took less than an hour to catch up with Misty. Rebecca pulled alongside of her and stopped. "Hello Rebecca, what brings y'all out this way?" Misty said as she smiled.

"Oh, I don't know, just felt like taking a ride," Rebecca exclaimed as she slid to the edge and climbed down. Misty put her bag to the ground and they tightly embraced each other. "I am really . . . really sorry for the way I acted. I can't hardly believe I could be that way, could you ever forgive me?" asked Rebecca.

"I love you Rebecca, I always will. You . . . Iz . . . Naomi are the best friends I'll ever have, I would never want to lose you." The two climbed into the buggy and headed for Mariah.

That afternoon they went riding. They rode as far as the meadows and sat there awhile talking about the many times they had all been there together, and how much they wanted to do it again. "Look at us Rebecca," Misty said laughing, "We're getting older, I'll be sixteen this spring, time seems to be going by so much quicker these days. You'll probably be married in a year."

"Married?!" Rebecca cried, "don't you think you're rushing things a bit? But he did tell me he loves me. Well, one never does know, does one?"

"No Rebecca," Misty laughed. "One never does."

They spent the evening in the house and the night in Isabelle's room. The next morning they said good-bye. Rebecca left early wanting to have the buggy home before her parents returned from the meeting. She tried to persuade Misty to come with her, but to no avail.

Henry had taken the elder Mrs. Tanner and Martha to the meeting and the big house was empty. She went out and gathered up half a dozen young children and brought them to the kitchen for breakfast. Afterwards she took them for a walk. Later that afternoon, Grandmother Tanner was napping in her room, Henry and Misty were playing chess in the family room and the house was as quiet as it ever was. The sound of horses was heard pulling up out front. Henry made his move and said he had better go see who it was. When he was almost at the door, it opened. Henry exclaimed excitedly, "Lor be! It's Miss Naomi!"

"Hello Henry," she said giving him a hug, "It's good to see you."

"Miss Naomi we weren't spectin you. Are ya alone?" he said looking for others. Misty wasn't sure she heard right and went to the doorway. Looking down the hall she couldn't believe it was true. Their eyes met at the same time. They rushed toward each other and gave each a long hard embrace. No words needed to be said. At that moment the void Misty had been feeling the past week was instantly filled and overflowing. Just the perfect day she needed. The coach pulled away and Henry went outside for her bags. It appeared she would be staying awhile.

"Oh Naomi," Misty said, "It is so good to see you. I've missed you so much. I've been missing everybody so much."

"I've missed you too Misty, and I've been homesick," she replied. "We weren't expecting y'all," Misty said as they walked into the family room. "Is everyone all right?"

"Everyone is fine," she said, "Zachary and I were gonna meet up with the family in Orleans and surprise everyone. But one of the ships was badly damaged and he had to take it to port along the coast to repair it."

"Was anyone hurt?" Misty asked.

"No, it hit against a reef and tore a hole in the side. It will take a month or so to fix. I thought I'd come home and visit Grandmother for a couple of weeks and then go to Orleans and see the family. Zachary will meet me there." She paused a moment and looking puzzled she said, "But why aren't y'all in New York with the rest of the family?"

"I had an accident and couldn't travel," she said not wanting to say more just now. "Now we get to spend the next two weeks with each other and we get to travel together! I can't think of anything better than that."

"How about a letter from Ros?" she asked. Misty's eyes opened wide. "Naomi, do you have one? Please tell me you do?" Misty asked.

"Well," Naomi said, "it's more like a book than a letter. He must have started writing it the night before he left."

"Do you have it?" Misty asked excitedly.

"Come with me sister," Naomi said as they rose up from the divan. "I'm afraid to make y'all wait any longer." Naomi opened a bag Henry had set in the hall and took out a large folder. "Ros sent this back with Zachary's father, I just received it the other morning. Look at this, a note for father. This one, about two and a half pages is for mother. Somewhere in here . . . oh this one is for me, and this card, isn't it pretty, is for Isabelle. Yours dear is this one." She handed her a large sealed envelope and laughed saying, "This is the history of Roscoe Tanner's journey. Misty you really don't want this do ya?"

Misty took it from Naomi and held it to her chest. "You could never know how much I love you," Misty said. "I'll make us dinner in a little while," She reached out and hugged her tightly, then quickly ran up the stairs and into Roscoe's room.

She emptied the contents on the bed, some were letters, some pictures, some were diagrams of things she had never seen before, those she tossed aside. She looked through the pictures first. Most were of landmarks and scenery, each with a note of description on the back, then at the bottom was what she was looking for, a picture of Roscoe. She looked intently at it as her emotions welled up inside her. After a moment she focused on the others in the picture with him. A tall distinguished looking gentleman and a very beautiful young lady. Flipping the picture over, the note on the back read, 'Misty, take a hard look at the people in this picture. What do you see? His name is Frederick Bordeau. His wife is mulatto. Her name is Lanya. I'll tell you more when I write.' Looking at the woman all Misty could see was that she was beautiful, but her curiosity was aroused. She hoped there was more about her in one of the letters.

Propped up against the pillows she started to read. All the letters were dated. Some were written while still on the ship. Some had been written over a two-and three-day period. All said how much he loved her and missed her. Finally, near the end, the gentleman's name in the picture came up again. Roscoe had met him at one of the local inns. One evening a week people gathered at this particular inn to play music and exchange ideas, and methods of play. He enjoyed Roscoe's style of guitar playing and invited him and several others to his home one evening. His wife's accent intrigued Roscoe and when he questioned her of her origins he learned she was a mulatto. Eagerly he shared his story with her and they quickly became friends. In his letter to Misty he wrote, 'Along with this letter I'm hoping to send you a picture. It was taken today. I won't get to see it for several days, but if it takes, you'll see Frederick and Lanya. Misty, I think he has the answer to our problem, and it seems so simple. Frederick is a genuine sort of fellow, very smart, a businessman trading in fabrics. You'd love seeing (and touching) the kinds of things he works with. He lives part of the time here and part of the time in France. That's where he met Lanya. Her father is French (white) her mother is Negro. I didn't ask if they were married, but Frederick and Lanya are, right

159

out in the open and no one even cares. He says I should bring you to England, buy a property and set up residence. Then we could legally marry. We would of course return to Mariah, but maintain our citizenship over here. Frederick says with my father's financial status and influence no one would dare challenge us in a legal way. I think he is right Misty, but even if he is not we can always live here, or anywhere. As long as I have you as my wife, that's all I really ever wanted. I love you more than life itself. If I could just hold your hand in mine right now. There are no words for me to express how much I miss you at this moment.'

Misty slid down the bed bringing her head to rest on the pillow and read the letter several more times. Then she closed her eyes and fell deep in thought. 'If I had the alchemists stone,' she mused, 'I'd be lying beside him this very moment, with my fingers on his chest feeling his heart beat.' She searched around the paper and found the poem again. She read each line slowly and reflected on his thoughts until her eyes grew heavy and she fell asleep.

Later that evening after dark a hand came down on her shoulder and shook her several times. When finally awakened she jumped away from the person standing over her, falling off the bed while letting out a frightful scream. "Misty!" a voice called out. "It's me Naomi! I didn't mean to scare you so." Looking from the other side of the bed she exhaled in a sigh of relief. "Oh Misty," Naomi said, "that was foolish of me, Henry told me what happened to you. I feel so stupid."

"It's all right Naomi," Misty said coming around to her; "Actually it's kind of funny, did you see how fast I went off the bed?"

"Right to the floor," Naomi said as they both began to laugh.

"I'm sorry I fell asleep, I did want to spend the evening with you," Misty said gathering up the letters and pictures. "Let's go to the kitchen and get a glass of juice. I'll show you the pictures Ros sent."

Misty squeezed a dozen oranges while Naomi looked through the pictures and read the notes on the back. The last one was of Roscoe and the Bordeau's. She flipped it to the back and read a portion of it and looked again at the front. "He says to take a look at them. Why?" Naomi asked.

"Take a look. What do y'all see?"

"She is very beautiful. Is she a stage performer?" Naomi asks.

"No," Misty said, "She is a mulatto, married to a white man. It's perfectly legal in England."

"You don't think he went up to them and said, would y'all mind having your picture taken with me? My friends back home in Georgia would like to see it," Naomi said laughing.

"No," said Misty. "He wrote in one of his letters about them."

With a coy look Naomi said, "I wonder what interest my little brother would have in a white man marrying a mulatto?"

Misty's response in an exaggerated southern accent was, "I dare say, I don't know."

The next morning after breakfast the girls went riding. The diagrams Roscoe sent were for Wendall, and he asked Misty to take them to him. She hadn't seen him for a while, thinking he was hesitant to come over after being questioned concerning her being attacked. He probably didn't even know she was home anyway. It was the perfect excuse to go to his house. They packed a lunch planning on making a day of it. For the next two weeks Naomi and Misty spent most of their time together. Wendall rode over a couple of times and Rebecca came to stay for several days.

Into the third week they began making preparations for their departure to New Orleans. Misty was growing more anxious with each day. One final weekend and the journey would begin. Rebecca came back on Saturday to stay till Monday morning. She and Naomi spent the day together while Misty went down back to say good-bye to her friends. The children particularly were sad to see her leave. No one gave them the kind of attention she did. Sarah walked with her all afternoon until she had seen everyone she wanted to see. Lastly she met up with Goldie and Leo as they came in from the field. After they deposited the bags of cotton in the storage bin they went together to their hut. Leo went off to gather some wood for a fire while Goldie kneaded bread and cut up some vegetables. Leo returned with the wood and started a fire for Goldie to cook on. He then went for a piece of fresh ham from a pig slaughtered that afternoon. They all ate stew and talked awhile before Misty said good-bye and returned to the main house.

Sunday morning they all went to the meeting together and then to the Myers' for lunch. Grandmother Tanner joined them and they all had a pleasant time. By mid-afternoon they were back home. Wendall was sitting on the veranda when they arrived. The girls had invited him for dinner. He remained there while they changed, reading and taking in the cool December air. Upstairs Naomi was commenting on how much Wendall has changed. "I didn't care for him much when he first moved here," she said.

"Nor did I," Misty said. "But he really is a nice fellow. I'm gonna miss him too."

Misty changed quickly and went outside to Wendall. "The others will be along shortly," she said. "My it's a lovely day, isn't it."

"It is," Wendall said, "just the way I like'em. I've got some good news and some bad," he continued. "It's actually all the same news, just has some good to it and some bad."

"Well Wendall," Misty laughed, "y'all gonna talk about it, or y'all gonna talk about it?"

"Okay," he responded, "I'm taking a bit of a holiday myself."

"Where are you going?" she asked.

"Boston," he replied with some excitement.

"Boston?" she said. "What are y'all gonna do there?"

"I told you I applied to several schools. I've got a calling from one. And it was really the one I wanted most. I'm pretty excited."

"I can see that," she said. I'm going to be excited too. I know how much you want this. So what's the bad news?"

"Bad news is, when you get back from Orleans I'll be gone. Don't know when we'll see each other again," he said.

"That seems to be my lot in life these days. Everyone dear to me is going off in a different direction," she lamented. "You will send me a letter won't you?"

"Of course I will," he answered her. The diagrams Ros sent, did you take a look at them?" he asked

"Not really. Well I did, but they don't make any sense to me," she answered.

"They're machines called turbines, powered by the force of water. I think he is starting to become fascinated with them also," he said.

"What are they used for?" she asked. He started to explain but the other girls arrived, and the conversation changed.

"It seems it was a good thing we invited Wendall for dinner;" Misty said. "He too is departing soon."

"Where are you going Wendall?" Rebecca asked.

"To school in Boston," he replied.

"That's wonderful Wendall, when will you leave?" she asked.

"Sometime around June. I don't have to start till October, but I thought I'd take a holiday first. See New York and some of the other northern states."

"I'm gonna be the only one left," Rebecca said.

162

"Not for long," said Naomi. "We're all coming back to Mariah, some sooner than others, but eventually we'll all be back to live here. There is just no finer place on earth."

That evening the girls prepared a dinner of roasted chicken with stuffing and corn, fresh baked bread and sweet potatoes. They followed that with warm pie and cream. They all ribbed Wendall relentlessly about how much he ate, and it showed as he walked to the family room slowly and uncomfortably. December evenings get dark early and a cloud cover hid the moon. They convinced Wendall to stay the night in one of the cottages. This allowed them to spend the remainder of the evening together, which they did mostly around the piano singing and enjoying themselves to the fullest.

The next morning everyone was up early. Lilly Mae prepared breakfast and served Wendall and the girls in the dining room. Henry and James had loaded the wagons and were having breakfast in the kitchen. They were joined by Lester and George. George is a young man in his early twenties who was born on the plantation and had never been off of it. He would be assisting them on their journey. The instructions were to bring two wagons. Mr. Tanner knew there would be much to take home.

After breakfast and just minutes short of their departure, Wendall asked Misty to come outside with them. They walked through the house and out the side leading to the courtyard. Sitting down on a bench Wendall said to her, "I want to tell you something. I've never really had a lot of friends. I think Ros and I would have become friends in time."

"Ros is your friend," Misty interjected.

"Well, I hope so," he replied. "But it's our friendship I want to talk about."

"Ours is impervious Wendall," she said with a smile.

"Beautifully put Misty," he said, "the words of a troubadour. Oh how I'm going to miss our conversations. I doubt there's anyone else I'll ever meet who speaks with such imagination."

"Wendall if I speak, shall I say, mellifluously, it is because you encourage it. Probably when I see you again you'll be introducing me to your wife, and I'll be so happy for her," Misty said putting her hand on his shoulder. Naomi stuck her head out of the door and called out to them. It was time to leave. They stood up and embraced each other then stepped back and smiled.

163

"Fare thee well my friend," Wendall said to her. Then in a sweet gentle tone he quoted a verse from a poem she had written, "When your darkest hour befalls you, and eclipses your light of life, fear not that you're alone, for in spirit I'll be with you on that night."

"Fare thee well also my friend," she said as tears came into her eyes. "May it go so very well with all you do." She covered her face with her hands now not able to keep from crying.

"No," he said, "don't do that or you'll have me crying." He took her arm and they walked back into the house. She almost got control of herself when Lilly Mae started crying and hugging her good-bye.

After a few moments she was in the wagon. A clicking sound and a light jolt and the wagon was pulling away. Rebecca would ride with them to town where there would be one final cry at the Myers' and then the journey would officially begin. It was just a few minutes down the road when they crossed through the covered bridge. "Oh my, what a feeling I just had," Misty said.

"A feeling of what Misty?" Rebecca asked.

"Like I will never cross the bridge again," she replied.

"It's just nerves and excitement Misty. You'll be back home in no time," Naomi reassured her.

By the time they stopped for lunch it was well past noon. They had already put many miles behind them. The plan was to be in Alabama by evening of the next day and the following day arrive for a surprise visit at Leesway. Misty wouldn't have done that if she were on her own, but with Naomi directing things she welcomed the idea. Their first night out they stayed at an inn and departed early the next morning. The second evening they had lost their bearings and a family on a small plantation put them up for the night. Naomi and Misty slept in a beautiful room in a large bed. A fire was made in the fireplace and they fell quickly off to sleep. Henry and the others slept in the barn.

It took two more days before they reached Leesway. What a surprise for Mrs. Tanner's sister finding her niece Naomi standing on the veranda, "I can't believe it, I just can't believe it," she kept saying.

"Go quick," she said to the servants, "find Master Eichner, send him here. Misty, I swear you're more beautiful now than ever. I am so happy to see you both." She sent another servant to find Jefferson. He arrived in a few moments and took Henry and the others, as well as the horses and wagons. Mr. Eichner came hurrying out to see what all the excitement was about.

"Lord above," he exclaimed throwing his hands up in the air, "do my eyes tell me the truth?"

"Hello Uncle Samuel," said Naomi giving him a hug.

"Where is that young man of yours. He's not letting you travel alone is he?"

"His work took him away for awhile. We're on our way to Orleans to meet up with the rest of the family," she said.

"Well, little girl," he said to Misty as he reached out to hug her, "I thought you couldn't get any prettier, but you proved me wrong."

"Come on everyone," Mrs. Eichner declared, "Let's go inside. I'm sure you girls want to freshen up." After four days traveling this was a welcome relief. The cook was told to prepare for two more. Others were sent to fill the bathing tub with warm water and prepare rooms for the guests. They would stay for three nights before setting out to complete their journey. The arrangement of sleeping quarters came as a surprise to them both. Naomi was given one of the guest rooms upstairs while Misty was given a room downstairs. These were normally used by servants. She would never have said anything about it, but when they were alone later Naomi told her how surprised she was by it.

The time spent there was both enjoyable and relaxing. The first two evenings were spent in the family room with lots of talking and singing and games. The final evening Misty departed quickly after dinner, she hadn't seen Henry or the others since they arrived.

She walked off toward the barn nearest the main house. Several Negro men were working inside and one gave her directions to the building Henry was staying in. She walked another few hundred yards before she reached the vicinity where most of the slaves were kept. This was not at all what she expected to find. Many slaves were returning from the fields and busying themselves gathering food and firewood. Believing she was white few would even look at her. No one spoke. Many of the faces wore blank expressions. Their clothes barely covered their bodies and a lot looked ill or moved with difficulty. The numerous huts in the area were all the same: not large enough to stand up in, none had working doors and the space between the boards could hardly keep the wind and rain from coming through. The roofs were tin and the dirt floors covered with straw. Clearly the number of slaves out numbered the huts and the sound of hungry children crying was relentless. Never had she seen a more pitiful sight. Many horrifying stories were told by slaves purchased and brought to Mariah, but having never seen it herself she never comprehended the reality of it.

She walked on a little further to another barn where she spotted their wagons, at the far end sat Henry and the others. She approached them with such a forlorn look on her face that Henry stood up quickly and had her sit on the wooden box he used as a seat. "Are you taken ill child?" he asked.

"No Henry, I'm confused, the Eichners aren't good masters?" she asked. Henry understood and he felt bad for her.

"Dey is no place like Mariah, Misty, dis place bad, other places worse."

George stood up and leaned against the back of the wagon saying, "Mariah t'aint no different. Nigger picks cotton from da sun up till sun down, hands crack and bleed, still pick cotton, and if'in y'all aint picks enough, Masser Louder whip ya good." Misty by this time was feeling ill. She rose up and walked out of the barn. Henry followed her out and stood alongside of her as she looked carefully at the surroundings.

"I am confused Henry, is it true what George says?" she asked.

"Da Negro pick cotton. Misty, dats what day do," he said.

"Poppa Tanner lets people be whipped if they're bad, but he wouldn't let Master Louder whip 'em for not pickin their share, I know he wouldn't," she said.

"Misty, Masser Tanner's a good master, but it's a big plantation and lots of cotton needs a be picked. He just don't mind Masser Louder's business none. And Masser Louder do his job, he don't let'em kill nobody. I hears tell der places that hang'em if'in a whip'en don't work," he said trying to be reassuring.

Looking around she said, "This is the most pitiful thing I've ever seen."

"I spects it is," he replied,"but don't you fret much about it, t'aint nothin you can do. I'm an old man. Didn't like it when I was a boy, don't like it no more now. But t'aint nothin you can do."

"I thought the stories I was told were exaggerated. I guess I didn't want to believe it could be so bad," she lamented.

"You never heard all what it's like, dem stories not told to the children," Henry said to her.

"Are you and James and George okay?" she asked.

"Yes'em, we's ta stay down here till we's sent for, dis always ta way it is here," he answered.

"Why didn't you say something?" she asked. Henry didn't answer and she realized it was a foolish question. "I suppose they don't like me the way they make like they do," she said.

"Da lady of da house is a kind person, she come from good stock. The master, the Lord will judge him. Best for you to be mindin to yourself, we be on our way soon enough."

Misty went back to the house and to her room, but many hours passed before she fell asleep. Her mind was fixed on the mother she never knew. What had her life really been like? What had she endured? Misty would only ever think of the time she spent at Mariah.

The next morning after breakfast the wagons were waiting out front. The girls said their good-byes and soon all were quickly on their way. Henry was driving the front wagon with George sitting alongside. Misty called out just a short distance down the road and Henry brought things to a stop. "George, might I sit up with Henry a bit?" she asked. George climbed down from the bench and Misty handed him a basket. "Share this with James," she told him. Naomi climbed out from the back of the wagon and joined Misty as she made her way up on the bench bedside Henry. "Did you have breakfast Henry?" she asked.

"No ma'm I didn't," he answered.

Misty handed him a package too. "Here," she said, "some things they sent us off with." This was the first real food they had in three days. Especially for Henry, who was use to eating from the main house, this food was welcome.

Once they were on their way again Misty started telling Naomi about the conditions the slaves endured at Leesway. "I didn't know about that," she said, "but I have seen things traveling about with Zachary that I've found most repulsive, and I'm certain I'm guilty of self-denial. It was always a way of life with us Misty. Owning a plantation means owning slaves. I do like to think we treat ours decently."

"I think they are," she replied, "but I don't know. It seems different to me now. Like all of a sudden my eyes have been unveiled."

"Me too, Misty," Naomi said, "It's easy to look at Henry and Martha and Willy Mae and not think about the rest."

"You couldn't believe that place," Misty went on, "and Henry says other places are even worse."

"Yes 'em dey is," Henry said. "Much more worse."

167

"Henry," Naomi said, "are you happy?"

Henry drew the word out long, "Well," he said, "Masser Tanner, and his father too, deys great men, no finer anywhere. It was good for Henry to be owned by them stead of some good for nothin man. And I's lived better than most slaves I's seen. I's happy in lots a ways Miss Naomi. I's bounced y'all on my knee when ya wez a baby, and I's see ya grow into a fine woman. Y'all has been like a family to me, but if'in a man's not free Miss Naomi, he's not fully happy. I's hear the white preachers all my life sayin the Negro meant to be a slave, but I's never believe it. If'in that was true then slaves won't be thinkin so hard on bein free, but that's all dat most Negro men think about."

"I always heard Poppa say you wouldn't want to be free," Naomi replied.

This made Henry laugh, "I spects he felt dat way cause he knows I's has it good," he said.

"Well, Henry, I know this is selfish but I'd never want you to leave," Naomi said.

"If'in I's was a young man and free I's would have left, with tears in my eyes, yes'em, but I's would have gone," Henry said to her, "but I's gettin on now and don't recollect I'd go anyway."

"Henry," Misty said having only been half listening and far off in thought, "will we pass the place where Mother Tanner took possession of my mother?"

"We be goin dat way Misty, but I's sure it's been a long time and I's don't know if'in I's would remember da spot."

"I'd like to find it if we could," she said.

"So would I," added Naomi.

"Well we sure gonna try then ain't we," he said nodding his head and sounding as reassuring as he could.

Several times along the way Henry thought he might have found the spot, but then he concluded it wasn't. Once he was sure they had to be past the area, he apologized, saying the landscape had changed much over the years and now he just couldn't be certain. Misty was noticeably disappointed, but it was only one of her quests regarding her mother, the other she knew would come about. She wanted to see the auction house where her mother had been sold. Henry reassured her this he could do.

It took another day and a half of travel before they reached the city of New Orleans. Misty was mesmerized. She had never seen anything like it. It is much more beautiful than the pictures she

168

kept saying. The streets were laid with stones and lined with gas lights and ornamental trees. Some streets were filled with houses the likes of which she had never seen before. The architectural style left her in awe. Some buildings were too big to be called houses, mansions were the more appropriate term. The lace ironworks, the perfectly landscaped patios overlaid in brick, other areas of shops and restaurants, hotels and offices were so much more than she had imagined it would be. Each time they rounded a corner it was like entering another new world.

They made their way to Chartres Street. This was a quiet section in the French Quarter. The Franklins had just had the house completed before they left to meet the Tanners in New York. On arriving they found the house empty. Disappointed, but not surprised, they had reached the city before the others. Naomi, though, knew just what to do. "Pull the wagons in off the street," she told Henry. "Take the horses to a stable. There must be one nearby." They drove the wagons to the rear of the property. There was a small carriage house not yet completed and several large shade trees.

"What are we gonna do?" Misty asked Naomi.

"We're on a holiday Misty. We're going to enjoy ourselves while we wait for the others to return." Naomi gave Henry money to purchase food for himself and the others. She also wrote passes for them saying they were on assignment and the address of where their owner could be found if necessary. The law of the south was very strict about these passes. There were many Negroes living in the city. They were required to carry certificates. Failure to have this could land them in jail for vagrancy. Henry and the others had to keep their passes with them at all times. Naomi had their bags brought to them and they departed.

Walking through the garden district was like being in a new world. Every corner they went around put them on a street more fascinating then the one before, and then suddenly there it was—The St. Charles Streetcar. This was a dream come true for Misty. Anyone who ever heard of or saw pictures of these streetcars wanted to ride one. Her time had come. They climbed up the stairs and into the car. Naomi wanted Misty to sit on the outside so she could have a full view of the city. They rode the entire length, up near the Tulane University and back to the downtown area. They exited as near as possible to the Histand Hotel. Mr. Tanner didn't know it yet, but he was treating the girls to a first rate holiday.

They took one of the suites on the third floor and made reservations for dinner.

The next morning they awoke well-rested, went to the dining room for breakfast and then out for an adventure. Misty suggested they see if the others had gotten back the night before, but Naomi felt if they had, they would have sent for them, so off they went to explore the city. Having been to New Orleans with her family on many past occasions Naomi acted as their tour guide. First place of interest, the Place d'Armes. "They call this the Pontalba now," she said. "Originally this whole area was made up of wooden buildings, but a fire took them all. A very wealthy Spanish merchant then contributed to the rebuilding of the area using bricks instead of wood, and so today we have one of my favorite places. We just refer to it as the shopping district."

"Mother always said if it wasn't sold here it probably didn't exist," Misty said. The girls walked up one side of the street and down the other. Admiring the many displays in the windows and on the tables and stands set up in front of many of the shops. But the shop that caught Misty's attention most was the one that sold books. On coming upon this one she hurried inside.

The walls were lined from floor to ceiling with shelves of books. Along the back wall a shelf of magazines. A doorway led to a small annex filled with cards, instruction manuals, calendars, writing paper and writing paraphernalia. Naomi said to Misty with a laugh, "You must be in heaven."

She looked back and smiled saying, "Did you ever see so many books in one place?"

"No dear I haven't," Naomi replied, "but we have lots to do today. You'll be back here soon enough I'm sure of that. Let's move on while the day is young." They ventured in and out of more streets and shops until past the midday mark. A streetcar took them to the *vieux carre*, the French Quarter, where they had lunch at a cafe that served its customers on tables outside. It was a beautiful day graced by a warm soft breeze.

They continued their tour the remainder of the afternoon walking in and out of streets that reflected the diverse culture that made up this fascinating city. Eventually they made their way to Chartres Street. They wanted to see if the family had arrived yet, and Misty wanted to be sure Henry was all right.

The house was still empty and the girls walked around back. Henry and James were sitting under a tree eating, accompanied by a young dog. "Done woke me up early dis mornin," Henry responded when asked about the dog. "Right playful young dog it is," he added.

"Twas a might hungry too," said James.

"Not a very pretty dog at all," Naomi commented. 'It looks like the offspring of two other ugly dogs. Y'all want to chase it off before the others get home."

"Where is George?" Misty asked.

"He walked off dis mornin, say he gonna go look about, t'aint seen hide nor hair of em since," Henry said. "Maybe I's better go look about fo him."

"No Henry," Naomi said, "it'll be dark soon. It's better for y'all to stay here. If he gets in trouble, and I think he's gonna, let it be his problem."

"Why do you think he is gonna get in trouble?" Misty asked.

"I saw the look in his eyes when we got here. I told him trouble was crouching at his door, but I don't think he listened," Naomi said. "If he's not back by mornin y'all go out and look about for him then." As they started walking away Naomi said, "But by then he could be long gone, if not dead."

The problem however, corrected itself. As the girls reached the street, George was there coming toward them. Naomi waited for him and asked, "Where've you been all day?"

"I's be down a bits workin on da house of da ladies of da lord," he replied.

"You've been where?" Misty asked.

"The ladies of the lord," Naomi answered. "They are the Ursuline Nuns, they have a house not far from here. We'll go that way, I'll show you."

"That was a good thing George," Misty said to him.

"Yes'em," he replied and started walking toward the back.

"You better stay around here, I wouldn't want Master Tanner coming back and finding you gone. He'd be right upset about that."

"Yes'em," he replied again.

"What's the matter Naomi?" Misty asked.

"I don't trust him, Misty. I think he is scheming," she said.

"Why do you think Poppa wanted him to come?" Misty asked.

"It was probably two-fold. I don't think they liked you traveling so far without enough protection. Also I'm sure they'll buy enough things to fill the two wagons and then some," Naomi answered.

The next several days were much the same. The girls went on various excursions throughout the day and to the theater in the evenings. Then they finally received the note they had been waiting for. "This afternoon at nearly five o'clock, one named Henry came to the hotel. His message is, your parents are here. They are waiting for you." It was signed by the day manager. Since it was too late to go traveling about, they decided to spend the night at the hotel and leave early the next morning.

It was before seven and they were both sound asleep when a sharp knock was applied to the door. Naomi arose, put on her robe, and opened the door. She was expecting to find a porter with a message from her family, but instead she found her sister Isabelle, who in one motion stepped forward and put her arms around Naomi and squeezed her tightly. The commotion awoke Misty who sat up and called out Isabelle's name. They were as excited as if they hadn't seen each other for a year. The girls hurried to get dressed, packed up their belongings and went to the dining room for breakfast.

"New York," Isabelle said, "is the most fascinating place in the world."

"Ros says England is the most fascinating place in the world," Misty replied. "But I have to believe it is New Orleans."

"Ah, but New York, Misty," said Isabelle. "The theaters are more numerous, and some of the shops are so large you get lost in them. The buildings are so big, and the streets so alive with activity."

"Did it snow?" Naomi asked.

"Snow," she said, "you wouldn't believe, everything was pure white. We built snowmen with the kids and rode on sleds that just flew across the top of the snow."

"Horse drawn sleighs too?" Naomi asked.

"They were everywhere. For a twenty-five-cent piece they take you almost anywhere you wanted to go. One day Susan and I took the kids to the park. It's just like we read it was, Misty, so beautifully landscaped and groomed. We bought ice skates and went on one of the ponds. It was like gliding on glass, so smooth, and hard when you fell."

"What were the people like?" Misty asked.

"That was a delightful surprise too. They were just as friendly and polite as anyone else. A lot of foreigners too."

172

"That's what makes the shopping in the cities so interesting," Naomi said.

"Indeed," Isabelle responded. "New York's shopping center is being divided into sections, entire blocks, and these blocks are huge. Some are devoted to fabrics, another may be machinery or food or any number of things."

"I'm going to order us a cariole," Naomi said and departed from the table. "I wished the whole time that you were there," Isabelle said to Misty.

"I did feel badly that I couldn't go, and several days after you were gone I realized I was feeling fine and I haven't had any problems since. But then Naomi showed up and we've had a truly wonderful time, especially here in Orleans, and now I hope you're gonna stay awhile," Misty said.

"I hope so too, but you know how Poppa is, he always thinks he wants a holiday, then he can't wait to get home."

"Y'all stopping at Leesway on your way back?" Misty asked.

"For a couple of days," she answered.

"We stopped on our way here," Misty said.

"I bet they were surprised by that," Isabelle responded. Naomi came back to the table and said a cariole would be out front in a moment. The girls left the hotel and were quickly on their way.

"Were y'all there when Henry told them I was here too?" Naomi asked.

"No, I wasn't," Isabelle said, "I wish I had been though. Mother was so happy when she was telling me. It's gonna be nice having us all together again." As they pulled up in front of the house, Mrs. Tanner was standing at the window. Before they could even disembark everyone was coming out of the door. After several minutes of everyone hugging and talking at the same time they entered into the house. Mrs. Franklin made a large pot of coffee. They had all purchased various varieties of beans from New York and were anxious to try some. They sat in the large family room for well over an hour and told of their varying experiences. Mrs. Franklin gave Naomi and Misty a tour of the house and put their belongings in the room they would share with their sister. Mrs. Tanner and Isabelle went to the food market while the men went out back on the patio.

That evening after dinner the new house had its first concert. The Tanners needed little coaxing to play and sing, and the excitement of being all together again made their hearts want to rejoice, and rejoice they did till well into the evening.

As the week progressed the men joked about living alone. This was in reference to the amount of time the women spent out and about. The other joke was, and this one solely Mr. Tanner's, was that so many items had been purchased he was shopping around for another wagon.

Late one afternoon toward week's end the girls came back from touring the Tulane University, and went to the patio looking for the others. As Naomi stepped out of the doorway, Zachary stood up smiling as broad a smile as one could muster up. She ran and threw her arms around him, "I didn't expect you for at least a fortnight," she said.

"Y'all won't believe the good fortune I had," he said as they all sat down. "I just finished telling about it once. I got a mind to wait till after dinner before I speak of it again."

"I know you Zachary Johnson," Naomi said, "when something's got you excited you can't keep it in even if you want to. So get it over with."

"By and by you have a way of making me tell even when I don't want to," he said laughing. "Well it happened like this here," he continued. "I took the damaged vessel to port like we had planned and who do you think is there but Abe Thompson."

"Who is Abe Thompson?" Naomi asked.

"He's the owner of the Laurington, a beautiful passenger ship he would like to sell."

"Is that the one you've told me about?" Naomi asked.

"The very one," he said.

"Is it a big ship," Isabelle asked.

"There's lots bigger out there, but this is no small thing. Thompson built his business on catering to the rich folk, it is pure luxury, and he wants a hefty price for it."

"So what happened?" Naomi asked.

"We got to talking and I sensed he wanted out a bit more than before, so I took'em along a little, see whether he might want to deal. I thought he did so I asked right out, did he want to sell me the business on agreement? You know, he would hold the paper a few years while I made the money to pay him off."

"You said that to him Zachary?" Isabelle asked as her excitement grew over this story.

"I sure did," he said. Took'em by surprise too, I know he didn't expect such an offer from me, being as young as I am, but I think he liked it, and I could see he was thinking. Then he assured me

174

he would think on it seriously. I'm to meet with him again come March. That tells me he's maybe got a timetable for what he wants to do, and that could be good too. Could be too, he wants to talk to my father first. I can understand it if he does."

"Naomi," Misty said lightly, "Queen of the Laurington. It sounds exciting to me."

"To us all Misty," Mr. Tanner said. "Zachary has the right idea. If y'all want something y'all gotta go and get it."

"Well, I hope you get it Zachary," Isabelle said. "Is it any different from commanding a cargo ship?" Misty asked.

"I can answer that," Naomi said with a smile of confidence. "The weight is different Misty, and add to that the size and that causes it to behave differently under varying situations." She turned to her husband and said coyly, "Anything y'all want to add to that dear?"

"No," he said laughing, "you've done quite well."

The next few days were important to all of them. Life was moving at a faster pace now. Time was separating them from each other and putting greater distance between them. These few days together were both relaxing and reassuring. On the final evening Mr. Tanner took his wife, the Franklins and the Johnsons out for dinner and a show. The two girls spent the evening home playing cards and talking. Most of the time for the past week they had been in the company of others and the conversation was generally about New York or Orleans, and the activities of the moment. This evening offered them what they both wanted, a chance to really talk to each other.

"The other morning at the hotel during breakfast your reaction puzzled me," Isabelle said. "When I said that you and I might be able to go to New York next year alone, and stay with Edward and Susan, I thought you would be excited. But it was a forced smile at best."

"I'd love to go, Iz, you know I would," Misty responded. "I don't know though if Susan would have it that way."

"Susan," Isabelle laughed, "will be dying for some family company in a year, and she always treated you the best when no one else was around. But I don't think that is all there is to it, I just can't believe you would let Susan stand in the way of you and I being on a holiday alone in New York."

"I guess I was just not ready for it when you said it. I couldn't think of anything I'd like to do more." The response Misty gave

175

sounded only half convincing. Isabelle knew her too well, but the conversation was left there when Misty added no more to it.

"Do you feel any different about staying now?" Isabelle asked.

"I do," she replied.

"You excited or just resigning yourself to it?" asked Isabelle as she dealt out the cards.

"I'm not as apprehensive as I was before leaving. I'm really looking forward to helping Gloria with the house, I'd like to do other things too, maybe work for some money."

"What might you do?" Isabelle asked.

"I don't know, there are so many things to do in the city. I'm going to get to know the place first and see what develops," Misty said.

"Poppa is going to leave y'all with money I heard him and mother talking about it," said Isabelle.

Misty laughed and replied, "After Poppa pays the bill Naomi and I made he might not want to leave anymore."

The girls were still up talking when the others got in. They sat about together for a while before going off to bed. Early the next morning Isabelle and Misty were downstairs in the kitchen making breakfast. They called in Henry and James to feed them first. George had not returned since the day past. He knew they were leaving this morning so it appeared he had run off. Isabelle suggested they not say anything till after her father had breakfast. The girls, having already eaten, set the table for the others and called them down. It's a special treat for the Franklins to have this southern style feast, flapjacks, grits, sausage and eggs. "I hope I can expect this once a week," Mr. Franklin says warmly to Misty.

"Every day if you like;" she responds, "I love cooking breakfast."

Mrs. Tanner ate lightly, then excused herself from the others. Walking over to Misty she touched her arm and said, "Sweetheart, let's you and I go talk for a few minutes while the others finish." They went into the parlor and sat in chairs they had turned to face each other. "Misty," Mrs. Tanner asked, "I want you to answer me honestly, would you like to leave with us this morning and go home?"

Misty's first reaction was a smile, then her eyes teared and she leaned forward and hugged her. "Oh mother," she said, "your timing as it usually is, is perfect. I really have to stay, but your asking me, that removes what might have been a stumbling block for me."

"Explain it to me dear," Mrs. Tanner said.

"I'm not sure I can," she said. "For the past couple of years people have been telling me how grown up I've become and I just accepted that I was. I guess it just seemed agreeable. Does that make sense to you?" Mrs. Tanner raised her eyebrows and shook her head reassuringly. "Inside of me," she continued, "it's hard to explain, like things are turning around and upside down. There's new understandings about things that I long thought I knew, and questions, so many questions that I want answers to, and there's Ros. I love him every minute of the day, with every breath I take, and I'm scared about the future and the many problems this could create."

"Misty," said Mrs. Tanner, "don't worry about the future to the point of interfering with the present. If we do that we don't do our best for either. It's like Hubert's saying you first have to make good tools, then you can build what ever you want the way you want it. I was very unsure about myself and leaving you here right up until this moment. Now I feel my prayers have been heard favorably. That this is the right thing, and that stumbling block, that's what would have happened if you stayed here just because I wanted you to. The time would have been wasted with you just waiting to come home. But now Misty I'm excited. You're like a cocoon slowly opening for the emergence of a magnificent butterfly."

Misty interrupted her with a smile "metamorphosis, mother, I like that."

But Mrs. Tanner looked at her seriously and said, "You are such, my dear. You have the right tools, and now an opportunity to work with them. Change the things that can be changed, accept the things that can't." Mrs. Tanner placed her hand on the side of Misty's face. "A few years back we thought of doing this so you could escape the stigma of being quadroon. Then as I watched Ros falling in love with you, I thought maybe the separation would send you two in different directions." Sitting back Mrs. Tanner smiled to Misty and added, "Foolish me, trying to make the future, you'd think I'd know better after all these years."

"I wouldn't have brought it up now Mother, but since you did, I've really thought about this a lot. At first I felt guilty that I didn't talk with you about my feelings."

Mrs. Tanner interrupted. "Sweetheart you don't have to explain anything. I never for a moment thought you did anything wrong."

"What are your thoughts, now that you've had time to think about it?"

"Well I've talked to Hubert about it," she started to say.

"Last night?" Misty asked excitedly.

"Oh no dear," said Mrs. Tanner, "while we were in New York. He actually brought the subject up."

"He never let on to me," Misty said.

"If he was going to be upset with anyone it would be Ros honey, not you," said Mrs. Tanner.

"Is he upset?" she asked.

"Concerned," Mrs. Tanner said, "concerned very much about you, dear."

"I hope he knows how much I love him, mother. I hope you both know. If you wanted me to go away, I mean really go away and not come back, I would. I could never stop loving Ros, but I couldn't place what I want above what you want," Misty said as she looked intently into Mrs. Tanner's eyes.

"That's not going to happen Misty," Mrs. Tanner said sitting forward with a reassuring smile. "Hugh wants to talk to Ros first, then perhaps both of you together. I'm taking his suggestion and you should too dear. We'll just let time run awhile, let Ros finish school and then all of us together, if you like, we'll work out what's best."

"I thought he would be so displeased. Sorry he ever allowed you to raise me," said Misty.

"Sometimes it appears that he's consumed with his work making it look as though it's so important to him, but nothing ever comes before his family, and he's a very strong-willed man. He has many times said, create solutions, and make your own paths in life, and don't waste too much time with other people's opinions. If you two let him help you, everything will work out for the good of all," Mrs. Tanner said.

"That takes a heavy weight off of me," said Misty.

"Hugh said something to me on our way down here. When you were just a small child you spent half your time, probably more, with us in the main house, but the time you spent with Willy Mae was at Hugh's urging. He said it was going to be hard enough for you because you looked white, but by the time you were ten or so you crossed between houses like there were no differences. By then though you had won his heart and he was telling me you

178

should have your own room here, but then I wasn't so certain anymore what was best. So he reminded me on the boat ride down here that it was he who said let the child go as she is and whatever comes of it we'll deal with. I'm sure you agree, Misty, this is an unusual situation," said Mrs. Tanner with a smile.

"I agree wholeheartedly with that," replied Misty.

Isabelle poked her head into the room and asked if she could come in. "Everyone is holding private conferences," she said.

"What are the others doing?" asked Mrs. Tanner.

"Poppa is in Scott's office with Zachary, and Gloria and Naomi are outside talking on the patio."

"I've told Iz about what Ros and I did," Misty said to Mrs. Tanner.

"I see it as a small family wedding," Isabelle said laughing, "under the trellis in the rose garden. A June wedding would be nice don't you think, mother?"

"I hope the sheriff gives us adjoining cells," said Misty as they all laughed.

A few moments later Henry came to the doorway to tell Mrs. Tanner the wagons were packed. "Is there anything we can do for you?" Mrs. Tanner asked Misty.

"Look after my little Sarah and don't let her forget me," she answered.

"I will, and she won't," said Isabelle. "There is one other thing. If you would, sometime, Mother, put down on paper my mother Lydia's life, from the time you first saw her in the wagon till she died."

"I'd be happy to dear. I'll do it soon and send it to you," she replied. "She's going to the auction house where Lydia was sold," said Isabelle.

"I'm sure I would want to do the same," said Mrs. Tanner. "I'm already longing for the day we'll be together again, there's going to be so much to talk about."

"I hope it comes soon," said Misty.

Mr. Tanner looked in and said they would be leaving in a couple of minutes. He then asked Misty to wait there for him. Returning to Scott's office they signed the document that had been prepared and handed it over to Zachary to take to his father. They shook hands and departed from the room.

Mr. Tanner went to the family room and asked to see Misty alone for a moment. Taking her by the hand they embraced. "I'm sure I can't give you any words of wisdom beyond what Emily already has," he said, "but I do know that Scott and Gloria are very excited about having you with them. It's going to be good for them, as well as you."

"You never said anything about what you were told, all week," Misty said.

Without changing his expression he said, "I'm sorry dear, congratulations."

Misty looked at him with a shocked look on her face, and then they both laughed. "Point well taken, poppa;" she said.

"Let's not be too concerned with things before we need to be, there's always plenty of time for that," he said in his usual reassuring manner. They embraced once more and spoke of their love for each other before joining the others.

So quickly it seemed they were in their wagons pulling away. Misty stood on the walkway waving good-bye with the others. Mrs. Franklin looked at her and saw her eyes welling up with tears. She put her arm around her shoulders and pulled her close. At this Naomi said to her, "What do we do Misty when things are overwhelming?"

"Get busy," Misty said. The wagon rounded the corner and out of their view. They all went inside and Mrs. Franklin suggested they do some shopping for material to make the many curtains needed for the new house.

Zachary, still excited about what had taken place in the office, wanted his wife to sit still a moment so he could share it with her. "You might as well listen to this, Gloria," said Mr. Franklin, "it involves you also.

"Your father," said Zachary, "has entered into the shipping business. If my father agrees with your father's proposal, and I believe he will, the four of us will buy ourselves a luxury liner."

"Scott are you the fourth person in this party by any chance?" asked Mrs. Franklin.

"Yes we are Gloria," he replied, "it was an offer I wouldn't refuse."

"Is this the boat you were looking at Zachary?" asked Misty.

"The Laurington, Misty," he answered. "A beautiful ship it is."

"Well tell us what happened," Naomi said.

"Yes, I'd like to hear what happened," said Mrs. Franklin. "It's not often we buy a passenger ship."

"Your father proposed that he, Scott, and my father each buy a share. I'll run the operation and we'll split the profit four ways," Zachary said.

"Oh my," said Naomi, "that's a wonderful idea."

Mrs. Franklin looked intently at her husband, not wanting to ask the question in the presence of the others, but hoping he would be able to read the meaning of her look. "You want to know how we can afford to do this," Mr. Franklin said to his wife.

"The thought crossed my mind."

"Hubert," he said, "is putting up two thirds of my share. He'll take my end of the profit for a few years. We figure by the end of five years we should all be making money."

"Think of the traveling we can do together," said Naomi.

"I still can't get over it," said Zachary. "I was ready to work years to save the money needed to buy such a ship."

"Did you propose it to him?" Naomi asked.

"No," he replied. "He said he wanted to talk to me privately before leaving."

"Did you know about this, Scott?" his wife asked.

"We talked some yesterday about it," he said. "We will have to leave tomorrow, Naomi. I want to be there when my father gets back. Within a fortnight I'm sure," said Zachary.

"Are you sure the owner is ready to sell?" asked Mrs. Franklin. "He's ready, and when he learns the money's coming up front I think he'll agree to the transaction quickly."

"Well," said Mrs. Franklin, "Hubert Tanner is not one to make a bad investment. I think we are all in for an enjoyable experience."

"Like I said to Zachary," said Mr. Franklin, "Hubert invested in that steel milling operation nearly seventeen years ago. Some people said he was crazy, was gonna lose everything. Now he owns three mills in two states and makes twice the money off of them than he does in cotton. I'm sure he is doing this one for Zachary and Naomi though."

As the conversation continued, Misty's thoughts drifted off. When the wagons rounded the corner a short while ago it was not the same as seeing them leave for New York. They were going home to stay and the thought of months passing by before she would see home again seemed like an eternity. She got up and poured herself a glass of ginger spice and went out to sit on the patio. Naomi would be leaving tomorrow she thought and she would be here

181

with strangers in a far away land cut off from everyone and everything she knew and loved. Sitting there her mind started racing. What am I expected to learn while I'm here? What if I don't do it right? What if it just doesn't work? What if the Franklins turn out to be like those at Leesway? What if Ros comes home and no one tells me or sends for me? Then, realizing what she was doing, she said to herself, "What if an earthquake opens the ground right next to me and I fall off this chair and down in the hole? Okay girl, you can either think yourself crazy or get up and do something." She went back inside and encouraged the others to ready themselves, suggesting they might go to the shopping district to purchase their supplies.

That evening after everyone retired Misty wrote the final portion of her letter to Roscoe. Naomi would take it in the morning and send it with one of the cargo ships headed for England.

* * * * *

A letter from Misty is what he needs. It's been months since he has seen her face or heard her voice. The excitement of being in England is wearing off now. Not one to waste time, he is applying himself to his studies. Most of it though comes easily and this just gives him more time to dwell on the things he misses.

He all but made up his mind to leave at the half point of the semester, but with some encouragement from his friends he decided instead to write to his father and ask him to come to England in the summer and to bring Misty and the family that they might all be together and tour the country. He also tells him of his plans to legally marry Misty, adding that if necessary they'll make a home in England. Added to the letter is a report on his recent visit to Lancashire. A full ninety percent of England's cotton mills are in this textile district and most all of the Tanner's exported cotton goes there. His report concludes with the statement that the possibilities of establishing a mill are most encouraging, added incentive he hopes, to bring his father sooner.

Early the next morning they said good-bye to Zachary and Naomi. Mr. Franklin had a busy day ahead of him and he too was quickly gone. Mrs. Franklin worked two mornings each week tutoring the children of French descent. She invited Misty to come along and meet the students but she declined. This day she would go to the auction house. Although she still wasn't sure why or what to expect when she got there, she just knew she had to do it.

The morning was chilly and overcast. Mrs. Franklin tried to persuade her to postpone this until later in the week when they could go together, but Misty was determined to do it today. So putting on a shawl and a hat she set out for her destination. The walk would take nearly an hour.

The auction house sat near the river on the outskirts of town. Not far into her journey a couple picked her up and drove her most of the way in their cariole. The short distance left that she had to walk felt like a hundred miles. She thought about that day in Mr. Moninghoff's store. The look in his eyes, his tone of voice. She thought about Leesway and the way people were made to live there. Each new thing she learned about slavery opened her mind a little wider. I hope George makes it all the way to Canada and freedom, she thought.

It was beginning to rain now. She pulled her shawl over her head and walked more quickly. Suddenly she was there. She knew immediately this was the place. Walking up close to the building she stood still and looked the place over carefully. How utterly ironic she thought, that it should rain this morning. The building was bigger than she had imagined it, but it was so quiet it was almost eerie. She walked up onto the large wooden platform and turned to look out at where the people would be. At first she felt numb. Her mother couldn't have been more than fourteen or fifteen years old, ill and pregnant, frightened beyond words and all alone in the world. From Mrs. Tanner's description, Misty long ago formed a picture in her mind of what her mother looked like. She now envisioned that face standing in a crowd of faceless people about to be sold like a horse or a carriage. Heavy bracelets on her ankles with a chain between them making each step loud and diffi-cult. The deafening sound of the crowd as they threw their arms out and yelled their bids. The sound of the auctioneer's mallet slamming down on the podium finalizing each sale. The chains jangling together and dragging across the wooden platform. The heartrending cries of mothers and children being torn apart. Did she know she was pregnant? Was she pleading in silence for some-one to save her? She was just a child, Misty said to herself. She was just a pitiful frightened child.

The vision so overwhelmed her she dropped down on her knees and covered her face with her hands and wept uncontrolla-bly. In her mind she took her mother, the young girl they called

Lydia, and held her to her bosom and mothered her and loved her until all around was silent.

The rain was coming steadily now and soaked her hair and clothing through. She stood up and backed against the wall under an overhang. She wanted to pray, but didn't, reasoning that God must loathe such places as this. She didn't want to call his attention to it here. But before the day was over she knew she had to talk to him.

Suddenly a door near her opened and an elderly man came out. It startled her and she stiffened her back against the wall. When the man caught sight of her he said, "My Lord child, are you all right?" Pushing the door open and motioning to her he said, "Come inside I'll make you a fire. You're gonna catch your death of cold out here. Did you lose your way?" Fearful of the man and the place she shook her head no and bolted off. Not looking back, she ran until she was far away. Then she walked the remainder of the way home in the rain.

For the next several days Misty was quiet and seemed tired and listless. The three would spend time together talking and playing cards in the evenings. After a week went by she was noticeably stronger and more willing to venture out. Soon she was back to herself, rising early in the morning and walking through the area with the dog that wouldn't go away. It's time she thought, to start taking advantage of the situation she's been placed in. She had earned money doing paperwork for Mr. Franklin and was going to the book store frequently purchasing magazines and stationery. Having previously inquired about employment, she was hired to work on Saturdays for which she would receive one dollar and fifty cents. Several days after that Mrs. Franklin secured her a job tutoring the children of a client, a plantation owner just outside of the city.

As January was coming to a close Misty was well settled into her new life and the city. Her two jobs and the work she did for Mr. Franklin earned her a fair sum of money. Her outgoing personality and charm made her well known and liked throughout the locality. February passed by quickly and by mid March trees were budding and early spring flowers were coming through. Most of the work inside the house was complete, the rest would have to wait. Mrs. Franklin and Misty were too anxious to work outside to wait any longer. Both a vegetable garden and a herb garden were planned, and flowers shrubs and trees had to be planted. Each afternoon when they returned to the house, they quickly changed and headed out back. On Friday the entire day was spent there.

The weather was perfect and Mr. Franklin told them during lunch that they needn't prepare dinner tonight. That meant dinner would be at his favorite restaurant, a place Misty enjoyed tremendously. The city had its own style of preparing food, some say unlike anywhere else in the world, but even more than the food Misty enjoyed the music. It had a life of its own, and the musicians play as if it's the most natural thing they do. During the course of the evening the band invited any in the room to join them. Some play along, others sing. On her last evening there the Franklins persuaded her to sing. She went up to the stage nervous but did as she was told to do the day of Naomi's wedding. Concentrate and feel the music she told herself. The band enjoyed it so much they called her back later for another song. She enjoyed it so much she has been eager to go back ever since.

The girls worked in the yard until nearly five o'clock before coming in to change. Misty wore an outfit she had made that week, using her own money to buy the material. She was thinking only of how much she liked buying and making it, but when the others saw her they had a different thought. Mrs. Franklin laughed as she said, "You went upstairs a dirty-faced girl. You've come down a stunningly beautiful woman. I couldn't make that change if I had all week."

"It's not too dressy for dinner is it?" she asked.

"No it's not," Mrs. Franklin replied, "and if you should sing with the band, it's not too dressy for that either."

"Is Scott ready?" Misty asked. "He brought a pitcher of bourbon and soda water out on the patio, he's waiting for us there," Mrs. Franklin answered as they left the room.

Sitting in a large wooden chair admiring the girl's work Mr. Franklin said, "This is beginning to look like paradise. I'm anxious to see things in full bloom."

"It won't really show till next year. A lot of the new plantings won't bloom the first year," replied Mrs. Franklin.

"Doesn't Gloria look lovely Scott," Misty said.

"Simply beautiful," he answered.

"And speaking of things blooming," said Mrs. Franklin, "hasn't Misty become quite the young lady?"

185

"Indeed she has," said Mr. Franklin. "Many are the inquiries concerning her when I'm out doing business. The gentlemen will be calling before long, that much I'm sure of."

"Mrs. Avery from the book store says business has noticeably increased since Misty began working there," Mrs. Franklin added.

"Oh I don't believe that," Misty said, "she seems prone to exaggerations."

"I don't know Misty," said Mr. Franklin with a smile. "I don't think I've ever seen so many young men carrying books about with them before." At first she considered what he was saying, then realized he was poking fun at her, and they all laughed awhile over it.

Later that evening at the restaurant after they enjoyed a meal they moved to a table closer to the band. The Franklins liked to dance and would do so often throughout the evening. While Misty sat alone listening to the band a girl came and sat down alongside of her. Having seen the girl before and having heard her sing she knew her to be the owner's daughter.

"Hello," the girl said, "my name is Genaset."

"I'm Misty Tanner," she replied, "I'm pleased to make your acquaintance."

"You're from Georgia," she said.

"Yes," Misty responded, "how did you know that?"

"Everyone around here wants to know everything about everybody and they ask questions."

"You sing beautifully in French, but you haven't much of an accent," Misty said.

"I've lived here since I was fourteen. I learned to speak English even before coming here, but songs sung in French are so much nicer I think."

"Well I can't understand what's being said, but it does seem much more romantic. This is one of my favorite places," Misty added.

"That's nice of you to say. Come on, I'll show you the rest of the place and we can get better acquainted."

When they returned, Misty introduced Genaset to the Franklins and told them she now had another job, working in the kitchen and waiting on customers Friday and Saturday evenings. Seeing her father, she motioned for him to come over. He joined the four of them for a drink and conversed for awhile. The musicians were returning now from their break. Maurice, Genaset's father, called

186

out to the piano player to come over. He was an older Negro fellow, blind, and was helped by another of the musicians.

"Calvin, I'd like you to meet our new friends." Genaset rose up and kissed him on the cheek. "Calvin is the best piano player in the world," she said.

"That's my girl," he responded with a deep loud laugh.

Genaset's father introduced the Franklins and then said as he introduced Misty, "This young lady sang most beautifully a fortnight back. Misty Tanner from Georgia, you were in Georgia weren't ya Calvin?"

"Yes sir I was, don't got no plans to goin back either,"
he said as he laughed again. "I wonder now Miss Tanner," he said, "if'in we don't be knowin some of the same old songs. We'll have to see won't we."

"Yes let's do that," said Misty. "That would be fun."

Throughout the rest of the evening Misty and Genaset sang several songs with the band. The Franklins danced and mingled with others until two o'clock in the morning when there was just a handful of people left. Most of the musicians had gone. Calvin and Misty sat at the piano playing and singing bits and pieces of songs they knew from back home. As Mrs. Franklin came to get Misty, Genaset called from the kitchen doorway reaffirming their plans for the following afternoon.

So many things happened over the next couple of months. Misty developed a bond with Genaset and her friends that helped fill the void she felt from being so long away from her family. Much of her free time was spent between working the grounds with Mrs. Franklin and going places with her new friends. But, free time, she had little of. Both the Saturday afternoon job at the book store and tutoring were given up. She was now working several days a week as Mr. Franklin's secretary, writing letters, filing documents and doing research through law books both at his office and the courthouse library. Mr. Franklin was defending a man charged with taking the life of another man in a business deal that went sour. Misty accompanied him to the trial each day to take notes that he studied that evening. Friday and Saturday evening she worked at the restaurant. Having grown up in a house where everyone was taught to work in the kitchen she learned to cook that combination of French, Orleans style that has become so popular in this part of the city.

Her friendship with the piano player Calvin has become important to her. When she has the time she visits him at his flat overlooking the river in the area of the docks. As she cleans and shines his little apartment, they talk at length about slavery and life in the south. Calvin is the only one who knows who she really is. He has become an oasis to her, and she has become like a daughter to him.

Through her work with Mr. Franklin she has been introduced to many of the city's more prominent citizens. One who befriended her is the assistant editor of the city's newspaper. Twice he has printed short poems she has written and requested more. A measure of time is also spent trying to learn the French language. While all of Genaset's friends are bilingual they most often speak in their own language. Both Mrs. Franklin and Calvin have picked up some, and so she frequently enlists their help.

A recent package from home brings with it news that is both good and disappointing. The good news is that she will be reunited with Isabelle and Rebecca, but not back home in Georgia. They are coming to New Orleans to stay for the month of June, then if Isabelle still hasn't convinced her father to let them go to New York the three will return home together. Misty hopes it will turn out that way. No matter how well things have worked out for her, she still wants more than anything else to be home. Along with the various letters from the family is a letter from Wendall. Misty is delighted to hear that he and Isabelle have become such good friends. Even Roscoe in his letters asks about him. Unfortunately he will be gone before she gets back home. Drawings from the child Sarah that she places in her photo album and assorted bits of news about people and events on the plantation will help to sustain her a little while longer.

The ugly dog that wouldn't go away has a name and a permanent home. Two cats and a half dozen caged birds add a pleasant touch to the big house that she affectionately calls her second home. Not all things are well for everyone though. Genaset was to journey with Misty and the Franklins on a business trip up the river to a Mississippi town called Natchez, but her father who had taken ill with a fever over the weekend is not doing well and she is needed at the restaurant. Another area of concern for Misty is caused by the attention she receives from several young men. Careful never to give any reason to think she may be interested, their persistence is constant and a source of trouble to her. Nice people from good families, she wonders just how quickly they would depart if they knew who she really was.

On this beautiful afternoon in May, Misty and Gloria are sitting in rocking chairs on the upper deck of a magnificent steamboat puffing and churning its way up the Mississippi. As they pass by another port Gloria remarks, "In all my life I've never seen so much cotton. Every port is as filled as the last one. Cotton bales five foot thick stacked on top of each other in row after row. We must be clothing the whole world," she mused.

Plantations along the river were plentiful, and most catered to cotton. Some farmed Indigo, some rice, some tobacco, but for the big money, cotton was the order of the day. It was what enabled the land owners to construct their glorious mansions.

The boat docked in the late afternoon. The Franklins and Misty remained on board for the night. The next morning they disembarked and ordered a cariole. The city of Natchez was built on a high bluff above the Mississippi. The ride would take an hour. But it could have lasted all day as far as the girls were concerned. The scenery was breathtaking, and at the top, more of the same. Houses could be seen in the distance, as big and beautiful as any in New Orleans or Georgia, and those working about them were everywhere.

Mr. Franklin's business was with a wealthy landowner who sold property in Orleans. The girls wandered about outside while he concluded his matters within. Sitting on a fence rail admiring the horses, their conversation kept going back to the topic on everyone's mind—the growing friction between north and south. This has been a very troubling subject for Misty Tanner. "All of those people working on the docks and in the fields, Gloria. There's so many of them. When I was a child I use to think that Mariah was such a big part of the world, and that most of the Negroes lived there, but that's so far from reality. What do the northerners think will become of this many people?"

"It would be so much better for everyone if they would just mind their own business," Gloria responded.

"I think a lot about what Henry said," Misty responded, "Freedom is worth anything. He said it's like making a man whole. I think of George too. The Quakers probably helped him get to Canada. Maybe he's working and getting paid real money. I bet any one of all those field hands could do the same."

189

"I'm not so sure of that Misty," Gloria said. "Not many have lived as Henry has. I'm sure I've seen a lot more of things than you have, and I'd be fearful that the northerners would make things worse for them than they are now." The conversation went back and forth and then to more light-hearted interests. Gloria well understood Misty's concern, and felt deeply for her.

By mid-afternoon they had secured lodging for the night. Mr. Franklin's business associate had invited them back for a concert that evening in his home.

The evening was very enjoyable. Misty mingled with many of the young adults after dinner, sometimes listening to the music, other times participating in conversation, but her mind wasn't fully there. She wondered why it should trouble her so much, being able to walk freely, being accepted by the rich upper class people of the south. It would be nice she thought, to have some time to think about all this. Perhaps the ride back down the river would offer some solitude. Regardless, things were going to be changing real soon. The month of June will bring Isabelle and Rebecca to New Orleans, and nothing could be better than that.

The next morning they boarded a boat being loaded with cotton. These large steamboats could carry hundreds of tons of cotton on its lower decks, but Misty would learn soon into the journey cotton wasn't the only commodity being shipped. While dining that evening she could hear clearly the conversation from a nearby table. Two handsomely dressed gentlemen were discussing the cargo. Though this kind of discussion was something she had heard before, it felt different. The particular cargo they spoke of was human cargo, slaves.

Trying to ignore the conversation and join in the one at her own table was not proving to be an easy task. "I don't like what I hear either," Mr. Franklin said to her, "but you have to sort of get used to it. They have their ways like we have ours."

"It's awful to think that just beneath this beautiful deck there are people chained to the wall, scared and hungry," Misty replied.

"Those men over there Misty," said Mrs. Franklin, "they couldn't change your mind could they?"

"No indeed," she answered.

"They feel just as strongly about their way of doing things and I dare say we won't change their thinking either."

After dinner the three sat out on the deck taking in a gentle warm breeze. Misty watched several porters bring trays back from those who dined in their rooms. Each tray held uneaten food. She excused herself after another went by and followed him down the walkway. When they were out of everyone's sight she stopped him and asked what would become of all the table scraps. On learning they would be thrown over the side of the boat she accompanied him into the kitchen quarters. There she began rummaging through and selecting as much edible food as she could find, she threw it all into a large pot. This she covered with a clean apron and took it with her.

As she walked up to the Franklins she couldn't keep the smile off of her face. "What are you up to girl?" Mr. Franklin said with a grin.

Not coming to a full stop she responded, "It's dinner time down below."

Once on the cargo deck Misty's smile quickly faded. It was her first real look at how the Negroes were transported. All were shackled at the ankles, the chain not long enough for anything more than very short steps. Even many of the older children were shackled and most of the men were also chained to a railing. Pausing momentarily, she scanned the whole area; then began to do what she set out to do. One by one she greeted each person and handed him or her something to eat. Each response was similar. The gratitude on their faces and in their voices touched her heart deeply. It was the children though with their empty stomachs and eyes red from crying, grateful for a mere meager handout who moved her the most. Some of the youngest ones she held to her chest and rubbed their heads while talking gently to them. Difficult it was, to walk away.

They arrived home the following evening, made a light meal and talked a short while. Then the Franklins retired. Misty sat at the piano and began to put music to the poem she had written while riding on the Mississippi River. Almost everything she ever wrote reflected the way she felt, and it was almost always upbeat and positive. But over the past year new experiences and perhaps new awakenings have caused her to write at times in a different vein.

The next morning she awoke to the sounds of birds singing outside her window. A warm breeze was gently moving her curtains. Thinking that it felt later than usual she sprang up and hurried to get ready for the day. Once downstairs she looked from room to room but found no one. A note in the kitchen read, "Good morning dear, Please purchase eggs and flour. Have a wonderful day. Gloria." The first thing she wanted to do was go over to Genaset's house. Her father was probably well now she thought, and it was such a lovely day to go about.

On arriving there what Misty found was anything but what she had expected. Greeted at the door by a woman she had never seen before she was asked. "Are you aware of what has happened?"

"No, I've been away for several days," she responded.

"Maurice passed away yesterday," the woman said.

"Oh my God, no!"

"It was yellow fever. Came on him so quickly," the woman said. "If you're a close friend of Genaset's I'm sure it would be good for her to see you. Come in child I'll go get her," the woman continued.

It was late afternoon before Misty would leave her friend. She went home to give this bad news to the others, but they had already heard. Yellow fever is not at all uncommon in the city, but it had seemed to abate some the past few years.

The following day was the funeral where Misty got more bad news. "The restaurant is going to be sold," Genaset said sadly, "Mother wants to go back home to France."

"I feel so bad for you both," Misty said putting her arm around her, "I will miss you terribly if you do."

"I don't know for sure that she will do it," Genaset responded. "Maybe it would be best for her." Misty stayed the night with them, making breakfast and fixing things up before going home.

Isabelle and Rebecca would be arriving any day. Misty busied herself getting ready for them and looking after Genaset as best she could. It was midweek now and Misty was determined to get Genaset out of the house awhile. With a large chicken pie, she took her friend to Calvin's apartment. He too had lost a friend. Life was made easier by Maurice's offer of steady employment, but for now he would put his sorrow and concerns aside. He was always able to make Genaset laugh, and even today would be no exception. For the next few hours after dinner the three sat about talking and singing and laughing until well past dark. On their walk home Genaset said she would look after Calvin while Isabelle and Rebecca were here. Misty saw that as a positive sign and went home feeling much better about her friend.

Another two days passed before they finally arrived. It was late afternoon on Friday when the back door opened leading to the patio where Misty was weeding a flower garden. Rebecca came out quietly and stood still for a moment. When she still wasn't noticed she started to sing a song the girls had often sung together. Misty's head shot around in an instant. Rising quickly to her feet, they went to each other and embraced. As the door opened again Misty expected to see Isabelle, but instead found Mrs. Tanner coming through the doorway calling out for the others to come out back. "Mother," Misty cried out as she went from Rebecca's embrace to the arms of Mrs. Tanner's. "Oh how good it is to see you!" Isabelle, who had gone upstairs looking for her, came out next. There were no dry eyes left as each one hugged her again. The final surprise for her was Mr. Tanner. "Hello sweetheart," he said pulling her into his embrace. "Where's Scott and Gloria?" he asked.

"I don't know, I'm sure they will be in soon," she answered. "Why didn't you tell me you two were coming? I just can't believe this?"

"By the time we knew we were coming, it was too late to write," Mr. Tanner said.

"Let's go inside and get something cool to drink. I've got a million questions. Is Henry with you?" she asked.

"No," Mrs. Tanner responded, "we didn't bring Henry. We're not going home directly."

This statement brought a look of disappointment that Misty couldn't hide. "I don't think I could bare parting from y'all again this soon," Misty sighed.

"Oh no Misty, you're going home!" Isabelle said with excitement, "by way of New York City!"

Mrs. Tanner looked at her expecting a joyful reaction but didn't see one.

"I'm sorry dear," she said, "we do know how badly you want to go home, we should have planned this out a little better."

"Not at all mother," she smiled, "I did expect it. I knew Isabelle would be working on Poppa all winter, and I would love to see New York."

The Franklins now entered the house. They didn't know either that Mr. and Mrs. Tanner would be accompanying the girls. The welcoming started all over again, after which, they all changed and went out for a fine dinner. The three girls sat at a separate table. It would take more than one evening to catch up on everything and the first thing they wanted to talk to Misty about was Roscoe. "It's been a month since his last letters," Misty said, "he is so homesick."

"Love sick," Isabelle laughed. "He sent Rebecca and me a gift with his last package and asked me to wrap this for you," she said as she placed on the table a small square package.

"What did he send you two?" Misty asked as she opened her gift.

"This ring," Isabelle said holding up her hand.

"He gave me a necklace. It's back at the house," Rebecca answered.

"This is beautiful," Misty said showing them her bracelet.

"They're scarab stones," Isabelle said.

"What a wonderful idea for a bracelet, it is beautiful," said Rebecca.

"Ros and Poppa have written each other concerning you. I'm not real sure what all has been said, but Mother keeps reassuring me that everything is gonna be good," Isabelle said with enthusiasm.

"I have to remain calm or I'll go crazy," Misty laughed. "You would think it would somehow get easier waiting for him to come home, but I go to bed every night and wake up every morning picturing his face, hearing his voice and longing all the more to be with him."

"It will be soon Misty," Isabelle told her. "Just to sit, all of us in the same room again will be a joy beyond comparison," said Rebecca.

After dinner they returned to the Franklins' and sat in the family room talking for another couple of hours. When they retired for the night the three girls shared Misty's room where they talked for another hour or so.

The plan as was related to Misty and the Franklins would have Mr. Tanner, and Mr. Franklin, if he could make time for it, leaving for the coast and meeting with his son-in-law. If all went as planned the transaction would take place giving them possession of the Laurington. Then off to New York for four to six weeks. This didn't sound quite so bad when she was told the three girls would have their own cottage to stay in. The only uncertainty was concerning Roscoe. Would he be coming home for awhile or would the family go to England to visit him, and if the family went was she going with them?

For now though it was enough to be with Isabelle and Rebecca again. The next morning they headed out early. Rebecca wanted to ride on the street car. Later in the afternoon Isabelle and Misty were sitting on a bench. Rebecca had walked off a distance and Isabelle asked, "Are you okay about going to New York?"

"I'm fine, why do you ask?" she responded.

"Before I left here, whenever we talked, or at least when I started talking about going, you seemed to act peculiar or something," Isabelle said looking concerned.

"I'd be lying if I didn't say I would much rather go home," Misty offered.

"Oh I know how much you want to go home, but I got the same feeling, when going to New York was talked about again," said Isabelle.

"Really, Iz," she responded, "I'm looking forward to the three of us having a holiday together, and what better place than New York City." Pausing for a moment then laughing she said, "Except England of course."

"Of course," laughed Isabelle.

Mr. Tanner was gone nearly a week. The girls were having a great time in the city, some of which was spent with Genaset. On one afternoon they had their pictures taken together. This was especially important now that Genaset's mother made a definite decision to sell the restaurant and return to France. One evening while they all were gathered in the family room talking and singing and laughing, Misty read her poem, most of it written while riding down the Mississippi. She said the title, "The Gift that Is" and began reading it with feeling and conviction.

"A time I was an eagle
sitting cliff high,
the water I watched,
carried her gently by.
The sound of the water
moved by the wheel,
kept me from hearing
what the lowly feel.
The gift is not in my ears,
but in my eyes,
I've let my gift fail me,
but I am sorry.

An owl I was,
perched nearby,
The waters I watched,

195

carried her gently by.
The sight of the water,
moved by the wheel,
keep me from seeing,
where the lowly kneel.
My gift is not in my eyes,
but in my ears.
I've let my gift fail me,
but I am sorry.

I was a man, I ruled,
starboard to port side,
I divided the waters
by and by.
The powerful wheel,
the strength of my hand,
on the backs of the lowly,
I've taken my stand.
I hear no cries,
I see no tears,
no deathly pangs,
do I fear.
I scoff at the gift.
Sorry? Not I.

Oh the gift I was, I am.
The waters I rode,
I laid out my heart,
I spread out my hand,
Decried the injustice
that enveloped the sad.
The offer was made,
clearly refused.
This great gift that is,
so seldom used.
A Negress Woman I Am!
And sorry for you.

The mood in the room was clearly changed. Isabelle broke the silence. "Tell us Misty."

"Tell you what?" she asked smiling.

"The ride down the river," said Mrs. Tanner, "Help us all to see what you see."

"My mind races off in so many different directions I don't know if I can make sense of it all that easily," she said.

"Your poem is very moving," said Rebecca.

"I think it expresses your feelings very well," added Mrs. Franklin.

"I'll tell y'all something interesting," said Mr. Franklin. "You gave the poem to Roger, right?"

"They won't print that one will they?" Misty laughed.

"Yes, they are going to print it," he said. "Mr. Derby, the editor, first wanted me to agree to it. This is going to be controversial."

"When I gave it to Roger he said Mr. Derby might not like it," Misty responded.

"What did he say about it Scott?" his wife asked. "Well, I've done some work for him. He was concerned that a bad reaction might hurt my business opportunities."

Mrs. Franklin and Misty both spoke at the same time. "I wouldn't think so," said Mrs. Franklin,

"I never thought that could happen," said Misty.

"Even if I thought it could, I would have still told Derby to print it. You're far from alone Misty in feeling the way you do," said Mr. Franklin.

"If it's true that controversy can sell papers, this should sell a few extra copies," said Mrs. Franklin.

"The other poems they printed were no less honest. They were of a light-hearted nature," said Mr. Franklin. "This is going to hit some hard. Besides Misty was accepted by everyone who met her. Some are going to feel they were intentionally deceived."

"Of course that's not the case," said Mrs. Franklin, "but I'm sure some aren't going to like it."

"Genaset thought the whole matter was quite amusing," said Isabelle.

"She's been such a good friend," said Misty. "I feel badly for her. I know I'm going to miss her greatly."

"I think we all understand what you're saying with this poem. Did the time spent on the boat have a big impact on you?" asked Mrs. Tanner.

"This is of course a rhetorical question, but does anybody want to feel like a slave does? Everyone would honestly answer no, but the feelings I have within me cause me to question things, and I haven't the answers yet," she responded.

"What made you feel different on the boat than at other times?" Rebecca asked.

"I realized I've never known how they feel, and that what I thought was true is really quite far from the truth," she answered.

"Like you can feel for them but not with them," suggested Rebecca.

"I guess," said Misty. "I think what's really sad is that I know they have known what I have known, but I could never feel what they do."

"I'm not sure I understand dear." Mrs. Tanner said to her.

"The greatest gift that anyone has ever given or received is of course . . . love . . . and I've had that in great abundance, more so than most. My mother Lydia, my mammy Goldie, Aunt Molly, Henry, my family, the Myers, Ros, the children back home, just an abundance. I really know the joy of it. I've seen the power of it. I can't imagine life without it, or being without the people who give it to me. Who would really feel differently than that? Yet it happens all the time to Negroes. Aboard the boat I talked to women whose hearts were broken by the selling of their children to other plantations, to men who were taken from their wives and children. One older man had it done to him twice." She broke down in tears covering her face with her hands. "All I could do was put my arms around him and tell him I was sorry."

Mrs. Tanner went to her and put her arms around her. Isabelle also hugged her tightly. Rebecca said as she wiped away tears, "God sent them an angel Misty, how you must have lifted their hearts."

"I wish I could have carried off their burdens; then maybe I would really be an angel," she answered.

"I know I've said it before, but you have been endowed with more perception and understanding than most. Just keep doing as you are, child. You'll bring the gift to a great many people," said Mr. Franklin with a fatherly smile. Soon the older ones retired for the night and the three girls played cards and talked for awhile before themselves bringing the day to its end.

Several more days passed by and Mr. Tanner returned. Everyone was anxious for the news. After they all gathered in the family room he told them of his trip. Zachary and Naomi were doing fine. Mr. Johnson was well, and the ship was theirs. "What else," he asked them, "would you like to know?"

"More about everything," said his wife.

"How does it feel to own a ship?" Mr. Tanner asked Mrs. Franklin.

"I guess it will seem more real when I see it," she mused.

"Not just see it, but sail in it," he said.

"When will that be dear?" Mrs. Tanner asked.

"We should know by the time we get back home. There's a possibility Naomi and Zachary will be waiting for us."

"Tell us more Father," Isabelle asked excitedly.

"The ship is at sea now. Zachary will take possession of it on its return. He'll take it to port where the cargo ships are maintained and have it refurbished while it is there. He'll advertise for a September departure to England. If everything is going well they would like to meet up with us at home in about six or eight weeks," Mr. Tanner responded.

"It would be so nice to go home and have them there," Misty said.

"But first it's off to New York," said Isabelle.

"Yes, what of our immediate plans Hugh?" asked Mrs. Tanner.

"I'd like to rest up tomorrow, talk a few things over with Scott, and we'll leave the following morning," he replied. Misty did her best to show enthusiasm for all of this, but that Roscoe's return wasn't mentioned in all of this troubled her. It would be an even bigger surprise if when they got home they found him there. She wanted to think it, but couldn't convince herself of it.

The following evening after dinner Misty presented the Franklins with an afghan she had crocheted for them. "I can never thank you enough for what you have done for me," Misty said.

"Misty this is always going to be your house and your bedroom," said Mrs. Franklin.

"And your dog," joked Mr. Franklin.

"But you can't take him with you," added Mrs. Franklin. "He's a part of the place now."

"I'm leaving with so many good things stored up in my heart - all the knowledge that you shared with me Scott, and all the time we worked together Gloria, on so many projects. It's been such a wonderful time," said Misty.

"Whatever the future holds for you it must always include reasonably long visits here," Mr. Franklin added.

"Oh the vicissitudes of life, isn't that what you say Scott?" Misty said as they both laughed.

"Vicissitudes are fine for young ones," Mr. Tanner interjected, "I would just like to stay home with my darling wife and enjoy the sun setting over the meadows."

"Soon," said Mrs. Tanner. "The sooner the better."

The next morning they said their good-byes and were on their way to New York City. Misty rode off with a heavy heart. Never had she imagined she would come to love the Franklins the way she did, nor did she ever think she would love any place other than Mariah, but New Orleans would always be a part of her now. Misty wasn't the only one to learn something new. The Franklins had come to love her as if she were part of their family, and in the weeks ahead they would defend her as such. The poem was printed, and controversial it was.

From the moment they stepped out of the train and into Grand Central Station, Rebecca and Misty were in awe. Never had they seen anything so massive. Nor had they ever seen so many people in one place. While Isabelle knew what they were in for, her only visit to the city had been in the wintertime. So many of the things they would experience would be new to her also.

First they would go to the house Mr. Tanner had purchased for Edward and Susan. This was not at all what the girls were expecting. As they were driven through the city streets they viewed many fine homes. Mr. Tanner commented that the brownstone houses were unique to New York City. On arriving at their destination it wasn't a house but an estate. A stone wall too high to see over surrounded the property. Entering through opened gates, a driveway with mature maple trees lined their way. The house was huge and made of stone. It was surrounded by spacious grounds and a small pond. Mr. Tanner pointed to a carriage house telling the girls that would be their home for the next four weeks or so.

Those weeks would go by quickly, but every minute was filled. For the three girls it was non-stop, sometimes with Mrs. Tanner and Susan, other times off on their own. They took in every show they could, visited every fabric shop they could find, went to the music shops and food markets and walked mile after mile. They made many jokes about how homesick Susan must be, but never was she nicer or more polite. As the weeks passed Isabelle noticed Misty would find reasons to avoid going to the main house. But when she was questioned she made light of it.

The time wasn't so enjoyable for Mr. Tanner. His days were long and what little they saw of him was enough to see things weren't what he had hoped they would be. One evening the girls slipped into the food pantry of the main house for something to snack on. They heard voices from another room arguing. It was apparent that Mr. Tanner and Edward were quite angry. The girls slipped back out unnoticed but talked at length about how badly they felt for Mr. Tanner. "I've seen some of the problems he's causing," said Isabelle of Edward. "Often times when I'm helping Poppa with paper work he gets such a troubled look about him. We all know if it wasn't for Susan and the children he would get Edward out of there quick. Poppa has a man he likes a real lot, he is the vice president of the company, but from what I've read and heard he spends most of his time running things and cleaning up Edward's careless mistakes."

"I wonder what it is that makes him like that? You would think with such good people around him and the opportunity he has been given he would want to do what is right," added Rebecca. "What do you think Misty?" she asked.

"I feel so bad for Susan. I know we all had the same feeling when they left, but it's apparent he is no different here than he was at home," she answered.

"I've got to say I never imagined your father's company was so big," said Rebecca.

"I don't think anyone imagined it would get so big," said Isabelle.

"Scott says the growth of it is extraordinary, but he also says Poppa is not like any other businessman he's ever met," responded Misty. "I miss them a lot already and I know I'll miss them more when I get home."

"I don't know Misty, there's gonna be so many people vying for your time," Isabelle said. Then looking at Rebecca she added, "And when Ros gets home, well that's a whole other story."

"Don't joke with me about it Iz," Misty countered. "That day just keeps getting moved back further."

"Yeah, but by continuing his studies straight through, he'll really be home for good a lot sooner," said Rebecca reassuringly.

"All he ever talks about is you," Isabelle said to Misty in a warm manner.

While the girls could easily distract themselves, Mr. Tanner could not. The company was fast becoming one of the largest steel producers in the country. His son-in-law was nothing more than a figure-head. What little he did was of no value. A board of directors oversaw all business transactions. Mr. Tanner uncharacteristically told his wife, "He's a drunk and a womanizer. He never did make any attempt at taking control of things. He just picked up where he left off in Georgia."

In spite of it all Edward will be left in his position for a time. He was given certain alternatives and had until spring to do what was required of him. Though at this point Mr. Tanner had little confidence it would matter.

Their day of departure arrived and Mr. Tanner now had another problem to solve—how would they ever travel with all that the girls had acquired? The season was in their favor, so rather than head south they went north, up through the green mountains of Vermont and into Canada. This was, as they all agreed, the most beautiful country they'd ever seen. They only stayed a few days, but it was long enough to visit some of the small towns along the train route. One event that meant a lot to Misty was meeting a Quaker family who participated in what was now known as the underground railroad, helping to bring runaway slaves to freedom. From there they traveled to the large lake above New York, down through the mountains, bypassing the city, and by train to Virginia. Another day and a half and they would be home. The closer they got the more Misty talked, the more her hands gestured, the more she got up and sat down. The girls had a great time making fun of her, but they too had been away a long time and were growing more impatient with each hour.

Finally, with the covered bridge in sight, she knew she was home. As their wagon pulled up in front of the house, the girls could sit still no longer. The wagon had barely stopped and they jumped off. People were coming from all different directions to greet them. Mr. Tanner sent for Lester, James, and others to unload the cargo. Misty hurried up the front porch steps. At the same time the door opened. "Henry!" she exclaimed loudly, throwing her arms around him. "Oh how much I missed you."

"My little girl," he said as tears filled his eyes. "I praise da good Lord you back at home. Jes everybody been missin you." Then stepping back to look at her he added, "Y'all done some growin too child. Look like a woman now ya do." Then he laughed and hugged her again. Isabelle kissed him on the cheek as he was still hugging Misty. "You can relax now Henry," she said smiling, "she's home." Soon Willy Mae and Lilly and a host of others were coming up on the porch. Men were unloading and young ones were carrying packages and a large group of people made there way into the house.

It didn't take long for everyone to head off in a different direction. Arrangements were made for someone to accompany Rebecca home and Isabelle went off to her room to unpack. Misty, after having a light dinner, was off to visit Leo and Goldie. First she would find the child Sarah, but not far into her journey she realized everything was different now. The warm greetings, the smiling faces didn't have the same meaning anymore. These weren't the happy people she had thought they were. She knew now that they were making the best of a sad and unhappy existence.

On finding Sarah she carefully looked her over too. This was a slave child, a pretty mulatto who would never have the opportunities that she did. Holding her hand and walking with her, Misty wanted so much to impart a warm and caring feeling, more so than ever in the past.

Later in the evening when they arrived at the hut Leo and Goldie lived in, Misty saw them too, as if for the first time. Their faces looked old, their hands were sore and cracked from long days of separating cotton. The only nice things they had were gifts from her from sometime ago. After sitting and talking awhile Goldie asked her, "Is someden a troublin ya child?" Then she added shrewdly, "Ya face has a smile, but cha eyes tellin someden wrong."

"Did you ever want to just leave here, go where you can be free?" Misty asked sincerely.

"Lor child, everyone wanta be free, but most runaway slaves dey kill, so ya thinks bout it den ya don't do it," she answered.

"I saw lots of free Negroes, Mammy. Some had lots of money too. Owned their houses, sent their children to school. Dressed in nice clothes."

"I's here tell deys Negro folk like dat, Lor I'd like to set dees here eyes of mine on such a thing just one time."

"So much of the talk these days Mammy is about the abolitionists. They're the folks up north who want to bring slavery to an end, set all people free," said Misty.

"Lor child what would become of us? We po Negroes know nutin but pickin cotton for Masser."

"The plantation owners would have to pay the worker just like up north. There would be no more whippings and youngins would go to school. I'm convinced it's the only right way," Misty said with conviction.

Leo, who had been taking it all in quickly said, "The white men of the south be strong and unruly. T'aint never listened to nobody before and t'aint gonna now. I's liked to be free like dem others ya see but I's know I t'aint gonna be free till I's see the Lord. I's see so many children die, even some of my own, and I thank the Lord just cause I knowd dey free," then with a smile he added, "I's just want to be with my sweet Goldie tills I die. Tis all I want just my sweet Goldie.

"I've seen other plantations now, and it's awful to think that families are sold apart. That's something Papa Tanner would never do, you know that don't you," Misty said reassuringly.

"Dey been good to us Misty," said Goldie for Misty's sake. "Best thing they ever do was saving y'all from being a slave. When I's go to be wit da Lor I tell em right quickly deys good people. I's know da love ya like ya Mammy doz."

"I love you both very, very much," Misty said as she hugged and kissed them both.

It was later in the evening before she returned to the main house. Her things were taken to Roscoe's room which she had already taken over before leaving. After putting Sarah to bed she joined the others in the family room. They were all so glad to be home and together in this room again. Zachary and Naomi had not yet arrived, but were anxiously being anticipated. Mr. and Mrs. Tanner made plans to ride into town and visit the Myers the next morning. Isabelle wanted Misty to go riding, and Sarah wanted her to go fishing. So with everyone's day planned they went off to sleep in their own rooms again, and there is nothing so good, as getting back into your own bed again.

The next day started a little later than normal with everyone but Sarah sleeping an extra couple of hours. The morning brought a steady rain, which in turn caused everything to move at a slower pace. It was nearly nine o'clock before they gathered at the kitchen table for breakfast. Mr. Tanner decided to work in his office for the morning and go to town later if the rain stopped. Mrs. Tanner wanted the girls to tend to their studies while being confined to the house. After everyone finished breakfast, Misty asked Mr. Tanner if she could talk with him in his study. Mrs. Tanner went off to check on the things that she takes charge of. Isabelle took Sarah with her to the library room and Mr. Tanner and Misty went to the study.

"Emily and I are quite proud of you young lady," Mr. Tanner said as he sat down at his desk. "There is something special about you, that's a fact. Scott and Gloria told us repeatedly how much they didn't want to see you go, and the way you took to the city, that was somewhat remarkable." The words made her feel warm and loved and that made her feel better about talking to him. Mr. Tanner never was too busy to talk to his children, and he could read them all fairly well.

"I came to love the Franklins like I'd been with them all my life. We had such wonderful times together, and I did love the city, more so than New York or any of the other places we visited. There's something different about New Orleans," Misty said.

"You've generally gone to Emily when something is on your mind. I'm happy you wanted to talk this morning with me, and I hope I can come up with the right answers for you," he said reassuringly.

"Well I really don't know where to begin, and I don't want to keep you from your work too long," she said.

"I'll never have enough time to do this paper work, so I don't let it concern me much," he replied.

"I want to say that I'm sorry for the problems you're having with Edward. We were in the pantry one night and overheard you arguing with him. We all feel bad about it," Misty said.

"You never did like him did you?"

"He's Susan's husband," she replied.

"Exactly how I feel," said Mr. Tanner "None of us realized how big the business up north was. Seeing it has helped me to understand why it is so important for Ros to get the education he needs." "With the things he's learning Misty, he'll have a lot easier time of it than I am. The technology of the next decade is going to demand being on top of things or being left behind," He said as he leaned forward and folded his hands as he always did when getting serious.

"There's a lot of talk about a war between the south and the north? Could that harm your business?" she asked.

He looked at her for several seconds before responding. "That's what's gonna make my son so successful. You're always going to be an asset to him and that's very important." Then looking at her with a warm smile he added, "One of the things we did while up there was to take precautions against that happening."

And then as though the words came out by themselves she said, "What about Ros and me, Poppa?" Immediately with a surprised look on her face she said, "Oh, I'm sorry, I shouldn't have asked that." He began to laugh, and she laughed with him.

"You have been remarkably patient," he said.

"Yes I have," she said as they continued to laugh.

205

After a few moments he sat back in his chair. "The boy has been givin me fits, Misty. Every letter has the same paragraph. Bring you to England so he can marry you there. But I still think it's better for him to finish school first. If there's a marriage before that he'll not get all he could from his time there."

"I know you're right, but I miss him more than I could ever say," she lamented.

"I'll know better what we're doing after I talk with Zachary. I'm sure everything will work out for the best. I've always found that what's right, works itself out," he said.

"There is one other thing, but I'm afraid of being presumptuous," she said.

"Speak your mind, child, if it's not for you to have, I'll tell you."

"When I was away I saw things differently. I mean, there were things that I always took for granted, but I've since learned differently."

"Slavery?" he said.

"Yes, I'm really confused," she said.

"Well, Sweetheart, I don't have an answer for you," was the reply that surprised her. He added, "I think it better that you continue to ponder it because the conclusion you arrive at is going to have a big impact on the adult you become. But I want to talk about this with you soon. I'm very interested in your viewpoint on this."

"This is a two part thought," she added, "I can't help but be concerned for my Mammy and Leo, they look so poorly to me now. I know it's not my place to ask, but I have too. Poppa couldn't they be used for domestic work. Maybe in the gardens, I could even teach Mammy to do housework."

"First let me suggest sweetheart, that you look carefully at all sides of this issue. With the owning of Negroes all my life, I've always accepted the practice, but, I've also always questioned it. It's a tough issue for a certainty, and I understand your feelings about your Mammy. For right now I can't do anything. There's too much work to do out there. But after the final harvest this year we'll take them out of there. God knows, girl, what we're gonna do with em," he laughed.

"Don't worry Poppa I'll see to them. All they know is hard work anyway," she said raising up with a happy smile on her face.

"Don't worry Poppa," he repeated to himself. "Whenever I'm told that I have to worry."

A few days later Zachary and Naomi arrived. Isabelle, Misty and Willie Mae were sitting on the veranda snapping the ends off a large basket of green beans. Henry came out and helped Zachary unload the baggage, then took the cariole to the barn. After they all greeted each other they went off in search of their parents. Within a short time the three girls persuaded their mother to go riding with them. Zachary stayed behind to wait for Mr. Tanner who was off somewhere in the fields. In late September some of the finest afternoon temperatures arrive, perfect for riding horseback or leisurely strolls through the gardens and trails. Zachary was soon joined by the old dog Digger and quickly lost all track of time as they meandered about along lush hay fields and tree lined fence rows.

It was dinner time before they came together in the same room. While dining, Zachary filled them in on all the various reports he picked up on his travels. Any news concerning England or the ever developing friction within the states was eagerly listened to. After a fine meal the girls went into the family room to talk and play music together. Mr. Tanner and Zachary went to the study to talk over their business arrangement. Later when they were all together the news was shared with everyone. The Laurington, now renamed the Anna Mariah after Mr. Tanner's grandmother and Zachary's great grandmother would make its maiden voyage at month's end, sailing to England. The news though got even better. The ship would make a return trip to England in late spring and come home in the early part of summer with Roscoe. All schooling completed, he would be coming home for good. As Misty listened to Mr. Tanner her heart filled with emotion. Just winter and spring she thought and they would finally be together again. The thought on Isabelle's mind was, when would they be passengers, and sail to England? Mr. Tanner was somewhat evasive on that, but with all the good news they had gotten, nobody thought much about it, nobody but his wife who would inquire more of it later. In the Tanner house good times always translated into good music, and the remainder of the evening was spent laughing and singing and enjoying each other's company.

After Zachary and Naomi left, Isabelle could not get the thought of sailing out of her mind. After again pressing her mother for more she was told privately of tentative plans for spring. Hearing this she was left with mixed feelings, as she was told her father had decided it would be best for Misty to remain at home. She knew this would be hard on her. Her father reasoned Roscoe marrying Misty in England was not a good idea. If it in any way jeopardized his inheriting the estate that would be reason enough to question the action. He also needed time to converse with friends whose influence could help determine the best way to challenge the law forbidding interracial marriage within the state. Also he had not had the opportunity to discuss the matter face to face with his son. However, until plans could be worked out further they all agreed it best not to mention it to Misty.

October and November passed quickly. By December things slow down a great deal. Everyone starts winter projects to keep busy and there is always something new coming up. Rebecca is engaged and a spring wedding is being planned. A young man is calling on Isabelle and the four of them spend at least one day at week's end together. Misty is reading as much as ever, playing the piano and writing music. Her highlights come when letters from Roscoe and Mrs. Franklin arrive. Also, the child Sarah occupies a large part of her time along with cooking, sewing, and a host of other hobbies.

The winter of '58' was a mild one, and uneventful for the most part. As the year moves into March and warm sunny days return so does the quickened pace reminiscent of spring. Suddenly everybody's schedule is overflowing with things that need to be done. Misty had long since been told of the decision made by Mr. Tanner. Though saddened much more than she let on, his decisions were always right in her eyes, so she set her mind to being patient knowing Roscoe's return was imminent.

With their plans to leave set for the first week in May, Rebecca's wedding was a top priority. The event would take place the last weekend in April. As always Mariah would be made as beautiful as possible, and it would be a wedding that would befit someone as loved by the Tanners as Rebecca is. Sadly though, Isabelle and Misty learned that Rebecca and her husband would be leaving the area. They planned to join a group of others and go west, but she was happy and excited about it. So the girls would be happy for her, though sad to see their childhood dreams altered in such a drastic way.

With the onset of April, each day was more beautiful than the last. Eight new colts were in the pasture, more than two dozen calves, a half dozen lambs and just as many baby goats. The fields were being planted, wagons and buildings being repaired, but all the magnificence of spring combined couldn't make Misty feel as good as when she stumbled upon Henry fishing with Sarah at his side. Henry's hair was all gray now, his back slightly bent and his movements a little slower. The child on the other hand was probably around five years old now, and as spirited and full of life as ever. Misty never said it, but everyone knew she had adopted her, and planned to raise the child as she had been. One other event would happen in April that had everyone excited. The Franklins, who were also going to England with the Tanners, would be arriving a fortnight before May. This would give Misty and Gloria time together, something they both wanted a great deal.

The days were quickly counting down now. Everyone was getting ready for something. Isabelle and Misty were invited to the Myers' for dinner. With the wedding day closing in fast it would probably be the last time the Myers' would spend with the three girls alone. That evening Rebecca showed the gift Roscoe had sent and read his letter, but not without tears. Her biggest regret was not having him there, and knowing she would be far off when he returned. "Well with Rebecca gone, and Isabelle too, we hope to see a lot of you," Mrs. Myers said to Misty.

"Maybe you could run an errand or two once in a while," laughed Doc Myers, jesting as they sometimes do about Misty's day in Moninghoff's store.

The Franklins arrived less than two weeks before the wedding, Word was quickly sent to the Myers'. There would be a dinner and gathering of friends tomorrow evening. Misty wanted time to race by, but not these last two weeks. Being with the Franklins was even better than she expected. But time with Rebecca was also very important. As it has to be though, time goes by.

The wedding was exquisite. Rebecca was never more beautiful, and Reverend Brown was in top form. Everything was perfect as every wedding should be. Shortly after the ceremony, Mr. Tanner and Doc Myers were outside talking when Rebecca approached them. Giving Mr. Tanner a large hug she said, "I love you Poppa Tanner and I'll never forget you as long as I live."

Kissing the top of her head and looking at Doc Myers with a smile he said, "Child, I wouldn't have it any other way."

As the evening drew to its close and Rebecca was readying to leave, Isabelle and Misty took her around to the outside wall of the patio. "We planted this maple tree this morning in your honor," Isabelle said.

"We'll meet here again before this tree is grown, okay?" Misty said.

"Okay," Rebecca responded. They shook hands on it, then tenderly hugged and kissed each other good-bye. Rebecca had been there from their earliest childhood. None of them even thought that one day they would part. If it weren't for the love the three girls had for each other the loss would have created an unbearable void.

The next week was both relaxing and refreshing, but it too ended too quickly, and it was the eve of their departure. Misty shared Isabelle's room while the Franklins occupied Roscoe's. Lying in bed that night they talked for several hours. Isabelle had fallen in love and her hope was to marry, build a large house at Mariah, and raise half a dozen children. They shared a common idea, that of seeing Roscoe and Misty in the big house with lots of children also, and watching them all grow together. "It's all taking shape now Misty," said Isabelle. "This time next year I think we'll both be married. We'll have a place to go in New York, friends to stay with in Orleans, a sail ship to travel about on."

"And the most beautiful place on earth to have as home," Misty interjected.

"Life is a wonderful thing," said Isabelle. "Wouldn't it be nice to one day go west and visit Rebecca? To see all of our children playing together."

"I think you're getting ahead of yourself Iz," Misty laughed, "but it does sound nice, doesn't it?"

"Are you wishing yet that you had pestered Poppa into letting you go?" Isabelle asked.

"I know I could have, and with you and Mother and Gloria after me about it so much it was real hard not to," she answered.

"There's still time, we can wake him up," joked Isabelle.

"I know in my heart this will be the last time I will have to wait alone. It may very well be the last really big thing that he asks of us. It's better to let it be; I'm sure of that," Misty responded.

The following morning everyone was up early. Misty helped Lilly Mae prepare a large breakfast, then went to the barn to get her horse. She placed Sarah on another and together they rode alongside the carioles as far as the covered bridge. On the other side of the bridge the girls disembarked and sat on the wall waving and watching as the others rode off. Climbing back onto their horses Misty said to Sarah, "When Ros rode off from here I had an awful feeling like I would never see him come back. I just had that feeling again. I guess I can't take it very well. Seeing those I love going away is something I'll probably never get used to."

May was always an active time on the plantation. The house usually bustled with energy and enthusiasm. But not this time. It was all so quiet in the big house.

Grandmother Tanner spends most of her time in her two-room area with Martha giving her constant attention. Misty has the entire upstairs to herself and, apart from Henry's room, the downstairs too. As the weeks slowly rolled by she and Sarah busied themselves with a variety of hobbies. Riding and schoolwork for the child and teaching her to play the piano is one of Misty's more enjoyable times. An occasional ride to town with Sarah to lunch with the Myers' is always a delight.

Time however, was moving much differently for Isabelle and the others. The ship was more beautiful than any of them imagined it would be and luxurious in ways they had only read about. Mr. Tanner was especially happy with what he was seeing. There was no doubt in his mind that this was going to be a very successful venture. Something he wanted far more for Zachary and Naomi than for himself.

Their arrival in England was a time never to forget. The ship no sooner was secured to the dock when Roscoe came racing on board. To his mother's outstretched arms he went, embracing her tightly and watching as his sister Isabelle came toward them. He hugged and kissed everyone as quickly as they came to him, then hugged most of them again. Many were the tears of joy that fell during those first few moments. Mrs. Tanner, looking at her son saw a handsome young man. As she watched and listened to him her heart welled up inside her. How many times has he mentioned Misty's name already she thought. If it were up to her she would untie the ship and take him home right now. Mr. Tanner too, looked on with pride. He saw a man before him, as well as his dream of working side by side with his son becoming a reality. As they left the ship he and Isabelle walked down the ramp arm in arm ahead of the rest. How different he looked to the Franklins now. "He's truly come into his own," said Mrs. Franklin to Naomi. "An awfully fine looking young man."

"I'm certainly impressed with how big he's gotten," said Mr. Franklin.

"He wrote that he and some others were doing weight training but I never expected him to look so big," his mother said.

211

"He's solid looking; that's a fact," said Mr. Franklin.

After reaching their hotel and unpacking they all met for dinner. Conversation went back and forth between what each had been doing individually and of the varied business interests. Roscoe had many questions to ask the Franklins concerning Misty's stay in New Orleans. He told them he looked forward to visiting them with her in the future. They would spend several days after this visiting with some of Roscoe's friends, including Frederick and Lanya. One day they visited the school for an in-depth tour and then rested and relaxed for several more days before leaving on a tour of the country.

Many conversations between Mr. Tanner and his son concerned Misty. These helped Roscoe endure this vacation that he really didn't want. The first boat home would have pleased him more, but with his father's assurance that nothing would keep them apart, he was better able to focus his time and enjoy it all to a greater extent. Often as they traveled the men discussed their business. Mr. Tanner was already making plans for a trip to New York with his son come spring. When at home the Tanners lived a simple easygoing life, but away, they traveled first class. For several days Zachary, Naomi, Roscoe, and Isabelle left the others. The pace set by the younger ones was taking its toll on Mr. Tanner. Pursuing different interests in different directions was a welcome and needed change.

By July's end they were heading for port. The trip home would take longer as the ship made several island stops before crossing back over the ocean. On their last day in England Roscoe and Isabelle went off to say good-bye to some of the many friends he had made. They had dinner that evening with Frederick and Lanya. Much of the conversation revolved around Roscoe's and Misty's relationship. The Bordeaus said repeatedly how much they wanted to be informed of the events after Roscoe's return stateside. With a promise to return with his wife in a year or so, they said good-bye. Roscoe and Isabelle went back to their hotel for their final night in England.

"It's over," Roscoe said to his mother as they stood on the deck watching the ship inch its way away from the dock. "It's finally over. I can't tell you how many times I wanted to leave. I think perhaps the thing that helped the most was having Misty in New Orleans. I wanted to be with her and I wanted to be with y'all, but knowing I couldn't do it at the same time helped me keep my focus." His hand rested on the railing and his mother placed her hand on his.

"I'm certain that helped, but I think even more than that, son, you always finish what you start, though sometimes later than sooner, and this was all too important not to see it through." Joined now by Mr. Tanner, the three stood there awhile and watched as the land disappeared. It took about two weeks of stops and layovers before finally getting underway for the long ride home. Roscoe and Isabelle told the others they would be traveling ahead of them after docking stateside. Coming home several days before the others would give Roscoe and Misty some quiet time to spend together.

As the passengers gathered for dinner this evening, much of the conversation concerned the impending storm. Not quite at the halfway point of the journey, they had been watching this storm build since early afternoon. Zachary and the crew had been through many storms on the open seas. He knew what to do as did his crewmen, and everyone was assured this was not going to get much worse. However, by midnight it had done just that. Mr. Tanner along with his son and Scott Franklin worked all evening with the crew securing the deck. Zachary and the ship's captain remained at the helm riding through what had now become a very turbulent and angry sea.

Everyone had been instructed to remain in their quarters. While Roscoe made his way back down to check again on the women, Mr. Tanner and Scott fought their way to the helm. It took all the strength they had to pull the door closed behind them. Holding on and standing next to Zachary they had to yell to each other to be heard over the sound of the wind. "This is a bad one sir," Zachary said to Mr. Tanner. "I don't think we can maintain it if it keeps up much longer." The ship slammed into the water again only to rise up high in the air as if the ship were a toy being thrown about by a child.

The waves grew even higher as the wind became one loud eerie whistle. The men could no longer hear their voices and the ship could barely be controlled.

Below in the cabin area Roscoe was holding tightly onto his sister who already had sustained injuries from being thrown against the walls. His mother was in a nearby room with Mrs. Franklin and Naomi. He too knew that the magnitude of the storm would overwhelm the ship if it kept up its fury.

Topside the men fought with all they had to keep the ship aright. Zachary, being a seamen from his earliest years, had been through hurricanes before, but never had he experienced anything like this. The wind was unrelenting. Everything was pitch black and the waves were so high they continually crashed down over the entire ship. Then a huge wave hit the ship with a force it could not withstand lifting them to an almost vertical position. At the same time another equally powerful wave hit them on the side. Like an explosion the force ripped the structure wide open, pieces of wood flew like arrows, and water entered in at all levels. The ship crashed into the water, this time on its side, but only for a moment as the waves threw it once again skyward. The ship tossed about now at the will of the hurricane was quickly coming apart and everyone on board knew they were going to die.

Roscoe had tied rope securely around him and his sister, and anchored them to a wall post but as the water started rushing in he managed to unfasten it and with his sister tied to him he crawled out into the corridor, only to be met there by an onslaught of rushing water that lifted and carried them to the end of the hall. Slammed against the wall and completely submerged, he groped frantically for something to pull them up above the water that was threatening their lives. As the ship's position changed, the water raced away, allowing him to brace his back against one wall and his feet against the other. Gasping for air he pulled his sister to his chest and held her as tightly as he could, within seconds they were submerged again. Only when the water covered them was there silence, then he felt a tremendous pressure, at the same time the wall he was pressed against disappeared, and they were gone.

The rage of the hurricane passed quickly, but its destruction was all too complete. As the morning light returned so did the calmness of the sea. Left behind were only remnants of the beautiful ship the Anna Mariah—a few pieces of splintered lumber, broken furniture, a trunk or two and some shredded clothing. These items would soon drift off in various directions disappearing and taking with them the story of what had taken place on the night of August 30th, 1859.

End of Part III

PART IV

A Travesty of Justice

Nearly a week to the day since the storm took down the Anna Mariah, a sighting is made from the vessel called Destiny. Off her portside and yet a distance out, there appears to be a raft of some sort carrying three people. The ship's direction is changed to make an investigation. Indeed, three people are floating on a loosely constructed raft. As the ship draws near the captain is told there are two men and a woman, all of whom appear to be dead. A crew is sent out to tow the raft in. The two men are alive, though barely. The woman is dead and has been for some time. The unconscious men are hoisted aboard, the body of the woman is set to sea. Being the kind of ship this is, and the kind of men that possess it, they conclude that the injuries sustained were the result of a losing battle that took their ship and left them refugees of the sea. They were perceived to be Englishmen, sailors in the Kings Royal Navy.

Taken below, they were looked after for the next several days. With their wounds bandaged and plenty of fresh water they slowly began to regain consciousness. Zachary Johnson lifted his head and looked about the room. There was nothing on his body that didn't hurt. Far too weak to stand, he tried repeatedly to focus his eyes on the figure lying still across the room. The last face he remembered seeing was his captain's. He called his name out, but it was only a whisper, and even this was too much for him. His head dropped down and he slipped back into unconsciousness.

The ship by now had carried them far from where it found them. The raft itself had also traveled a considerable distance. It was unlikely that any other survivors, if there were any, could be rescued by this vessel.

As the morning's light entered the room, Zachary was awakened by someone shaking him. He opened his eyes slowly. So many days without food has left him not only weak, but confused about time and events. Trying to focus his eyes he brought his hand up to block the blinding glare of the sun hitting his face. The person sitting over him kept talking and repeating his name. The face was partially covered by a full unkempt beard and mustache. One eye was swollen and black. He had a loosely tied bandage around his head. "Zachary, Zachary, you have to wake up. You have to eat," the voice kept saying. As his eyes focused he recognized the face and he grabbed onto the arm that was holding him. "Naomi? Is she all right?" he asked.

"I don't know," the man answered. Then shaking his head he said again, "I don't know."

"I'm all right," Zachary said. "Go look for her . . . please." He realized Zachary thought they were still on their own ship. Perhaps he thought it hadn't gone down.

"Okay, but first eat some of this," he answered feeding him some warm stew.

He scanned the room from end to end. "I have to find her," he said trying to rise up.

"She's not aboard this ship, Zachary. Perhaps another ship rescued the others." At that the door opened and a man entered carrying more food and fresh water. "I'd like to speak to the captain."

"I'll tell him mate. You wait here till you're sent for." The look on Zachary's face showed things were becoming clearer to him now. He closed his eyes and lay back on the pillow. He lay still for a long time.

After a while Zachary was helped to a table and the two ate and talked about what they could remember of their ordeal. They weren't sure of the ship they were on, but of the people they met so far they felt a need to be cautious. By late afternoon they had shaved and cleaned up as much as possible. Zachary lay down again and fell off to sleep while his partner waited for an audience with the ship's captain. This took place early that evening when he was brought to the captain's quarters to dine with him. "Now that it appears you're going to live, let me officially welcome you to my ship," the captain said. Extending his hand he continued,

"I'm Captain William Duffy, and you are a guest aboard the valiant ship Destiny."

Grasping the captain's hand he replied, "My name is Roscoe Tanner from America. I need to know sir, were any others besides us rescued?"

"We found no others, Roscoe Tanner of America. That you were found could only be by the hand of God," he replied. "Was the young woman a wife to one of you?"

Hesitating a moment he lamented, "My sister, Isabelle. She died some days back. I couldn't bring myself to set her to the water. I thought death was a foregone conclusion for us as well."

"As it should have been," replied the Captain.

"It's imperative that I get to America. Whatever the cost to you or your government, it will be repaid. I give you my word of that," Roscoe said confidently.

"You say it like you mean it, and so I believe you do," the captain responded sitting back in his chair. "But I, too, am a man with a mission, and I'm afraid I can't accommodate your wishes at this time."

"Where then is this ship bound?" Roscoe asked.

"We've a cargo to deliver to the West Indies," the captain said as he resumed eating.

"Surely you can deliver us to a port sooner, for that sir I would see you rewarded well," said Roscoe speaking earnestly.

"Aye my friend, don't look so dejected. I'll see to it you're taken care of. But understand, we're not on a mission for his Majesty the King. Quite the contrary," he continued. "He doesn't hold a warm place in his heart for me and my mates, and this can be an encumbrance when seeking a safe port to enter."

"Is this not a ship belonging to the King's Navy?" asked Roscoe.

"It was," he replied.

"You're an outlaw, Captain Duffy?" Roscoe asked.

"Aye my friend, if I am indeed an outlaw it's because my hand was forced, not because I chose it," he responded quickly.

"Are you being hunted?" Roscoe inquired.

"You'll be treated as a guest and safely put ashore. You've no need to be rescued," the captain assured him.

"Forgive me Captain, the question was inappropriate."

"In light of your circumstances it's a valid question. Twice we fought on the open sea and twice we won. The first, lost everything, the second retreated, though looking badly beaten."

"You must have a crew of valiant men, Captain Duffy," said Roscoe.

"Aye, some good seafaring men aboard, but the difference, Roscoe, is that the navy was fighting for the King; we were fighting for our lives." He sat back again, "Always bet on those fighting for their lives."

Roscoe spent the next hour listening to the captain relate his history and his plans. He figured the man was around thirty years old, his intelligence was never in question. Trying to appear interested in what he was hearing, Roscoe listened, but his thoughts were on other things. How could he get to America as quickly as possible? Had his family survived the storm? Would Zachary recover? And Isabelle. He fought every minute not to let his mind dwell on her death, but his heart ached beyond what words could describe.

The word the captain wasn't using was pirate. As he explained himself and his purpose it was apparent to Roscoe that getting off this ship could be just as important to his life as getting on was. He had counted on his inner strength to keep focused and alert. He said little in response to what he had heard that evening. His objective was to gain the captain's friendship.

As the days passed by, both men regained a good deal of their strength. They learned the cargo onboard consisted of two hundred barrels of ale stolen from its owners a week before, a large arsenal of swords and knives, and human cargo—several hundred men, women, and children, Negroes captured from their homeland to be sold into slavery. This was, as one crewman stated, not the usual cargo, but there was a profit in it and they were going there anyway so they were purchased for resale.

One afternoon as they neared their destination they sat on the deck hoping that sometime soon there would be land in view. For many hours a steady stream of Negroes were brought up topside to be cleaned. Several men continuously hauled buckets of water up over the side and doused the men and children who had been confined to the hull of the ship for nearly two weeks. Some were brought up dead and thrown overboard, many of the women were kept by and passed around with the crewmen. Seeing the look in the eyes of these men as they stood naked with excrement and vomit dried to their skin, eating rarely, and at that, food that others would consider refuse, caused Roscoe to think of Henry. Had he suffered a like fate? And what about his father? His attention was

drawn away from this thought by loud voices coming up from below. A young Negro was fighting those who were bringing him up.
He was a man of twenty-five years or so, at the point of starvation,
yet two men could not control him. It couldn't be understood what
he was saying, but Roscoe and Zachary watching nearby knew, if
not the words, the meaning. This man wanted to be home with his
family as badly as they did. However, when they could not bring
him under control, the order was given to throw him overboard,
which they did. This was accompanied with much laughter and
cheering as the crew made their way to the side of the ship to make
sport of the event by throwing things at the man. Zachary jumped
to his feet in disbelief. Roscoe rose up also, but he walked in the
other direction. In a moment he returned and made his way over
to the crowd. "Get back," he demanded loudly and threw a rope
down to the young man. "Help me pull him up," he ordered. As
the rope went tense, "Help me I said," he shouted again as he began
to pull. The laughing had ceased but no one made any attempt to
assist him until Zachary took hold of a piece of the rope and the
two began to pull the man out of the water. Only then did two
others take hold and lift him up over the side. No sooner was the
man on his feet, when several men threw him head first back down
into the hull of the ship. That night, as Roscoe lay in bed thinking
about his family, he thought also about the young man he rescued
that day, about the conditions in which they were surviving down
there, and about all the talk of war over the whole issue. But still
he didn't as yet feel a link between the atrocities on board ship and
the plantations at home.

It was late before he finally fell asleep, but his rest was short.
Disturbed by nightmarish dreams of the hurricane as he was every
night, he was back on his feet at six o'clock. As he stood on deck
drinking coffee with a fellow named Tyler, Roscoe told him about
the storm and how he found Zachary dazed and clinging to a piece
of the ship. "With the rope I had tied around us, I was able to use
some of the wood we were on and some he was clinging to, to tie
up a makeshift raft. "But when he began to talk about Isabelle he
was overwhelmed and he walked to the side and began to weep.

The captain had been summoned to the front of the ship. Roscoe noticed the commotion and made his way over to the captain's
side. A group of them were peering through eye scopes at a ship a
good distance off. With the early morning mist it was impossible
to determine the flag it was sailing under. Captain Duffy decided

to move closer for a better look. "Perhaps," he said to Roscoe, 'they will add to our delights."

"What if they are pirates and want to add to their own booty?" Roscoe asked him.

"I've no friends out here, mate. If they wish to pass by so be it. If not we'll take them down as we would anyone else," he answered.

Within an hour the ships were in plain view of each other. What they now observed left them perplexed. Not a soul could be seen. The ship appeared to be drifting and lifeless. The lieutenant asked if he should take a crew and board the vessel. "Not if you want to see the sun set," the captain answered. "Tell the men to prepare for a fight, and when it's over I want the captain brought to me." With that the word spread quickly throughout the crew, the ship was turned broadside and everyone waited for the command to fire. Roscoe and Zachary stood near the doorway leading down under. They still weren't sure this was a trap as Captain Duffy insisted. After several hours had passed Roscoe approached the captain. "If someone is laying a trap, why the silent standoff?" he asked.

"Oh, for a certainty there is a very smart captain looking through a hole in the wall and counting his time. He thinks one of two things is gonna happen. One, that we might start thinking like you and say to ourselves, maybe nobody is here. They could have all eaten something rotten and died," the captain laughed, then he added more seriously, "But more likely friend, he's hoping to lull us into a false sense of security. It's a Navy ship. They can take down the symbols and markings, but up this close I know what it is."

"What if it's not you they're looking for? Why not just pass it by?" suggested Roscoe.

"Every captain knows that taking us down will make a name for himself. Maybe he wasn't looking for me, but he found me. Besides," he laughed, "we're always up for a good fight, and additional cargo." Roscoe walked back and sat down with Zachary.

"What do ya think Ros?" Zachary asked.

"I think we better be prepared to jump ship when the fighting begins," he answered.

"A ship that size can carry an awfully large arsenal."

"I know what you're saying Zachary, and I sure don't want us to die with this dastardly group. I think we better start looking at this like there is going to be a fight. Do you think we could lower a boat if the standoff goes into the night?" Roscoe asked.

"It's too risky, Ros. It's hard to get these boats down quickly and quietly. If they see us they can fire on us easily, and we can't be sure the other ship wouldn't do the same."

"What do ya suggest then brother? I know you can get us off this ship," Roscoe said with confidence.

"We'll go to the tool room and get a couple of saws. Then we'll find a room on the opposite side of the ship about mid-level. If the fighting commences it should take us about ten minutes or so to cut a porthole large enough to get through," Zachary responded.

"Then what?" Roscoe asked.

"Then hope we pick the right time to jump in," he said.

"Unless of course this crew wins," said Roscoe.

"In that case," answered Zachary, "we go upstairs and congratulate the scoundrel."

The men found their saws and a large hammer. After finding a suitable room they hid the tools and went topside. "What makes him think you won't fire first?" Roscoe asked Captain Duffy.

"Between you and me and that water out there, I ain't sure mate, but this is an interesting situation, and as the hours wear on I become more intrigued with what he's doing over there," replied the captain.

"You know, captain, as a guest aboard your ship, I think it not very hospitable your involving us in a battle," Roscoe said with a grin.

"Something to tell your grandchildren," the captain retorted as he walked off laughing.

The sun was setting and still not a sign of life from the ship. Captain Duffy had his ship sail off another hundred yards to be out of firing range during the darkness. No one slept well that night and morning only brought more of the same. By now though the crew was starting to get anxious. More were beginning to think that something had occurred aboard the mysteriously silent ship, leaving it unoccupied. This resulted in the men letting their guard down more and more. But noticeable to Roscoe and Zachary was Captain Duffy's growing frustration. He stood for long hours staring at the other ship. By mid-afternoon a restless spirit had affected nearly the entire crew, and many were starting to doubt the Captain's judgment, feeling the ship was there for the taking, and wanting to take it.

That evening Roscoe and Zachary dined with the captain and his lieutenant. The captain made his decision. In the morning he would fire three shots near the ship to see if he could stir any action. If no response was made he would send a dozen men over to investigate. As with the night before, he ordered his ship to withdraw from firing range. That night all onboard slept better. Most, no longer feeling there was any threat, went quickly and soundly to sleep. However, there was a threat, a serious one. During the late hours of the night men from the other ship who had remained quiet and out of sight for two long days, carried out their plan flawlessly. Paddling small boats half the way, then swimming, they climbed up over the side of the Destiny and easily overtook the small crew standing watch. A signal was sent to the Navy ship, and its captain ordered his ship moved forward. As the night gave way to the morning's light, Captain Duffy's crew were making their way topside to be captured and placed in a line face down on the deck, bound and gagged. When enough men were taken, and more navy men came aboard, the order was given to go down and bring the captain and any others to the deck. With great expediency and force they routed everyone including Captain Duffy. Some put up a fight and paid with their lives. Both Zachary and Roscoe tried to explain their circumstances but found no hearing ear. They were bound and gagged and laid on the deck.

After some time the Negroes held captive below were brought up and gathered at the ship's end. Some of Captain Duffy's men were ordered to haul water up for them to clean themselves with. When the captain of the navy ship came aboard, he ordered the flag replaced with the flag of England. He then ordered Captain Duffy hung. As they put the rope around his neck the decree was read declaring his death sentence for treason. When asked if he had any final words he replied with a smile, "I applaud your ingenuity captain. I hope we meet again someday."

The captain responded, "I think that highly unlikely," then nodding his head he gave the order and in a swift second Captain Duffy hung by his neck . . . dead. Some of his own men were commanded to cut him down and pitch him over the side.

Roscoe now relaxed though he was still lying on the deck. It would be only a short time now and he would be set free, and once he explained who he was and what had happened he would be on his way home. What's more he thought, maybe the captain knew of the Anna Mariah and of other survivors. However, things didn't move too quickly. They all were left to lie on the deck the entire day. Most of the cargo was removed to the other ship. The Negroes were transported over presumably to be returned to their homeland.

When evening arrived the men were brought to their feet three at a time. Stripped of shirts and shoes they were told to go to the side of the ship and relieve themselves. Then they were fitted with ankle braces and given something to eat. At no time were any allowed to talk. On several occasions both Roscoe and Zachary were struck with fists for trying to explain who they were. Finally, for refusing to follow orders they were chained together by their ankle braces and literally thrown down into the hull of the ship.

The air was so heavy and the stench so strong that both men vomited and nearly panicked. Groping in near total darkness they immediately searched for the door. Unable to force it open they began making their way to the far end of the hull where a stream of light was coming through a hole, slipping and falling repeatedly in the vile left by those who had been held captive there. When they finally reached the hole they took turns placing their mouth over it to suck in fresh air. Again getting somewhat stabilized they started digging at the hole with their fingernails, working at it until darkness fell.

Early the next morning they were awakened by the sound of the door opening. Too far away to reach it quickly, they could only look on as three men chained together were pushed in, and the door once again slammed closed. "Come this way," Zachary called out several times as the three tried to walk in the direction of his voice. After a long struggle they arrived, covered in the same disgusting slim as Roscoe and Zachary from repeatedly falling. "We've been trying to enlarge this crack," Roscoe told the men. "If we work in shifts we can open it enough to bring in fresh air."

"There are two port holes somewhere. They've been sealed shut. If we find em we can breakem open," said one of the men.

"Why were they sealed closed?" Roscoe asked.

"I don't know mate, I just know they're here," he answered. It took a considerable time to locate one, but when they did, it was ripped open in seconds. Along with the much needed fresh air, came light. The light sent the rats running for cover; it also exposed the source of the stench that was still so overbearing they had yet to get accustomed to it. Along with the feces and vomit were two badly decaying bodies.

Their main concern now was the two corpses they were imprisoned with. The portholes were too small to push them through, and there were no containers or separate rooms to place them in. They decided to make a wooden box with the boards they could rip loose, and wrap the bodies with pieces of burlap that were strewn about.

After this was done they sat under one of the portholes in an area they had cleaned. "What's going on up there?" Roscoe asked.

"During the night we cut our way out of the room we were in, thought we might get a boat lowered and drift off," one man stated.

"Never even got it free before they had us," said another.

"We've been sailing all night. Where they taking us?" Roscoe said impatiently. "If we live long enough, they're taking us to a penal colony," one answered. "We'll be guests of the King on one of his little islands."

"Shaping rocks for his majesty," said another.

"We've got to get word of who we are to the captain," Zachary said to Roscoe.

"Forget that happening mate," one of the men said, "the captain is on his own ship heading for England to be richly rewarded for getting William Duffy, and if you cause any more trouble with those up there, well, they'll hang ya I'm sure."

"There will be a trial when we get to port won't there?" Roscoe said in a half statement, half question.

"The trial's over," one laughed. "That took place a couple years ago. Guilty of treason, and we are ya know. That's life at hard labor mate. We just wanna be hopin the men up top take the ship back somehow, but I don't think so."

"There'll be someone we can talk to Ros. We just need to take care of ourselves till we get there," said Zachary as he slumped back and rested his head. "I can give all the needed information concerning the Anna Mariah's registry. I just need to talk to the right person."

That evening the door was opened briefly and food was dropped to the floor. Landing in the mire that covered everything rendered it useless, but before evening came round again the men had pulled more boards loose and made a shaky platform to catch the food the next time. However, some of this was lost when a fight broke out between them concerning the distribution of the small amount of food they had been given. The third day no one brought them anything. After several more days had passed, they could see land from a porthole. Weakened and filthy, they thought their ordeal was over, that they would be freed once taken ashore. But by the time the ship set anchor it was dark. Nothing would happen until morning.

Those back at home are filled with fear. A messenger arrived from Zachary's father. It offered little in the way of information only that the Anna Mariah is seriously late. Mostly, the messenger was looking for information. Perhaps they had to dock elsewhere or were delayed at a port of call. What the message didn't say, and the messenger shouldn't have said, was that all those in the shipping business in that area knew about the hurricane. Many suffered major damage when it reached shore. If they were on schedule they met this storm on open seas. Mr. Johnson knew he had reason to be very concerned. He had only one of his cargo ships in port. He sent that out and leased two smaller vessels to form a search party.

Misty was frantic. She had gone to Doc Myers' that day and every day after as he tried to get word from Mr. Johnson. After too many days, Misty decided she had to go to Mr. Johnson herself. Even if they got home while she was gone he would be able to tell her they were all right she reasoned.

The next morning she arrived at the Myers' commanding a small horse-drawn cariole. Not wanting to let her go without a driver, Dr. Myers did his best to persuade her, but he could see she was now distraught with fear and so he gave her some money and told her which road to travel. Immediately upon her departing he went to a reliable old fellow he'd known for many years and hired him to catch up with her and escort her to her destination safely.

* * * * *

It was mid-morning aboard the ship and the prisoners were being prepared to exit onto boats for the short ride to the island. The five men in the hull watched for several hours as small groups of men were taken ashore. When the activity stopped and only the sounds of a few people walking about up top could be heard, they realized they had been forgotten. This was good news for the three pirates, but not for Roscoe and Zachary who wanted to be taken ashore to be set free.

The three men said they would oppose with every means any attempt the others made to be found. Saying they wanted the opportunity to break out of the hull under cover of night, they reasoned there would only be perhaps a couple of men left on board to keep watch while the others stayed ashore the night and replenished their supplies. If they could get free of the chains and gather some food, they could stow away aboard the ship and wait for an opportunity to escape. The two thought it best to not try and fight it out with them, so they all agreed to wait until that night and force the hatch open. Roscoe and Zachary planned to surrender when they reached the top. The others knew that would be a good distraction for them. They all sat back saying nothing and waited the hours away.

When the time arrived they had little difficulty removing the hatch. First Roscoe and Zachary climbed through, then the other three. "You go that way; it leads to the deck," one of them said to Zachary and Roscoe. "And remember mates," he added, "if you say anything we'll all be on that island together." With that the three headed for the tool room. The others for the stairs. It took several minutes to reach the deck, but only seconds to be apprehended. The rustling of the chains coming up the stairwell alerted the guards who were waiting one at each side with pistols drawn. "We were coming to surrender," Roscoe stated when confronted by the guards.

"Ya lyin cut throats," a guard said as he struck the side of Zachary's face with his fist. "Ya thought ya was escapin." Roscoe lunged for the man only to tangle in the chain as Zachary was dropping to the floor. Scrambling to turn around, Roscoe found himself face to face with the other guard's pistol. "If you want to see daylight lay flat on that floor and don't move," he said.

"I'm okay Ros, don't antagonize him," Zachary said. "Let em take us to shore in the morning. There's no point in trying to talk to them." So there they lay for the remainder of the night, the better part of which rained steadily. A few hours after daybreak the men were ordered to lower a boat into the water. One of the guards sat at the rear and held his pistol on them as they rowed to shore. Having not eaten for days and being a week without bathing or shaving they looked no different than any of the others that had been brought to shore. Taken to a stockade and fastened in, they were told someone would come for them . . . sometime . . . and then rubbing his dirty hand around Roscoe's face he laughed and said, "Welcome to your new home boys."

By afternoon they were baking in the hot sun. Many guards went by, but nobody offered them any relief. It was late afternoon when a group of men passed by, along with the one that brought them ashore. "This is the scum we forgot in the hull," he laughed, "but they didn't wanna miss out on comin here, so they come up to remind us."

As they all stood there laughing another of them said, "Where are the three I threw down there?"

"We didn't see any others," he replied. Walking over to Zachary and lifting his head by his hair he asked, "Where's your mates at my friend?" He moved his mouth but no words could be heard. Lifting Roscoe's head he asked the same question. Roscoe's only reply was to ask for water. "They're still on board," he said dropping Roscoe's head. "They might of gotten out of the ankle chains. If they did they're probably armed. Send a dozen men out to get them."

Shortly after midnight two men came and released Roscoe and Zachary from the stockade. Neither of them had the strength to stand. A cup of water was handed to each of them. Most of it ran down the sides of their faces as they tried to drink it. After that they were made to walk to a nearby building. The door was opened for them and they were practically pushed inside. There they met up with the three men who had just been brought in from the ship. A tall man with cold eyes who had been sitting behind a desk stood up and said, "You have been sentenced to life at hard labor for your acts of treason. The only possible change to that decree would be . . . death . . . for attempted escape. That you're not being hung right now, is only due to the fact that your foolish behavior occurred before you were turned over to me."

Pulling himself up in his chair Roscoe attempted to address the man saying, "My name is Roscoe Tanner from America, shipwrecked on the Anna Mariah."

"Shut up!" the man shouted. "You're a liar and a scoundrel. You'll speak to me when I give you permission to do so."

But again Roscoe said, "I'm from America; it can be verified."

The man came around from behind his desk, walked over and standing in front of him turned to the others and said, "Is this man not one of you?" Thinking that Roscoe and Zachary had turned them in they replied by nodding their heads yes. Perhaps if he had not been so weak and dehydrated his accent might have helped his cause, but his voice was hardly above a whisper. The man placed his foot squarely across Roscoe's chest and pushed him over backwards. "If you speak again, you hang." Then addressing them all he said, "If I permit you to speak to me, you will address me as Master Shot." Then turning to the guards he said, "Take them to the barracks, except this one, (pointing to Roscoe); he goes to the hole for ninety days, needs to learn some manners."

The hole was a ten foot deep pit with a large wooden door that lay flat over it. No blankets or other provisions were provided. The floor was mud and the temperature was well below fifty degrees at night. Only once a day when food was thrown in would he see light.

The days went by slowly for Roscoe, but the weeks went by quickly for Zachary. As he became more accustomed to the way of life there he was able to get around some, looking for possible advantages with some of the guards, and sometimes making his way over to the hole to talk with Roscoe. He kept trying to get more food to him, but had only little success. Finally, somewhere near the end of December the ninety days passed. The door opened for what Roscoe thought was his daily allotment of food, but a voice called for him to come out.

The day's light was at first blinding and no one offered a hand to help him scale the dirt wall and reach the top. Ninety days living in his own wastes and neither bathing or shaving had left him in such a way no one wanted to be near him. Once out of the hole he was taken to a bathing area. What was left of his clothes he discarded, and he bathed for as long as they let him. Walking to the barracks naked, he was given a shirt, pants and a pair of boots, assigned a bunk and told to remain there until the others returned from work detail that evening. It was nearly dark before they arrived.

Zachary helped Roscoe up and brought him to the feeding area. There he began to tell him of life on a penal island. "This Master Shot," Roscoe asked, "do ya see much of him?"

"Very little. He spends most of his time on the other side where most of the work is being done," said Zachary.

"I've got to get to him somehow, and make him listen," Roscoe said.

"I've heard he has left men in the hole half the year. We've got to come up with something real good," Zachary replied.

"You say some supplies come in from that side of the island?" Roscoe asked.

"It seems from what I've heard, many of the building projects are completed on the exterior. The king has been steadily sending furnishings and building materials to finish the inside of the main house. I've never been over there, but it sounds like it's gonna be quite a retreat for the old boy," related Zachary.

"We've got to get over there," said Roscoe.

"I figure that won't be so hard for you, with both mason and carpentry skills they'll want to use you there," Zachary said.

"I've got to get my strength back, but God knows how you can do it on this stuff," Roscoe said looking at his bowl.

"There are wild boars all over this island, Roscoe. Everybody is scared to death of em. I've seen some, and they're big all right. I've been working on a hole near where I'm digging rocks. I know if I catch one it'll make an awful noise until I club it. I've got my guard to agree to a fifty-fifty split. I don't think they get to eat much better than we do," Zachary told him.

The next morning at sun-up the guards were there to route everyone out. To the first guard near him Roscoe said, "I'm a skilled carpenter. I could work on the other side." Without looking at him the guard said as he passed by, "Today you're busting rock," and for the better part of twelve hours he did, and again the next day and many more to follow. Each day he would say the same thing to the guards. After many days they had explained their story to most of the guards hoping one would take it to Master Shot, but each day brought more of the same.

* * * * *

A world away she sat with pen in hand. This was not her first attempt, and again hours have gone by with only tears touching the paper. Her long hair unbrushed, she held her other hand to her forehead. All the responses from all the ports they could have gone to, have come in. Their last port of call had them leaving on schedule, and that placed them right in the hurricane's path. Mr. Johnson knew there was no mistake, and no longer any hope. The sea had taken his only child and everyone with him. It was nearly daylight before Misty completed her letter.

Dear Dr. Myers,

Only through the strength God gives those crushed of heart can I write this letter. How can I even say the words. I would rather have it that I fall asleep in death and await God's glory, and her arms that lovingly held me from my infancy.

Oh Dr. Myers, all of them are gone. I have been sitting here for days because I could not bring myself to say those

231

words. The ship went down in the storm. When I arrived here I could not believe the devastation of the land, what must it have been like at sea?

I can't write anymore for my hands shake and I can't make it stop, but please if you can, when you go to see Grandmother Tanner, please tell Henry and Willy Mae with your own mouth.

In my heart I feel him Dr. Myers, calling, reaching to me. Love is stronger than fire, stronger than death.

Misty

She stayed down there until spring, helping the many poor families who had lost everything in the storm. She sewed mostly, and tended gardens. She rarely smiled. For the first time in her life music was gone from her heart. Every day she would walk alone and cry. The passing of time offered no solace. One evening she had a woman cut her hair to just beneath her shoulders. The eyes that once glowed were reddened and sad. Kind words were offered but nothing could be said that would ease so great a loss.

"Come sit with me; I have something for you," said Mr. Johnson who had sent for her. "I have a letter from your friend Dr. Myers. Before you read it I want you to think about something. You know the sale of my business will be finalized in a week or so, and I've nothing to stay here for. I've been to many beautiful places, and I think I am going to go back to some of them. I'd gladly take you with me child. You need only tell me you want to come. But I think it would be better for you to go home. I understand your not wanting to be with their daughter, Susan. Perhaps the doctor will have you stay with him. He is very concerned you know."

"You've been very kind Mr. Johnson, I wish I could have been as comforting to you as you have been to me. I know I must go home now. I just don't know how I'm going to bear the emptiness," Misty said.

"There are those there who need you, probably more than you realize," said Mr. Johnson.

"My heart aches for little Sarah, and Henry too, and my Mammy whom I dearly love," Misty said and then began to cry.

"Oh you poor child," said Mr. Johnson.

Later she read Dr. Myers' letter. Actually it was written by Mrs. Myers who encouraged her to come home and invited her to stay with them. Mr. Johnson made arrangements for an escort, and the following day Misty was on her way home.

* * * * *

The predicament Roscoe and Zachary were in would not change. Their repeated requests to speak with Master Shot became an annoyance to him, so he ordered that any guard who spoke of them would spend time in the hole with them. Zachary had just spent thirty days in the hole for a confrontation with one of the lying men they were imprisoned in the hull with. Roscoe was still splitting rocks and waiting for a time when he would be taken to the other side. He wondered now if Master Shot's dislike for him was keeping him from being used in the other areas. The guards liked them though. On three occasions a wild boar had been caught and roasted in an area far from the view of others. By the time the third was caught, four guards were raiding the food bin and bringing rum. Since they were getting extra food on an almost regular basis, both Roscoe and Zachary, (until he went in the hole), had been able to build themselves back to fine form.

The time drags on ever so slowly. They know in their minds no one else had survived the storm, but their hearts won't let go or allow them to accept it. At times Roscoe's heart burns so badly he calls her name out loud. Other times he weeps over the loss of the family that was his life. Having each other to talk to is what keeps them from giving in to the rage within them against those holding them captive. They know if they're patient they will find a way. They also know the only one on the island who can match their intelligence is Master Shot, and he is so rarely seen he offers little threat to the various ideas they're considering.

The guards stay for six months at a time. They're trying hard to befriend one enough so as to get a letter off the island. The problem with this is, most of the guards are no more intelligent than most of the prisoners. One thing is certain. They are imprisoning the wrong man, not in the sense that they have an innocent man, but in that they're holding Roscoe Tanner against his will, and his will is unbreakable. He has accepted the fact that he'll do whatever is necessary to free himself, and that makes him the wrong man to oppose.

* * * * *

The weather was good on the morning she started for home

233

and in a week's time she was crossing the covered bridge, and in sight of Mariah. She went directly to the barn and put the cariole away, then bridled Roscoe's horse and headed off to Goldie's. From there she sent a young boy to bring Sarah. News spread quickly of her return, and soon Henry and Lester arrived as she knew they would. Willy Mae would be along as soon as she could, Misty was told, and all of them sat in the hut and ate the food Misty had purchased earlier in the day.

Listening to them talk only added to her pain. Life on the plantation was becoming increasingly harder under the headship of Edward, and a look of fear was constant in the eyes of the slaves. Willy Mae lamented how she had no time for other things anymore, that Susan wanted her there constantly to care for her needs, and that of her children. Only when the conversation focused on the growing likelihood of war did any of them get excited. For the first time in any of their lives there was a reason for hope and the word freedom was being spoken often.

Misty stayed that night with Goldie and Leo, with Sarah at her side. In the morning after everyone went to the fields she took the child on her horse and rode off to the meadows. She talked without let-up to the child about the times she and Roscoe had with Isabelle and Rebecca. Sometimes Naomi would be there too. The old dock wasn't safe to walk on anymore, and the boat was partly submerged. Misty would have stayed longer if Sarah had not been hungry.

She did not want to go to the main house and prolonged it as long as she could. That evening after dark she went in. Leaving Sarah with Lester she went to the house entering through the kitchen. Quietly she made her way to Grandmother Tanner's room. The old woman looked more frail than when Misty had last seen her. Sleeping with pillows propping her up to an almost sitting position, she was motionless. "Mrs. Tanner," she whispered and gently shook her arm.

The old woman opened her eyes and a faint smile appeared on her lips, "I knew you'd be back child. I've been waiting for you."

"Are you well?" Misty asked.

"My bones are tired, but my mind won't rest. You're the only one I can trust to tell me the truth," she said.

"You do understand, don't you?" Misty asked her as she fixed the pillows more comfortably behind her.

"Those fools think because the body's worn out the mind is gone too. Even those little devils they call children don't say a kind word," Mrs. Tanner lamented.

"I'm so sorry for you," Misty said touching her hand softly.

"I know you are child, and I doubt I deserve it from you," she said with a smile adding, "I was told you got back several days ago. Why you didn't come into the house is your business. If you don't want to see Susan and that jackal she married, even me for that matter, I couldn't blame you." Misty looked toward the floor and tried to interrupt but Mrs. Tanner continued. "No child, let an old woman speak her mind. When I was finally told I lost them I sent for you, but of course, by then you were gone. Some of them thought it was consoling when they said Susan was coming home, but it wasn't. They loved you as much as anyone of their children, and Misty," the woman said with tears in her eyes, "you're the only one left who emanates their wonderful qualities." Misty knelt down at the side of her bed and still holding her hand lay her head on it and cried. The old woman cried some too, and with her other hand touched Misty's head conveying what she couldn't say with words. After some time Misty stood up. Bringing a chair to the bedside she sat down and said, "We can help each other, Mrs. Tanner. I don't want to stay in the house anymore, but if you let me set up a cot in here with you, I'll take care of the things you need help with."

"I won't live much longer, I'm sure you're aware of that, and after I die it will be best for you to leave here. I'll give you a certificate of freedom and one for the girl. You take her with you, and I'll give you what you need to take care of your needs," said Mrs. Tanner.

"Please don't talk of dying, there are so many things we can talk about. I need your friendship now," Misty said.

"But it will come to pass child, and they would expect nothing less of me," Mrs. Tanner said. Misty helped her get ready for the night, then took a pillow off her bed and an afghan from the closet and spent the night peacefully on the divan.

The next morning she helped Mrs. Tanner to dress and together they went to the dining room. Not long afterwards, Edward arrived. "Well . . . well . . . well . . . ," he said, long and drawn out. "The chicken has come back to the coup." He walked around the table and greeted Mrs. Tanner with a kiss on the cheek, though she barely acknowledged his presence. "Misty I declare, you're the most beautiful creature, you just keep getting prettier all the time." Though she had no words for him, the look on her face said a great deal, both to Edward and old Mrs. Tanner.

Soon the children were at the table and Willy Mae served breakfast. Edward sat in Mr. Tanner's chair at the head of the table. Misty had no appetite when she came into the room, and seeing him sitting there made her feel sick. How pathetic she thought. Mr. Tanner was more of a man on his worst day than Edward has ever been. She never took a bite of her breakfast, only waited for Mrs. Tanner to finish so she could help her back to her room.

She was about to leave the house when Willy Mae called to her, "Miss Susan want y'all ta go ta her room, Misty."

"How is she doing?" Misty asked.

"Tain't come out of her room much. Po child took it hard. Even I's felt bad fo her some, but she a miserable person, not notin like ho sweet mama." Misty went upstairs to find Susan. She had stayed away from that part of the house intentionally. At the top of the stairs she stood as if unable to move another step. Staring down the hallway at Isabelle's door, one scene after another flashed through her mind. How many times they had raced up these stairs and into that room. Without even thinking about it she walked to the doorway. "If only I could open the door and find her there," she said to herself. If only it were all a bad dream. She opened the door, went in and closed it behind her. Everything was the same as the last time she had been there.

She walked over and sat down at the vanity. Sliding the small drawer completely out, Misty slipped her fingers into the opening and reached onto a ledge Roscoe had made for his sister to use as her secret compartment. With all her heart Misty hoped they were still there. The first two things to come out of this little hiding place had been put there by Isabelle. Reaching in again her fingers touched it. Pulling out the cherry ring Roscoe had made on the night they married, she placed it on her finger and looked at it intently. After a few moments she reached again inside the compartment. This time she brought out a golden earring. Emily Tanner long ago had given Misty this. It was the remaining one of the set her husband had purchased, and she had used to save the life of her mother Lydia. With the ring on her finger and the jewel in her hand she squeezed her fist tightly, closed her eyes and prayed to God to give her the strength to go on. After a while she rose up and walked across the room. Sitting on the side of the bed, she cried and said, "Oh Isabelle, Isabelle, how can you be gone, how can I live and never talk to you again? Oh the times we had in this room. The dreams we dreamed, the secrets we shared. I love you Isabelle,

I hope you can hear me." Then she lay back on the bed and thought about happier times. Closing her eyes she thought of the many nights when they were younger and Rebecca would spend the weekend and how the three of them would sleep in the bed together, talking until late into the night.

More than an hour passed before she rose to her feet again. For several minutes she sat at Isabelle's vanity and brushed her hair. Carefully, she replaced all the items she had removed from the secret compartment and put the drawer back in its place. She then moved on in search of Susan. She wasn't ready to go into Roscoe's room, and would have passed by if the door hadn't been open. Looking in didn't bring her the sadness it might have had she seen his room untouched as Isabelle's was. What she saw though made her sad in a different way. Susan's oldest boy had taken the room for his own. Many of the things Roscoe made for his room were missing, some were even broken. This room had the same feeling as the rest of the house. All but Isabelle's room seemed devoid of life. The warm greetings, the sound of laughter and music were gone.

"Misty," a voice called bringing her back to the present. "What did you do to your hair?"

"Hello Susan, I was coming to see you," Misty replied.

"How did I come to be the last one you should greet?" she asked as she walked toward the master bedroom.

"I'm sorry Susan, I just couldn't bear coming into the house," Misty answered as she followed her into the room that once was her parents.

"There are days still when I just don't want to get out of bed. Sometimes I can't eat in the dining room because they're not in there with me. What a travesty of justice. I ask God why? Why? But I get no answer. As for that silly Reverend Brown—the audacity of the man, coming out here telling me God loved them so much he took them to be with him. Did the fool think I would be consoled by telling me God drowned my mommy and daddy!" Susan said fighting back tears.

"The slaves understand it's the devil that makes bad things happen to good people, and that Jehovah only does what is right and good for people," Misty told her.

"You are gonna stay here in the house, just like always, Misty," Susan stated, though it sounded more like a question.

"Yes, I'm going to stay in Grandmother Tanner's room and look after her needs," Misty said.

"By and by life is just giving me one surprise after another. I would think you were chiding me if I didn't know you so well. I'll have a talk with her. She already has Martha for a nursemaid, and I want you to have dear Isabelle's room. You would like that wouldn't you?" Susan asked.

"Thank you, Susan, but I volunteered to stay with her, and she has already sent for a bed for me," said Misty.

"Misty!" Susan said in an excited tone, throwing up her hands, "she doesn't need you. I do! surely you can see that? I'm just not strong enough to tend to the children the way they need to be. I want you to be a nanny to them, an auntie, like Molly was. Y'all can teach them so much more than anybody else around here."

Misty didn't feel like being in the same room with Susan at this point. Selfish thoughts, she said to herself, they have consumed this girl, and not a redeeming quality left. "I'll help you with the children," Misty responded as she walked toward the door, "but I'll stay in Grandmother Tanner's room." Nothing more was said about it and Misty left the house quickly.

In a short time, with Sarah sitting behind her, they rode her horse through the covered bridge and into town. The Myerses weren't home when they arrived so Misty did as she had been told and went in and made herself comfortable. She tried to sit down and relax but she couldn't, so the two of them walked to Moninghoff's to purchase items for dinner. Misty still had a portion of the money Mr. Johnson had given her for her trip home. She bought fabric to make Sarah a dress and some candy which they ate while walking back.

When the Myerses returned, they were delighted to find the girls in the kitchen preparing dinner. It was a tremendous loss for them also, and with both their daughters so far from home, it was all so different for them now. Again they asked Misty if she would like to live with them, but she declined telling them how much she loved them, but she wanted to look after Sarah and Henry and the others. Knowing this is the best thing for her they reassured her their home was always open to her.

Many dinners were shared together over the next few months. Sarah was made a part of this new family and nothing could have pleased Misty more.

Lots of time too, was spent in the gardens. This was a way she could spend a great deal of time with the child and at the same time feel close to Mother Tanner, who used to spend countless hours and days with the girls from planting to harvest.

The hot summer days of August were passing slowly. As often as she could Misty would take Susan's boys and a group of slave children to the fishing pond to swim. The activity with the children was bringing a measure of joy back to her heart. Laughing more often and sometimes singing with them made her happy, as it did them.

One evening while fishing, she and Henry started singing to Sarah the songs they used to sing together when she and Isabelle were growing up. Soon, they were exchanging memories and talking freely about things they had kept locked up in their hearts. They laughed and talked till nearly dark before they started for home.

"What an awful mess it's become," Misty said to Henry as her voice turned serious. "It would break their hearts to see what's taking place here now. I dread to think what's gonna become of it all."

"Masser Edward, he don't care. Tain't got a lick of sense anyways. Keep sayin more cotton being grown now dens before. But he ain't takin care of da fields, and dey workin people ta death. How's he spects to keep gettin dat good money ifin da cotton tain't good like it usea be," replied Henry.

"I tried to talk to Susan again last night about the way the slaves are being beaten and shackled, but I might as well talk to one of these catfish," said Misty.

"Deys makin it real bad fo demselves. Everybody know it was da Negroes dat burn dem storage sheds. I's never seen things like this, peoples not acting da same anymore. Dey could do sometin bad to Masser Edward or Masser Louder. I's think dey could," Henry said.

"That will only make it harder on everyone. I hope that doesn't happen," Misty said.

It could happen, and she knew it. The slaves were being pressed harder and harder all the time. The buildings that were burned and the equipment that's being broken so frequently are acts of rebellion that were once rare on Mariah. Any books, paper or pencils that the Negroes had, have been taken away. The allotment of clothing has diminished greatly, and the longer hours in the fields make it difficult to gather food at the days end. However, what the Negroes consider the greatest injustice against them, more so than any beating, is the constant abuse of their teenage daughters by Edward and Tom Louder, something that everybody but Susan is aware of.

Misty never had a problem keeping herself separate from Tom Louder. Mr. Tanner set certain rules when he took on Louder as field overseer, and when Misty was attacked a couple of years back, he was one of the ones Mr. Tanner thought of first. His questioning of him was rough, leaving a lasting impression.

Edward on the other hand was a constant problem. She avoided him as often as she could, but at times he made it difficult. Whenever he saw her alone he would approach her. His rude manners and speech were repulsive to her. At times when he had been drinking a lot he would try to touch her. On several occasions she had to push him away from her with force. Even though his obnoxious behavior was becoming more frequent, she said nothing to Susan. No matter what she thought of her, she was still Emily Tanner's daughter, and Misty out of her deep love and respect for Mrs. Tanner would always treat Susan properly.

Signs of autumn were setting in. The days were busy with harvest activities. The sun was disappearing much earlier and the evenings were cool. It's been a year already since the tragedy at sea. Misty, as well as some of the others, are still having a hard time of it. Though it's been a year it can feel just like yesterday if she thinks about it too long.

Lying in bed this night she had something else to think about. Another piece of her world was about to change. The Myers had her come in for dinner that evening to share their plans with her. As Rebecca's letter to Misty stated, they had completed building their house and were diligently clearing ground for spring planting. Her sister and husband settled nearby, and they wanted badly for their parents to join them. The Myers told Misty that evening they had decided to go. The political instability and constant talk of war left little doubt in Dr. Myers' mind that life as it had once been is slipping even further away. He told her he had sent letters to several medical schools informing them of the need for a replacement doctor. He couldn't leave until that was taken care of. With the news of their eldest daughter expecting another child, a change in their plans was arranged, and Mrs. Myers decided to leave ahead of her husband to be of assistance. Within a fortnight, they told her, she would be leaving.

This was not totally unexpected. They had expressed a desire on other occasions to be with their children. What was a surprise though, was their determined effort to convince her to go with them, even offering to bring the child Sarah if Susan would permit it. Of course, she wanted to go and to be with Rebecca again, and help the Myerses to settle into a new area. Even more important, she wanted to see Sarah grow up without the stigma of being an orphaned slave. But she couldn't say yes. There were Leo and Goldie, Willy Mae and Lester, and most importantly, Henry. There was also old Mrs. Tanner, who Misty wanted to look after. In doing so she felt she was doing something for those who had loved her, and there was the feeling in her heart, the one she talked about only to the child, the feeling she couldn't believe was true, but couldn't convince her heart it wasn't, that Roscoe was alive and would one day return to her.

The next couple of weeks were good ones. Lots of time was spent with the Myerses helping to pack and sort things, to write poems and letters to Rebecca, sleeping many of the nights in her room. Together she and Mrs. Myers made baby clothes for children born already and those to come.

The day before her departure they dressed in their Sunday best and were photographed. Some of the pictures were for Misty, others were for Rebecca. She stayed that night and rode with Dr. Myers to the depot to see his wife off. Mrs. Myers made her promise to look after the doctor until he left. She made Dr. Myers promise he would not stop trying to change Misty's mind about going out west with them. Misty's promise was easy to keep and she did it with joy. His was hopeless, and he knew it. Still he never stopped trying, even though he could tell she wasn't about to leave, not yet anyway.

It took about three weeks for the doctor to settle his affairs. The new doctor seemed like a nice fellow. He purchased the Myers' house and most of the furnishings. The final few days before departing, Doc Myers stayed at Mariah in one of the cottages and one afternoon he went fishing with Henry. Misty and Sarah joined them with a basket of food and cider. As they ate and talked Henry said, "I's remember da day she was born jes like it was yesterday."

"So do I," said Dr. Myers, "and I'm sure gonna miss her. I do feel good knowin you'll be lookin after her Henry."

"Dats bout da only joy left in dis old heart," he said.

Misty leaned over and hugged him tightly saying, "I can't ever lose you Henry," then turning to Dr. Myers she said, "Whenever I want to feel good, I only have to think of Henry and all the years we've come here fishing, or riding in the boat singing songs. You know when I was little, Dr. Myers, it didn't matter if I asked Henry every day to walk to the covered bridge, he would take my hand and go, always teaching me about God, and good manners, and telling me all my favorite stories no matter how many times I asked him to."

"And now we's tell em together ta dis sweet little girl," Henry said smiling to Sarah.

"You love your Henry don't you Sarah," Misty said to her. Without saying a word she went over and hugged him as Misty had done.

The following morning Dr. Myers had breakfast with old Mrs. Tanner, Misty, Edward, and Susan. After saying good-bye to them he and Misty went to the stable where a cariole was hitched and waiting for him. Henry was waiting there too. "Henry my good friend," he said shaking his hand, "It's been a pleasure knowing ya. I'll never put a fishin pole in my hand and not think of you my friend."

"I's sure have enjoyed knowin y'all Dr. Myers, I's praise da Lord for dat."

Dr. Myers stood still for a moment and the smile turned to a serious look as he said, "Henry, you're as honorable and as decent a man as I have ever met," then shook his hand a second time.

"Thank you sir," Henry said, then nodding his head he said again, "Thank you sir."

Misty rode off with Dr. Myers as far as the covered bridge. There they sat for a few moments and Misty said, "Seems like I wind up here saying good-bye to everyone."

"The day will come when there is no longer any reason to stay my child. That's when we will all be together again. I know it seems far off now, but when it comes we'll help you get settled where we are. You have a long life ahead of you and there will be years of happiness in it for you." They embraced each other and he kissed her tenderly on her forehead. She kissed him on his cheek and told him she loved him dearly. As he rode off she walked through the bridge to the other side watching and waving as he disappeared from her view. Parting from those she loves will never get easier, but it has become a sad fact of life.

She walked in his direction about a hundred yards to the big beech tree they had all carved their names into. Even Mr. and Mrs.

Tanner's names were cut in many year ago. It appears that Wendall and Addie must have stopped one day and added theirs also. She placed her hand over Roscoe's name, then Isabelle's, Rebecca's, and Naomi's. She kissed each one of them, then walked back over the covered bridge and slowly made her way home.

1860 was drawing to a close. It was late December and the plantation was in its quietest time of the year. Everywhere you went people were talking about the changes in government. Some were happy about it, some were weary of it. Most were confident that breaking away from the union and forming a confederacy would maintain the south's right to choose its own standards of living. But, talk of emancipation or Abraham Lincoln made people uncomfortable, and acts of slave rebellion were on the increase.

Most evenings Misty spent the time after dinner with Sarah and Willy Mae's daughter. Coming back to the house late, she would check in on Mrs. Tanner and retire. She returned this evening and went first to the kitchen, hoping not to run into Susan, knowing that could mean listening for an hour about her aches, pains, and other complaints. As she finished making a small bowl of potato salad the door behind her opened and someone entered the room. Without turning around she asked if they would like some. Expecting to hear Susan's voice or that of her children she was taken back when Edward answered, "That's right nice of y'all to be fixin a little somethin special to make my evening more pleasurable." Misty hesitated for a moment then placed the fork into the bowl, set it down on the table and headed for the door. Stepping in front of her he said, "Now hold on there pretty girl." He tried to touch her face with his hand, but she pulled her head back. "No need to hurry off girl, I like somebody to talk to when I'm eating."

"Let me by Edward, Mrs. Tanner is waiting for me," Misty said trying to step around him.

"Waiting for you? I don't think the old lady is even awake. Why disturb her?" He stepped in front of her again.

"Let me by, I don't want to talk to you," she demanded. The smell of alcohol was heavy and the look in his eyes frightened her. She tried again to go around him but he pushed her back. When she tried to exit through another door he loudly said, "When I'm talkin to you, wench, you stand still!" He grabbed her by the arm and pulled her back, then shoving her to the table he made her sit down. "Now don't y'all get me upset with ya, I want to talk to someone when I eat. I want to talk to someone intelligent for a

243

change, and lookin at a pretty face never did a man no harm," he said as he started to eat the salad she had made. "My, my, this is good Misty," he said, "I'll bet everything you make is good." Then he laughed a bit. "Y'all ever drink any whiskey girl?" he asked. Not replying she stood up and started to leave the room. He quickly jumped up and in two large steps grabbed hold of her arm and hair, forcing her back to the table. Neither of them was aware of Susan opening and closing the door. She stood silently, listening outside of the room. Misty protested loudly that he leave her alone, he snapped at her, 'Y'all might think you're some high and mighty princess, but cha ain't." His hand slapped the back of her head, "You're just another nigger girl here. You're my nigger girl. I own you and you will do as I say. I'll have you like I have any other nigger girl, you understand me?" She lay her head down on the table and covered it with her hands fearing he was going to strike her again. Instead he reached down gently and removed her hands from over her head and lifted her head upright. "No, no, girl," he said trying to sound differently, "I don't want to hit you. I want to be nice to you. Wouldn't you rather have it that way too?" She shook her head free of his hands and again demanded he leave her alone. Ignoring what she said, he ordered her not to get up and sat down to finish his bowl of potato salad.

For the next five minutes he rambled on not making a lot of sense. Misty sat on the edge of the bench waiting for an opportunity to run. She had reason to believe if she didn't make it out of the room he would become quite violent. But before she had a chance he was back on his feet and standing behind her. Placing his hands on her shoulders he said, "Misty, I've never seen a woman as beautiful as you are. I could be real good to you." She shook to get his hands off of her, but it only made him grab tighter. "Behave yourself girl, I could send y'all into the cotton fields if I had a mind to. You wouldn't look so pretty after awhile. What do ya think of that?" After he said this he started to slide his hands down over her shoulders.

She pushed his hands off and turned part way around, pushing him again, and knocking him back a step. Rising quickly to her feet she grabbed the fork from the bowl on the table. Lifting it up high she said, "You're a despicable fool, you come near me and I'll put out your eye. If you ever force yourself on me, I'll kill you!"

Edward stepped back out of her reach and began laughing loudly and saying, "I should have hit your head a little harder that night. Maybe you wouldn't be so squirrely. I'm gonna have you, wench, sooner or later. Y'all might as well consign yourself to that fact."

"You stupid thing, I didn't tell it was you because of the pain and the trouble it would have caused everyone, but there's nobody to protect anymore. I'll go to the sheriff," she said. This only caused him to laugh more.

"You can't go to no sheriff, you're property. I can do what I please to you," he said. Though she didn't really, she said, "I know where Olivia's body is. I'll say I saw you kill her. I know you beat her and she died, just like you tried to kill me!"

The laughter quickly stopped and the look on his face turned meaner and uglier than she had ever seen. "There's a way of taking care of niggers that get out of line," he said walking right up and placing his face in front of hers, "and you been out of line far too long." He walked to the door and pulled it open hard. Susan back stepped six feet or so when she heard him coming. "What'd you hear woman?" he said in a loud voice.

"I didn't hear anything. I was coming for some juice," she replied. He looked at her hard for a second then brushed by her and went upstairs. Susan entered the kitchen and found Misty still with the fork held up in the air. She lowered it to her side and looked at Susan without speaking. "He's not a bad man Misty, he has some problems. He needs time to work them out. I can't be without him, y'all understand what I'm saying, I . . . I . . . just can't be," Susan said with a very worried look on her face. Misty didn't respond, she placed the fork on the table and left the room.

Since Misty's return to Mariah, she had been careful never to be in a vulnerable position with Edward. She always felt he was less of a threat because he believed she didn't know he was the one who attacked her. Now she knew it was dangerous. Unfortunately, she didn't realize the greater danger was Susan.

During the next few days nothing more was said. What little Misty saw of Susan was awkward. They spoke little and the fearful look in Susan's eyes made Misty very uncomfortable. After helping old Mrs. Tanner back to her room, Misty went to the kitchen to talk with Willy Mae.

"Jes after breakfast," she was saying to Misty, "she had James fetch the cariole and off dey went, didn't say where's she goin or nothin. I's know she ain't gone nowhere alone in a coon's age."

"Maybe she's going to town to buy something," Misty offered.

245

"I's speck she goin to da doctor. She lookin somein awful dey past few days. I's know she ain't a eatin much a'tall cause I's bring jes much food back as I give to her. Ders somethin a troublin her aright." Then she paused to laugh and say, "Maybe she gettin so mean she be scarin herself." Misty didn't know what it was, but Susan never left the plantation and most certainly not alone. She worried that Susan might go to the sheriff, believing that what she had heard was true. Maybe she would try to discredit her before she said anything. She couldn't be sure, but she knew it had to have something to do with the other night.

Later that afternoon she saw Henry walking up from the stable area. "Is Susan back, Henry?" she asked.

"Tain't seen em since dey left dis mornin," he answered.

"Did James say where he was taking her?" she asked.

"I's see's em wit da buggy, but tain't talk to em none," he replied.

"Seems awful strange her going off like that," Misty said.

"Yes'em it do," Henry said as they sat down on a bench, and said further, "took wit her a travel bag, I specks she won't be back directly."

"Are you sure, Henry? She didn't say anything to Willy Mae or me about being away," Misty said sounding confused.

"Yes'em, I sure of it, saw it with my own eyes," he said in a matter-of-fact manner. This added information really had her concerned now. It appeared that only Edward knew what she was doing, and nobody was going to ask him.

That day and all of the next Misty stayed away from the big house. The few times she checked on old Mrs. Tanner she had Henry stay close by. On the third afternoon Susan returned. Without saying a word to anyone she went up to her room and remained there. Henry found Misty and told her of Susan's return. Together they went to see James, hoping to learn of his whereabouts the past three days.

"I's don't really know where she go, I take her to the big town-a-yonder ways off. She tell me stay at de barn till she come back. I's stay dar two nights till she come, dens I bring her home. She don't speak narry a word der or back."

"You don't know who she went to see?" Misty asked hoping for more.

"I's don't know nothin Misty. She's sure weren't lookin like diz was a holiday, lookin all down in da face, like sometin troublin her bad."

246

Misty looked at Henry. "I've got more questions now, but no answers."

"Maybe you can trick her into sayin. Girl never had a lick of smarts anyway," Henry said, and the two of them left together. "I's always did believe it's cause she turned blue when she's a baby," he said.

"I know you do, Henry," she responded smiling, "but babies do that sometimes, and it doesn't seem to leave them hurt any."

"Molly would say to me when there weren't nobody around, she thought dat the girl died when she see her on dey floor, she was blue and Molly picked her up. She lay like she was dead in her arms. Mistress Tanner grab da baby and shook da dickens out of her. Molly say da devil got in her and dats why she was not a good baby no mo."

"I have heard that story before Henry, and I wonder if maybe it did hurt her some, but I don't know about Aunt Molly's idea," Misty said as they walked to the big house together.

That evening she had dinner with Mrs. Tanner and Susan's boys. Edward never came in and Susan had Willy Mae bring her dinner to her room. Shortly after dinner Misty went up to Susan's room. She was invited in and found her sitting in a chair by the window. "Is there anything I can do for you?" Misty asked.

"Would you like to sit and talk for awhile?" Susan asked her quietly.

Misty turned a chair around and pulled it closer to Susan. "Did you have a good trip?" Misty asked, but got no answer.

"Isn't this a lovely room Misty. I left almost all Momma's things here. She had beautiful things, and knew just how to place everything to make it look so nice. I think of her all the time. She used to sing to me when I was a child. Do you remember when I used to play school with you and Isabelle and Naomi? I'd make believe I was the teacher, do you remember Misty?" said Susan with a far away look in her eyes.

"Yes I do Susan. It was a very nice time," Misty replied softly.

"Yes it was a nice time. Mother liked me to help her. She would always say I was a good girl," Susan said.

"She loved you very much, Susan," Misty said. She reached over and touched Susan's hand. "You look tired, Susan, perhaps you should rest," she added.

"I will dear," she said as she walked to her bed. "You were always a sweet girl Misty, I'm sorry." Though Misty thought it a peculiar thing to say, Susan's entire behavior was worrisome to her and she felt it best to just let her rest.

As she was leaving the room Susan said, "Would you come to me tomorrow after you have your lunch? I'd like you to do something for me."

Misty talked that evening with Mrs. Tanner about Susan. She felt there was nothing anybody could do for her, that Susan had always been odd and Edward had only contributed to her problems. Ironically, she again told Misty she was going to make her a document proclaiming her free, and that she should take the child and leave when she herself died.

The following afternoon Misty went up to Susan's room. Susan brought her in and handed her a sealed envelope with no inscription on it. "I want you to take this to someone for me," she said.

"In town?" Misty asked.

"No. About halfway someone will meet you. Give him the envelope. Tell him it is from me and tell him who you are," Susan said in a strange emotionless voice. "I don't want anyone to know what you are doing, so it is better if you walk . . . alone."

"I don't understand Susan, won't you tell me what this is all about?"

"You loved my mother didn't you," Susan stated.

"You know I did," Misty responded.

"You would do anything to protect her," Susan said in almost a childish manner. Misty stood with the envelope in her hand looking at Susan. She could make no sense out of what was being said. At first she was frightened by the strange request, but the more she looked at Susan the more she felt this was all something just taking place in her mind, and there would be nobody to receive the envelope. Before Misty could say anything else Susan surprised her further by saying, "I know she loved you very much. You will always have that." Then she turned her back to Misty and walked to the window.

Of all the things she had said, this by far was the most perplexing. Susan had never acknowledged Misty as a sister the way the others did, and many told her over the years that Susan was jealous of Mrs. Tanner's love for her. She left the room to carry out her assignment, but believed it was a futile effort.

Downstairs Sarah had been told to wait in old Mrs. Tanner's room. Misty would do as Susan asked and not tell anyone what she was doing, but she didn't see any harm in bringing the child with her. They each took a handful of cookies from the kitchen and started for the front door. As she passed a family portrait that hangs in the hall she paused to look at it. Almost by habit her eyes saw everyone's face but Susan's. At that moment she thought about that and looked at the teenage girl standing with her parents and began to feel sorry for her. Sarah tugged her arm and off they went.

The late December air was chilly. It didn't take long to reach the covered bridge where they rested a few minutes then walked to the old beech tree. Sarah could read most of the names carved into it. This delighted Misty and she told her on their return they would cut her name in the tree also. After walking a half mile or so Misty decided to sit on the roadside and wait awhile, becoming more convinced that Susan was succumbing to her emotional stress. However, they hadn't been waiting long when a covered wagon rounded the bend and rode up to them. Even when it stopped Misty didn't think there was a connection. Two men climbed down and greeted her. "Afternoon Missy," one said.

"Good afternoon," she replied. "Is there some way I can help you?"

"Well, we're to pick up a package along the way here. I don't recollect you know anything about that, do ya?"

Now a little confused again she said, "From Susan?"

"Yes Maam, a Miss Susan Ramsey," he said.

"Well I do declare," Misty said being quite surprised, "I didn't think, I mean I wasn't sure you were coming."

The other man spoke up saying, "Oh little missy, we wouldn't pass this up." Then he laughed and said to the other fellow, "but something ain't quite right here."

At that Misty said, "Oh, I'm sorry," and pulled out the envelope, "I was to give this to you." The man took the envelope and opened it. He displayed what looked to Misty like five or more pieces of currency. While she couldn't discern the amount, the look on the other man's face indicated he was well pleased. As the man read the paper that was with it, he looked at Sarah, then Misty, then read it some more.

"Now someone got something mixed up here. Your name is Misty, little honey?" he said looking to Sarah.

"That's who I am," Misty responded, getting very uneasy. The man looked again at the paper then scratched at the back of his head. "Now that makes sense, then it doesn't make sense," he laughed. "You're Misty, then who is this?" he said pointing to Sarah.

"Just a child from home I'm walking with," she replied as her mind started racing. "If you have a message you want me to bring back please give it to me now, as I have to be going," Misty said while reaching out her hand for Sarah to come to her.

"Just hold on a spell Miss till I talk to my brother." The two walked off a piece and talked quietly while reading the paper again. After just a minute they walked back and the one doing most of the talking said, "I can look at this little one and safely say this is a Negro child. Now this here piece of paper says you're a Negress woman, but I ain't so sure that someone ain't trying to pull the wool over my eyes." A cold and frightened feeling went all the way to her feet as she stood frozen in disbelief. She couldn't move or speak, but knew what was taking place. "I want you to be telling me the truth ya hear, are you a Negro?" Without answering Misty started to back up pulling Sarah with her.

Seeing the look on Misty's face Sarah became frightened and started to cry. The other man said to the first, "I reckon this is on the up and up, let's take the little one too, she's worth at least two hundred." By this time the girls had backed up several feet. With one hard pull Misty spun the child around and began to run with her. Had she been alone maybe she could have outrun them, but she stood no chance with Sarah. The men easily caught them and pulled them to the ground, but they found out quickly this would be no easy task. They tried holding her arms and she kicked. If they held her legs she punched and scratched. If they didn't hold her head back she bit. To get Misty under control they had to let go of Sarah and put all their effort into subduing her.

"Run Sarah! Go for Henry!" she kept screaming until the child fled. She fought with everything she had until they finally tied her hands and feet and placed a gag over her mouth. They threw her face down into the wagon. One placed his knee into her back to hold her down, while the other took the reins and quickly turned the wagon around and hurried off down the road.

For several hours she squirmed and rocked back and forth until she exhausted most of her strength. Fearful of what was going to happen to her, she forced herself to concentrate. Once she was still for awhile the man tied her to the side of the wagon and climbed up front with the driver. With her head lying close to the front she could hear most of what was being said. "It's too bad we lost the little one. She'd have fetched a good sum," he said to the driver.

"No matter brother, did you ever see one that looked like that one sell for less then seven hundred, maybe even nine. I thought the lady was simple minded, wanting to pay five hundred dollars to get rid of a slave, but I'll bet all five of it I know why now," the driver said. "Whatcha thinkin?" he asked.

"That's her husband's mistress, it's as plain as the hand in front of your face," the driver replied. "Maybe she's gonna have his baby."

The wagon rode long into the night before stopping. The men came to the back of the wagon and pulled out blankets and pillows. She tried by making noise to get them to remove the cloth from around her mouth, but they paid her no mind as they prepared their dinner over a fire and set up their blankets for the night. If she slept at all she didn't know it. By daylight her body was becoming stiff and sore. By kicking and making as much noise as she could they were awakened and brought to the wagon. The driver climbed in and removed the gag. "You can make it easier for yourself if you don't do anything stupid," he told her.

"Won't you please untie me? I have no feeling in my arms or legs," she asked him.

After he thought about it a moment he untied her and helped her sit up.

"Where are you taking me?" she asked as she rubbed from her knees to her feet.

"We were paid to take you to North Carolina. There we can sell you to whoever wants to pay the most," he answered, as he climbed back out of the wagon. Slowly she got to her feet and made her way to the back of the wagon. There seemed to be no opposition to it so she climbed down to the ground. "If you try to run, the rest of this journey will see you tied to a board," the driver said as he searched a compartment on the outside of the wagon.

"I need privacy for a minute sir," she said. He looked at her with uncertainty then said, "You go over to those trees, but don't stop talking to me ya hear," he responded pointing to where he wanted her to go. When she returned she sat down by the fire the other one was rebuilding. He didn't say much, but what little he offered revealed a plebeian personality, and so she knew this one was to be feared more. They prepared coffee and grits and shared it with her.

The early morning hours were very chilly and she sat quietly wrapped in a blanket close to the fire. As they talked to each other she studied them. Their conversation indicated at least two, maybe three days traveling. Somewhere she had to find a means of escape. That letter of freedom, even freedom itself she always took for granted. Now her very life depended on getting back to Mariah and old Mrs. Tanner. With letter in hand she would confront Susan. She tried for awhile to convince them she was free, and they'd be put in jail for kidnapping. She told them she could clear their names of any wrong doing, that they could keep the five hundred and get a thousand more if they brought her back to Mariah. The one that had done most of the driving the day before seemed to be the smart one. His brother referred to him as Wes. It was this one she tried to appeal to, but his response was, "Ya talk smart for a Negro, but if ya don't shut up a while I'm gonna hog tie ya again, and stuff a rag in your mouth."

The day's journey began early. They traded off driving to keep a swift pace going, hoping to get half way through South Carolina by nightfall. Later in the day they stopped to rest the horses. Misty followed Wes around as he checked the horses and the wagon. "Is selling people the way you make all your money?" she asked.

"I sell other things too, cattle, sheep, tobacco, indigo, anything I can profit from," he told her.

"You don't see any difference between selling cattle and selling people do you?" she said. "I don't sell people. I sell niggers. Does that answer you all right little miss?" he returned indignantly.

"You don't think I'm a person?" she asked. He looked perplexed for a moment then said, "Well I know you're not a steer, because they don't ask any questions. Now get back in the wagon and be quiet." Any other attempt to talk with him he ignored. His brother who he called Toad repeatedly made crude remarks, and looked at her in a vulgar manner. This one seemed to lack any intelligence at all, and she started to think maybe he could be tricked and used somehow to gain her freedom. So now instead of being harsh with him she would smile sometimes when the other one wasn't looking. She knew how dangerous this could be, but she also knew if they got to North Carolina and sold her into slavery she might never get free.

They rode again till nearly dark. She was allowed to come out of the wagon and eat by the fire. The two men sat off a distance, but she could hear most of their conversation. They figured on

252

making their destination by the following evening. The thought of what could happen kept her strong. She had never been so scared before, but she knew she couldn't give into it. If she were still in their hold this time tomorrow it would be too late. They would sell her easily, and she knew what she would be purchased for.

After eating they allowed her a few minutes of privacy, but only a very short distance from them. She thought about running and taking her chances of getting away in the dark, but felt the two of them had too good a prospect of catching her, and then she'd probably be shackled the remainder of the way. When she came back to the wagon she was ordered to get in and was then tied for the night. The one called Toad volunteered to do it. Inside Misty spoke nicely to him and asked if he would sit with her awhile. He tied her, then sat down. "Do you know what is going to happen to me?" she asked.

"I reckon I do," he answered.

"Nobody is gonna buy me to pick cotton. I'm gonna be somebody's mistress," she said. This caused him to laugh and say, "I reckon you're right. Was ya mistress to that lady's husband like Wes says ya was?"

"Yes I was. She knew it for a long time, but I cook real good, and I make clothes good, and so she didn't want to sell me off," Misty replied.

"Then why did she?" he asked.

"Because he started to love me more than her. You don't have a wife do you?" she asked.

"I ain't never did," he said.

"Why don't you keep me? You have the papers. As of right now you own me. Your half of five hundred is two hundred and fifty dollars. Why not give it to your brother and tell him he gets the money, and you keep me?"

It was obvious he liked the idea. For a long time he quietly listened as she reasoned the matter out to him. When Wes came to the wagon for his sleeping gear he called for Toad to come out. Misty hoped he would tell his brother what she had told him to. At the least she wanted them to argue. If he was told no, like she knew he would be, then he would believe it was the two of them against his brother. She hoped she could then convince him to let her sneak off and let him think they would meet somewhere. After about an hour Misty could hear a heated exchange taking place.

However, it didn't last long and silence set in. She lay awake nearly the entire night hoping he would attempt to kidnap her.

When she awoke it was morning and Wes was tugging at the rope to untie her. "I'm gonna let you have some food, then I'm gonna tie you up again. You're a little too smart for your own good. I sure wouldn't want to be the one that puts out any money for you. You ain't gonna stick around long. I can see that okay," he said with a smile. She sat up and rubbed her ankles and wrists then began to climb down. When Wes came out she said to him, "The day will come sir, when Susan will have to look me in the eye. You can bet your five hundred dollars on that."

She poured water into a large bowl and washed her face and hands. The men had made coffee and were about to eat some dried beef sticks. Misty went to the side of the wagon where the food stuffs were and gathered what she needed to make corn toast and oatmeal, enough for the three of them. "Ya know girl, this is business. It's a buy and sell world. You're pretty smart, you understand this don't you?" Wes said to her.

"I'm not sure I understand what your point is," Misty replied.

"Never mind girl, it don't matter anyway," he said.

"I didn't make you this food to make you feel guilty or did I think it would gain me any special favors from ya. I've been taught to love my neighbor. If I fail in that it's not only my defeat, but a reflection on my teacher," she said.

He sat rubbing his chin for a moment. "I've sold many a nigger girl, but none like you I'll say that."

"Oh no sir you're mistaken, they were all like me. They wanted to be free, to love whom they choose to, to live a quiet life with dignity and self respect. My poppa taught me there is a lesson in everything, and that knowledge is a great comforter, but wisdom is to be desired more than anything. I had much knowledge about slavery, but now I truly understand. I do forgive you. If you're to be judged adversely it will be by God, not by me." After saying this she quietly ate her breakfast, the brothers didn't speak for a while either.

When the time came to depart she asked not to be tied, but Wes would take no chances with her. He did agree to tie her hands in front of her, and didn't place anything over her mouth.

As the day wore on the men felt certain they were now in North Carolina. Misty had long ago loosened the ropes on her wrists and ankles and with the afternoon well along she knew something had to happen soon. However, what was about to take place was not in any way what she had been praying for. The men brought the wagon to a stop near a stream and unhitched the horses. After watering and feeding them Wes walked off in search of a deeper area to bath in. When Misty realized this she knew it had to be now. She called Toad to the wagon and said, "By tomorrow morning at the latest, your brother will have me sold. I'd like to stay with you, I'd be good to ya."

"There's no way Wes is gonna let that much money get by em, and you wouldn't stick round long anyway. I'm not gonna get myself fooled by no nigger girl," he said looking into the wagon.

"If I have to belong to someone; why not you. Wouldn't you like that?" she said. Her feet were free of the ropes and her wrists were loose to the point of slipping them out. She concealed this from him as she tried to move closer to the rear of the wagon.

"I'm not gonna get myself in no trouble, girl, and I can get you as my mistress right now, and maybe I have a mind to," he said. Misty stopped where she was.

"Your brother will come back soon, and won't like it, and then you'll be in trouble anyway," she said.

"I don't always do what he wants ya know. He ain't be'in back for a spell, so maybe y'all better just stop ya talkin' for awhile," he said as he climbed into the wagon. "Don't be a fussin or nothin ya hear," he told her as he reached out and took hold of her arm. At that point she pulled her other hand free of the rope and slapped him across the face as hard as she could. Then with both of her feet she pushed him hard knocking him over. She got to her feet and was at the rear of the wagon when he grabbed her dress and pulled her down. With the weight of his body he pinned her to the floor and tried to hold her still.

Earlier that day she had found a broken ax handle and hid it near where she was sitting. During their struggle she freed her hand and groped about for it. After several attempts her hand found it and her fingers wrapped firmly around it. There wasn't the room to swing it hard, but she managed to hit his head with enough force to daze him temporarily. Pushing him aside she got to her feet, he tried to do the same. He was nearly straight up when she drew her arm back and swung, hitting his forehead with a loud thud. His eyes disappeared up into his head, and he fell over backwards. When he came down his head struck an empty oak beer barrel that was banded with steel straps, a loud grunt came out of him as his body rolled over and came to rest on his side. She had only wanted to disable him, to gain a slight edge in her endeavor to escape, but as she stood over him, the broken ax handle in her hand, she knew she had killed him. A large wound on the back of his head was bleeding profusely. He had a cut on his forehead, and blood was coming from his mouth. Opening her hand the handle fell to the floor. She climbed quickly out of the wagon hoping not to see his brother returning.

The horses were tied nearby eating. She loosened them and fastened one rope as a bridle. She jumped up onto the horse, took hold of the rope on the other one, and rode off leading it with her. For several miles they rode at a fast pace. Coming upon a large open field she removed the rope from the horse she had been riding and released it. Climbing up on the other one she quickly took off down the road.

It soon became too dark to ride. She tried to walk leading the horse, but there was no moon at all and she was forced to stop for the night. Not for a minute did she sleep, her heart wasn't pounding anymore, but her mind was racing. Is he on her trail? Would he kill her if he found her, or take her to the sheriff? Which of the scenarios was worse? Where could she go? They'd be looking for her at Mariah she thought. If only she had her letters from Rebecca she could find her way out there. But even that she thought might be dangerous. Susan would tell him to look for her there.

At the very first sign of light she was on the horse and moving. As soon as the sun started coming over the horizon she left the road and started riding through the woods and fields. Somewhere along the way she decided there was only one place she could go for help . . . Wendall Cambridge. But all she had to go on was the name of the school, and that was in Boston, Massachusetts!

She rode for the entire day stopping occasionally to rest the horse and search for things to eat. Mostly she cracked open acorns on rocks and ate the bitter food they contained. It was now the beginning of January. The shawl she wore offered little comfort during the cold dark hours of the night. She had slept little since being abducted, and eating even less has left her weak and susceptible to illness.

When daylight came she had no choice but to ride. Even with two days lost in the woods and many miles between her and the wagon, she was still constantly looking over her shoulder. After two more days of the same she was starting to lose hope that she would survive this ordeal. Even the afternoon sun wasn't so warm anymore, and when the following night brought a heavy frost she was forced to ride in cold and wet clothing. Having lost so much strength it was hard to keep up any kind of pace, and the fear of not finding a way out of the forest was increasing.

Late that afternoon she came down the side of a mountain she had crossed. Looking ahead through the trees she could see a bright area before her. If this was an open field she decided she would stop for the day and let the horse eat and rest. She too would rest, knowing she would sleep better while it was still somewhat warm. This was the first good thing that had happened in many days. She was able to sleep until after dark before the cold woke her. Staying under the branches of a large white pine tree kept her dry and a little warmer than the previous night.

In the morning she gathered acorns and berries before riding on. Going back into the woods she rode only a short distance before coming onto another field. This one was fenced in with cows. That meant a farm nearby, and hopefully food and shelter. She went from one field to the next looking for a road or trail. Instead of finding the farmhouse, she found the farmer, with a horse and cart. He was cutting firewood at the edge of a field.

"Good day sir," she said as she approached him, "could you help me? I seem to be quite lost." He was an older man in his sixties. He looked at her carefully as he put his bow saw down. She had the look of not only being lost, but frightened, and extremely undernourished. "You come on down from that horse young lady, it looks like you both need a rest," he said in a reassuring manner. Misty climbed down and nearly fell over. He told her to sit on the cart, then tied the horse to it. Next he opened a small wooden box and gave her an apple. He talked to her nicely as he loaded the wood he had cut. A few minutes later they were riding off.

When they arrived at the house he drove around to the rear. The door opened and a small gray-haired lady came out to greet them, and saying his name like a question said, "Frank, who did you find?"

"She found me, Libby," he said climbing down.

"Well it looks like a good thing she did," she responded as she took Misty's hand and helped her from the cart. "Poor child, you come right in the house." Inside she was given a wash basin to clean her face and wash her arms and hands. Then a bowl of warm stew and bread with milk to drink. Misty told them she had been kidnapped and managed to run free. She didn't say how or reveal her true identity. They could see she was very troubled, and that what she needed most was a few more good meals and a warm bed to sleep in.

The heat coming from the wood stove drew her close. She sat wrapped in a blanket not saying much until she finally lay back on a pillow and fell fast asleep. She slept till almost ten o'clock the next morning. When she awoke she discovered her throat was swollen and sore, and her chest was badly congested. Lying on the floor in the warm blanket with a fire next to her she didn't want to get up.

"Good morning child," Libby said coming in with hot soup. "There is nothing better than chicken soup for what ails ya."

Misty found it hard to talk but said, "You've been more than kind to me and I've no way to repay you."

"We don't see too many people living a way out here, so even if they're a little sick we try to keep them a spell," she smiled.

"Am I still in North Carolina?" Misty asked. "My goodness girl you must have been traveling for some time. You're in Virginia now," she answered.

"I really must be going today. I have to get to Boston as quickly as possible," she said. "It's better to get to Boston late than not at all. You wouldn't get very far in your condition, and do you know the further up you get the colder it gets. Winter is a lot different up there," Libby said to her.

"I must get there. He is the only one who can really help me, and I can't be a burden to you folks," she said.

"Why not stay two or three days. If you don't rest up some you'll only get worse," Libby suggested. Misty could only smile and nod yes. She felt so sick she didn't even want to stand up. Another day's rest sounded real good to her. As Libby and her husband suspected, two days quickly turned into five, and only then did she start to really feel better.

With her strength back and the cold subsiding she was able to help out both inside and outside of the house. It was easy to become comfortable with these people. Their kindness and generosity helped her to relax mentally, and to begin to accept all the things that had happened. Most mornings now saw a thick covering of frost on the ground and occasional snow flurries were not at all unusual. Libby did not want Misty to leave under these conditions. She suggested waiting until spring when traveling would be safe.

258

Her husband agreed, and offered to bring a letter to town. "Write to this fellow," he told her, "have him come and get you here." It was an offer too good to pass up. That evening she wrote to Wendall telling him everything, and asked him to come for her. The letter went to town the following week. Misty felt greatly relieved after that.

February passed. It was much colder than winter in Georgia. March brought almost two weeks of rain. They thought the sun would never shine, but finally it did, and it caused things to come to life everywhere. Misty was helping outside as much as she could, and in between her chores, trying to finish an afghan she was crocheting for them before Wendall arrived. There was so much to do that the days were going by quickly. With March giving way to April, seeds were now being planted, but still there was no sign of Wendall.

On the fourteenth day of the month, Frank made the journey with his wife to town. They were picking up supplies, and Misty hoped they would also find a letter from Wendall. They returned without a letter, but the news they had heard in town was probably the reason he had not come. On April twelfth the confederates fired on Fort Sumter in South Carolina, and the Union was preparing for war. They didn't have a great deal of news, but what information they did relate did not sound good. Misty told them if this meant a war she wanted to leave quickly to find Wendall, who was hopefully still in Boston.

The next day was to be her last. The uncertainty of what was happening would force her to move on. Though they didn't have any money to spare, they sent her off with a blanket and clothing, and enough food to take her quite a ways. It was difficult to say good-bye to such nice people, knowing she would probably never see them again, but the uncertainty of what Wendall would do in the advent of war made it vital she leave right away.

The fact remained that she would be wanted for murder, and the theft of two horses. In an attempt to make herself harder to recognize she traded her horse for one of theirs. Though she got the lesser of the deal she was happy for them, and more relaxed not riding the stolen horse.

Soon into her journey she realized that at least for now she was safe. No one was thinking about anything but the war. In every small town or village she passed through, people were preparing to fight. For her safety, Misty developed a story about her parents dying, and her need to reach Boston and her Grandmother. She feared saying she was a southerner might hinder her ability to travel freely. Doing her best to hide her accent she said she was from Kentucky whenever she was asked.

Riding hard day after day she made her way out of Virginia and into Maryland. On the nineteenth day of April she entered Baltimore. Tension was thick in the air, a strong minority of secessionists were concentrated there. With her food stuffs almost depleted it was necessary to enter town to find a way to replenish them. This however, proved to be a costly mistake. Troops from the sixth Massachusetts regiment were passing through on their way to Washington, and a riot occurred. The city was thrown into confusion, all she could do was run for cover. The remainder of the day, and most of the night, the fighting was fierce. Finding a half-filled coal bin she crawled to the rear and sat quietly until just before dawn.

Her horse she had left staked on a small piece of ground in the area where she entered the city. Cautiously making her way in the dark, she retuned only to find the animal was gone, and with it what few things she had been given. There was no point in looking for it, she knew someone had taken it to flee the city. There was no point despairing over the situation either. She simply began walking back down the road that had brought her there.

A couple days on foot and she was back in Virginia. The war movement was progressing so rapidly she now doubted Wendall would still be in Boston. He wouldn't fight for the North she reasoned, because his family was in the South. However, she didn't think he would side with the South since he opposed their politics. But no one expected the war to last long, and even if he was not there now, he might return. Or at the very least she could try to find out where to reach him. Plus, no matter how anything else turned out, Boston is most likely to remain in a free state.

For a young woman wanted as a runaway slave, a horse thief, and a murderer, to chance finding a friend was worth everything. On the advice of someone she met, she traveled to the Potomac River hoping to ride a ferry up river toward Washington and then go by train to Boston. Under normal circumstances perhaps this may have worked out, but nothing was as it used to be.

It was now nearly June and reports of large military troops being assembled were spreading like fire. The only activity on the river was war-related. Misty managed to get on a boat going north by hiring herself as a cook and a maid. This allowed her to once again eat three times a day and procure clean clothing and a cot to sleep on. When the boat reached its destination, the captain encouraged Misty to continue on to Manassas Junction where she could help the other women sew uniforms.

Crossing over to the North was becoming more difficult, as well as dangerous. If she stayed and worked, it meant food and shelter, and with a little help she could secure a train ticket to Boston. The days quickly turned to months and as the seasons changed, Misty's duties changed with them. As the war raged on, she was moved to various locations to perform the tasks of a nurse. Her training was quick and raw. The atrocities being inflicted by both sides was beyond anything she could have imagined. Working at times eighteen hours in a day, she cared not only for the Confederate soldiers, but the wounded Union soldiers taken captive as well.

In the spring of 1862 the news came that New Orleans had been taken by the Union. This was a major defeat for the Confederates, and everyone took the news badly, but Misty thought differently. She could only think of the Franklins and the beautiful city they shared with her and of her good friend Genaset, thankfully safe in France now. As for Calvin, she could only pray he was alive and well.

As time went on there were new locations for her to apply her skills. Moving steadily through Virginia, then into Tennessee, and up to Kentucky she saw the reality and cruelty of war. She had, on too many occasions, watched people die as she tried to help them. Many times she completed the amputation of arms and legs struck by cannon fire, sewing up wounds, knowing there was still metal inside that couldn't be removed. The South seemed to be coming apart and the slaves were escaping into Union lines with more and more frequency. Some were forced to return while others were declared a contraband of war and used in the fight against their former owners. Still others escaped altogether and continued on to Canada.

The war seemed by now to have no end. The number of dead and wounded men was staggering. It was as though there would be no one left to put the land back together again. A country of widows is what the war weary nurses and aides were predicting. Misty didn't care what side called itself the winner. She often thought of Mr. Tanner's words: "You judge the quality of your work by what it accomplishes." All she had seen and experienced told her the war was wrong. She would stay and help the suffering, but she told anyone who wanted more than that, that she was neither rebel nor yankee, and wanted no part of their war.

In the spring of 1863 she was taken back to Virginia, first to Fredericksberg, then to Williamsport. Near the beginning of June she was in Pennsylvania. At no other time did she feel so strongly about leaving and making her way to Boston. Never had she been so close. But as before, the thought of those suffering kept her waiting for the war's end. Though she paid little attention to the talk and speculation of military movements, she knew for a certainty that Commander Lee was nearby, and what she heard again raised her hopes that it was all coming to its end.

Not many miles from Gettysburg, Pennsylvania in the opening days of July, a fierce battle broke out. As the wounded were brought back, it sounded like the battle that would end it all. Not just her hopes, but everyone's were running high. They all eagerly awaited the victory call. But on July 4th there was a call for retreat. Devastated to be moving south again, she found herself pushing through the South Mountain passes, and back to Williamsport. Another week and they were falling deeper south into Virginia. More battles, more wounded, as the months turned into years.

It is now 1864. In Richmond it appeared that Grant was coming not for Richmond, but for Lee himself. Misty felt the tide had turned to the North. She realized that reports spread amongst southerners were too biased to be considered accurate. By now it didn't matter anyway. What did she care if the South were defeated. The years had changed everyone, including Misty. No one can experience these things and not be adversely affected. If the North abolished slavery and freed Henry and Sarah and all the others from the likes of Edward Ramsey and his cohorts, then at least some good would result. But again things turned the other way. The defeat suffered by General Grant at Cold Harbor on June 23rd, was one of the worst the Union had endured. About seven thousand northern men lost their lives, while less than fifteen hundred southerners perished. The Confederates' hopes were again high. Back and forth the war raged on. As 1864 ended, much of the land was controlled by the Union, and by now its once beautiful landscape was marred by cannon fire, and covered with blood. Whatever the outcome, Misty was certain things would forever be changed.

Five long hard years have passed. They've lived with the uncertainty and degradation that makes up the life of a prisoner. News of the war comes in on occasion, never accurate and always months after its occurrence. Being so far from home it is hard to believe any of it is true. Every story only heightens their desire to escape from this island and return home to protect their land and loved ones. Though all his concern focuses on Misty and her safety, he is confident her intelligence and ingenuity will carry her through the horrors of war.

After five years of breaking rock from the quarry, Roscoe was finally moved to the other side of the island. There he found a much easier way of life. He was first assigned to the masonry crew working on walkways throughout the compound. Later he was assigned to the carpentry detail building barrels for rum and ale, boxes for the transfer of furnishings and other related items the king and his royal family would be sending to this island retreat.

The boxes were four feet wide and five feet long, and packed with stones unique to the island when the ship went out. This offered Roscoe his best opportunity yet for escape. Master Shot would regularly leave the island for two to four months at a time leaving a deputy as ignorant as himself in charge. Roscoe hoped each time he left he wouldn't return, but he always did. Many of the buildings had been completed for some time now, and when they were to be used by any of the king's family or guests all but a few prisoners would be confined to the far side of the island.

It was early May on a Sunday morning when the deputy entered the barracks calling for everyone's attention. He proceeded to pick five men, of which Roscoe was one, for a work detail on the other side. Everyone was sent back on Friday so they knew a ship was coming in soon with the king or some other high ranking family for a holiday. Had Master Shot not been off the island at this time, Roscoe would not have been picked, but the deputy gave it no thought and picked him, along with four other muscularly built men. After being taken outside, they were ordered to wait for the guards who would lead them to their work assignment. When the deputy departed, Roscoe told one of the other prisoners that he knew and trusted to go back inside and send out Zachary. When the guards came and led them off, they were taken to the other side and there boarded transfer boats to be taken to the ship anchored off shore. Roscoe and Zachary had no intention of overpowering the guards. They were both cautious and fully armed. Nor was there any chance of overtaking a ship the size of the one they were about to enter. But there had to be something they could exploit in this. Something that would help gain them their freedom.

Whatever royalty came on the ship was taken ashore prior to the prisoners' arrival. Only the ship's guards and the cook remained. For the better part of an hour the men carried heavy wooden boxes from below to the transfer boats. The remaining items were from the ship's kitchen. It was there that Roscoe saw his first opportunity.

While packing the box with various cooking utensils he tried to tell his story to the chef. The man at first seemed to be listening, then interrupted by saying, "I could almost believe such a thing. It's too absurd a tale to think you could contrive it." But he refused to listen any further and left Roscoe to his work and the two guards watching him.

When everything was packed and loaded onto the boats, they started rowing back to shore. The chef stayed with the kitchen goods, and that put him in the same boat with Roscoe and Zachary. Again Roscoe tried to explain who they were, but the chef didn't believe any of it. As they unloaded the boxes he directed Roscoe and Zachary to carry his things to the kitchen. This was a small building separate from the main living quarters. When out of earshot of the guards, Roscoe said to him, "We trap wild pigs and garnish and roast them southern style. We can get you one for the king or whoever it is that's on the island." For the first time the man looked like he heard something he wanted to hear. Then he dismissed them without saying anything at all. Walking away Zachary said to Roscoe, "I'll slip away the first chance I get and set the traps. We'll take the cook a fresh liver. He wanted what you said to be true. He will probably find favor with whoever brought him here if he could offer a roasted boar."

"If they keep us on this side of the island overnight, they'll shackle us I'm sure," Roscoe said.

"Something's got to happen this time. It could be another five years before we get any kind of opportunity again," Zachary said as they met with the others.

"These two stay, the others go back," was the order given by the guard. Zachary and another were to remain to perform house chores for the visitors.

"Good hunting mate," he said as Roscoe was led away. No workers were sent back over when anybody from the motherland was there.

Roscoe was sent to the quarry everyday to cut stones. At least once during each day he checked the traps. This required his absence for an hour or more. If he found one trapped he was obligated to share it with the guard on duty that following Sunday when they would slaughter and roast it. That he reasoned he could work out with the chef if he could win his favor.

It was a Friday afternoon when Roscoe discovered a boar had fallen into one of the traps. He secured the opening to keep any others from falling in. If two were in there together they would kill each other and the meat would be useless. On Saturday he waited until the work day was close to over before returning to the trapped boar. This one was a male and quite large. He likened them to the cows they had back home.

To kill these animals was always a difficult task. He first had to hit its head with a large rock to at least daze it. Then he jumped into the pit and clubbed it to death. Had he a knife he could cut its throat, but the sharpest thing he had was a rock sharpened like an Indian arrowhead. This he used to cut out the liver. From this time on his life hung in the balance. With a fresh and bloodied liver he took off running as fast as he could go. He had to first get away without his guard missing him too soon, then elude any guards on the other side, and slip into the kitchen area. Even if he did all that he still didn't know if the chef would listen to him or summon the guards. What he didn't know was that Zachary had already convinced the chef they had been trapping the boars, and the chef was waiting to hear they had one for him.

Roscoe slipped into the compound unnoticed and quickly made his way to the kitchen area, only to find he was alone. He placed the liver in a pan and put a lid on it, then sneaked around the prisoners' cottages in search of Zachary. At the far end of the row he saw a guard stationed outside. With no other prisoners on that side of the island he knew Zachary had to be in there. The cottages are built up off the ground on poles so climbing under them was an easy way to move quickly and not be detected. Because there were only two prisoners, and they were locked in, only one guard was there for them. Roscoe knew by now they would be searching for him on the other side, and in only a short time they would come over to this side looking. If he were caught he would be hung. He had to be very cautious while time was in his favor.

Lying on the ground under the building he tapped repeatedly with a stone until he got their attention. "Who's there?" a voice called.

"Zachary, it's Ros. Don't speak too loudly," he said.

"Did you get a boar?" Zachary asked.

"I brought the liver to persuade him with, but he's nowhere to be found."

"Go back to the kitchen area and wait, Ros. I told him we would do it. He'll know why you're there when he sees ya," instructed Zachary.

Roscoe crawled back under the row of buildings and quickly made his was to the kitchen. All the while he was hoping the chef would be there. The building that was the kitchen was a large square room made of stone connected to a spring house that stored the fruits and vegetables. There was only one entrance, but several large open window areas along the sides. Roscoe slipped in through one of them quickly to avoid being seen by a passing guard. As his feet touched the floor, someone else's nearly left it. A young girl of about eighteen years was startled and jumped backwards into a cabinet. They frightened each other and froze for a moment.

"I'm not supposed to be here, I won't hurt you, I brought the cook a pig's liver. If the guards find me before I talk to the cook they will hang me. They really will," Roscoe said quickly as he backed away from her and went to the pan to show her the liver. To his surprise she began laughing. If she thought this was funny he reasoned, maybe she wouldn't scream. "Do you think my hanging is funny?" he asked and smiled.

"Oh no not at all," she said. "I'm not supposed to be here either. My uncle won't let me out of the house alone."

"Who is your uncle?" Roscoe asked.

"He's the earl, and a cousin of the king," she said.

"I don't want you to be frightened, I wouldn't harm you," Roscoe said trying to sound reassuring.

"I'm not frightened. Besides, if I cry out guards will come." As he looked at her he could see she really wasn't frightened. She had been looking for food when he came in.

"Do you know where the chef is?" Roscoe asked.

"Uh huh," she answered with a smile.

266

Smiling back he said, "It would be real good for me if you would get him."

"I can't," she said. "I'm not supposed to be out alone." Then hesitating and smiling more she said, "They're always saying, what if one of the prisoners escapes and finds me unprotected? Anyway, what would I say? There is a runaway criminal waiting to cook you dinner? Really now, do you want me to get in trouble just because you are?"

"I assure you young lady, you're not in the presence of a criminal, but I need help to prove it to those who can help me," he said.

"Never a guilty man hung, that's what the earl says," she responded.

"Will you help me?" asked Roscoe in a worried tone of voice. She talked with him a short while more then went off to carry out his request. He wanted to believe he could trust her, but had too much to lose to leave himself entirely in her hands.

When she left the building a nearby guard saw her and insisted on escorting her back to the main house. Roscoe took the opportunity to slip off a distance into the dark and watch for the chef's arrival. He wondered if the man would just report the incident, or if the girl would tell someone else and cause his capture. If he had to wait too much longer, he thought it might be better to get back to the other side and fake an injury. To be found lying in one of the open pits might get him out of his predicament and give him the opportunity to try again at another time.

When he saw two guards coming in his direction he dropped to the ground and pulled himself by his elbows into a thicket. Even though they didn't look like they were doing anything unusual he was growing very concerned that his whole plan was failing. Had it not started to rain he would have continued to draw back and make his way around the island. However, the downpour kept him there long enough to see the chef and the girl appear and enter the kitchen. Being cautious he waited awhile to see if any others were following behind them. After a few minutes the girl came out and looked about. It was obvious she was looking for him and no one else, so he quickly ran to the kitchen building and slipped inside.

"I thought they caught you," the girl said looking relieved.

"Your friend told me you would catch one. Where do you have it?" the chef said as he stood over an open fire frying up the liver.

"Can you help me to talk with the Earl?" Roscoe asked.

"Tonight I'll tell him, with the help of you and your associate, they will all enjoy an unusual feast. If all goes well for me, it will go well for you also," the chef responded.

"Can you be certain he will be interested in this?" Roscoe asked.

"This man pushes the scale over the three hundred pound mark," the girl mused. "He lives to eat."

"Is the animal clean and hanging?" the chef asked.

"Not exactly," Roscoe replied in a coy kind of manner. "I'll need Zachary's help to remove it from the hole it is in and carry it back. Can you arrange that?" Turning to the girl the chef told her to return to the main house. This however, brought quick opposition, and for the sake of time he relented and the three went for Zachary.

Not far from the kitchen they were confronted by three guards with two barking dogs. Their rifles pointing at Roscoe, they commanded he lie on the ground. "This man is no runaway, I specifically sent for him today. Why weren't you informed of this?" the chef asked. One guard looked to the other and none had an answer. "He is here on assignment by orders of the Earl of Wyndham." At that the chef dismissed them then turned his attention to Roscoe. "You risked your life hoping I could help you. I'm convinced that there is more than an ounce of merit to your story. But I won't make you any promises you know."

"Everybody on the island knows we're not like the others, but none of em have the decency to care. If we don't take a chance when we think there's an opportunity we'll be left here to die," Roscoe said.

"If I even suspect you're up to something not good, I'll have ten guards on you in a minute," the chef responded as they walked on to the cottage Zachary was in.

The chef eventually introduced himself as Edward Foraker. At about five foot five or so, and a little pudgy, he looked like someone who knew what to do with food. Roscoe was beginning to think he was not as hard as the man wanted him to believe.

The girl's name was Jocelyn. To her this was a much needed distraction. She had told Roscoe that her parents sent her off frequently with relatives while they traveled alone to more interesting places. Whether he was a criminal or not, he knew she really didn't care. This was the most exciting thing to happen to her in some time, and it appeared she considered Mr. Foraker a friend, and trusted his judgment.

There was no opposition from the guard, and he released Zachary to the chef's custody. After this Mr. Foraker made Jocelyn stay at the main house and the three went to retrieve the wild boar. With ropes and muscle they pulled the animal out of the pit. Mr. Foraker did what he could to eliminate any excess weight. The rainfall early that evening made carrying this heavy animal even more difficult. It was past midnight when they returned to the kitchen. Another hour was spent cleaning and preparing the boar before hanging it for the night.

The chef escorted them back to the cottage and gave directions. They would be allowed to bathe and be brought to the kitchen at nine o'clock the following morning.

When they arrived back at the kitchen, breakfast was there for them with food they hadn't seen in five years, and of course, Jocelyn was there eager for the day's events. Roscoe proceeded to work with Mr. Foraker preparing the many appetizers and other dishes that would accompany the roasted boar. Mr. Foraker tapped a five gallon barrel of ale that was stored in the adjacent spring house and he freely partook as he worked. Zachary built a large pit and a spit to turn the boar above it. The sky was clear and a gentle sea breeze blew in off the water.

Around four o'clock Zachary started the fire. The Earl and all his guests came around to see the men fasten the boar to the spit and turn it over the fire. In the course of the next four hours while the pig roasted to perfection, several more kegs of ale were opened.

Roscoe and Zachary stayed in the kitchen or at the fire pit serving all evening. Jocelyn spent much of her time around them, listening to their stories of America and telling her own sad tales of life with ones who cared so little.

At Zachary's bidding she went to where the three musicians had performed and brought back a guitar. Though it had been five years, Roscoe played as if it had been but a day. Jocelyn was enthralled. She never heard that kind of music before, and she liked it. She wasn't alone. Quite a few of the others joined around them, and so he played a half an hour of the best Negro pickin' and stompin' they had ever listened to.

When the evening was over and the party was through Roscoe and Zachary were told to clean it up. Mr. Foraker offered to help, but he had had far too many mugs of ale to be of any assistance.

Jocelyn was taken back to the main house with the others, but just as quickly slipped out another door and returned to be with them. As she worked at cleaning up she talked even more openly with Roscoe. "I know it's no consolation," she said, "but you did have a beautiful family that loved you. You'll always know what that felt like, and you have your Misty to return to. I'd give up half my life to be loved like you love her. I know at eighteen what so many never learn in a lifetime. Riches and royalty do not equate to happiness. I've seen many servant girls my age in total bliss because of the love and attention of a lowly stable boy, and children with barely enough to clothe them looking into their mothers' eyes and smiling. Some day soon they'll come to me and tell me I'm to marry some hollow hearted enigma with the charm of one of your wild boars, and the wit of a jackal."

At that Roscoe stopped what he was doing and looked intently at her, and together they started to laugh. "Well I don't know who I'd feel more sorry for," he responded.

"For him I dare say," she retorted with a grin.

As they worked an occasional guard would come by. Roscoe greeted each one by bringing him to the ale barrel. This went on until nearly eleven o'clock when they were finished. The three of them sat and drank a mug of ale themselves and talked for another hour before the guard walked her back. They laughed as they went, joking about the prisoners protecting her from the guards. After she left they went into the first cottage they came to and slept the remainder of the night.

These buildings were sealed up pretty tightly, and kept most of the morning light out. After two days of exhausting activity it was easy to sleep until noon, and they might have slept longer had they not been awakened by two guards standing over them loudly demanding they get up. Things all too quickly changed. Roscoe was told he was being taken back to the other side while Zachary would remain and perform various duties with the other prisoner. Roscoe immediately protested and demanded they see Mr. Foraker first. This almost got him the butt of a rifle but he ducked in time. Zachary quickly told him to be smart and not wind up in the hole. Roscoe knew he was right, and left the cottage quietly.

After four days and no word from anyone, Roscoe was growing uneasy. If the Earl of Wyndham were going to help them he would have sent for him by now. Every day he looked for a way to get word from Zachary. On the fifth morning while out in the quarry a guard came for him saying he was needed to reload the visitors' belongings onto the ship. As they made the trip over the island his heart beat rapidly. Was he going to be free, or left here again without hope. The answers came quickly when he arrived.

Zachary and two others were already loading the large wooden boxes on carts to wheel them to the transfer boats. "Send that one up here," Mr. Foraker called. "Roscoe, I'm sorry young man, the truth of the matter is, he just doesn't care enough to want to get involved. I think maybe it would be an embarrassment to tell the American government the king has held two innocent men for nearly six years."

"Are you saying this Earl will let us die so they can save face?" Roscoe asked in disbelief.

"I suspect it's so," he replied.

"There has to be something more you can do," Roscoe said angrily. "We have a plan," he said.

"No, Jocelyn has a plan, but if it doesn't work, I'll hang along-side of you two. Do you understand?"

"I wish there was a way of reassuring you. I give you my word, that's all I can offer. I'd go to my death before I'd implicate you or Jocelyn. Tell me what we need to do," Roscoe said.

"Jocelyn had two boxes brought to her room. You have to be the ones to carry them out," Mr. Foraker told him.

"What'll be in them?" Roscoe asked.

"Nothing, that's why you two have to carry them and stay with them until they're unloaded onto the ship. Jocelyn will be there to help you at that point. I'm going to cross over and request two prisoners to help transfer the goods. I'll take the men personally to the ship, and leave them in the kitchen to unpack what's being taken out now. Then I'll come back and wait for the final run. That'll be you, Zachary and the two boxes," Mr. Foraker said con-fidently.

"But a guard always escorts the boat going out," Roscoe said.

"I'll send him on some bogus errand so he won't be there to see who is on the boat with me. I'll send some guards from the ship to bring back the two men that'll already be out there," he replied.

"And we get into the boxes," Roscoe said.

"From then on friend, you're Jocelyn's responsibility. I'll put a knife in each box. I don't know how much air you'll get, so you'd better cut a hole. You may be in there a while." With that Mr.

Foraker departed and Roscoe joined Zachary in loading the guests' belongings.

They didn't see Mr. Foraker again until late in the afternoon. When all else was loaded he instructed them to pick up the last two boxes from within the house. As planned, he sent the guards off to meet someone who wasn't going to be there. The men hurried the boxes onto the boat and quickly rowed away from shore. Once on the ship Mr. Foraker had them bring the boxes down below one at a time. In the presence of two crewmen he said to Roscoe and Zachary. "We'll go to the kitchen and finish unloading, and I'll give you something to eat," he then sent the crewmen off.

He now said to Roscoe and Zachary, "Move those boxes to the back of the room, and put a few in front of them. Then climb in. It will be couple of hours before we sail." They both shook his hand and thanked him, then went to work rearranging the many boxes to secure theirs in the back. Eventually they got in the boxes, pulled the lids over and proceeded to cut a small hole for fresh air.

The time spent waiting for the ship to sail seemed worse than all the time they were imprisoned. Not knowing if the plan had failed, if someone were going to come in searching the boxes for them, and knowing it would mean their death if the plan did fail. However, when they felt the boat move they knew they were free. With each passing hour they felt their strength renewing. They weren't sure how they would get off the ship, but after all they had been through, that didn't concern them at all. Nothing could stop them now.

Early the next morning the door opened and someone came into the room. They lay still and quiet, listening for a voice. Faintly they heard someone fooling with the boxes. Soon they heard Jocelyn quietly calling Zachary's name. Cautiously they each lifted the tops of the boxes they were in and peered out into the room. What a beautiful sight they saw—the pretty young girl with food in each hand, smiling with a look that said, "we fooled them all." The men quickly jumped out and hugged her.

"You may be the Earl's niece to everyone else, but to us you're a princess. You saved our lives. Do you realize that. How can we repay you?" Roscoe said.

"Repay me? This is the most fun I've had in all my life. When you live close to the top as I do, you see the injustice innocent people suffer. So this is fun. But it's also right, and that feels good," said Jocelyn.

The three sat and talked while the men ate and replenished themselves. Jocelyn had secured a room away from most activity, saying she wanted to work on her painting. Her uncle had the room emptied and protected with a lock. After giving them directions she departed, and they went back in their boxes to await the time to make their move. Jocelyn would be back to help them.

Once inside the safety of her room they began to feel like themselves again. Jocelyn supplied pillows, blankets, and fresh clothing. Mr. Foraker sent her each day with more than enough food.

For eight days they sailed. Being ardent fishermen, the Earl and his friends made the thee-day journey last more than a week. Much of this time the three of them spent together in this room. There was a lot of talking and laughing. Card-playing and chess helped pass the time, as well as watching Jocelyn paint pictures of vases, the cups, sunsets, and whatever else they could dream up. Roscoe spent a lot of time just looking out of the porthole waiting for land, or lying on the floor staring at the ceiling, his thoughts a thousand miles away.

Zachary more often sat with Jocelyn as they shared stories of their past, and Jocelyn in particular, her hopes and dreams of the future. The men never stopped telling her what an incredible girl she was, and though she repeatedly made light of it, in her heart she rejoiced with every word of kindness and praise. Jocelyn was a girl who had everything but the thing she wanted most, to be valued and loved by the parents who had no time for their child.

Late into the night of their eighth day of freedom they sat anchored about a mile out from a port in English waters. Deciding it was better to swim tonight than risk being caught the next day, they prepared what few items they would take, and waited for Jocelyn to return from checking the upper deck. Around four thirty, she slipped down to the room with the news they had been waiting for. She handed them some food and a small amount of money. Some of it hers, the rest Mr. Foraker's, whom they hadn't seen since he helped them onto the ship. Roscoe took hold of both of her hands. "Jocelyn, my dear Jocelyn," he said as they smiled. "We've laughed and joked a lot this past week, but I tell you now in all sincerity, you've given me back my life. I can never balance the scale between us, but I want you to know I'll cherish my love for you always." As they embraced each other affectionately she cried with mixed emotions—feeling good about what she had done, and at the same time feeling sad because she was saying good-bye forever.

After that Roscoe stepped out into the hallway and left Zachary alone to say good-bye. Though they hadn't spoken, Roscoe understood the troubled feelings Zachary experienced during the past week. After nearly six years they had long laid to rest any hope that others had survived the sinking of the Anna Mariah. Still his love for Naomi was just as strong as it ever was, and only after going back to America and receiving an official word of her death would he be able to start life new again. Still, this girl who exhibited so many of the same fine qualities, and was so beautiful in her own right had begun to touch his heart. After a few minutes passed the door opened, and the two men made their way to the deck. Securing a rope to a post they threw it over and climbed down into the water and began their long swim to total freedom.

Once ashore their situation continued to improve. Within the week they had hired themselves onto a ship bound for America, and could see the end of what had seemed a never-ending nightmare.

It was finally over. Wide awake and standing strong, they planted their feet firmly on rich southern soil again. Something like eight years had passed since Roscoe Tanner departed. He left as a young lad full of dreams and desires. He returned a man, one who would have to greatly alter those dreams and desires, and one also, who would have to accept the greatest loss of all. As was confirmed for them, the others were gone.

* * * * *

The war is over. The guns have been silent for several months, but it will certainly be many years before the anguish and visions of horror subside. Each waking day retells the same sad story as women open their eyes to be reminded they slept alone, and young boys struggled to perform their fathers' tasks. Many had lost not only their loved ones, but their land as well. Others who were able to hold onto it had to contend with the damage done, and the almost total loss of revenue. But however sad it was for them, whatever devastation they had to face, they were still a far cry better off than the Negroes. They had gained their freedom, the thing they wanted the most, but now new and in some ways even more difficult obstacles greeted them. Many were those who showed themselves to be gallant men, unreservedly going to fight in the war to win their own freedom only to be enslaved again by an even greater enemy . . . death.

The white people of the south were the ones who lost the war. It would take years to rebuild what had been destroyed, and few concerned themselves about the effects all this had on the Negro. If there was no longer such a thing as a slave, then there can no longer be applied the title, "runaway slave." The posters and notices and newspaper ads were quickly disappearing. This made the word . . . FREE . . . ring even louder for some.

But, not for her. An indictment of murder and the theft of two horses is not about to leave her mind. In 1863 when the war was ravaging the country, the law still found time to hang a woman in Texas for horse thievery. How much more so a part Negro who killed a white man, then stranded his brother without his horse.

It was clear to her there was no going back. However, this wasn't as hard to accept as it once was. The abolishment of slavery meant that those she loved at home were probably gone. She couldn't imagine anyone staying on with Edward running Mariah. Yet in her heart she cried and longed for home. Too many years had passed. She knew there was no point in pursuing Wendall in Boston. She wanted very much to write to him at home, but feared his parents might intercept the letter and turn her in to the authorities.

Though she was totally alone in a physical sense, she was well endowed spiritually. With a memory full of Biblical verses Mrs. Tanner had taught her, and the numerous hymns sung to Jehovah the slaves had taught her, she never felt that she couldn't go on. With her strong faith in God and the abundance of practical wisdom supplied by Mr. Tanner she would survive. Indeed she awoke one morning realizing that she alone would carry on the teaching and meaning of the lives of Hubert and Emily Tanner.

She rose to her feet that morning with a different outlook on everything and a new revitalized meaning to her life. The war was over, but the suffering was not. Misty was encouraged by one of the field doctors to go to a nearby hospital and continue her nursing duties since the need was so great. So for the better part of that year she did what she could to help many recuperate and adjust to the hideous aftermath of the war.

She lived a quiet life renting a room from a family not far from the hospital. Though many tried to involve her socially she preferred to keep to herself. Everything seemed to be going so well that she finally started to relax her guard some. The better she felt, the more outgoing she became, until one afternoon like a recurring nightmare, she was confronted with her past.

Asked to come to the administrator's office she found herself seated with him and another gentleman she had never seen before. "Victoria, this is Abe Shelco," the administrator said to her, "he would like to ask you a few questions. He thinks you could be someone he is looking for." She immediately choked up, unable to speak.

"I'm in the business of finding people," he began. Misty knew that meant bounty hunter. "Would you read this notice for me?" he asked, handing her a piece of paper. When she started to read it to herself he asked her to read it out loud.

<u>REWARD</u>
**Paid for any information that leads to the
discovery of MISTY TANNER.
Description as follows:
Swarthy complexion, long black hair and green eyes.
Small mole just above the corner of the mouth on left side.
Twenty-six years of age. May be using a fictitious name.
Slight scar on left temple.
Please refer all information to local sheriff.**

When she completed the reading she handed it back to him, but said nothing.

"I had been informed that a girl fitting this description was residing here. I checked on you from a distance first, and you have to admit you fit the bill all right," he said as he reached out to push back the hair that covered the temple area.

"Please sir," she said pulling away from his hand. "I don't know you. I would have it that you not touch me. I am quite a bit older than the girl described on that paper, but if it would please you I have proof of who I am back at my room." Saying this she rose and began walking toward the door. "It will not take me twenty minutes to get it." Just that quickly she was heading down the hallway. Mr. Shelco looked at the administrator and said, "That's the girl. She sure acts like she doesn't want to be found."

He thought he would give her the benefit of the doubt, but he planned to follow her as she went to her home. For several minutes the men stood in the window waiting to see her leave. That never happened, not by the front entrance anyway. That five minutes or so was all she needed. She was already off the hospital grounds moving quickly toward a wooded area where she could disappear.

One thing she had learned during the war years was, know your enemy's whereabouts, and watch for his next move. It was this thought that kept her from running off blindly. Once into the woods she stopped to collect her thoughts and devise a plan. It was hard to concentrate. The wanted poster kept flashing in her mind. If her next move was the wrong one, it could mean her very life.

After an hour of waiting near the edge of the woods she slipped back into the hospital, and returned to the administrator's office. Without giving him too many details she quickly told him the truth. She trusted he was a decent man, and took the chance he would help her, which he did.

"If that story weren't true you wouldn't have told it," he said. "You have been such an asset to us here, Victoria. We are all going to miss you."

With the help of other staff members they brought Misty to his house and prepared her for travel. Any money or clothing at her room had to be left behind. The little money she had in the bank, the administrator exchanged for her. Others supplied a few pieces of clothing and a carrying bag. That night she was taken from the small city she had made her home and brought to a nearby town to await the morning stagecoach.

For many months after that she stayed on the move, never remaining in any area more than a week or so, always fearful of being confronted with another poster or being apprehended without an opportunity to escape. Eventually her travels brought her back into Tennessee. Like everywhere else she had been, they too, were still recuperating from the war.

Most often when entering a town she would seek out employment as a chambermaid in one of the many hotels that were springing up in the growing cities. This offered room and meals with a small commission for a week's work.

One other thing Misty had to do whenever she was going to stay in an area to work was check the information boards. On more than one occasion she was forced to leave quickly after finding the wanted poster attached.

There were times like this one, when she found work by reading the information on the boards. This time she found employment

277

teaching piano to the children of a wealthy family. For room and board she exchanged household chores.

Here she was able to once again enjoy this beautiful instrument. Whenever left alone in the house she would play the songs she loved the best, the ones she had grown up playing and singing. Sometimes, even when it hurt badly, she would continue to play. It was the music more than anything else that brought back the living memories of her past.

In this large house there were many Negro servants. Though she could say nothing, she was appalled to see and hear them being treated so badly. In time as she befriended the servants she spent more of her free time with them, teaching them basic reading and writing skills, as well as basket-weaving, a trade she was taught in Virginia.

It was only in the company of the Negroes that she could be totally relaxed, be called by her real name, and be surrounded with family love. It became her oasis even though she had to keep it a secret from her white employers.

Most of the time when Misty moved on it was for reasons beyond her control. This time was different. She had an opportunity to be a school teacher. A notice at the town hall had been posted by residents of a town about thirty-five miles north of there. Along with a note from her employer she sent a resume seeking the job. Within two weeks she was asked to come and start immediately.

Using the name Emily Myers, she arrived at what would be the most enjoyable employment she had yet to experience. A small cottage was provided for her to live in. There was ample ground for a garden and a chicken house in need of chickens. The salary was small, but adequate for her needs.

The school house had one medium sized room with desks and a blackboard, a wood stove to warm it during the winter months, and five boys and eight girls with ages varying from eight to fifteen.

In just a few days the children knew they had a good teacher. Never had they been so enthusiastic about going to school. Learning became a joy to them as they were introduced to new ways of doing things.

From the outset Misty asked for a piano. All involved insisted it was beyond their means, and with none to even borrow from any of the parents, it was considered an impossibility. Misty saw it as a challenge for her and her pupils, as well as a lesson for them to learn as she had.

At the next meeting of the town fathers she requested a ten foot log and several of the larger branches from a freshly cut green white oak tree. She told them it was for a class project that would raise money for a piano. Unfortunately, she was turned down, and told that reading and writing and maybe some arithmetic was all her pupils needed.

The next day however, brought a surprise. One of the local men who had heard about her strange request saw it as maybe a good opportunity to win the favor of the very pretty and unattached school mistress. Douglas Grist came riding in with two large work horses pulling a wagon heavy with a fresh cut white oak tree, and a look of rescue in his smile. Misty and all the children went out to greet him.

"Good afternoon Ma'am," he said lifting his hat. "I don't know why you want it or whatcha gonna do with it, but here it is."

"It's perfect," she responded. "It's going to do just perfectly."

"Where bouts do ya want it unloaded?" he asked. By now the younger children were climbing all over the wagon and the excitement of the event was bringing laughter from them all.

After unloading the tree Mr. Grist was invited in for some iced tea and an explanation. The oak tree he was told would be used to make baskets they could sell to purchase a piano. "Many Negroes did this in Virginia after the war," she said. "They taught me how to do it."

"Why not use a pine tree?" he asked, "it's a whole lot lighter to work with."

"I don't know if pine would work. They showed me how to pull strips off a white oak that's still green. You can strip it by hand once you get it started right," she said.

One hour each day was spent in the classroom learning the art of basket weaving. Mr. Grist kept up a ready supply of oak wood, and the baskets were beginning to pile up by month's end. After two months they had enough baskets to sell. Mr. Grist offered to bring the items to the nearby city to market them, if Misty would accompany him. Never did she give any reason for him to think she was interested in anything more than his friendship. But, it was obvious to her and most others that he was serious about her.

About every two months they rode to the city selling their baskets. The goal was to purchase a piano in two years time. However, the enthusiasm of the young ones rubbed off on some of those much older and they came to contribute their time to basket-making as well as teaching other crafts that added to their items to sell.

Then it happened again . . .

If you're a banker you want to be the best banker you can be, if a newspaper man, then the best possible, and so it goes down the line. Not so if you're a fugitive from justice. To forget for a moment when life has you feeling vivacious is daring. To forget for an hour is dangerous.

On their fourth trip to the city they had one of the older children with them, Jennifer, a fifteen-year-old who was more a teacher's aide than a student. The three split up to carry out different errands. One went to the grist mill, another to the fabric shop, the third, Jennifer, to the general store. When they all met back at the wagon and deposited their supplies Jennifer said, "I saw a picture Miss Emily that looked just like you. I couldn't believe it. I just kept staring at it."

"You telling me there is someone else as pretty as Miss Emily, Jennifer?" Mr. Grist said making the girl shyly respond.

"I swear it. She looked just like her," she said.

"We better hurry if we are to get back before dark," Misty said. While Mr. Grist and Jennifer joked about it, they climbed onto the wagon and started to move.

Had they not had to pass in front of the general store nothing more would have been said. Misty was uneasy about Jennifer's report, but didn't take it too seriously having never seen a poster with her picture on it. Passing by the store Jennifer said, "It's over there," pointing to a bulletin board. "You should see it Miss Emily, maybe it's a relative of yours."

"Oh, I don't think so Jennifer. It's just a coincidence I'm sure," Misty responded.

"Well I sure gotta take a look," said Douglas, bringing the wagon to a halt. "Come on Emily you must be curious."

"No Douglas, I'm really only concerned about getting home," she said.

Douglas jumped down from the wagon followed by Jennifer who wanted to see it again. Several minutes passed and they returned. Getting himself back into the seat he handed her the poster saying, "She certainly was right, Emily. More right than she knew." Unrolling the paper Misty couldn't hide her surprise. It was her picture, taken from one of the charcoal sketches the painter Milo

280

Topaz had done. This also meant that the ones looking for her had gone to Mariah to get the picture.

Seeing her discomfort Douglas started the wagon moving and drove outside of town before stopping to talk. "A ten thousand dollar reward Emily, that's an awful lot of money. Who wants to find you that badly?" Douglas asked.

"That really is you Miss Emily?" asked Jennifer in a confused way.

"Yes, I'm afraid it is sweetheart, I just don't know what to say," she answered.

"It doesn't say why they're looking for you. I'd like to know, I want to help you if I can," Douglas said.

"No one can help me Douglas, I'm guilty of what they say I did," she said softly.

"But Emily they don't say you did anything, what is it you did?" he asked.

As they both sat and listened almost in disbelief, Misty told them her story. She felt so bad about doing this to people who had so unconditionally made her a part of their lives. When it was all told, Jennifer cried. Douglas needed a few minutes to adjust to such a revelation.

Hugging Jennifer, Misty too began to cry. This was the best life had been for a very long time, and all she wanted to do was continue with it. The thought of leaving her pupils and the little school house she had grown to love was considerably harder than anything she had done for quite some time.

"The townspeople will back you up Emily. It wasn't your fault the man died, and you didn't take the horses to profit from them. I'm sure a judge would understand. I know you want to stay here, and everyone will want you to," Douglas said.

"Yes, Miss Emily," Jennifer added, "you can't leave, you just can't."

"I'll go to the sheriff first," Douglas said, becoming more convinced as he listened to his own words. "Talk to him about how to straighten this whole mess out. With the townsfolk behind you I know we can settle this thing." It all sounded so good, and so right, that Misty wanted to believe it. The wagon began moving again as Douglas in his excitement talked faster and faster. After promising not to say anything until the following afternoon, Misty agreed to his plan. She wanted only to tell her pupils herself first.

On their ride home and well outside of the city they came upon a wagon that had broken down. A large family of Negroes with all their worldly goods in tow were stranded by a broken wheel. They had already repaired the wheel, but they weren't strong enough to lift the wagon and slip the wheel back on. Douglas continued to ride right by them. Only at Misty's urging did he stop and walk back to help, and this he did as she could see, reluctantly.

That one little display of truism brought her back to reality. The townsfolk would not back her, not unanimously. She was a Negro, and the controversy over her teaching their children could easily lead a judge to want to remove her.

That night she packed what she could carry and wrote a note to Douglas to thank him, and to Jennifer to be read to the class in the morning. After placing them on her desk in the schoolhouse, she stood for a moment and looked about. Not allowing herself to be saddened at this time, she smiled. It was a brief encounter with happiness and she wanted to remember it as such.

Then, as had been done so many times before, she disappeared into the darkness of the night . . .

If only she could have known how close she had come, close to bringing it all to an end, to seeing with her eyes what she felt with her heart.

Shortly after leaving the area one of the townspeople went to the sheriff and reported on the wanted poster. His instructions were to send a notice to the one who was responsible for having the posters placed. A letter was immediately sent to Mariah. Misty's fear of being wanted by the law was what kept her thinking that the wanted and missing notices were life threatening. She had no reason to question the fact that they never stated what she was wanted for. At the same time Roscoe couldn't have known she thought she was running from the law. If he had, the notices could easily have been worded differently.

When Roscoe and Zachary returned to America they went first to Zachary's home. Finding it now occupied by others they started gathering the information they needed. Shortly after this they parted company. Zachary set out to find his father first, then planned to return for Jocelyn. Roscoe headed for Mariah and the longed for reunion with his beloved Misty. How sad he was to find his homeland so devastated. Passing from one town to the next were the constant reminders of a long and brutal war.

Prior to reaching home he sent a letter to Misty. He did not want to just appear as though he had returned from the dead, nor did he want to confuse anyone about the fate of the others. This of course, caused quite a commotion. Susan intercepted it, and the word spread quickly.

On arriving the following day he was greeted just before reaching the main house by a face he didn't at first recognize. Bringing his cariole to a stop the girl said to him, "I didn't sleep all night just hoping ya was bringing her back."

As he climbed down to meet the child who was obviously waiting for him he said, "Sarah? It is you isn't it? I've sure been gone a long time." Pulling her to him he hugged her tightly. "Many were the days I thought of you Sarah. You couldn't know how pleasant you are to my eyes."

"She's not with you is she?" the young girl asked.

"No Sarah, they're all gone," he replied sadly, though thinking she meant Isabelle.

"But, you can find her, I can help too," she said, now becoming teary eyed. He smiled a little, thinking that she had never seen anything larger than the fishing pond, and could never comprehend the magnitude of an ocean.

"You loved Isabelle didn't you?" he asked. "Yes I did," she answered and added, "but, I miss Misty more." He thought at the outset that it was odd Misty wasn't there waiting for him. Now a cold fearful chill raced through his body. "Where is Misty, Sarah?" he asked.

"I's don't know sir. She's been away a long time," the girl responded.

"Why did she go away Sarah, do you know?" he asked. "The men took her away," she answered. Getting her into the cariole and quickly driving it to the main house he questioned her further, but could not understand what she was telling him.

Standing at the bottom of the front porch steps and eagerly awaiting the cariole to stop was the one he knew would best answer his questions. With tears in his eyes he clasped Roscoe's hand firmly while trying to get his words and emotions in order. "I had to see it wit my own eyes to believe it," said Henry as he shook his hand repeatedly.

"I can't tell ya how glad I am to find you here Henry. Sarah says Misty's gone. When did this happen?" Roscoe asked, his voice sounding both confused and worried.

"Jus a bits before da war started. Da child come home one mornin tellin a story bout two men takin Misty away. Miss Susan tells us to find her. We look for a week son, but we didn't know which way dey went, and nobody tells nutin to help us. I's came and wait for her, and I's still doin da same," he explained.

Even though his only concern was Misty, he couldn't help but notice the conditions around him. Everything was in a state of deterioration, there were no signs of any work force, and no faces that he recognized.

As Henry and he continued their conversation they made their way up into the house. Roscoe wasn't expecting to find the house the same as when he left it. It was somewhat rundown on the inside, but not as bad as he anticipated. As he called out for his sister Henry told him of her misfortune. Edward had gone off to fight in the war and was killed somewhere in South Carorlina.

Hearing his voice Susan came out of the study and quickly fell into her brother's arms. For a long time they held each other as she repeated his name many times. Eventually the two of them went into the family room and talked for many hours. During this time all four of Susan's children came in and out of the room. The boys, David and Wesley, were teen-agers now, the girls Desiree and Miranda he had never met.

Susan claimed to know nothing about Misty's disapperance, and Roscoe had no reason not to believe her. Because of the many things he learned that night he could feel only compassion for his sister. Their grandmother passed away during the war years, and Lester with Willy Mae and their children left after it ended. Henry stayed on hoping Misty would one day return. It was obvious too, that Henry was older than they had thought he was, and far beyond being able to do the kind of repairs needed after the war was over. Sarah was taken in by a couple with children of their own, former slaves who staked out a plot of land on Mariah and worked out a meager existence. The rest of the land had lain barren for nearly six years.

The very next morning Roscoe was up early and in his father's study. His first priority was of course, to find Misty. This was the beginning of what would be a long and expensive search, one that would encompass nearly a dozen states and involved numerous private investigators and bounty hunters, and the invaluable assistance of a very good friend.

Another priority was to sort out the massive confusion the plantation's legal affairs were in. The second task was as difficult as the first. Their land holdings in Georgia, New York and Pennsylvania were all intact. But he was able to locate only about half of the money they had had prior to the war.

Much of Mariah he leased out in forty acre plots to sharecroppers. This was the new way of farming plantations. The rest he put back under cultivation with hired laborers.

Only on the occasions when word came to him about someone seeing Misty, did he leave Mariah. During the next two years he restored his home to its former splendor, and returned the fields to their once productive state.

By selling all their interests in the New York enterprise, and a larger share of the steel mills in Pennsylvania, he obtained a considerable fortune. More importantly to him though was his freedom of both mind and time to focus more on finding Misty, something that was much harder than everyone involved could understand.

Two other things Roscoe did shortly after arriving home. He made headstones for the family cemetery bearing the names of his grandmother, his parents, Naomi and Isabelle, along with Scott and Gloria Franklin. The other thing was to hang the portrait that was painted by Mr. Topaz of Misty when she was a teenager. Never a day went by that he didn't sit at least for a moment and gaze at her beautiful face and wonder when he would find her.

Perhaps finding her would have been easier had she stayed in one place longer, but she rarely did. Much of the past two years was spent in Kentucky moving about with the Negro population. Schooling was inadequate at best and Misty found the children everywhere eager to learn. On more than one occasion she helped the sharecroppers to avoid being cheated by the landowners. A white girl amongst the Negroes stood out, and was far too noticeable. This kept her on the move. Many of those she stayed with had benefited from the underground railroad movement that had helped runaway slaves escape to the north before the war. With what they learned they had no trouble keeping her safe.

A chance meeting one day while she was working at a hotel would change her life forever. An elderly woman of German decent, Hilda Schickna, arrived on the afternoon stagecoach. A porter brought her baggage to the room and Misty brought an extra blanket that she had requested. They exchanged greetings and a few kind words.

The following morning when the woman came down for breakfast Misty waited on her. Again they exchanged kind words as Misty helped her remove her shawl. A short while after giving the woman her breakfast she came back to inquire of her needs. Seeing the woman had barely touched her food Misty asked if everything was all right. "I'm afraid I haven't been feeling very well lately. Would you please help me back to my room? I feel a little light headed this morning," the woman commented. After taking her to her room Misty went to the hotel owner and told him Mrs. Schickna would be staying another day.

That evening after work Misty went upstairs with a bowl of soup to check on the elderly woman. "Are you feeling better this evening?" she asked. "They told me downstairs you didn't send for any dinner."

"This is very thoughtful of you young lady. I am feeling a little better, and this soup smells delicious," the woman responded.

"Oh I'm happy to hear that," said Misty. "Is there anything else I can do for you?"

"If you think your employer wouldn't mind, perhaps you could sit for a few minutes while I eat this bowl of soup," Mrs. Schickna requested.

"That would be fine," Misty replied. "My work day was over a half hour ago. I would be happy to stay for a few minutes." Obviously impressed with her kindness the woman introduced herself and asked Misty for her name. The few minutes quickly turned into a couple of hours as they talked about life during the war years.

Mrs. Schickna, an intelligent, discerning woman, was a widow whose husband had left her financially secure. She told Misty the reason for her recent trip to New York. She had for some time suffered from an illness yet to be diagnosed. Unfortunately the doctors there could offer no answers either.

As she listened to Misty she realized she was being deliberately careful about explaining her past. She could easily see she was a kind and loving person who knew pain of heart very well. When Mrs. Schickna learned that Misty lived alone with no relatives in the city she offered her a proposition. If Misty traveled the remainder of the trip with her, she would pay her well and also help her get a job in the area hospital.

What little Misty had she gave to those who had been her friends, and once again said good-bye. At nine o'clock that morning she boarded the stage with Mrs. Schickna and set out on a trip that would bring her back into the deep south, into the state of Mississippi.

Journeying back she saw first-hand what many who had fled to the north had told her. The vast majority of the Negroes suffered unendingly. The plantations were for the most part rebuilt and run by hired slave labor, meaning the little they were paid was quickly taken back through cheating, and over-charging for even the simplest of staples. Misty was relieved to know Mrs. Schickna, having grown up in Germany, had never owned slaves and deplored the conditions they were forced to live in. By the time they reached home in Mississippi, Misty had developed a great deal of respect and admiration for this sweet elderly woman.

The original plan was that Misty would stay with Mrs. Schickna until she could save enough money to make her own way. However, she was offered another proposition. The elderly woman knew she wasn't getting any better, and while her good days were fine, there were times that she couldn't function as well as she needed to, so she offered Misty not only her room and meals, but a substantial salary too.

Perhaps because of the responsibility in this, and the respect Misty felt for the woman, she decided to tell the truth about herself first, and give Mrs. Schickna the opportunity to make a decision based on that. After making them a pot of tea Misty asked to talk frankly with her. Feeling that this was going to be a shock she spoke carefully. When she was finished Mrs. Schickna smiled slightly and said, "I knew you were troubled by something big, though my dear, I would have never guessed at all of this. You've been through enough, and it's time to put it behind you. For as long as you want to stay, you may do so. I probably need you more than you need me. We'll say you're my niece, the daughter of my deceased sister. What shall we call you? How about Chrissy? I've always been fond of the name."

Sitting back in her chair, and taken by surprise, Misty at first didn't know what to say. "I'm so tired of running and hiding and being frightened. I've also learned what an awful thing it is to be lonely. Every time I thought it would end, something would happen, and I would be looking over my shoulder again. If you can help me make it stop I would be forever grateful, but never able to repay you."

The old woman sat forward in her chair and said, "Getting old was not nearly as bad as being alone. And I have been alone too long. Oh, I've got some friends, but without family there is a sense of being alone," she smiled and added, "It will be good for the both of us." So the arrangement was made and over the next few weeks Aunt Hilda introduced her niece, Chrissy Reed to her friends and associates.

One person in particular was very happy for old Aunt Hilda, a man named Ned Prickett, the grandson of one of Mrs. Schickna's close friends. A college-educated young man, his mother had died of yellow fever, and his father was a casualty of the war. From the outset he began pursuing her, stopping by at least once a day bringing flowers for her, and Aunt Hilda, a name he freely called her by. Misty was, of course, flattered by the attention, but refused to participate in anything that might indicate a date, always insisting that they do things with a group. On many occasions Aunt Hilda spoke to her about the need to let go of the past, and to begin to think about the rest of her life.

As the months went by Ned spent more and more time at their home, until his eating dinner there became a nightly occurrence. His ambition was to be a state legislator. His first run for office was only a year away. At that time he would try for the Mayor's position.

Aunt Hilda's words began having an effect on Misty. She told Misty that love would eventually follow if she married Ned. She believed that after another year or so all the wanted posters would have disappeared and even if her situation ever did come to light no one would make trouble for a legislator. She further reasoned that she probably wouldn't live much longer. Her illness was rapidly growing worse and she wanted to know that Misty would be taken care of.

Before that month was over Ned proposed. Misty had suspected this was coming, and influenced by Aunt Hilda she said yes. It was a most difficult thing for her to do. She wanted to believe she loved him, but the countless nights of little sleep along with the vivid memories of Roscoe, and the strange feeling in her heart that he still called to her, left her in a constant state of emotional distress.

The day arrived quickly and a small wedding took place in the home of their Aunt Hilda. The house was a large stone building with spacious grounds for a small reception. The couple honeymooned away for several weeks, then returned to Aunt Hilda's to live while Ned more actively pursued his political career. Prior to their marriage Aunt Hilda had decided to leave her estate to Misty. She really had no one else, and the care Misty provided was on a level equal to anything she had ever seen between a mother and a daughter. However, by the time the will was drawn up the marriage had taken place, so for the sake of legalities everything was put in Ned's name.

The following year brought many unexpected changes. After a long and painful illness Aunt Hilda passed away. Ned campaigned vigorously, but lost a close race, and Misty delivered a baby girl. It was in a sense, the fulfillment of half a dream. From her earliest years she had envisioned her and Roscoe having this baby and naming her Molly. This made her realize all the more she would never love Ned the way she should.

With the money that Ned now had in his possession he was able to run a better campaign and win a position as a representative of his voting district. This meant many new people entered their lives. Entertaining on a weekly basis became a way of life. Along with all of this came many unpleasant realities. Before these changes occurred Ned expressed his feelings in a compassionate way, for the abuse of the freedom the Negros were granted. He didn't know the truth about his wife, but he understood how she felt on that subject. It was now becoming clear Ned was not the person he championed himself to be, and worse, he openly joked in her presence about the value of a beautiful wife on the campaign trail.

As life with this man continued to deteriorate, and Molly reached her third year, Lydia was born. This was a tremendous joy to Misty's heart, as well as a legitimate excuse to spend as little time as possible with her husband's friends.

To the public they were the perfect family. Growing more successful in his political career, and now with an opportunity to be Lt. Governor if his good friend won the race.

Misty was as youthful and beautiful as she ever was. The two girls resembled her in most ways; both had long flowing black hair and rich shining skin. The only times Misty and Ned were together were for the sake of his career. He rarely saw the children. Misty knew he had a mistress; something he didn't try to hide. However, this arrangement did not disturb her, for it allowed her to spend all her free time with the children, and not have to share too often, her bed.

As the race for the Governor's seat heated up they were forced to make more and more public appearances together. This meant more photographs in more newspapers and magazines, a thing that still frightened her a great deal. As events would bear out, this was not an unfounded fear.

Two events began to unfold simultaneously; one came about as a direct result of their public life, the other by sheer chance. One was motivated by the greed and the insensibility of a worthless, dastardly man. The second was carried on by a love so strong and undying that no amount of time could ever change it.

Jacob Cobb, a hotel owner in Kentucky, had lived in this small city all of his life. Helping a friend move his belongings to a new house he chanced upon a box filled with old papers taken from the town's bulletin board a few years back, when keeping this information organized was his friend's responsibility.

While the men were amusing themselves with the old news, Mr. Cobb's attention was caught by a pretty face on a wanted poster. "There's something about her that looks familiar," he said to his friend Jeffrey. "I'm certain I've seen her somewhere."

Taking the poster from him, his friend said, "A ten thousand dollar reward, and a pretty face is a hard combination to forget."

"I've got it," Mr. Cobb said slapping is leg, "that girl worked for me. Now how long ago was that?"

"This poster has to be at least three years old. I haven't had charge of the board in that long," Jeffrey said.

"No, this seems older than that," Mr. Cobb replied taking hold of the picture again. "Now I know when it was," he said rising to his feet. "I remember it angered me that she left so abruptly, told me that night she was leaving and boarded the stage with an overnight guest. Yes I remember it now!" he said excitedly.

"A fellow was it, Jacob?" Jeffrey asked.

"No, I believe it was an old woman. Can't imagine what she could have done. Never stole nothing from me. Worked hard too," he said.

"Ten thousand dollars right under your nose Jacob. Whatcha think of that?" Jeffrey mused.

"Maybe it's not all lost, she might still be wanted. I'm gonna look back through my registry, see if I can't find the woman's name she left with. That information might be worth a couple of thousand," he reasoned.

The following day Jacob Cobb went to the sheriff with the poster of Misty and the name of Hilda Schickna. The only other information he had was the next stop the stage would have made, a nearby town. This was sent to Mariah according to instructions. For the first time in a long while Roscoe had a positive lead, and he acted quickly so as not to lose it.

A private investigator was hired to meet him there to try and uncover as much information as possible.

While Roscoe was heading for Kentucky, someone else was on his way to Mississippi, armed also with a wanted poster, and a strange story to tell Ned Prickett. The man's name was Wes Shocklar. Through newspaper photos he recognized the girl who killed his brother and stole his horses, and he was looking for compensation.

They met in Ned's office, in the evening at the man's request. His motive was clear—to blackmail Ned for a large sum of money. Everything the man said made sense to Ned. Nobody knew his wife's life prior to coming here, except maybe Aunt Hilda, and she wasn't around any longer to say.

Ned asked the man who had paid for the posters and offered the reward. "I traced it back to the place I got her from. But I never went there myself so I don't know why they want her."

"Why is it you never went to the sheriff about what you say she did?" Ned asked.

"My brother was a simpleton, Mr. Prickett. He put his head where it didn't belong, and she cracked it for him. I never doubted that there was some truth to her story, but I did have a legal docket saying I could sell her. Y'all know what kind of money a girl like that was worth. I don't want any trouble. I buried my brother and recovered one of my horses, nothin more worth doin," he replied.

"What makes you so sure I won't call the law in after you? I'm a very respected man around here?" Ned asked.

"I say you don't want to jeopardize your good name. I say, too, I'm not here to make you any problems. We are both reasonable men. I could turn the girl in and collect the ten thousand dollars, but then you would be without a political career. I think there's a better way, one that's good for all," he said.

291

Carefully Ned studied this man as he listened. He felt the biggest mistake the fellow was making was thinking that he loved his wife, and would want to protect her, as much as his political career. The man could never have known what Ned was thinking. "This is what I'll do," Ned told him. "I'll give you five thousand dollars, and see you go away happy and safe."

"Well, you see," Wes said shifting in his seat, "I don't think that's gonna make me happy."

Slamming his hands down on the desk Ned jumped up in a rage, "I don't think you understand. For two thousand dollars I can pay somebody to hang you. I'm being generous with you my good man, don't trifle with me, do you understand me now?"

Standing up and looking quite unsure of himself Wes said, "It could be a mistake on your part. You can't be sure what I might do." At that he walked toward the door.

Ned had only wanted to bait him and scare him. "Well now maybe I did act a little hastily Mr. Shocklar. This is all coming too quickly. If you would sir, at my expense, check into the local hotel for a couple of days and put it on my account. Just stay out of sight, that's all. I'll put something together and come see you," Ned said in a more relaxed tone of voice.

On the third evening at nearly ten o'clock Ned met again with Mr. Shocklar, this time in his hotel room. "I've decided, my friend, you are worth more than ten thousand dollars. I think fifteen is what you can leave here with, does that sound good to you?" Ned asked him.

"That's an expensive change of heart you've had, Mr. Prickett."

"Oh it gets even better sir. You can leave with fifteen thousand dollars, and avenge the murder of your brother," said Ned opening a leather bag to display more one hundred dollar bills than Mr. Shocklar had seen in his entire life.

"If I understand what you're saying here correctly, I'm not sure I like it."

"Perhaps you're misunderstanding me," he replied.

Leaving the bag sit open on the bed Ned walked to a chair and made himself comfortable. "My friend, inside of a month I'll be the Lieutenant Governor of this great state. From there I'm going to the house of representatives, and from there . . . well . . . I've got my plans. Now this Misty Tanner, this outlaw that you have so kindly brought to my attention is a threat to my very existence. I am quite frankly, ready to have her killed. You can see this doesn't bother me at all. But, at the same time we should discuss the dilemma you have created for yourself," said Ned Prickett.

"The dilemma seems to be yours not mine," Mr. Shocklar responded.

"Quite the contrary. You have decided to play a dangerous game without knowing all the variables. I'm gonna fill you in on them. I don't care in the least what happens to that woman. You have unknowingly given me the perfect way out, and that's fine. But, sir, you have also made yourself a threat to me, leaving me with only two options. One is to have someone trail you a distance out of town and then see that you go no further. I doubt anyone would ever come looking for you. The other is to have something to hold against you, to assure me that you won't get greedy or decide to talk about what you know. You do understand what I'm saying?" said Mr. Prickett in a very cold, unemotional tone.

As he stood across the room looking at Ned he believed the man would carry through on his word. Nothing was more important than his career. That was easy to understand. Fifteen thousand dollars was a lot of money. He had worked many long, hard years and never realized that kind of reward. Figuring it was in his best interest to agree, he said he would do it and listened as Ned gave him the details.

It was well past midnight when Ned returned home. He immediately went to his wife and shook her forcefully until she awoke. When she sat up in her bed he handed the wanted poster to her. She didn't have to read it having seen it before. She just looked at him.

"I don't have to tell you what this means. I know you're smart enough to have known all along. But I am gonna tell you this: nothing or nobody will interfere with my life. I love you Chrissy, or Misty, or whoever you are, but you're not capable of keeping up with me. We just don't see the things that are important to me, eye to eye. You understand? As I have come to learn, we truly are of a different breed. I've made arrangemeents, for the good of my career of course, and the good of the children. Y'all will be leaving here . . . tonight . . . alone," said Ned looking down on her with a cold look on his face.

"You can't do this to me! I won't go! I won't leave my children! You can straighten this problem out, Ned. You have to for the children," she said as she rose to her feet.

293

"I think what I'm doing for them is already quite generous. You're the one jeopardizing things. Without you around to be found by someone with a poster like this here, no one will ever know they have Negro blood. I'm sure you're aware how quickly I'd be voted out of office if it were discovered my children were of Negro descent," he said.

"You can't possibly ask me to leave my children here with you. You never showed any interest in them before, and now that you know the truth you'll despise them. I know you," she responded trying not to lose control of her emotions.

"They will be looked after. I'm not an evil person, Chrissy, but I'm not about to try and explain the disappearance of all three of you," he replied.

They argued for several more minutes. Misty knew it was in the best interests of her children to try and appease him at this time, and when he threatened to hide the girls away in an orphanage if she didn't cooperate she was sure he could do them harm. She listened intently to his instructions.

When Misty walked out of the house that night Ned thought it was into a well-planned trap. The cariole that was waiting for her, she was told, was going to take her to a train depot where she was to disappear into the north. Ned's plan was to have her delivered to Mr. Wes Shocklar who was to silence her forever. It didn't go quite as planned.

Mr. Shocklar was not the nicest man you would meet, but he was far from being capable of murder. Just outside of town where she was to be delivered to him, he sat in his wagon. Misty had been crying the entire time, and with the night without much moonlight she didn't at first recognize him when he approached them.

He told the driver to wait by his wagon and climbed up alongside of her. When she got a good look at him she knew who he was. By the look on her face he knew that she recognized him also. "Jus call it a simple twist of fate," he said. "You have increased in value a great deal over the years, but this time I've been paid to get rid of you permanently, like you did my brother." Misty slid over to the edge of the seat, but the fear she felt had nothing to do with her own safety. If Ned could have her killed, then her children were in grave danger. It was more obvious than ever before that he would stop at nothing to realize his goals.

294

"Don't get out girl. It wouldn't be wise not hearing me out. I'll take some chances for fifteen thousand dollars, but not one that gets a rope around my neck. Y'all listen real good. You go back makin trouble for that man and the next person he hires won't be as big-hearted as I am, and he won't think twice about getting rid of those children. You understand that? I know you do. I'm gonna let this fellow take you to the train depot just like you thought he was. Y'all get on that train and don't look back, and those kids of yours will grow up fine." Having said that he climbed back down and talked briefly with the other man then boarded his wagon and drove away.

They rode through the night and part of the day before coming to the train depot. The man waited until Misty was on board and the train was gone before leaving.

Sitting, staring out of the window, she was already making plans for the rescue of her girls. What was needed first was a safe haven to escape to once she had them. When the train made its first stop she disembarked and the search began.

Finding Misty had never been more promising. It took nearly two months from the time Roscoe received word from Kentucky to get a private investigator to confirm the truthfulness of it, and then get there himself.

Sitting in the very hotel she had once worked in, they laid out a strategy to cover as much ground as possible. The stagecoach driver couldn't be located, and trying to consider the many directions they could have gone was frustrating. Each was armed with a picture of Misty and the old woman's name. Setting off on different trails they went from one stop to another trying to find someone who knew Hilda Schickna.

This went on for another two months until word finally reached Roscoe in Tennessee that he was to come immediately to Mississippi. On arriving the news he was given was both good and bad. The private investigator, Joshua Larue, met him when the stage came in. He took him quickly to his hotel room to fill him in.

"She was here, Roscoe, not more than six months ago. There's something funny about it, though I'm not sure yet what it is. I didn't want to be snoopin round too much, least till you got here anyway. I've got to tell ya, she married a local fellow." As Mr. Larue said this Roscoe felt the words like a weight on his heart. "But, there's something not right about it," he continued. "They have two children."

At that Roscoe exclaimed without even thinking, "Children? Misty has children!"

"Two little girls maybe five years for the oldest one," Mr. Larue responded.

"You've seen the children, but Misty's not here?" Roscoe asked.

"Her husband is a kinda would-be politician, secretary to the governor or something. From what I gathered she came here as Chrissy Reed, the niece of this Hilda Schickna. He's still living in her house, the old lady died some time ago," said Mr. Larue.

"Get to the heart of it Joshua. Where is Misty? Is she all right?"

"He claims she ran off with another fella, broke his heart the way he tells it," said Mr. Larue.

"He's lying Joshua, if Misty has children she didn't run off and leave em," Roscoe said matter-of-factly.

"Well Roscoe, the years have been many and hard. People can change ya know," he offered. Roscoe didn't bother responding to that.

"I want to get a look at the children. When can we do this?"

"We can get close enough to the house I guess. We'll go tomorrow and watch for em," he answered.

There never was any doubt in his mind that Misty had been, for whatever reason, forced to leave her children. Seeing them, he knew something bad must have happened to her. If he could he would have put his arms around them and never let go. To anybody who knew her, they were Misty Tanner.

After that he set up an appointment with Ned Prickett. Using a fictitious name he presented himself as a lawyer sent by a steel company in Pittsburgh, Pa., to set the ground work for a land purchase from the state for the purpose of a mining operation. In an attempt to discern the man's character, Roscoe made several suggestions about large cash payments to helpful individuals with inside connections. Mr. Prickett readily responded.

At the conclusion of their meeting, arrangements were made for dinner that evening. Choosing the most expensive place in the area Roscoe made every effort to impress him and put him at ease. During dinner the conversation was strictly business. Afterwards they relaxed and enjoyed several glasses of bourbon. Roscoe now started to steer their conversation toward family life.

First inquiring of his children, he found the man had little interest in their lives. Then commenting on photos he had seen, he said how beautiful his wife was, and how sorry he was to hear she had gone. Roscoe became the most troubled when Ned said he had told the children their mother had fallen ill and died. At this he asked him how he could be so certain that she wouldn't return. He simply smiled and said that would never happen.

It was apparent to Roscoe and Mr. Larue that Ned was lying about many things. Fearing the worst, Roscoe had a difficult time being patient over the course of the next couple of weeks.

They decided to follow through on the land deal. Roscoe wired Pittsburgh about his intentions. The necessary documents were sent to make it look like a legitimate business transaction. This bought Roscoe time to get to know Ned, and look for any clues that would lead them to Misty.

During the first week Roscoe went to Ned's house almost daily. He would wait until Ned left then go there under the pretense of looking for him. His motive was to see and talk with Misty's children. However, the children were kept upstairs a great part of the time, and Roscoe could not get past the housekeeper no matter what excuse he tried. Finally, during the second week he spotted the woman walking in town with them. He approached them as the housekeeper was about to enter a store. He greeted them all and followed them in.

A small counter with stools was there for customers to enjoy soda pop and other treats. He invited the girls to have a snack with him. This gave him an opportunity to be alone with them since Negroes could not sit at the counter. As they cheerfully talked with Roscoe he repeatedly wiped tears from his eyes. "Molly is a very pretty name, did your mother know someone named Molly?" he asked.

"Mommy had an Auntie named Molly when she was a little girl," she answered.

"Lydia is a pretty name too. I like Isabelle, I think that is pretty." As he said this he saw the look on her face change. "Did your mommy know Isabelle?" he asked.

With a puzzled look she asked, "Do you know the secret?" He knew he should let it go, but his heart overruled it.

"Did you keep mommy's secret and never tell anyone?" he asked. She nodded.

"I know the secret, Molly, but you can't tell anyone I know. Your mommy wouldn't want you to," he said placing his hand on the side of her face.

Looking down she said sadly, "My mommy died." He leaned over and kissed her head tenderly, then started to weep. "You're sad too aren't you?" she said, then climbed down from the stool and leaned her head against his side.

It took several more days to conclude the land deal. A large financial reward was given to Ned Prickett for his part in undermining the others who wanted the same piece of land. With everything carefully recorded they now had in their possession the necessary documents detailing Ned's illegal activity.

It was now time for the second part of the plan. Joshua Larue who, up until this time had remained out of the picture, now approached Ned at his home on Sunday afternoon, and presenting himself as a federal agent sent down from Washington, gave Ned copies of the land deal transaction. "I'm not here today in an official capacity Mr. Prickett. To the best of my knowledge only my boss and I have seen these things in their entirety. I might add, my boss is also my uncle. We feel very strongly that individuals should be compensated for their hard work in behalf of the people. You know what I mean? So from time to time something like this comes to our attention. We're not so inclined to go looking for . . . um . . . well deeds of misconduct. Most often this sort of thing can be swept under the table. I think you'll agree it's best for everyone."

"Well, ya know what I always say sir, what good would all that money be? And that is what we are talking about here right?" Ned asked.

"I believe you understand perfectly," responded Mr. Larue.

"Yes, that money could cost me more in the long run if my reputation were tarnished. I'd be better off to not have so much now, don't you agree?" Ned said.

"Absolutely sir, and I am on your side, I want you to know this. Ya see here it is in a nut shell. If this were the only time your name had come to our attention why, we would have just taken care of it back home. But we did that once already for you sir. To do it again quite frankly, will require some compensation."

"For the life of me I don't know what you're talking about. You will have to make yourself clear," Ned responded.

As Mr. Larue reached into his attaché case he was saying, "We're a sort of internal affairs office. We gather information on people. We want to make sure only those deserving are elected into an office of oversight." From his attaché he handed him a wanted poster with Misty's picture on it. What happened next couldn't have been planned.

Roscoe and Mr. Larue expected Ned to think he was being confronted with the fact that his wife was a Negro, but Ned jumped too quickly to the wrong conclusion, believing he was being blackmailed for murdering his wife. He assumed that the fellow he paid had actually done it, then talked about it to others.

Rising up out of his chair he exclaimed, "Now I'm gonna tell y'all the truth on this matter. I paid this fellow a goodly sum to put her on a train north. That's all I told him to do. Then I come to learn he's got an ax to grind with my wife. I hear tell she killed his brother and he, unbeknownst to me, takes his revenge and kills her. Now I can prove that all I wanted was for her to be on a train. I paid a local fellow to drive her there. This other man, he took her from my driver. There wasn't nothing he could do about it. Now, I can get him. Yes, that's what I'll do. You meet me here tomorrow evening and I'll get him here to straighten this problem out."

Mr. Larue sat quietly for a moment. He had no reason to believe that Misty was alive. He was thinking how he would tell Roscoe and keep him from killing this worthless man who stood before him. Departing, he told Ned to make arrangements. He was not about to let anyone involved get away with taking Misty's life.

Roscoe was staying in a nearby town, so Mr. Larue figured it best to carry through with the meeting the following night, gather all the information and then meet up with Roscoe.

Mr. Larue knew that Ned and his associate would have the evening well-rehearsed before he got there. Listening intently to the other man's story he knew he was nervous about presenting these lies as facts. With every discrepancy in his story Ned jumped in to put things right. Both men were adamant about not knowing the name of the fellow who took Misty. When everything was said Mr. Larue thanked them and told Ned he would see him one more time before returning to Washington. He then departed.

Ned thought he was coming back for money and that everything was going to be okay. Mr. Larue waited a short distance from the house and followed the other fellow to his home. Nothing more was done that night.

The following day Mr. Larue joined Roscoe in his hotel room and delivered the news as carefully as he could. Roscoe's reaction was not what he expected. He told him matter-of-factly, "Misty is not dead. I would feel it if she were," he told him. "Joshua we have got to go back and pay this man a visit. He will tell me what I want to know." There was no doubt he could supply more information, and that Roscoe would get it out of him was easily believable.

The next day Roscoe went to a lawyer and had some legal documents drawn up. That night, well into the late hours, the two of them paid an unexpected visit on the man who had driven the cariole that took Misty away.

While Roscoe didn't believe that Misty was dead, he was very concerned that she might have been beaten and threatened, thus keeping her away from her children. Even at this point he didn't understand that she had killed a man and was still believing she was wanted for murder.

With one forceful kick the door not only swung open, but broke completely free from its hinges and crashed into a table making a frightful sound. Before the man and his wife could get out of their bed Roscoe was standing over them. Joshua lit a lamp and Roscoe punched the man with a good deal of force laying him flat out on his back. "I want the man's name that you turned the girl over to. If you tell me you don't know, I'll break both of your arms before asking you a final time," Roscoe demanded. The man didn't know Roscoe, but he knew who Mr. Larue was, and he knew what was being asked of him.

"I lied about it," he said trying to back away from Roscoe. "Prickett wanted me to say those things but he don't know the truth either. I lied to him too. I never wanted to get involved anyway, but he paid me good." Roscoe grabbed him and pulled him to his feet, then pushed him back against a wall and warned of the consequences if he didn't make everything clear quickly.

As the man told what happened that night, a great feeling of relief came over both Roscoe and Mr. Larue. After getting the whole story from the man, they all agreed it was in everyone's best interest to let Ned Prickett think it had gone according to his plan.

When the two men arrived at Ned's house it was nearly five o'clock in the morning. Not wanting to frighten the children they forced open a window and entered the house from the rear. Just inside Joshua turned to Roscoe and asked him to hand the pistol over for his own sake because he was far too wound up and should think about the children. This Roscoe declined to do saying, "This man is going to be given only one option."

Mr. Larue went upstairs in search of Ned while Roscoe waited in the study. In a few minutes they came in, Ned protesting in a loud angry voice as he entered the room. Roscoe stood behind the door until they were both into the room. Pushing the door closed he stepped forward. A surprised look came over Ned's face as he stared briefly at him.

"My name is Roscoe Tanner," he said, then delivered a hard solid punch sending Ned backwards across the room. Before he could collect himself Roscoe was there striking him with another blow. This caused Ned to fall over his desk crashing onto the chair which came apart under his weight as he fell to the floor. With considerable force Roscoe pressed his boot down onto Ned's chest and held it there. He was dazed with blood coming from both his nose and mouth.

Roscoe reached down and placed his one hand over Ned's bloody face the other behind his head and lifted him to his feet. "The decisions you make over the next sixty seconds are going to determine whether you live or die tonight," said Roscoe as he pulled the pistol from his pocket.

"If it's money you want I'll give it all back. I'll give you more if you want it," Ned said trying to get some distance between himself and the pistol.

"You had your wife murdered. The man who did it is ready to testify that you arranged it, and paid for it. I can see that you're hung for that," Roscoe said in a loud voice.

"Just wait a minute here, there's things you don't understand. She lied to me. She was a nigger. Ain't nobody gonna care about this, we can . . ." Before he could complete the sentence Roscoe let his fist go with such force that Ned dropped to the floor, out cold. It took several minutes to revive him and get him to his feet again. It was apparent that his nose was broken as it bled profusely. Pushing him down in a chair he was told not to speak another word.

Roscoe motioned to Joshua who handed him a round case that was protruding from his back pocket. After removing the lid, papers were pulled from within. They were unrolled and placed on the desk, and a pen was laid next to them. Roscoe demanded that Ned come to the desk. Holding a handkerchief to his nose he quickly did as he was told. "You are going to sign these adoption papers giving me uncontested custody of Misty's children," Roscoe told him.

For a brief second Ned thought he was going to say something, but as he opened his mouth Roscoe pointed the pistol at him and said, "Whether you live or die, her children are going home with me." As he was signing the papers Mr. Larue added, "If you ever make mention of this, the next time your name appears in the newspaper there'll be a picture above it . . . of you hanging." Ned was made to sit in the chair with Mr. Larue guarding him. Roscoe went upstairs for the children.

All the commotion downstairs had awakened Molly. When Roscoe entered the room he found her sitting frightened on her bed. Sitting down alongside of her he said, "Don't be afraid sweetheart. When mommy told you the secret about Isabelle did she tell you about Mariah?"

The child looked at Roscoe and said, "Mommy lived there a long time ago. Did you live there too?"

"I still live there Molly. There's been a terrible mistake. Your mommy didn't die. She got lost and I'm going to find her. But first I'm going to bring you and Lydia to Mariah, and then I'll bring your mommy back," Roscoe said in a soft reassuring voice. Molly moved over to him and put her arms around his neck and held onto him tightly. After filling two pillow cases with clothing, he picked Lydia up from her bed and carried her down the stairs.

The door to the study was closed. When Roscoe reached the front door he called for Mr. Larue to come, and the four departed.

Now Mr. Larue had to begin mapping the almost endless possibilities of where Misty might have gone after being placed on the train. They both agreed she would not have let too great a distance come between her and the children. A reliable man was hired to watch for her, knowing she was bound to return for her little girls. Mr. Larue boarded the train the next morning to search out leads. They knew this time they were close.

As their cariole neared Mariah the covered bridge came into view. Molly stood straight up, excitedly pointing to it saying, "Mommy told me about that. Isabelle was there too!"

A short distance from the bridge the cariole was brought to a stop. After helping Molly down he picked Lydia up and they walked to the old beech tree. "You see this here?" Roscoe said pointing to the many names carved into it. "This one is your mommy's name, this is my sister Isabelle's, here is my name, and Rebecca's." At that Molly interrupted and asked where her name was. "You weren't born yet sweetheart. Would you like me to make your name there now?" She responded yes and pointed to a spot next to Misty's. As he cut their names into the tree he said, "Do you see that number?" referring to the number twelve next to Misty's name.

"That was how old mommy was the first time we put her name onto the tree. For you I'll put a five, right?" After cutting the girls' names in the tree he brought them home to Mariah.

Several days after that Roscoe was visited by an old friend, a friend who over the years had offered his services many times tracking down leads that were sent to Mariah. Along with his wife and children he met Misty's little girls. Then he heard about the events of the previous month. After listening he persuaded Roscoe to remain at home with the children and wait for word from Mr. Larue.

He postponed his return trip to New York and set out that very day for Mississippi!

The time has gone by quickly for Misty, for her every moment is devoted to the rescue of her children. After disembarking from the train she walked for several days until coming upon a town of moderate size. Filling every minute of her days she eventually obtained work to fill the entire week. Mostly she cleaned houses and washed clothes. Some evenings she played piano and sang at a local saloon, and other nights she stayed up until the late hours weaving baskets. Misty knew she needed enough money to travel a great distance quicky once she had possession of her children. Her plan was to go directly to Canada believing he would never be able to trace her there.

Wanting to keep as low a profile as possible she made no friends in town at all. She did eventually secure a room a short distance outside of town. This came about after a sharecropper, Matthew Thomas, a Negro man in his late fifties, found her early one morning at the edge of one of his fields eating raw corn off the cob.

After bringing her home and allowing her to fix a meal for herself she told him of her plight. He offered her a place to live in exchange for some field and housework. They were both very careful to keep this arrangement secret.

Over the course of the next several weeks Matthew became very fond of Misty, and at considerable risk to himself, offered to help her retrieve her children.

When the time finally arrived Misty packed what few belongings she had and set out early in the morning with Mr. Thomas. After a full day's journey they arrived at the edge of town. Misty waited until late into the night and carefully walked the rest of the way. She had Mr. Thomas wait for her; she did not want to jeopardize his safety should anything go wrong.

Going to the home of Ned's housekeeper, Misty gave her quite a shock when she opened the door and found her there. "Lord help me . . . Miss Prickett . . . I never thought I would see you again," the woman exclaimed. "I need your help Mildred. I need a key to get into the house. I don't want to awaken Mr. Prickett. I'm going to take my children away with me," she said.

"You come sit down here for a minute Miss Prickett. I's afraid I have to tell y'all something dats not good," Mildred said bringing Misty to a chair.

"Please, tell me my babies are all right. He didn't hurt them did he?" Misty asked with a worried voice.

"Da girls is gone Miss Prickett, been so fo some time. I goes da work one day and Mr. Prickett tell me da girls go away for awhile, but when I's clean up der room, I's find all dar clothes still in the drawers. I's think it wrong, but Miss Pricket I's can't say nothin bout it." After saying that she paused a moment then looked to the floor and added, "Mr. Prickett's not dar no mo Miss Prickett. He dead child. Man done shot him in de back. I's hear tell it was at one of dem poker games he go to at night. Dey man be in jail right now, dats all I know. Lord Miss Prickett ifin' I's can help ya I will." Misty just sat back in the chair and didn't say anything. All she could think of was Ned saying he would put the girls in an orphanage.

Concern for her children kept her from giving into the rage she felt inside. "Slavery was suppose to be abolished. How is it that someone could take my babies away from me?" Misty said as she covered her face with her hands and cried. "I'm glad he's dead. God forgive me, but I'm glad he's dead!"

Once again Misty had to summon strength from deep inside. She gained her composure and collected her thoughts.

With Mildred's key she went to the house to search for any clues that would lead her to the girls. Over many hours, and well into the dawn's light she looked but found nothing. Blood stains in the study only added to her worries, and the girls clothing was all there minus only a few items.

Packing the photographs and several dolls the children had, Misty left in despair. She next went to two of Ned's close friends and revealed to them the truth in hopes of finding out anything that would give her a clue to their whereabouts. Both were sympathetic but unhelpful.

By midmorning she walked back to Mildred and told her all of the truth about herself, including the information about Mr. Thomas and that Mildred could get any word of her children to her there.

As they rode home together Misty was already planning to use the money she had saved to take her to every orphanage in the south if need be, saying she would never . . . ever give up until she had her children back.

Once they returned she began quickly to gather information about the many orphanages in the state of Mississippi. Her doing this brought attention to herself from the sheriff and other citizens of like mind.

Many small groups of white men had formed by this time throughout the south. Their primary fixation was to keep the Negroes oppressed, and in fear. Lynchings were becoming more common, as well as night raids on Negro land owners bringing destruction to their belongings.

For this reason it was kept secret that Misty was living in the home of Matthew Thomas. During her long years on the run she had made few mistakes, but in her grief over her children she neglected to be as cautious. When it came to be known by certain ones that a white woman, a beautiful white woman, was living with a Negro man, plans were formulated to correct the matter and punish those involved.

Such a serious offense would be dealt with quickly. After Sunday morning services a small group of men gathered in a room in the rear of the church to discuss and finalize the plan. The time of action was set for the following evening.

That very Sunday afternoon in the town where Misty had lived with her children, a stranger arrived. A rather big man about six foot two and weighing two hundred pounds. He wore black boots with black riding pants and a black round-brimmed hat. His chestnut brown eyes stared out through small wire rim glasses. He spoke as a man on a mission.

After checking into the hotel and dining he began the task for which he had come. This was not a hard callous man by nature, but having been close before, he understood what it took to get this job done. He also learned of the great changes that had occurred and this added to the urgency.

The biggest difference would prove to be, he knew her; Mr. Larue and the others didn't. He knew how she thought, and what her priorities would be. While the others went off in search of her elsewhere, he immediately found the housekeeper and talked with her at length. After convincing her of his credentials and purpose she told him what they had waited years to know—where to find Misty!

Early the next morning he was on the trail. His directions were faulty, and on more than one occasion he had to backtrack a distance to get his bearing straight. He arrived around dinner time and went to the Sheriff's home asking for directions to Mr. Thomas' farm. The Sheriff, knowing what was to take place there this very night, became noticeably concerned, and began asking more questions, but gave fewer answers. Not wanting to do anything that would frighten Misty off before he got there, the stranger was offering very little information. This made the Sheriff even more uneasy and reluctant to help. The stranger was then told to go to the Sheriff's office and wait there for him, at which time he would be escorted to the Negro's home.

It was easy to see that the problems he presented to the Sheriff were of serious concern. He went just far enough to be out of view then watched the Sheriff's house. In a couple of minutes the Sheriff came out and quickly rode away. The only sense the man could make out of all this was that for some reason the Sheriff wanted to get to Misty before he did. The Sheriff for his part thought the man was a federal agent who must have learned of their intentions to do Mr. Thomas harm.

Going back to the Sheriff's house the man informed the Sheriff's wife that her husband was in grave danger, and she quickly gave him directions so that he could help, the Sheriff's wife being ignorant of the evening's plan.

At first he thought that she had deceived him, as he was told to go in the opposite direction he saw the Sheriff leave in. He could only hope he was going to get there before anything bad happened.

The Sheriff had gone in the other direction hoping to catch the men before they headed out for the Thomas place, wanting to warn them and call it off for now. However, he missed them by more than ten minutes and knew they would reach their destination before he could catch them. The Sheriff at this point turned about and went home, not wanting to have any responsibility for what was going to take place on this night.

Matthew Thomas and Misty were inside and unaware of what was taking place around them. The four men had left their horses a short distance away and quietly made their way to the house. Misty had gone up into the loft which served as her sleeping quarters to get her sewing box. Matthew was finishing his dinner when the door opened and the four men entered in. With large wooden clubs in their hands they quickly began smashing everything in the room while hurling obscenities and false accusations about the relationship between Mr. Thomas and Misty. Matthew jumped from his seat and grabbed hold of one of the men, but before he could do anything else he was struck on the back and dropped to his knees.

At this Misty began screaming at the men from the loft. Her demanding they stop what they were doing and leave them alone only caused them to become more violent. Again they struck Matthew with their wooden handles. One man went up the ladder and forced Misty to come down. When she wouldn't stop swinging her hands and kicking at them they struck her too, knocking her to the floor.

Having been clubbed repeatedly Matthew was lying unconscious and bleeding badly, Misty attempted to crawl to him but was pushed over again and again by the feet of those who stood over her laughing. Grabbing at her clothing and hair they brought her to a standing position and began shoving her from one to another, never allowing her a second to plant her feet. All her attempts to strike out at them failed as they laughed and ripped at her clothing.

After nearly a minute of this she was able to get hold of the shirt of one of them and pull herself close. She then bit into his shoulder breaking through the skin and holding him there for several seconds. When he finally got free he became so violent the others had to pull him away from her and hold him back until he calmed down some.

"We'll take care of her after we show her what happens to niggers who touch white women," one man said as they tied Mr. Thomas' hands behind his back. With blood coming from the corner of her mouth she continually stated that she was a Negro woman. Each time she said it the man whose hand held the back of her neck would strike her face with his opened hand.

Mr. Thomas was dragged across the floor and out into the yard. Two of the men then carried him to a large tree and placed a long rope around his neck. At this Misty panicked and fought with a strength beyond what she possessed. Breaking free of the man's hold she ran screaming toward those holding Mr. Thomas. Kicking and gouging in total hysterics it took all four men to subdue her, striking her repeatedly on her face and body. A large gash just above her right eye sent blood streaming down her face considerably impairing her vision.

"Tie her up! Tie her up!" one kept repeating until a rope was wrapped around her and the tree they were all beneath. Unable to wipe the blood from her eyes she could only shake her head in a desperate attempt to see what was happening to Matthew.

The rope was thrown over a low but sturdy branch, and the men began to pull it tight. As the rope was getting tight around his neck Mr. Thomas began to regain consciousness. Scrambling to get to his feet, broken up and bloodied he raised himself erect and felt the rope begin to lift him up off of his feet. The man standing in front of Misty ripped off a piece of her dress that was torn and hanging. He wiped the blood from her with one hard swipe across her face, then grabbed her jaw and turned her eyes toward his. "After we hang that nigger I'm gonna show you what a real man is like," he said with his face close to hers. As he was looking her dead in the eye she spit a large amount of saliva and blood into his face. At that he reared back and let go with a powerful force, the back of his hand hitting her squarely between her eyes. But as the force of his hand struck her face, a force of far greater magnitude struck the tree about ten feet above their heads, showering bits of bark and wood down on them. Misty was not aware of it, having been knocked unconscious, but the others quickly turned to see what had happened.

Sitting tall and looking mean on a large dark horse, a man dressed in black pointed a rifle at them. The four men were frozen in place. For a long moment no one spoke. Then the man on the horse said, "Cut them free!" Which they did without any hesitation. He then told them to clear out of there if they wanted to remain alive. Quickly they turned to leave, but the man on the horse called out again, "YOU," he said, pointing to the one that struck Misty last. Climbing down from the saddle he walked toward the man with his rifle pointing at the ground. The other men had hurried off a safe distance then turned to see what would happen.

The stranger stood directly in front of the man, peering down through his small round glasses. Fearing for his life the man began to plead that he not be hurt. "I should kill you where you stand. If any harm comes to anyone out here, I'm holding you personally accountable. Do you understand what I'm telling you?" he said. Backing away the man assured him he did, then turned around and quickly fled.

Mr. Thomas was badly beaten and bleeding. He had gotten to Misty and was holding her head in his lap pressing a piece of cloth to her wound as the stranger approached. "You saved our lives Mister," Mr. Thomas said looking up at him. Without responding the man looked intently at her for a moment. "You know her don't you," Mr. Thomas stated.

"Yes, I do," he replied. Then looking at Misty he said, "It's been a very long time, my friend."

After getting them both into the house he began wiping Misty's face clean with a wet cloth. She quivered a few times and lightly moaned, then opened her eyes. First she had to focus, then she had to realize that what she was seeing was true. Looking into his eyes she softly said, "Oh Wendall, I always knew you would come for me." Wendall then smiled and spoke that same verse of poem that he had quoted to her when they had last parted so many years ago.

"When your darkest hour befalls you and eclipses your light of life, fear not that you're alone. For in spirit I'll be with you on that night." With that he put his arms around her. She embraced him back, then she lay her head on his shoulder and cried for the longest time.

The next days were spent with Mr. Thomas. They could not persuade him to leave, so Misty did her best to nurse his cuts and bruises while Wendall repaired his badly damaged house.

Misty knew she was going back to Georgia with Wendall, but didn't as yet know where or why. Roscoe and Wendall both agreed that her life had ended for the two of them when she left Mariah, and so it would not begin again until she was home.

Most of their conversation at Matthew's was centered on the war years and Misty's life over the last several years. She didn't ask too many questions about where he was taking her. He had asked her not to, wanting her to trust him for just a little while.

In the morning Wendall went to town and purchased a small cariole. Misty had nothing to take with her but a small bag of clothing and a wooden box with her children's pictures in it. While she trusted him completely she needed to hear him promise repeatedly that she would have her girls back with her very soon.

Sitting in the cariole next to Wendall and waving good-bye to Matthew she felt a strange mix of emotions, all of them good, but none of them fully understood. Wendall slapped the reins on the horse and said, "Come on boy, take us home." This made her want to begin questioning him again, but she didn't. He had already shown with words and laughter that keeping their destination a secret was something that brought him a great deal of satisfaction.

For several days they traveled at a quickened pace. And then they were back in Georgia.

End of Part IV

PART V

The Final Crossing

By now Misty knew she was heading for Mariah. Though Wendall didn't say it directly, she could sense it in his conversations and feel it in her heart.

Through the course of the days she learned that Edward had gone off to fight in the war and died, that Susan was well and Mariah had been restored to its former stately manner, that Mrs. Tanner had passed on shortly after Misty had been abducted, and that Wendall wasn't sure of Goldie's and Leo's fate. Everything else he was deliberately vague about.

Misty concluded that it was Susan who had kept up the search for her. Living all alone with just her children she was certainly frightened and most likely lonely. Misty even wondered if perhaps Susan was sorry for what she had done and wanted to make it right again.

At Misty's request Wendall swore never to tell anyone the truth about her disappearance and Susan's involvement. How she would react to Susan she wasn't sure, but all the things she always told herself she would say and do were quickly forgotten. To Misty, Susan was, and always would be, Emily Tanner's daughter.

It was late afternoon when they entered the town Misty had known so well. Bigger and busier now, it had undergone many changes. One that brought a big smile to her face, was a big sign that read, MONINGHOFF'S GENERAL STORE. "Is Amy still here Wendall?" she asked.

"Yes she is," he replied. "Three or four children now I think. I'm sure you'll run into her sometime."

"You are awfully sure I'm going to stay here. But I'm really not. I certainly won't stay to look after Susan and her children," she said.

"Oh you'll stay all right, I'd bet everything on that," he responded with a grin.

Wendall brought the cariole to a stop on the other side of town. Summoning a young man who was passing by on his horse, he took him aside for a moment. Misty watched as Wendall wrote out a note and handed it to the fellow along with a sum of money. The young man quickly rode off ahead of them. Misty tried to get out of him what it was all about, but he only smiled and said, "I'm just following instructions."

From there they rode to the end of town where Misty had him stop in front of the Myers' house. After looking at it for several minutes she said, "I'll be able to make contact with them again. Maybe I'll even go to live where they are."

"You've waited this long Misty. Go with it one more hour and I promise all things will be made clear," Wendall said reassuringly.

The cariole was purposely driven slower now. Misty's anticipation of seeing Mariah again took her mind back through years of love and laughter. For the first time on their entire trip back she was silent. Wendall began to sing a song they once knew, and this brought her to the present again. "I can picture riding up and down this road a thousand times," she said interrupting him. "We were really quite young when we began riding to Rebecca's. It was such a peaceful time then. We hadn't a care in the world. All we ever wanted was to be together." Wendall looked over and smiled.

"When you were in New Orleans I rode down this road a couple of times with Isabelle, riding into town to purchase things," he said.

"Isabelle was the prettiest girl I've ever seen," Misty said, "so kind and loving. I can hear her voice like it was yesterday."

"I'd give anything to be there when you and Rebecca see each other again," Wendall said.

"To have my children is what I want the most; then to be with the Myers' again. If I can have that I'll never be in want again, and I'll always feel safe and secure knowing that I have you as my most special friend," said Misty as she leaned over and kissed his cheek.

As they rounded the next turn Misty rose up from the seat. In full view now was what she waited so long to see. There in the distance was the covered bridge. Fearing it had been destroyed in

314

the war, she hadn't asked about it. "So many things ended at that bridge. So many good-byes. It was one of our favorite places. Ros and I would ride out to the bridge when it looked like it was going to rain and let it trap us there. Sometimes the rain came down so hard you couldn't see down the road. It felt so good being in there. I've long ago accepted the deaths of the others, Wendall, but my heart won't let me do the same with Roscoe," Misty said as her emotions welled up within her. "I don't believe I've ever had a moment I didn't feel him reaching for me. I tried for a long time to deny it, but I know now it will never leave me."

Wendall brought the cariole to a stop just before the bridge. With a warm smile he said to her, "You've truly come full circle, Misty. I, too, waited many years to see this day, but I'm afraid we have to part company for a while."

"You're leaving me here?" she asked. "Someone will be along for you shortly. I suspect they're on their way right now," he answered.

"You have certainly made a mystery of all this, Wendall, and you didn't hide the fact that you've enjoyed it," she said.

"Enjoyed it immensely, my friend," he laughed.

"I'll stay here because you want me to, but I am scared, Wendall. I wish you would tell me more."

"Tomorrow Misty, I'll introduce you to my wife and children. We'll have a lot more to talk about then," he said as he stepped down and walked around the cariole. Taking her hand he helped her down and said, "It's as if time has had no effect on you at all. You are as exquisite now as you ever were. I wish I could stay to see you welcomed home, but that time unfortunately does not belong to me." Misty reached out and hugged him tightly saying, "Oh, Wendall, my most valued friend. You pertinaciousness in finding me meant my very life. I've finally reached a time when I have no words to express to you what I feel. To say I'll always love you is inadequate to say the least, and if you have rescued my babies . . ." Unable to finish the sentence she began to cry as he held her head on his shoulder.

"I wish I could have been the one who did that," he said hugging her tightly. "Everything is all right now, Misty . . . everything."

After a few words and several minutes Wendall climbed back onto his cariole and said good-bye. Misty watched him ride

315

through the bridge and down the road before sitting down on the stone wall to await whatever the next event would be.

It was early in the evening and the sun was beginning to make its way toward the hillside, a distance off from the other side of the bridge. After sitting only for a few moments she got back up and began walking to the old beech tree to once again read the many names carved into it. When she got there she knew right where to look to see the name she wanted to see first. In big bold letters he had carved his name next to hers. Looking at it she thought how strange it was to be back again and how quickly the events of the past few days had unfolded. Wendall had rescued her, brought her back, left her and was gone. Laughing to herself she thought, I'm probably dreaming. Looking over all the other names she reached out and touched Isabelle's, then she saw something unexpected. A little higher than the others were the names Molly and Lydia. She knew they weren't there before. At first she thought only of her mother Lydia, and Aunt Molly. Then she saw the number five next to Molly's name and a two next to Lydia's. She became confused. The thought of her children overwhelmed her. Could Wendall have already found her children, or Susan? She was more confused now than at anytime during the journey home.

For a long time she just stood and stared at their names. With her back facing the bridge she hadn't noticed the cariole coming in her direction. When it came onto the bridge it stopped. Three people got off. Standing with a child on each side of him, Roscoe Tanner looked on at the sight he had waited for what seemed like a lifetime to see again. With her back facing him he looked at her long black hair and watched as she repeatedly wiped away tears. He was about to call out to her when she sensed someone was behind her. She turned around to see three figures standing just inside the bridge, but there wasn't enough light under the roof to make out who it was. With her emotions and thoughts running at a rapid pace she started walking toward them.

When she was about halfway there she realized the children were hers. She began to run calling out Molly's name. The child could wait no longer and darted from Roscoe's side and out into the light toward her mother. Lydia too, began to run crying and calling out to her mother.

Roscoe waited and watched as Molly and Misty reached each other. With Molly's long shiny hair bouncing and flying about behind her it was as if he were seeing Misty as a child again.

When they reached each other Misty dropped to her knees and threw her arms around the child. "Oh my baby, my baby!" she kept saying. Then Lydia fell into her mother's arms and the three of them hugged each other tightly, kissing each other, and crying with a joy so overwhelming it was as if time were standing still, waiting for them.

Roscoe stood watching, feeling almost guilty that he alone was alive to see this. How much his mother would have loved those children. Naomi and Isabelle too should be here. Looking at Misty's face it was as youthful and beautiful as it had been the day he left for England.

Though it was only several minutes, it seemed like a long while that he stared at her. When finally she looked up, he believed she could see him clearly, but the sun setting behind him blinded her and all she could see was the figure of a man. Not knowing what else to think, she called out Wendall's name. "No mommy," Molly said as she tenderly kissed her mother's cheek again, "It's him, he didn't die."

In a voice filled with emotion she looked at her child and spoke her name as if she was asking a question, "Molly?" Then she looked up again. He stepped out from the bridge and blocked the sun's rays with his back. Staring up at his face she spoke his name softly. "Roscoe," then rose to her feet. After all those years, her eyes were telling her what her heart had never stopped believing, Roscoe Tanner was alive.

Standing before her was the only man she had ever loved, the only one she ever could have loved. Releasing the hands of her children she said his name again. Then closing the short distance that separated them she fell into his arms.

"I love you Misty," he said as he tightly, yet tenderly wrapped his arms around her. "I've lived for nothing else but this moment. We will never be apart again."

Roscoe Tanner is a big man, the children have already come to know and love him, and as he has repeatedly held them in his arms they have learned how secure and safe a place that is.

Molly didn't fully understand what it meant to her mother and Roscoe as they held and kissed each other and cried, but as she stood holding her sister's hand and watching, she knew her mother was safe now, and never had she seen her, or anyone else, express such happiness.

317

After some time elapsed he helped them all into the cariole. As he turned it around to cross back through the covered bridge he said, "You're going home now Misty, to take your rightful place as my wife, and Mistress of Mariah."

He had told her within the first few minutes of their being together again, that the rest of the family had not survived. The words, though sad to hear, were not in any way unexpected. She had long ago mourned the loss of the family. She realized he was only worried that seeing him she might believe they too were alive.

Her questions never stopped coming for the entire ride home. Some he answered, some he purposely evaded. There was still several more surprises in store for her.

He drove at a slow but steady pace allowing Misty to take in the sights she once knew so well. The sky was bright blue with soft white clouds moving slowly above them. When Mariah came into view her heart beat even faster. The house loomed before her as big and magnificent as it had ever been. The thought of being there again with Roscoe was so overwhelming she asked him to stop. Pulling Lydia onto her lap, Misty said she felt afraid. He reached over and took hold of her hand and said, "We can sit here for a moment Misty. I know this has been a lot for you."

But after he said that, Molly put her arms around her mother's neck and said, "We can't stay here mommy. Aunt Sarah is waiting for you."

"Sarah, Ros?" she said excitedly. "Do you have Sarah? That's why you wouldn't answer me. You do have her don't you!"

"It was to be a surprise. It was all I could do to keep her from coming to the bridge," he said. Then turning to Molly he added, "Don't tell her any more." Now Misty wanted to ride quickly. She thought she would never see the child again, and yet another dream was about to become a reality.

They were now on the plantation riding between the massive oak trees that line each side of the road leading to the main house.

A young couple with a small child about three, and a newborn baby were sitting on the front steps waiting. When the girl stood up and began first walking quickly, then running toward the cariole Misty knew it was Sarah. As Roscoe brought the cariole to a stop Misty made her way from the seat to the ground in one clean jump and began running. They called each other's name as they embraced. It didn't matter that Sarah was a young lady now. Misty hugged and kissed her as if she were the child she had taken for her own, and lost so many years ago.

It was just a short distance now to the house. Roscoe drove the cariole around them and went on to the porch where he disembarked with the children and waited for the girls to walk to them.

After a long emotional greeting they walked hand in hand toward the others. Sarah was indeed a young woman now, with long wavy red hair and high cheek-bones. She had grown into a very beautiful young lady, as they all knew she would. On reaching the others Misty looked at the little girl who came to them and held onto Sarah's leg. Misty again began to cry and dropped to one knee to touch the child.

"This is your child, Sarah," Misty said softly. Sarah too knelt down and turned the child to face Misty.

"I've wanted more than anything for you to see my little girl. Her name is Margaret. She is three."

"She is beautiful," Misty said gently bringing her close and kissing her, "and a baby too," Misty said looking at the infant that was being held by the young man whose proud smile said without words the children were also his. Misty stood up and he handed her the baby. Holding the baby close to her heart she reached out and pulled Sarah to her and tenderly kissed her.

Sarah, one arm still around Misty, turned toward the young man and said through her tears, "This is my husband, Russell," but couldn't say anymore.

Misty handed the baby over to Sarah and hugged the young man so tightly he finally laughed and said, "Y'all better save some of your strength now. I think everyone gonna wanta hug you again."

Molly lay her head on Misty's hip and reached her arms around her legs. Roscoe came close holding Lydia and kissed her. "How does it feel to be home?" he asked.

"Like heaven Ros. There can't be anywhere else that can feel this good," she replied. For the next several minutes they stood together and talked. Misty held the baby and kissed her over and over again. She could not stop crying her tears of joy.

When slavery was abolished after the war most of those on the plantation left. Leo and Goldie were gone and no one ever knew what had become of them. Sarah in time fell in love with Russell who came from a nearby plantation, and so she stayed behind to marry and become a sharecropper with him. When Roscoe returned

319

home he provided them with a double portion of land and paid them well for their crops.

"If only my dear Henry were still with us. How happy he would have been to see our children," Misty said to Sarah.

"What did you tell Misty, Ros?" Sarah asked.

"Oh, I know he is dead. Every time I asked him he changed the subject," Misty said.

"Henry was apparently much older than any of us thought Misty," Roscoe responded. "When I got home he was much older looking. What hair the old fella had left was all gray, and he was bent over pretty hard, and moving real slow, didn't expect him to be around much longer."

"Well at least he got to see you, to know you were still alive," said Misty. At that Sarah, Russell and Roscoe all began to laugh.

"He stayed around a little bit longer than that Misty," Sarah said looking at Roscoe.

"When did Henry die Ros?" Misty asked.

"He didn't my dear," Roscoe responded with a smile. "I think he's holding on, waiting for you to come home."

"Why didn't you tell me Ros? I can't believe it! I gave up the thought of ever seeing him again," she exclaimed.

"I wanted us to be together when he saw you again," Roscoe said to her.

"Is he well?" Misty asked.

"He can't get out of bed any more, and he only has sight in one eye, and I don't think that's very good. But most of the time he is very alert. Sarah looks after him and helps us with him quite a bit."

"Is he here in the main house?" she asked.

"Would you like to see him now Misty?" he replied nodding yes to her question.

Together they made their way up the steps and crossed the porch to the large front doors. Just as they reached them someone pulled the door open. For a second Misty froze. She was face-to-face with Susan. Over the years, and especially during the most difficult of times she had felt great anger for Susan, and she wondered countless times what she would say and how she would react if ever she saw her again. But being in her presence now, and seeing a woman who looked much older than her years, with eyes filled with loneliness and despair, Misty could feel only compassion and sorrow for her. They stared into each other's eyes in silence for a moment, until Misty smiled and spoke her name, then reached out and hugged her affectionately. "I'm so sorry for what I've done to you," Susan said.

Still holding her Misty said quietly, "We shall never speak of it. Love will reign in this house the way it was meant to be."

From there they walked through the hallway to a room that had always served as servants' quarters. Roscoe opened the door and entered first, followed by Misty, then Sarah and Russell. Roscoe called to Henry, waking him up as the children gathered in around his bed. "Are you awake?" Roscoe asked. Henry turned his head to look in the direction of his voice.

"Henry, who was here to see ya today?" he asked.

"Sarah," responded Henry.

"Was the little girl in too?" Roscoe asked.

"She was in dis mornin," he answered referring to Molly.

Convinced that Henry was awake and alert Roscoe said to him. "I've found her Henry, she's come home."

He understood perfectly what was being said and immediately covered his right eye with the back of his hand allowing his other eye to focus on Misty who stood near the bottom of his bed. As he spoke her name a tear came from the corner of his eye and rolled down the side of his face. "You're all grown up," he said. "You're a woman now." The others stepped back as Misty walked to his side and knelt down. She took his hand with hers and lay her head lightly on his chest. Neither of them could speak as they held onto each other and quietly cried.

Roscoe who wanted more than anything to have her to himself, knew he would now have her forever, and so he motioned the others to leave Misty and Henry alone.

After a short while Henry fell off to sleep and Misty followed the sound of their voices into the family room. Her portrait hung over the fireplace where Josiah's once did. On another wall hung Isabelle's. Misty stood and stared at her for a moment then said, "Whenever I want to I can hear her laughter, or see her smile. We were so close we were like one person. We shared every thought we had. I really believe I love her even more today than before."

Roscoe walked over to Misty and tenderly holding her face in his hands, he kissed her and said, "For the rest of our lives Misty, we will share our thoughts about them."

She looked affectionately into his eyes smiled and said, "We will always have them. They will live in our hearts forever."

Soon Russell and Sarah said good-night. They collected their children and promised to return for dinner the following day. While Misty was with Henry, Sarah had put Lydia in her crib. Molly was sleeping at the bottom of the divan next to Roscoe. Sitting on his other side she slid down to rest her head on his shoulder as he pulled her close. "It just seemed that everything reminded me of you. It never got easier in any way at all, but I think the worst had to be spring time, when I smelled the lilacs in the air. That always made me think of how beautiful you were when you braided them into your hair," he said softly.

"Tell me I'm not going to wake up and find this is all a dream," Misty said.

"If it's a dream Sweetheart, it's mine. I keep asking myself Misty, how did you do it? To hurt so badly for so long, but not give up?" he said as he gently kissed her cheek.

"There was always something in me that kept moving me on. But there were times that my heart burned so badly, it should be ashes by now. There are so many things I want to ask, I don't even know where to begin," she exclaimed.

"Why not put this little girl to bed? Tomorrow will be a good day to talk," he offered. All the traveling she had done over the past several days, all the excitement of this day, was starting to take its toll.

After picking up the sleeping child she turned to him and asked, "Which room did you give them?"

"The girls' room, Misty, the one you would have given them," he smiled. She stepped forward and kissed him then turned and walked out of the room and up the stairs.

When she entered Isabelle's room she looked about slowly. Most of the furniture was still there, but most importantly, the bed. As she tucked the child in, her eyes opened, Molly asked her mother to lie down beside her, which she did. Lying on her side facing her daughter and brushing her hair with her hand she said, "I'm going to tell you so many stories Molly, all about the times Isabelle and I slept in this bed together when we were children, and the many things we laughed about." They talked until Molly fell asleep. Misty covered her securely then stood looking down on her child. For the first time she thought of Isabelle without mourning. At that moment she knew that Isabelle would have approved of her girls having her room as their own. Almost in a whisper she said, "My dear sweet Isabelle."

Turning away from the bed she walked to the vanity. Sitting down she carefully removed the drawer that hid the secret compartment of their youth. One piece at a time she brought out its contents until five items were before her. Three pieces of jewelry that belonged to Isabelle, two that were her own. She gently dusted off the cherry wood ring and placed it on her finger, then holding the gold nugget in her hand and thinking of Emily Tanner she softly said, "You alone gave me life. Every breath I take, every joy I know is because of you. I'll give to him the fullness of your love, Mother, as well as my own, for as long as I live."

Leaving the room she found herself standing in the corridor looking at the light coming from the open door of the master bedroom. When she left Mariah this had been Edward and Susan's room. No one had to tell her it wasn't so anymore. Stepping inside she looked at Roscoe who was lying on the large bed that she had so many times climbed into as a child to curl up next to Mother Tanner. A feeling so warm and good came over her she felt her entire body relax.

"Mrs. Tanner," Roscoe said with a smile, "Your husband has been desiring your presence here for a very long time." Misty smiled, and closed the door behind her.